More praise for
THE SILENT CRY

"Monk and Hester...keep us enthralled with their bold intellectual assaults on the hypocrisy of Victorian moral standards. With her grimly detailed descriptions of the match factories, sweatshops, paupers' hospitals, and tenement 'rookeries' crowded into these slums, Perry brings a rank sense of reality to the wretched living conditions of the working poor....Her early-Victorian series...has deepened and darkened its insights into the social evils that burdened London's underclasses."
—*The New York Times Book Review*

"The brainy, passionate Latterly is good company, as ever. "
—*The Washington Post*

"Reads like a firsthand account of the life and customs of that distant time."
—*Cincinnati Post*

"A wonderful historical mystery series...William remains an intriguing, brooding hero, and the support cast is top rate."
—*www.amazon.com*

"Richly detailed...By the novel's end, revelations of corruption and depravity break through the severe conventions of upper-class Victorian prudery in a dramatic courtroom scene....Highly recommended."
—*Library Journal*

By Anne Perry
Published by Fawcett/Ivy Books:

Featuring Thomas and Charlotte Pitt:
THE CATER STREET HANGMAN
CALLANDER SQUARE
PARAGON WALK
RESURRECTION ROW
BLUEGATE FIELDS
RUTLAND PLACE
DEATH IN THE DEVIL'S ACRE
CARDINGTON CRESCENT
SILENCE IN HANOVER CLOSE
BETHLEHEM ROAD
HIGHGATE RISE
BELGRAVE SQUARE
FARRIERS' LANE
THE HYDE PARK HEADSMAN
TRAITORS GATE
PENTECOST ALLEY
ASHWORTH HALL

Featuring William Monk:
THE FACE OF A STRANGER
A DANGEROUS MOURNING
DEFEND AND BETRAY
A SUDDEN, FEARFUL DEATH
THE SINS OF THE WOLF
CAIN HIS BROTHER
WEIGHED IN THE BALANCE
THE SILENT CRY
A BREACH OF PROMISE

THE SILENT CRY

Anne Perry

IVY BOOKS • NEW YORK

An Ivy Book
Published by The Ballantine Publishing Group
Copyright © 1997 by Anne Perry

All rights reserved under International and Pan-American Copyright Conventions. Published in the United States by The Ballantine Publishing Group, a division of Random House, Inc., New York, and simultaneously in Canada by Random House of Canada Limited, Toronto.

http://www.randomhouse.com

Library of Congress Catalog Card Number: 98-96344

ISBN 0-8041-1793-4

Manufactured in the United States of America

First Hardcover Edition: October 1997
First Mass Market International Edition: March 1998
First Mass Market Domestic Edition: September 1998

10 9 8 7 6 5 4 3 2 1

For Simon, Nikki, Jonathan, and Angus

THE
SILENT
CRY

1

JOHN EVAN STOOD shivering as the January wind whipped
down the alley. P.C. Shotts held his bull's-eye lantern high so
they could see both the bodies at once. They lay crumpled and
bloody, about seven feet apart on the icy, cobbled alleyway.

"Does anybody know what happened?" Evan asked, his
teeth chattering.

"No sir," Shotts replied bleakly. "Woman found them and
ol' Briggs came an' told me."

Evan was surprised. "In this area?" He glanced around at
the grimy walls, the open gutter and the few windows, blacked
with dirt. The doors he could see were narrow, straight onto the
street, and stained with years of damp and soot. The only lamp-
post was twenty yards away, gleaming balefully like a lost
moon. He was unpleasantly aware of movement just beyond
the perimeter of light, of hunched figures watching and waiting, the myriad beggars, thieves and unfortunates who lived in
this slum of St. Giles, only a stone's throw from Regent Street
in the heart of London.

Shotts shrugged, looking down at the bodies. "Well, they
obviously in't drunk or starved or freezin'. All that blood, I
reckon as she likely screamed, then were afraid someone 'eard
'er, an' she din't wanter get blamed, so she went on screamin',
an' other folk came." He shook his head. "They ain't always
bad about lookin' arter their own around 'ere. I daresay as
she'd 'a kept walkin' if she'd 'ad the nerve, an' thought of it
quick enough."

Evan bent down to the body nearest to him. Shotts lowered the light a little so it showed the head and upper torso more clearly. The victim was a man Evan guessed to be in his middle fifties. His hair was gray, thick, his skin smooth. When Evan touched it with his finger it was cold and stiff. His eyes were still open. He had been too badly beaten for Evan to gather anything but a very general impression of his features. He might well have been handsome in life. Certainly his clothes, though torn and stained, had been of excellent quality. As far as Evan could judge, he was of average height and solid build. It was not easy to tell because he was so doubled up, his legs splayed and half under his body.

"Who in God's name did this to him?" he asked under his breath.

"Dunno, sir," Shotts answered shakily. "I in't never seen anyone beat this bad before, even 'ere. Must 'a bin a lunatic, that's all I can say. Is 'e robbed? I s'pose 'e must 'a bin."

Evan moved the body very slightly so he could reach into the pockets of the coat. There was nothing in the outside one. He tried the inside and found a handkerchief, clean, folded linen, roll-hemmed, of excellent quality. There was nothing else. He tried the trouser pockets and found a few coppers.

"Button'ole's torn," Shotts observed, staring down at the waistcoat. "Looks like they ripped orff 'is watch an' chain. Wonder wot 'e was doin' 'ere. This is a bit rough fer the likes of a gent. Plenty o' tarts an' dolly mops no more 'n a mile west. 'Aymarket's full of 'em, an' no danger. Take yer pick. W'y come 'ere?"

"I don't know," Evan replied unnecessarily. "Perhaps if we can find the reason, we'll know what happened to him." He stood up and moved across to the other body. This was a younger man, perhaps barely twenty, although his face also was so badly beaten only the clean line of his jaw and the fine texture of his skin gave any indication. Evan was racked with pity and a terrible, blind anger when he saw the clothes on the lower part of the torso soaked in blood, which still seeped out from under the body onto the cobbles.

"God in heaven," he said huskily, "what happened here,

2

Shotts? What kind of creature does this?" He did not use the name of deity lightly. He was the son of a country parson, brought up in a small, rural community where everyone knew each other, for better or worse, and the sound of church bells rang out over manor house, farm laborer's cottage and publican's inn alike. He knew happiness and tragedy, kindness and all the usual sins of greed and envy.

Shotts, raised near this uglier, darker slum of London, found his imagination less challenged, but he still looked down at the young man with a shiver of compassion and fear for whoever could do this.

"Dunno, sir. But I 'ope we catch the bastard, and then I trust they'll 'ang 'im. Will if I 'ave anything ter do with it. Mind, catchin' 'im won't be that easy. Don't see nothin' ter go on so far. An' we can't count on much 'elp from them 'round 'ere."

Evan knelt beside the second body and felt in the pockets to see if there was anything left which might at least identify the victim. His fingers brushed against the man's neck. He stopped, a shiver of incredulity, almost horror, going through him. It was warm! Was it conceivable he was still alive?

If he was dead, then he had not been so for as long as the older man. He might have lain in this freezing alley bleeding for hours.

"What is it?" Shotts demanded, staring at Evan, his eyes wide.

Evan held his hand in front of the man's nose and lips. He felt nothing, not the faintest warmth of breath.

Shotts bent and held the lamp closer.

Evan took out his pocket watch, polished the surface clean on the inside of his sleeve, then held it to the man's lips.

"What is it?" Shotts repeated, his voice high and sharp.

"I think he's alive," Evan whispered. He drew the watch away and looked at it under the light. There was the faintest clouding of breath on it. "He is alive!" he said jubilantly. "Look!"

Shotts was a realist. He liked Evan, but he knew he was the son of a parson and he made allowances.

"Maybe 'e jus' died after the other one," he said gently. " 'E's 'urt pretty dreadful."

3

"He's warm! And he's still breathing!" Evan insisted, bending closer. "Have you called a doctor? Get an ambulance!"

Shotts shook his head. "You can't save 'im, Mr. Evan. 'E's too far gorn. Kinder ter let 'im slip away now, without knowin' anything about it. I don't suppose 'e knows 'oo dun 'im anyway."

Evan did not look up. "I wasn't thinking of what he could tell us," he replied, and it was the truth. "If he's alive we've got to do what we can. There's no choice to make. Find someone to fetch a doctor and an ambulance. Go now."

Shotts hesitated, looking around the deserted alley.

"I'll be all right," Evan said abruptly. He was not sure. He did not wish to be alone in that place. He did not belong there. He was not one of those people, as Shotts was. He was aware of his fear and wondered if it was audible in his voice.

Shotts obeyed reluctantly, leaving the bull's-eye behind. Evan saw the constable's solid form disappear around the corner and felt a moment's panic. He had nothing with which to defend himself if whoever had committed these murders returned.

But why should he? Evan knew better. He had been in the police long enough—in fact, over five years, since 1855, halfway through the Crimean War. He remembered his first murder. That had been when he had met William Monk, the best policeman he knew, if also the most ruthless, the bravest, the most instinctively clever. Evan was the only one who had realized also how vulnerable Monk was. Monk had lost his entire memory in a carriage accident, but of course he dared tell no one. He had no knowledge of who he was, what his skills were, his conflicts, his enemies or even his friends. He lived from one threat to another, clue after clue unfolding and then meaning little or nothing, just fragments.

But Monk would not have been afraid to be alone in that alley. Even the poor and the hungry and the violent of that miserable area would have thought twice before attacking him. There was something dangerous in his face with its smooth cheekbones, broad, aquiline nose and brilliant eyes. Evan's

4

gentler features, full of humor and imagination, threatened no one.

He started as there was a sound at the farther end of the alley, at the main street, but it was only a rat running along the gutter. Someone shifted weight in a doorway, but he saw nothing. A rumble of carriage wheels fifty yards away sounded like another world, where there was life and wider spaces, and the broadening daylight would give a little color.

He was so cold he was shaking. He ought to take his coat off and put it over the boy who was still alive. In fact, he should have done it straightaway. He did it now, gently, tucking it around the boy and feeling the cold bite into his own flesh till his bones ached.

It seemed an endless wait until Shotts returned, but he brought with him the doctor, a gaunt man with bony hands and a thin, patient face. His high hat was too large for him and slid close to the tops of his ears.

"Riley," he introduced himself briefly, then bent to look at the young man. His fingers felt expertly and Evan and Shotts stood waiting, staring down. It was now full daylight, although in the alley between the high, grimy walls it was still shadowed.

"You're right," Riley said after a moment, his voice strained, his eyes dark. "He's still alive . . . just." He climbed to his feet and turned towards the hearselike outline of the ambulance as the driver backed the horses to bring it to the end of the alley. "Help me lift him," he requested as another figure leaped down from the box and opened the doors at the back.

Evan and Shotts hastened to obey, lifting the cold figure as gently as they could. Riley superintended their efforts until the youth was lying on the floor inside, wrapped in blankets, and Evan had his coat back, bloodstained, filthy and damp from the wet cobbles.

Riley looked at Evan and pursed his lips. "You'd better get some dry clothes on and a stiff tot of whiskey, and then a dish of hot gruel," he said, shaking his head. "Or you'll have pneumonia yourself, and probably for nothing. I doubt we can save the poor devil." Pity altered his face in the lantern light, making

5

him look vulnerable. "Nothing I can do for the other one. He's the undertaker's job, and yours, of course. Good luck to you. You'll need it, around here. God knows what happened—or perhaps it would be more appropriate to say the devil does." And with that he climbed in behind his patient. "Mortuary van'll come for the other one," he added as if an afterthought. "I'm taking this one to St. Thomas's. You can enquire after him there. I don't suppose you have any idea who he is?"

"Not yet," Evan answered, although he knew they might never have.

Riley closed the door and banged on the wall for the driver to proceed, and the ambulance pulled away.

The mortuary van took its place and the other body was removed, leaving Evan and Shotts alone in the alley.

"It's light enough to look," Evan said grimly. "I suppose we might find something. Then we'll start searching for witnesses. What happened to the woman who raised the alarm?"

"Daisy Mott. I know where ter find 'er. Daytime in the match fact'ry, nights in that block o' rooms over there, number sixteen." He gestured with his left arm. "Don't suppose she can tell us much. If them what done this 'd bin 'ere when she come, they'd 'a killed 'er too, no doubt."

"Yes, I suppose so," Evan agreed reluctantly. "Since she screamed, they'd have silenced her at least. What about old Briggs, who fetched you?"

" 'E don't know nothin'. I asked 'im."

Evan began to widen his search, going farther away from where the two bodies had been, walking very slowly, eyes looking down on the ground. He did not know what he was looking for, anything someone might have dropped, a mark, a further bloodstain. There must be other bloodstains.

"In't rained," Shotts said grimly. "Those two fought like tigers fer their lives. Gotter be more blood. Not that I know what it'll tell us if there is. 'Cept that someone else is 'urt, an' that I can work out fer meself."

"There's blood here," Evan answered him, seeing the dark stain over the cobbles towards the central gutter. He had to put his finger into it to be sure if it was red, and not the brown of

6

excrement. "And here. This must be where at least some of the struggle took place."

"I got some 'ere too," Shotts added. "I wonder 'ow many of them there was."

"More than two," Evan replied quietly. "If it had been anything like an equal fight there'd have been four bodies here. Whoever else was here was in good enough shape to leave . . . unless, of course, someone else took them away. But that isn't likely. No, I think we're looking for two or three men at the least."

"Armed?" Shotts looked at him.

"I don't know. The doctor'll tell us how they were injured. I didn't see any knife wounds, or club or bludgeon wounds either. And they certainly weren't garroted." He shuddered as he said it. St. Giles particularly was known for the sudden and vile murders by wire around the throat. Any dirty and down-at-heel vagrant could be suspected. There was one notable occasion when two such men had suspected each other and had almost ended up in mutual murder.

"That's funny." Shotts stood still, unconsciously pulling his coat a little tighter around him in the cold. "Thieves wot set out ter rob someone in a place like this usually carry a shiv or a wire. They in't lookin' fer a fight, they wants profits and a quick getaway, wi' no 'urt to theirselves."

"Exactly," Evan agreed. "A wire around the throat or a knife in the side. Silent. Effective. No danger. Take the money and disappear into the night. So what happened here, Shotts?"

"I dunno, sir. The more I look at it, the less I know. But there in't no weapon 'ere. If there was one, they took it with them. An' wot's more, there in't no trail o' blood as I can see, so if they was 'urt theirselves, it weren't nothing like as bad as these two poor souls the doc and the mortuary van took away. I know they was dead, or as near as makes no difference, wot I mean is . . ."

"I know what you mean," Evan agreed. "It was a very one-sided affair."

A hansom went by at the far end of the street, closely followed by a wagon piled with old furniture. From somewhere in the distance came the mournful cry of a rag-and-bone man. A beggar, holding half an old coat around himself, hesitated at the mouth of the alley, then thought better of it and went on his way. Behind the grimy windows there was more movement. Voices were raised. A dog barked.

"You have to hate a man very much to beat him to death," Evan said in little more than a whisper. "Unless you're completely insane."

"They didn't belong around 'ere." Shotts shook his head. "They were clean ... under the surface, well-fed, an' their clothes was good. They was both from somewhere else, up west for certain, or in from the country."

"City," Evan corrected. "City boots. City skins. Country men would have had more color."

"Then up west. They wasn't from anyw'ere near 'ere, that's for certain positive. So 'oo around 'ere would know 'em to 'ate 'em that much?"

Evan pushed his hands into his pockets. There were more people passing the end of the alley now, men going to work in factories and warehouses, women to sweatshops and mills. The unknown numbers who worked in the streets themselves were appearing, peddlers, dealers in one thing and another, scavengers, sellers of information, petty thieves and go-betweens.

"What does a man come here for?" Evan was talking to himself. "Something he can't buy in his own part of the city."

"Slummin'," Shotts said succinctly. "Cheap women, moneylenders, card sharps, fence a bit o' summink stolen, get summink forged."

"Exactly," Evan agreed. "We'd better find out which of these, and with whom."

Shotts shrugged and gave a hollow laugh. He had no need to comment on their chances of success.

"The woman, Daisy Mott," Evan began, starting towards the street. He was so cold he could hardly feel anything below his ankles. The smell of the alley made him shrink tighter and feel queasy. He had seen too much violence and pain in a short space of hours.

"The doc were right," Shotts remarked, catching up with

8

him. "An 'ot cup o' tea wi' a drop o' gin wouldn't do yer no 'arm, nor me neither."

"Agreed." Evan did not argue. "And a pie or a sandwich. Then we'll find the woman."

But when they did find her she would tell them nothing. She was small and fair and very thin. She could have been any age between eighteen and thirty-five. It was impossible to tell. She was tired and frightened, and only spoke to them at all because she could see no way of avoiding it.

The match factory was busy already, the hum of machinery was a background to everything, the smells of sawdust, oil and phosphorus were thick in the air. Everyone looked pallid. Evan saw several women with swollen, suppurating scabs, or skin eaten away by the necrosis of the bone known as "phossie jaw," to which match workers were so susceptible. They stared at him with only minimal curiosity.

"What did you see?" Evan asked gently. "Tell me exactly what happened."

She took a deep breath but said nothing.

"In't nobody cares w'ere yer was comin' from," Shotts interposed helpfully. "Or goin'."

Evan made himself smile at her.

"I come inter the alley," she started tentatively. "It were still mostly dark. I were near on 'im w'en I saw 'im. First I reckoned as 'e were jus' drunk an' sleepin' it orff. 'Appens orften down 'ere."

"I'm sure." Evan nodded, aware of other eyes staring at them, and of the supervisor's grim face a dozen yards away. "What made you realize he was dead?"

"Blood!" she said with contempt, but her voice was hoarse. "All that blood. I 'ad a lantern, an' I saw 'is eyes starin' up at me. That were w'en I yelled. Couldn't 'elp it."

"Of course. Anyone would. What then?"

"I dunno. Me 'eart were goin' like the clappers an' I felt sick. I fink as I jus' stood there and yelled."

"Who heard you?"

"Wot?"

9

"Who heard you?" he repeated. "Someone must have come."

She hesitated, afraid again. She did not dare implicate someone else. He could see it in her eyes. Monk would have known what to do to make her speak. He had a sense of people's weaknesses and how to use them without breaking them. He did not lose sight of the main purpose the way Evan too often did. He was not sidetracked by irrelevant pity, imagining himself in their place, which was false. He did not know how they felt. He would have said Evan was sentimental. Evan could hear Monk's voice in his mind even as he thought it. It was true. And people did not want pity. They would have hated him for it. It was the ultimate indignity.

"Who came?" he said more sharply. "Do you want me to go around every door, pulling people out and asking them? Would you like to be arrested for lying to the police? Get you noticed. Get you a bad name." He meant it would make people think she was a police informer, and she knew that.

"Jimmy Elders," she said, looking at him with dislike. "An' 'is woman. They both come. 'E lives 'alfway along the alley, be'ind the wood door wif the lock on it. But 'e don' know wot 'appened any more'n I do. Then ol' Briggs. 'E went for the rozzer."

"Thank you." He knew it was a waste of time asking, but he had to go through the motions. "Had you ever seen either of the two men before, when they were alive?"

"No." She answered without even thinking. It was what he had expected. He glanced around and saw that the supervisor had moved a little closer. He was a large, black-haired man with a sullen face. Evan hoped she was not going to be docked pay for the time he had taken, but he thought she probably would. He would waste no more of it.

"Thank you. Good-bye."

She said nothing, but returned silently to her work.

Evan and Shotts went back to the alley and spoke to Jimmy Elders and his common-law wife, but they had nothing to offer beyond corroborating what Daisy Mott had told them. Elders denied having seen either of the men alive, or knowing what they might have been doing there. The leer in his face suggested the obvious, but he refrained from putting words to it. Briggs was the same.

They spent all day in and around the alley, which was known as Water Lane, going up and down narrow and rotting stairs, into rooms where sometimes a whole family lived, others where pale-faced young prostitutes conducted their business when it was too wet or too cold outside. They went down to cellars where women of all ages sat in candlelight stitching and children two or three years old played in straw and tied waste bits of rag into dolls. Older children unpicked old clothes for the fabric to make new ones.

No one admitted to having seen or heard anything unusual. No one knew anything of two strangers in the area. There were always people coming and going. There were pawnshops, fencers of stolen goods, petty forgers of documents, doss houses, gin mills and well-hidden rooms where it was safe for a wanted man to lie for a while. The dead men could have come to do business with any of these, or none. They might simply have been entertaining themselves by looking on at a way of life different from their own and immeasurably inferior. They could even have been misguided preachers come to save sinners from themselves, and been attacked for their presumption and their interference.

If people knew anything at all, they were more afraid of the perpetrators, or of their peers, than of the police, at least in the form of Evan and P.C. Shotts.

At four o'clock, as it was growing dark again, and bitterly cold, Shotts said he would make one or two more enquiries in the public house, where he had a few acquaintances, and Evan took his leave to go to the hospital and see what Dr. Riley had to say. He had been dreading it because he did not want to have to think of the younger man again, the one who had been still alive in that dreadful place. The memory of it made him feel cold and sick. He was too tired to find the strength inside himself to overcome it.

He said good-day to Shotts and walked briskly in the general

11

direction of Regent Street, where he knew he could find a hansom.

In St. Thomas's Hospital he went straight to the morgue. He would look at the bodies and deduce what he could for himself and then ask Riley to explain to him what else there was to learn. He hated morgues, but everyone he knew felt the same. His clothes always seemed to smell of vinegar and lye afterwards, and he never felt as if the damp were out of them.

"Yes sir," the attendant said dutifully when Evan identified himself. "Doc Riley said you'd be 'ere some time, prob'ly today. I only got one body for yer. Other one in't dead yet. Doc says as 'e might pull through. Never know. Poor devil. Still, I suppose yer want ter see the one I got." It was not a question. He had been there long enough to know the answer. Young policemen like Evan never came for anything else.

"Thank you," Evan accepted, feeling a sudden surge of relief that the young man was still alive. He realized now how much he had been hoping he would be. And yet at the same time it meant he would wake up to so much pain, and a long, slow fight to recover, and Evan dreaded that, and his own necessity for being part of it.

He followed the attendant along the rows of tables, all sheet covered, some with the stark outline of a corpse beneath, others empty. His feet rang in the silence on the stone floor. The light was harsh, beaming back from bare walls. It was as if no one but the dead inhabited the place. There were no concessions to the living. They were intruders here.

The attendant stopped by one of the tables and pulled the sheet off slowly, uncovering the body of a middle-aged, slightly plump man of average height. Riley had cleaned him up very little, perhaps so Evan could make his own deductions. But with his clothes absent it was possible to see the terrible extent of his injuries. His entire torso was covered in contusions, black and dull purple where they had bled internally while he was still alive. On some the skin was torn. Several of the misshapen ribs were obviously broken.

"Poor devil," the attendant repeated between his teeth. "Put up one 'ell of a fight afore they got 'im."

Evan looked down at the hand nearest him. The knuckles were burst open and at least two fingers were dislocated. All but one of the nails were torn.

"Other 'and's the same," the attendant offered.

Evan leaned over and picked it up gently. The attendant was correct. That was the right hand, and if anything, it was worse.

"Will you be wanting to see his clothes?" the attendant asked after a moment.

"Yes, please." They might tell him something, possibly something he could not already guess. Most of all he wanted to know the man's name. He must have family, perhaps a wife, wondering what had happened to him. Would they have any idea where he had gone or why? Probably not. Evan would have the wretched duty not only of informing them of his death, and the dreadful manner in which it happened, but where he had been at the time.

"'Ere they are, sir." The attendant turned and walked towards a bench at the farther end of the room. "All kept for yer, but otherwise just as we took 'em orff 'im. Good quality, they are. But you'll see that for yourself." He picked up underwear, socks, then a shirt which had originally been white but was now heavily soiled with blood and mud and effluent from the gutter in the alley. The smell of it was noticeable, even there. The jacket and trousers were worse.

Evan undid them and laid them out on the bench. He searched them carefully, taking his time. He explored pockets, folds, seams, cuffs. The fabric was wool, not the best quality, but one he would have been happy to wear himself. It was warm, a rather loose weave, a nondescript brown, just what a gentleman might have chosen in which to conduct an expedition into an unseemly quarter of the city—not, perhaps, one as dangerous as St. Giles. No doubt for his normal business he wore something better. The linen of the shirt would suggest that his taste and his pocket both allowed a greater indulgence.

All that told him was that the man was exactly what he'd thought, from somewhere else, seeking either pleasure or a dishonest business in one of London's worst slums.

The suit had been damaged on the knees, presumably when

13

he had fallen during the fight. One knee was actually torn, the threads raw; the other only pulled out of shape, a few fibers broken. There was also a badly scuffed patch on the seat and it was still wet from the gutter and deeply stained. The jacket was worse. Both elbows were torn, one almost completely gone. There was a rent in the left side and a pocket all but ripped off. However, even the most thorough search, inch by inch, revealed no damage which could have been done by a knife or a bullet. There was a considerable amount of blood, far more than could be accounted for by the nature of the injuries to the dead man. Anyway, it appeared to have come from someone else, being darker and wetter on the outside of the garment and having barely soaked through to the inside. At least one of the man's assailants must have been pretty badly hurt.

"D'yer know wot 'appened?" the attendant asked.

"No," Evan said miserably. "No idea, so far."

The attendant grunted. "Come in from St. Giles, didn't 'e? Reckon as yer'll never find out, then. Nobody from there says nothin' on their own. Poor devil. 'Ad a few garroters in from there. 'E must 'a crossed someone proper ter get beat like that. Don't need ter do that ter no one just ter rob 'im. Gambler maybe."

"Maybe." The name of the tailor was on the inside of the jacket. Evan had made a note of that, and the address. It might be sufficient to identify the victim. "Where is Dr. Riley?"

"Up on the wards, I s'pec, if 'e in't bin called out again. Fair make use of 'im, you rozzers do."

"Not of my choice, I promise you," Evan said wearily. "I'd much rather not have the need."

The attendant sighed and ran his fingers through his hair. He said nothing.

Evan went up the stairs and along the corridors, asking, until he found Riley coming out of one of the operating theaters, jacket off, shirtsleeves rolled up, his arms spattered with blood.

"Just taken out a bullet," he said cheerfully. "Damn fool accident. Marvelous thing, this new anesthetic. Never saw anything like it in my youth. Best thing to happen in medicine

14

since . . . I don't know what! Maybe it's just the best thing—straight and simple. I suppose you've come about your corpse from St. Giles?" He shoved his hands into his pockets. He looked tired. There were fine lines crisscrossing his face, and a smear of blood over his brow and another on his cheek where he had rubbed his hand without realizing it.

Evan nodded.

A medical student walked past them, whistling between his teeth until he recognized Riley, then he stopped and straightened his shoulders.

"Beaten to death," Riley said, pursing his lips. "No wound from any weapon . . . unless you count fists and boots as weapons. No knife, no gun, no cudgel as far as I can judge. Nothing to the head more than a flat concussion from falling onto the cobbles. Wouldn't have killed him, probably not even knocked him senseless. Probably just stunned and a little dizzy. Died of internal hemorrhage. Ruptured organs. Sorry."

"Could one man alone have done that to him?"

Riley thought for quite a long time before he replied, standing still in the middle of the passage, oblivious of blocking the way for others.

"Hard to say. Wouldn't like to commit myself. Taking that body alone, without considering the circumstances, I'd guess more than one assailant. If it was only one man, then he was a raving lunatic to do that to another man. He must have gone berserk."

"And with considering the circumstances?" Evan pressed, stepping to one side to allow a nurse to pass with a bundle of laundry.

"Well, the boy's still alive, and if he survives tonight, he might recover," Riley answered. "Too soon to say. But to take on both of them, and do that much damage, I'd say two assailants who were both big and well used to violence, or possibly even three. Or else again, two complete lunatics."

"Could they have fought each other?"

Riley looked surprised. "And left themselves damn near dead on the pavement? Not very likely."

15

"But possible?" Evan insisted.

Riley shook his head. "Don't think you'll find the answer is that easy, Sergeant. The younger man is taller. The older one was a bit plump; he was well muscled, quite powerful. He'd have taken a lot of beating, considering he was fighting for his life. And there was no weapon to give the advantage."

"Can you tell if the wounds were made attacking or defending?"

"Mostly defending, as well as I can judge, but it's only a deduction made from their position, on forearms, as if he were putting up his arms to protect his head. He may have begun by attacking. He certainly landed a few blows, judging from his knuckles. Someone else is going to be badly marked, whether it is anywhere that shows or not."

"There was blood on the outside of his clothes," Evan told him. "Someone else's blood." He watched Riley's face closely.

Riley shrugged. "Could be the younger man's, could be someone else's. I've no way of knowing."

"What condition is he in now, the younger man? What are his injuries?"

Riley was distressed; he looked overwhelmed by his knowledge, as if it were something he would have gladly put down.

"Very bad," he said almost under his breath. "He's still senseless, but definitely alive. If he pulls through tonight he'll need a lot of careful nursing, many weeks, maybe months. He's badly injured internally, but it's hard to tell exactly what. Can't see inside a body without cutting it open. As much as I can tell, the major organs are terribly bruised but not ruptured. If they were, he'd be dead by now. Luckier than the other man where the blows landed. Both his hands are badly broken, but that hardly matters, compared."

"Nothing in his clothes to say who he is, I suppose?" Evan asked without any real hope.

"Yes," Riley said quickly, his eyes wide. "Apparently he had a receipt for socks with the name R. Duff on it. Must be his. Can't think why you'd carry a receipt for another man's socks. And he has the same tailor as the dead man. There's a very slight physical resemblance about the shape of head, way the

16

hair grows, and particularly the ears. Do you notice a man's ears, Sergeant Evan? Some people don't. You'd be surprised how many. Ears are very distinctive. I think you might find our two men are related."

"Duff?" Evan could hardly believe his good fortune. "R. Duff?"

"That's right. No idea what the *R* stands for, but maybe he'll be able to tell us himself tomorrow. Anyway, you can try the tailor in the morning. A man often knows his own handiwork."

"Yes—yes. I'll take a piece of it to show him. Can I see the boy's clothes?"

"They're by his bed, over in the next ward. I'll take you." Riley turned and led the way along the wide, bare corridor and into a ward lined with beds, each gray blanketed, each showing the outline of a figure lying or propped up. At the farther end a potbellied stove gave off quite a good heat, and even as they walked up, a nurse staggered past them with a bucketful of fresh coals to keep it stoked.

Evan was reminded sharply of Hester Latterly, the young woman he had met so soon after his first encounter with Monk. She had gone out to the Crimea and nursed with Florence Nightingale. He could not even imagine the courage it must have taken to do that, to face that raging disease, the carnage of the battlefield, the constant pain and death, and to find within oneself the resources to keep on fighting to overcome, to offer help and to give some kind of comfort to those you were powerless even to ease, let alone to save.

No wonder such an anger still burned inside her at what she perceived to be incompetence in medical administration. How she and Monk had quarreled! Evan smiled even as he thought of it. And yet when Monk had faced the worst crisis in his life it had been she who had stood beside him, she who had refused to let him give in, had fought for him when it looked as if he could not win, and worst of all, did not deserve to.

She must have rebelled against rolling bandages, sweeping floors and carrying coals when she was capable of so much more, and had done it in the field surgeons' tents when all the

17

doctors were already doing all they could. She had wanted to reform so much, and the eagerness had got in her way.

They were at the end of the ward now, and Riley had stopped by a bed where lay a young man, white-faced, motionless. Only the clouding of his breath on a glass could have told if he was still alive. There was nothing for the eye to see.

Evan recognized him from the alley. The features were the same, the curve of eyelid, the almost-black hair, rather long nose, sensitive mouth. The bruising did not hide that, and the blood had been cleared away. Evan found himself willing the young man to live, aching with the tension in his own body, as if by strength of his feeling he could make it happen—and yet at the same time he was concerned about the pain the young man would feel when he woke.

Who was he—R. Duff? Was the older man related to him? And what had happened in that alley? Why had they been there? What appetite had taken them to such a place on a January night?

"Give me the trousers," Evan whispered, a wave of horror and revulsion returning to him. "I'll take them to the tailor."

"You'd be better with the coat," Riley replied. "It's got the label on it, and there's less blood."

"Less blood? The other man's coat was soaked in it."

"I know." Riley shrugged his thin shoulders. "With this one it's the trousers. Maybe they all went down together in a scrum. But if you want the tailor to be fit for anything, take the jacket. No need to give the poor man a turn."

Evan took the jacket after he had examined both pieces. Like the dead man's clothes, they were torn in several places, filthy with mud and effluent from the gutter, and stained with blood on coat sleeves and tails, and the trousers were sodden.

Evan left the hospital horrified, exhausted in mind and spirit as well as body, and now so cold he could not stop shivering. He took a hansom home to his rooms. He would not get in an omnibus with that dreadful jacket, and he had no wish to sit among other people, decent people at the end of their day's work, who had no idea of what he had seen and felt or of the young man in St. Thomas's who might or might not awake again.

He found the tailor at nine o'clock. He spoke personally to Mr. Jiggs of Jiggs and Muldrew, a rotund man who needed all his own art to disguise his ample stomach and rather short legs.

"What may I do for you, sir?" he said with some distaste as he saw the parcel under Evan's arm. He disapproved of gentlemen who bundled up clothes. It was no way to treat a highly crafted piece of workmanship.

Evan had no time or mood for catering to anyone's sensitivities.

"Do you have a client by the name of R. Duff, Mr. Jiggs?" he asked bluntly.

"My client list is a matter of confidence, sir—"

"This is a case of murder," Evan snapped, sounding more like Monk than his own usually soft-spoken self. "The owner of this suit is lying at death's door in St. Thomas's. Another man, who also wore a suit with your label in it, is in the morgue. I do not know who they are . . . other than this . . ." He ignored Jiggs's pasty face and wide eyes. "If you can tell me, then I demand that you do so." He spilled the jacket onto the tailor's table.

Jiggs started backwards as if the garment was alive and dangerous.

"Will you look at it, please," Evan commanded.

"Oh, my God!" Mr. Jiggs put a clammy hand to his brow. "Whatever happened?"

"I don't know yet," Evan answered a trifle more gently. "Will you please look at that jacket and tell me if you know for whom you made it?"

"Yes. Yes, of course. I always know my gentlemen, sir." Gingerly Mr. Jiggs unfolded the coat only sufficiently to see his own label. He glanced at it, touched the cloth with his fore-finger, then looked at Evan. "I made that suit for young Mr. Rhys Duff, of Ebury Street, sir." He looked extremely pale. "I am very sorry indeed that he seems to have met with a disaster. It truly grieves me, sir."

19

Evan bit his lip. "I'm sure. Did you also make a suit in a brown wool for another gentleman, possibly related to him? This man would be in his middle fifties, average height, quite solidly built. He had gray hair, rather fairer than Rhys Duff's, I should think."

"Yes sir." Jiggs took a shaky breath. "I made several suits for Mr. Leighton Duff; he's Master Rhys's father. I fear it may be he you are describing. Was he injured also?"

"I am afraid he is dead, Mr. Jiggs. Can you tell me the number in Ebury Street. I am obliged to inform his family."

"Oh—why, of course. How very terrible. I wish there were some way I could assist." The tailor stepped back as he said it, but there was a look of acute distress in his face, and Evan was disposed to believe him, at least in part.

"The number in Ebury Street?" he repeated.

"Yes . . . yes. I think it is thirty-four, if my memory serves, but I'll look in my books. Yes, of course I will."

Evan did not go straight to Ebury Street. First he returned to St. Thomas's. There was a sense in which it would be kinder to the family if he could tell them at least that Rhys Duff was still alive, perhaps conscious. And if the young man could speak, maybe he could tell them what had happened, and Evan would have to ask fewer questions.

And there was part of him which was simply not ready yet to go and tell some woman that her husband was dead and her son might or might not survive, and no one knew yet in what degree of injury, pain or disability.

He found Riley straightaway, looking as if he had been there all night. Certainly he seemed to be wearing the same clothes with precisely the same wrinkles and bloodstains on them.

"He's still alive," he said as soon as he saw Evan and before Evan could ask. "He stirred a bit about an hour ago. Let's go and see if he's come around." And he set off with a long-legged stride as if he too were eager to know.

The ward was busy. Two young doctors were changing bandages and examining wounds. A nurse who looked no more than fifteen or sixteen was carrying buckets of slops, her shoulders bent as she strove to keep the buckets off the floor. An elderly woman struggled with a bucket of coals and Evan offered to take them from her, but she refused, looking nervously at Riley. Another nurse gathered up soiled laundry and brushed past them with her face averted. Riley seemed hardly to notice; his attention was solely upon the patients.

Evan followed him to the end of the ward, where he saw with a rush of relief, overtaken instantly by anxiety, that Rhys Duff lay motionless on his back, but his eyes were open— large, dark eyes which stared up at the ceiling and seemed to see only horror.

Riley stopped by the bed and looked at his patient with some concern.

"Good morning, Mr. Duff," he said gently. "You are in St. Thomas's Hospital. My name is Riley. How are you feeling?"

Rhys Duff rolled his head very slightly until his eyes were focusing on Riley.

"How are you feeling, Mr. Duff?" Riley repeated.

Rhys opened his mouth, his lips moved, but there was no sound whatever.

"Does your throat hurt?" Riley asked with a frown. It was obviously not something he had expected.

Rhys stared at him.

"Does your throat hurt?" Riley asked again, "Nod if it does."

Very slowly Rhys shook his head. He looked faintly surprised.

Riley put his hand on Rhys's slender wrist above the bandaging of his broken hand. The other, similarly splinted and bound, lay on the cover.

"Can you speak, Mr. Duff?" Riley asked very softly.

Rhys opened his mouth again, and again no sound came.

Riley waited.

Rhys's eyes were filled with terrible memory; fear and pain held him transfixed. Momentarily his head moved from side to side in denial. He could not speak.

Riley turned to Evan. "I'm sorry, you'll get nothing from

him yet. He may be well enough to answer yes and no to-morrow, but he may not. At the moment he's too shocked for you to bother him at all. For certain, he can't talk to you or describe anyone. And it will be weeks before he can hold a pen—if his hands mend well enough ever."

Evan hesitated. He needed desperately to know what had happened, but he was torn with pity for this unbearably injured boy. He wished he had his father's faith to help him understand how such things could happen. Why was there not some justice to prevent it? He did not have a blind belief to soothe either his anger or his pity.

Nor did he have Hester's capacity to provide the practical help which would have eased the aching helplessness inside him.

Perhaps the nearest he could strive for was Monk's dedication to pursuing truth.

"Do you know who did this to you, Mr. Duff?" he asked, speaking over Riley.

Rhys shut his eyes and again shook his head. If he had any memory, he was choosing to close it out as too monstrous to bear.

"I think you should leave now, Sergeant," Riley said with an edge to his voice. "He can't tell you anything."

Evan acknowledged the truth of it, and with one last look at the ashen face of the young man lying in the bed, he turned and went about the only duty he dreaded more.

Ebury Street was quiet and elegant in the cold morning air. There was a slick of ice on the pavements and housemaids were indisposed to linger in gossip. The two or three people Evan saw all kept moving, whisking dusters and mopheads out of windows and in again as quickly as possible. An errand boy scampered up steps and rang a bell with fingers clumsy with cold.

Evan found number thirty-four and, unconsciously copying Monk, he went to the front door. Anyway, news such as he had should not go through the kitchens first.

The bell was answered by a parlormaid in a smart uniform.

Her starched linen and lace immediately proclaimed a household of better financial standing than the clothes worn by the dead man suggested.

"Yes sir?"

"Good morning. I am Police Sergeant Evan. Does a Mr. Leighton Duff live here?"

"Yes sir, but he isn't home at the moment." She said it with some anxiety. It was not a piece of information she would normally have offered to a caller, even though she knew it to be true. She looked at his face, and perhaps read the weariness and sadness in it. "Is everything all right, sir?"

"No, I'm afraid it isn't. Is there a Mrs. Duff?"

Her hand flew to her mouth, her eyes filled with alarm, but she did not scream.

"You had better warn her lady's maid and perhaps the butler. I am afraid I have very bad news."

Silently she opened the door wider and let him in.

A butler with thin, graying hair came from the back of the hallway, frowning.

"Who is the gentleman, Janet?" He turned to Evan. "Good morning, sir. May I be of assistance to you? I am afraid Mr. Duff is not at home at present, and Mrs. Duff is not receiving." He was less sensitive to Evan's expression than the maid had been.

"I am from the police," Evan repeated. "I have extremely bad news to tell Mrs. Duff. I'm very sorry. Perhaps you should remain in case she needs some assistance. Possibly you might send a messenger for your family doctor."

"What . . . what has happened?" Now the butler looked thoroughly horrified.

"I am afraid that Mr. Leighton Duff and Mr. Rhys Duff have met with violence. Mr. Rhys is in St. Thomas's Hospital in a very serious condition."

The butler gulped. "And . . . and Mr. . . . Mr. Leighton Duff?"

"I am afraid he is dead."

"Oh dear . . . I . . ." He swayed a little where he stood in the magnificent hallway with its carved staircase, aspidistras in stone urns and brass umbrella stand with silver-topped canes in it.

"You'd better sit down a minute, Mr. Wharmby," Janet said with sympathy.

Wharmby straightened himself, but he looked very pallid. "Certainly not! Whatever next? It is my duty to look after poor Mrs. Duff in every way possible, as it is yours. Go and get Alfred to fetch Dr. Wade. I shall inform Madam that there is someone to see her. You might return with a decanter of brandy . . . just in case some restorative is needed."

But it was not. Sylvestra Duff sat motionless in the large chair in the morning room, her face bloodlessly white under her dark hair with its pronounced widow's peak. She was not immediately beautiful—her face was too long, too aquiline, her nose delicately flared, her eyes almost black—but she had a distinction which became more marked the longer one was with her. Her voice was low and very measured. In other circumstances it would have been lovely. Now she was too shattered by horror and grief to speak in anything but broken fractions of sentences.

"How . . ." she started. "Where? Where did you say?"

"In one of the back streets of an area known as St. Giles," Evan answered gently, moderating the truth a little. He wished there were some way she would never have to know the full facts.

"St. Giles?" It seemed to mean very little to her. He studied her face, the smooth, high-boned cheeks and curved brow. He thought he saw a slight tightening, but it could have been no more than a change in the light as she turned towards him.

"It is a few hundred yards off Regent Street, towards Aldgate."

"Aldgate?" she said with a frown.

"Where did he say he was going, Mrs. Duff?" he asked.

"He didn't say."

"Perhaps you would tell me all you can recall of yesterday."

She shook her head very slowly. "No . . . no, that can wait. First I must go to my son. I must . . . I must be with him. You said he is very badly hurt?"

"I am afraid so. But he is in the best hands possible." He leaned a little towards her. "You can do no more for him at present," he said earnestly. "It is best he rests. He is not fully sensible most of the time. No doubt the doctor will give him herbs and sedatives to ease his pain and help him to heal."

"Are you trying to spare my feelings, Sergeant? I assure you, it is not necessary. I must be where I can do the most good, that is the only thing which will be of any comfort to me." She looked at him very directly. She had amazing eyes; their darkness almost concealed her emotions and made her a peculiarly private woman. He imagined the great Spanish aristocrats might have looked something like that: proud, secretive, hiding their vulnerability.

"No, Mrs. Duff," he said. "I was trying to find out as much as I can from you about what occurred yesterday while it is fresh in your mind, before you are fully occupied with your son. At the moment it is Dr. Riley's help he needs. I need yours."

"You are very direct, Sergeant."

He did not know if it was a criticism or simply an observation. Her voice was without expression. She was too profoundly shocked from the reality of what he had told her to touch anything but the surface of her mind. She sat upright, her back rigid, shoulders stiff, her hands unmoving in her lap. He imagined if he touched them he would find them locked together, unbending.

"I am sorry. It seems not the time for niceties. This matters far too much. Did your husband and son leave the house together?"

"No. No . . . Rhys left first. I did not see him go."

"And your husband?"

"Yes . . . yes, I saw him leave. Of course."

"Did he say where he was going?"

"No . . . no. He quite often went out in the evening . . . to his club. It is a very usual thing for a gentleman to do. Business, as well as pleasure, depends upon social acquaintances. He did not say . . . specifically."

He was not sure why, but he did not entirely believe her. Was

25

it possible she was aware that her husband had frequented certain dubious places, perhaps even that he'd used prostitutes? Such behavior was tacitly accepted by many wives, even though they would have been shocked if anyone had been vulgar and insensitive enough to speak it. Everyone was aware of bodily functions. No one referred to them; it was both indelicate and unnecessary.

"How was he dressed, ma'am?"

Her arched eyebrows rose. "Dressed? Presumably as you found him, Sergeant. What do you mean?"

"Did he have a watch, Mrs. Duff?"

"A watch? Yes. Oh, I see. He was . . . robbed. Yes, he had a very fine gold watch. It was not on him?"

"No. Was he in the habit of carrying much money with him?"

"I don't know. I can ask Bridlaw, his valet. He could probably tell you. Does it matter?"

"It might." Evan was puzzled. "Do you know if he was wearing his gold watch yesterday when he left?" It seemed a strange and rather perverse thing to go into St. Giles, for whatever reason, wearing a conspicuously expensive article like a gold watch, so easily visible. It almost invited robbery. Was he lost? Was he perhaps taken there against his will? "Did he mention meeting anyone?"

"No." She was quite certain.

"And the watch?" he prompted.

"Yes. I believe he was wearing it." She stared at him intently. "He almost always did. He was very fond of it. I think I would have noticed were he without it. I remember now he wore a brown suit. Not his best at all—in fact, rather an inferior one. He had it made for the most casual wear, weekends and so forth."

"And yet the night he went out was a Wednesday," Evan reminded her.

"Then he must have been planning a casual evening," she replied bluntly. "Why do you ask, Sergeant? What difference does it make now? He was not . . . murdered . . . because of what he wore!"

26

"I was trying to deduce where he intended to go, Mrs. Duff. St. Giles is not an area where we would expect to find a gentleman of Mr. Duff's means and social standing. If I knew why he was there, or with whom, I would be a great deal closer to knowing what happened to him."

"I see. I suppose it was foolish of me not to have understood." She looked away from him. The room was comfortable, beautifully proportioned. There was no sound but the crackle of flames in the fireplace and the soft, rhythmic ticking of the clock on the mantel. Everything about the room was gracious, serene, different in every conceivable way from the alley in which its owner had perished. Quite probably St. Giles was beyond the knowledge or even the imagination of his widow.

She turned towards him slowly. "I suppose you want to know how my son was dressed also?"

"Yes, please."

"I cannot remember. In something very ordinary, gray or navy, I think. No . . . a black coat and gray trousers."

It was what he had been wearing when he was found. Evan said nothing.

"He said he was going out to enjoy himself," she said, her voice suddenly dropping and catching with emotion. "He was . . . angry."

"With whom?" He tried to picture the scene. Rhys Duff was probably no more than eighteen or nineteen, still immature, rebellious.

She lifted her shoulders very slightly. It was a gesture of denial, as if the question were not answerable.

"Was there a quarrel, ma'am, a difference of opinion?"

She sat silent for so long he was afraid she was not going to reply. Of course it was bitterly painful. It was their last meeting. Father and son could never now be reconciled. The fact that she did not deny it instantly was answer enough.

"It was trivial," she said at last. "It doesn't matter now. My husband was dubious about some of the company Rhys chose to keep. Oh . . . not anyone who would hurt him, Sergeant. I am speaking of female company. My husband wished Rhys to make the acquaintance of reputable young ladies. He was in a position to make a settlement upon him if he chose to marry, not a good fortune many young men can count upon."

"Indeed not," Evan agreed with feeling. He knew dozens of young men, and indeed older ones, who would dearly like to marry but could not afford it. To keep an establishment suitable for a wife cost more than three or four times the amount necessary to live a single life. And then the almost inevitable children added to that greatly. Rhys Duff was an unusually fortunate young man. Why had he not been grateful for that?

As if answering his thought she spoke very softly.

"Perhaps he was . . . too young. He might have done it willingly if . . . if it had not been his father's wish for him. The young can be so . . . so . . . willful . . . even against their own interests." She seemed barely able to control the grief which welled up inside her. Evan hated having to press any questions at all, but he knew that she was more likely to tell him an unguarded truth at present. The next day she could be more careful, more watchful to conceal anything which damaged—or revealed.

He struggled for anything to say which could be of comfort, and there was nothing. In his mind he saw so clearly the pale, bruised face of the young man lying first in the alley, crumpled and bleeding, and then in St. Thomas's, his eyes filled with horror which was quite literally unspeakable. He saw again Rhys's mouth open as he struggled, and failed to utter even a word. What could anyone say to comfort his mother?

Evan made a resolve that however long it took him, however hard it was, he would find out what had happened in that alley and make whoever was responsible answer for it.

"He said nothing of where he might go?" he resumed. "Had he any usual haunts?"

"He left in some . . . heat," she replied. She seemed to have steadied herself again. "I believe his father had an idea as to where he frequented. Perhaps it is known to men in general? There are . . . places. It was only an impression. I cannot help you, Sergeant."

"But both men were in some temper when they left?"

"Yes."

"How long apart in time was that?"

"I am not sure, because Rhys left the room, and it was not until about half an hour after that when we realized he had also left the house. My husband then went out immediately."

"I see."

"They were found together?" Again her voice wavered and she had to make a visible effort to control herself.

"Yes. It looks as if perhaps your husband caught up with your son, and some time after that they were set upon."

"Maybe they were lost?" She looked at him anxiously.

"Quite possibly," he agreed, hoping it was true. Of all the explanations it would be the kindest, the easiest for her to bear. "It would not be hard to become lost in such a warren of alleys and passages. Merely a few yards in the wrong direction . . ." He left the rest unsaid. He wanted to believe it almost as much as she did, because he knew so much more of the alternatives.

There was a knock on the door, an unusual thing for a servant to do. It was normal for a butler simply to come in and then await a convenient moment either to serve whatever was required or to deliver a message.

"Come in?" Sylvestra said with a lift of surprise.

The man who entered was lean and dark with a handsome face, deep-set eyes and a nose perhaps a trifle small. Now his expression was one of acute concern and distress. He all but ignored Evan and went immediately to Sylvestra, but his manner was professional as well as personal. Presumably he was the doctor Wharmby had sent for.

"My dear, I cannot begin to express my sorrow. Naturally, anything I can do, you have but to name. I shall remain with you as long as you wish. Certainly I shall prescribe something to help you sleep and to calm and assist you through these first dreadful days. Eglantyne says if you wish to leave here and stay with us, we shall see that you have all the peace and privacy you could wish. Our house will be yours."

"Thank you . . . you are very kind. I . . ." She gave a little shiver. "I don't even know what I want yet . . . what there is to be done." She rose to her feet, swayed a moment and grasped for his arm, which he gave instantly. "First I must go to St. Thomas's Hospital and see Rhys."

"Do you think that is wise?" the doctor cautioned. "You are in a state of extreme shock, my dear. Allow me to go for you. I can at least see that he is given the very best professional help and care. I will see that he is brought home as soon as it is medically advisable. In the meantime I shall care for him myself, I promise you."

She hesitated, torn between love and good sense.

"Let me at least see him!" she pleaded. "Take me. I promise I shall not be a burden. I am in command of myself!"

He hesitated only a moment. "Of course. Take a little brandy, just to revive yourself, then I shall accompany you." He glanced at Evan. "I am sure you are finished here, Sergeant. Anything else you need to know can wait until a more opportune time."

It was dismissal, and Evan accepted it with a kind of relief. There was little more he could learn there. Perhaps later he would speak to the valet and other servants. The coachman might know where his master was in the habit of going. In the meantime there were people he knew in St. Giles, informers, men and women upon whom pressure could be placed, judicious questions asked, and a great deal might be learned.

"Of course," he conceded, rising to his feet. "I shall try to bother you as little as possible, ma'am." He took his leave as the doctor was taking the decanter of brandy from the butler and pouring a little into a glass.

Outside in the street, where it was beginning to snow, Evan turned up his coat collar and walked briskly. He wondered what Monk would have done. Would he have thought of some brilliant and probing questions whose answers would have revealed a new line of truth to follow and unravel? Would he have felt any less crippled by pity and horror than Evan did? Had there been something obvious which his emotion had prevented him from seeing?

Surely the obvious thing was that father and son had gone whoring in St. Giles and been careless, perhaps paid less than the asking price, perhaps been too high-handed or arrogant showing off their money and their gold watches, and some ruffians, afire with drink, had attacked them and then, like dogs at the smell of blood, run amok?

Either way, what could the widow know of it? He was right not to harry her now.

He put his head down against the east wind and increased his pace.

2

$R_{HYS\ DUFF\ WAS\ KEPT}$ in the hospital for a further two days, and on Monday, the fifth day after the attack, he was brought home, in great pain and still without having spoken a word. Dr. Corriden Wade was to call every day or, as Rhys progressed, every second day, but of course it would be necessary to have him professionally nursed. At the recommendation of the young policeman on the case, and having made appropriate enquiries as to her abilities, Wade agreed to the employment of one of the women who had gone out to the Crimea with Florence Nightingale, a Miss Hester Latterly. She was of necessity used to caring for young men who had suffered near-mortal injuries in combat. She was considered an excellent choice.

To Hester herself it was an agreeable change after having nursed an elderly and extremely trying lady whose problems were largely matters of temper and boredom, only slightly exacerbated by two broken toes. She could probably have managed just as well with a competent lady's maid, but she felt more dramatic with a nurse and impressed her friends endlessly by likening her plight to that of the war heroes Hester had nursed before her.

Hester kept a civil tongue with difficulty, and only because she required the employment in order to survive. Her father's financial ruin had meant she had no inheritance. Her elder brother, Charles, would always have provided for her, as men were expected to provide and care for their unmarried female relations, but such dependence would be suffocating to a woman like Hester, who had tasted an extraordinary freedom in the Crimea and a responsibility at once both exhilarating and terrifying. She was certainly not going to spend the rest of her days in quiet domesticity being obedient and grateful to a rather unimaginative if kindly brother.

It was infinitely preferable to bite one's tongue and refrain from telling Miss Golightly she was a fool . . . for the space of a few weeks.

Hester thought, as she settled herself in the hansom that was to take her to this new position, that there were other very considerable advantages to her independent situation. She could make friends where and with whom she chose. Charles would not have had any objection to Lady Callandra Daviot; well, not any severe objection. Callandra was well-bred and had been highly respectable while her army surgeon husband was alive. Now, as a fairly wealthy widow, she was becoming rather less so. Indeed, some might have considered her a trifle eccentric. She had made a pact with Monk when he became a private agent of enquiry that she would support him financially during his lean times as long as he shared with her his more interesting cases. That was not in any sense respectable, but it was enormously diverting, at times tragic and always absorbing. Frequently it accomplished, if not happiness, at least a resolution and some kind of justice.

The hansom was moving at a brisk pace through the traffic. Hester shivered in the cold.

And there was the agent of enquiry himself. Charles would never have approved of William Monk. How could society possibly accept a man without a memory? He could be anyone! He could have done anything! The possibilities were endless, and almost all of them unpleasant. Had he been a hero, an aristocrat, or a gentleman, someone would have recognized him and owned him.

Since the one thing he knew about himself for certain was that he was a policeman, that automatically placed him in a social category somewhere beneath even the most regrettable trade. And of course trade was beneath any of the professions. Younger sons of the gentry went into the army or the church or

33

the law—those who did not marry wealth and relieve themselves of the necessity of having to do anything. Elder sons, naturally, inherited land and money, and lived accordingly.

Not that Hester's friendship with Monk could easily be categorized. Pressing through the traffic in the rain, she thought of it with a mixture of emotions, all of them disturbingly powerful. It had lurched from an initial mutual contempt to a kind of trust which was unique in her life, and she believed in his also. And then, as if suddenly afraid of such vulnerability, they had been quick to quarrel, to find fault and keep little rein on temper.

But in times of need, and the mutual caring for some cause, they had worked together in an understanding that ran deeper than words, or the need or time for explanations.

In one fearful hour in Edinburgh, when they had believed they faced death, it had seemed to be that kind of love which touches only a few lives, a depth of unity which is of the heart and mind and soul, and for one aching moment of the body also.

In the lurching of the cab and the hiss of wheels in the rain she could remember Edinburgh as if it had been yesterday.

But the experience had been too dangerous to the emotions, too demanding for either of them to dare again.

Or had it only been he who would not dare?

That was a question she did not want to ask herself; she had not meant to allow the thought into her mind . . . and there it was, hard and painful. Now she refused to express it. She did not know. She did not want to. Anyway, it was all irrelevant. There were parts of Monk she admired greatly: his courage; his strength of will; his intelligence; his loyalty to his beliefs; his passion for justice; his ability to face almost any kind of truth, no matter how dreadful; and the fact that he was never, ever, a hypocrite.

But she hated the streak of cruelty she knew in him, the arrogance, the frequent insensitivity. And he was a fool where judgment of character was concerned. He could no more read a woman's wiles than a dog could read Spanish! He was consistently attracted to the very last sort of woman who could ever make him happy.

Unconsciously, she was clenching her hands as she sat in the cold.

He was bewitched, taken in again and again by pretty, softly spoken, outwardly helpless women who were shallow of nature, manipulative and essentially searching for comfortable lives far from turmoil of any kind. He would have been bored silly by any one of them within months. But their femininity flattered him, their agreement to his wildest assertions seemed like good nature and good sense, and their charming manners pleased his notion of feminine decorum. He fancied himself comfortable with them, whereas in truth he was only soothed, unchallenged, and in the end bored, imprisoned, and contemptuous.

They were pressed in on all sides by hansoms, drays, carriages. Drivers were shouting. A horse squealed.

Most recently Monk had fallen under the spell of the deliciously pretty and extremely shallow Countess Evelyn von Seidlitz. Monk had seen through the countess eventually, of course, but it had required unarguable evidence to convince him. And then he was angry—above all, it seemed, with Hester! She did not know why. She recalled their last meeting with twinges of pain which took her unexpectedly. It had been highly acrimonious, but then so had a great many of their meetings. Normally it caused her irritation that she had not managed to think of a suitable retaliation at the right moment, or satisfaction that she had. She was frequently furious with him, and he with her. It was not unpleasant; in fact, at times it was exhilarating. There was a kind of honesty in it, and it was without real hurt. She would never have struck at any part of him she felt might be genuinely vulnerable.

So why had their last encounter left her this ache, this feeling of being bruised inside? She tried to recall exactly what he had said. She could not now even remember what the quarrel had been about: something to do with her arbitrariness, a favorite subject with him. He had said she was autocratic, that she judged people too harshly and only according to her own standards, which were devoid of laughter or humanity.

The hansom lurched forward again.

He had said she knew how to nurse the sick and reform the dilatory, the incompetent or the feckless, but she had no idea how to live like an ordinary woman, how to laugh or cry and experience the feelings of anything but a hospital matron, endlessly picking up the disasters of other people's lives but never having a life of her own. Her ceaseless minding of other people's business, the fact that she thought she always knew better, made her a bore.

The sum of it had been that while her qualities were admirable, and socially very necessary, they were also personally unattractive; he could do very well without her.

That was what had hurt. Criticism was fair, it was expected, and she could certainly give him back as much in quality and quantity as she received. But rejection was another thing altogether.

And it was completely unfair. For once she had done nothing to warrant it. She had remained in London nursing a young man desperately damaged by paralysis. Apart from that, she had been occupied trying to save Oliver Rathbone from himself, in that he had undertaken the defense in a scandalous slander case and very nearly damaged his own career beyond repair. As it was, it had cost him his reputation in certain circles. Had he not been granted a knighthood shortly before the affair, he could certainly abandon all hope of one now! He had shed too ugly a light on royalty in general to find such favor anymore. He was no longer considered as "sound" as he had been all his life until then. He was suddenly "questionable."

But she found herself smiling at the thought of him. Their last meeting had been anything but acrimonious. Theirs was not really a social acquaintance, rather more a professional friendship. He had surprised her by inviting her to accompany him to dinner and then to the theater. She had accepted, and had enjoyed the evening so much she recalled it now with a little shiver of pleasure.

At first she had felt rather awkward at the sudden shift in their relationship. What should she talk about? For once there was no cause in which they had a common interest. It was years since she had dined alone with a man for other than professional reasons.

But she had forgotten how sophisticated he was. She had seen the vulnerable side of him in the slander case. At dinner and at the theater he was utterly different. There he was in command. As always, he was immaculately dressed in the understated way of a man who knows he does not need to impress, his position is already assured. He had talked easily of all manner of things—art, politics, travel, a little philosophy and a touch of trivial scandal. He had made her laugh. She could picture him now, sitting back in his chair, his eyes looking at her very directly. He had unusual eyes, very dark in his lean, narrow face with its fairish hair, long nose and fastidious mouth. She had never known him so relaxed before, as if for a space of time duty and the law had ceased to matter.

Once or twice he had mentioned his father, a man Hester had met several times and of whom she was extraordinarily fond. He even told her a few stories about his student days and his first, disastrous cases. She had not been sure whether to sympathize or be amused. She had looked at his face and ended laughing. He had not seemed to mind in the least.

They had nearly been late for the theater and had taken their seats almost as the curtain rose. It was a melodrama—a terrible play. She had sat trying not to acknowledge to herself how bad it was. She must keep facing the stage. Rathbone, sitting beside her, would be bound to be aware if she gazed around or took more interest in the other members of the audience. She had sat rigidly facing forwards, trying to enjoy the play.

Then she had glanced at him, after one particularly dreadful sequence of lines, and saw him wince. A few moments later she had looked at him again, and this time found him looking back, his eyes bright with rueful amusement.

She had dissolved in giggles, and knew that when he pulled out a large handkerchief and held it to his mouth, it was for the same reason. Then he had leaned across to her and whispered, "Shall we leave before they ask us not to disrupt the performance?" and she had been delighted to agree.

Afterwards they had walked along the icy street still

laughing, mimicking some of the worst lines and parodying the scenes. They had stopped by a brazier where a street peddler was selling roasted chestnuts, and Oliver had bought two packets. They had walked along together trying not to burn their fingers or their tongues.

It had been one of the happiest evenings she could remember, and curiously comfortable.

She was still smiling at its recollection when the hansom reached her destination in Ebury Street and set her down with her luggage. She paid the driver and presented herself at the side door, where a footman helped her in with her case and directed her to where she should wait to meet the mistress.

Hester had been told little about the circumstances of Rhys Duff's injuries, only that they had been sustained in an attack in which his father had been killed. She had been far more concerned with the nature of his distress and what measure she could take to help him. She had seen Dr. Riley at the hospital, and he had professed a continuing interest in Rhys Duff's case, but it was the family doctor, Corriden Wade, who had approached her. He had told her only that Rhys Duff was suffering from profound bruising, both external and internal. He was in a state of the most serious shock and had so far not spoken since the incident. She should not try to make him respond, except insofar as to make his wishes known regarding his comfort. Her task was to relieve his pain as far as was possible and to change the dressings of his minor external wounds. Dr. Wade himself would care for the more major ones. She must keep her patient clean and warm, and prepare for him such food as he was willing to take. This, of course, should be bland and nourishing.

She was also to keep his room warm and pleasant for him, and to read to him if he should show any desire for it. The choice of material was to be made with great care. There must be nothing disturbing, either to the emotions or the intellect, and nothing which would excite him or keep him from as much rest as he was able to find. In Hester's view, that excluded almost everything that was worthy of either the time or effort of reading. If it did not stir the intellect, the emotions or the imagination, what point was there in it? Should she read him the railway timetable?

But she had merely nodded and answered obediently.

When Sylvestra Duff came into the room she was a complete surprise. Hester had not formed a picture of her in her mind, but she realized she had expected someone as anodyne as Dr. Wade's regimen for Rhys. Sylvestra was anything but bland. She was, very naturally, dressed entirely in black, but on her tall, very slender figure, and with her intense coloring, it was dramatic and most flattering. She was pale with shock still, and moved as if she needed to be careful in case in her daze she bumped into things, but there was a grace and a composure in her which Hester could not help but admire. Her first impression was most favorable.

She stood up immediately. "Good morning, Mrs. Duff. I am Hester Latterly, the nurse Dr. Wade engaged in your behalf to care for your son during his convalescence."

"How do you do, Miss Latterly." Sylvestra spoke with a low voice, and rather slowly, as if she measured her words before she uttered them. "I am grateful you could come. You must have nursed many young men who have been terribly injured."

"Yes, I have." Hester considered adding something to the effect that a large number of them had made startling recoveries, even from the most appalling circumstances, then she looked at Sylvestra's calm eyes and decided it would be shallow and sound as if she were minimizing the truth. And she had not yet seen Rhys Duff; she had no idea for herself of his condition. Dr. Riley's pinched face and anxious eyes, his expressed desire to hear of the young man's progress, indicated that his fears were deep that Rhys would recover slowly, if at all. Dr. Wade had also seemed in some personal distress as he spoke of it to her when engaging her.

"We have prepared a room for you next to my son's," Sylvestra continued, "and arranged a bell so that he can call you if he should need you. Of course, he cannot ring it, but he can knock it off onto the floor, and you will hear." She was thinking of all the practical details, speaking too quickly to cover her emotion., "The kitchen will serve you meals, of course, at whatever time may prove most suitable. You must advise Cook what you think best for my son from day to day. I hope you will be comfortable. If you have any other requirements, please tell me, and I shall do all I can to meet them."

"Thank you," Hester acknowledged. "I am sure that will be satisfactory."

The shadow of a smile touched Sylvestra's mouth. "I imagine the footman has taken your luggage upstairs. Do you wish to see your room first and perhaps change your attire?"

"Thank you, but I should prefer to meet Mr. Duff before anything else," Hester replied. "And perhaps you could tell me a little more about him."

"About him?" Sylvestra looked puzzled.

"His nature, his interests," Hester answered gently. "Dr. Wade said that the shock has temporarily robbed him of speech. I shall know of him only what you tell me, to begin with. I should not like to cause him any unnecessary annoyance or distress by ignorance. Also . . ." She hesitated.

Sylvestra waited, with no idea what Hester meant.

Hester took a breath.

"Also I must know if you have told him of his father's death. . . ."

Sylvestra's face cleared as she understood. "Of course! I'm sorry for being so slow to understand. Yes, I have told him. I did not think it right to keep it from him. He will have to face it. I do not want him to believe I have lied to him."

"I cannot imagine how difficult it must be for you," Hester said. "I am sorry I had to ask."

Sylvestra was silent for a moment, as if she too was stunned even by the thought of what had happened to her in the space of a few days. Her husband was dead and her son was desperately ill, locked in his own world of isolation, hearing and seeing but unable to speak, unable to communicate with anyone the terror and the pain he must feel.

"I'll try to tell you something about him," Sylvestra replied. "It . . . it is difficult to think of the kind of things which would help." She turned to lead the way out of the room and across the hall to the stairs. At the bottom she looked back at Hester.

"I am afraid that because of the nature of the incident, we have the police returning to ask questions. I cannot believe they will trouble you, since naturally you can know nothing. When Rhys regains his speech, he will tell them, but of course they don't wish to wait." A bleakness came over her face. "I don't suppose they will ever find who did it anyway. It will be some pack of nameless ruffians, and the slums will protect their own." She started up the stairs, back very straight, head high, but there was no life in her step.

Following after her, Hester imagined that Sylvestra was barely beginning to lose the numbness of shock, and only in her mind did she turn over and over the details as their reality emerged. Hester could remember feeling the same when she first heard of the suicide of her father, and then, within weeks, of her mother's death from loneliness and despair. She had kept on worrying at the details, and yet at the same time never really believed the man responsible for her family's ruin would be caught.

But that was all in the past, and all that needed to be retained in her mind from it was her understanding of the changing moods of grief.

The Duff house was large and very modern in furnishings. Everything she had seen in the morning room and in the hall dated from no further back than the accession of the Queen. There was none of the spare elegance of the Georgian period, or of William IV. There were pictures everywhere, ornate wallpaper, tapestries and woven rugs, flower arrangements and stuffed animals under glass. Fortunately, both the hall and the upstairs landings were large enough not to give an air of oppression, but it was not a style Hester found comfortable.

Sylvestra opened the third door along, hesitated a moment, then invited Hester to accompany her inside. This room was completely different. The long windows faced south and such daylight as there was fell on almost bare walls. The space was dominated by a large bed with carved posts, and in it lay a young man with pale skin, his sensitive, moody face mottled with blue-black bruises and in several places still scabbed with dried blood. His hair, as black as his mother's, was parted to

41

one side and fell forward over his brow. Because of the disfigurement of his injuries and the pain he must feel, it was difficult to read his expression, but he stared at Hester with what looked like resentment.

It did not surprise her. She was an intruder in a very deep and private grief. She was a stranger, and yet he would be dependent upon her for his most personal needs. She would witness his pain and still be detached from it, able to come and go, to see and yet not to feel. He would not be the first patient to find that humiliating, an emotional and physical nakedness in front of someone who always had the privacy of clothing.

Sylvestra went over to the bed, but she did not sit.

"This is Miss Latterly, who is going to care for you now you are home again. She will be with you all the time, or else in the room along the landing, where the bell will ring to summon her if you need her. She will do everything she can to make you comfortable and help you to get better."

He turned his head to regard Hester with only mild curiosity, and still what she could not help feeling was dislike.

"How do you do, Mr. Duff," she said rather more coolly than she had originally intended. She had nursed very awkward patients before, but for all her realization, it was still disturbing to be disliked by someone for whom she had an instinctive pity and with whom she would spend the next weeks, or months, constantly—and in most intimate circumstances.

He blinked but stared back at her in silence. It was going to be a difficult beginning, whatever might follow.

Sylvestra looked faintly embarrassed. She turned from Rhys to Hester.

"Perhaps I had better show you your room?"

"Thank you," Hester accepted. She would change into a plainer and more practical dress, and return alone to try to get to know Rhys Duff and learn what there was she could do to help him.

Her first evening in the Duff house was unfamiliar and oddly lonely. She had frequently been among people who were profoundly distressed by violence or bereavement, even by crime.

She had lived with people under the pressure of investigation by strangers into the most private and vulnerable parts of their lives. She had known people whom dreadful circumstances had caused to be suspicious and frightened of each other. But she had never before nursed a patient who was conscious and yet unable to speak. There was a silence in the whole house which gave her a sense of isolation. Sylvestra herself was a quiet woman, not given to conversing except when she had some definite message to impart, not talking simply for companionship, as most women do.

The servants were muted, as if in the presence of the dead, not chattering or gossiping among themselves, as was habitual.

When Hester returned to Rhys's room she found him lying on his back staring up at the ceiling, his eyes wide and fixed, as if in great concentration upon something. She hesitated to interrupt him. She stood watching the firelight flickering, looked to make certain there were enough coals in the bucket for several hours, then studied the small bookcase on the nearer wall to see what he had chosen to read before the attack. She saw books on various other countries—Africa, India, the Far East—and at least a dozen on forms of travel, letters and memoirs of explorers, botanists and observers of the customs and habits of other cultures. There was one large and beautifully bound book on the art of Islam, another on the history of Byzantium. Another seemed to be on the Arab and Moorish conquests of North Africa and Spain before the rise of Ferdinand and Isabella had driven them south again. Beside it was a book on Arabic art, mathematics and inventions.

She must make some contact with him. If she had to force the issue, then she would. She walked forward to where he must see her, even if only from the corner of his eye.

"You have an interesting collection of books," she said conversationally. "Have you ever traveled?"

He turned his head to stare at her.

"I know you cannot speak, but you can nod your head," she went on. "Have you?"

He shook his head very slightly. It was communication, but the animosity was still in his eyes.

43

"Do you plan to, when you are better?"

Something closed inside his mind. She could see the change in him quite clearly, although it was so slight as to defy description.

"I've been to the Crimea," she said, disregarding his withdrawal. "I was there during the war. Of course, I saw mostly battlefields and hospitals, but there were occasions when I saw something of the people and the countryside. It is always extraordinary, almost indecent to me, how the flowers go on blooming and so many things seem exactly the same, even when the world is turning upside down with men killing and dying in their hundreds. You feel as if everything ought to stop, but of course it doesn't."

She watched him, and he did not move his eyes away, even though they seemed filled with anger. She was almost sure it was anger, not fear. She looked down to where his broken and splinted hands lay on the sheets. The ends of the fingers below the bandages were slender and sensitive. The nails were perfectly shaped, except for one which was badly torn. He must have injured them when he had fought to try to save himself . . . and perhaps his father too. What did he remember of it? What terrible knowledge was locked up in his silence?

"I met several Turkish people who were very charming and most interesting," she went on, as if he had responded wishing to know. She described a young man who had helped in the hospital, talking about him quite casually, remembering more and more as she spoke. What she could not recall she invented.

Once, during the whole hour she spent with him, she saw the beginning of a smile touch his mouth. At least he was really listening. For a moment they had shared a thought or a feeling.

Later she brought a salve to put on the broken skin of his face where it was drying and would crack painfully. She reached out with it on her finger, and the moment her skin touched his, he snatched his cheek away, his body clenched up, his eyes black and angry.

"It won't hurt," she promised. "It will help to stop the scab from cracking."

He did not move. His muscles were tight, his chest and

shoulders so locked that the pain of it must pull on the bruises which both Dr. Riley and Dr. Wade had said covered his body.

She let her hands fall.

"All right. It doesn't matter. I'll ask you later and see if you've changed your mind."

She left and went downstairs to the kitchen to fetch him something to eat. Perhaps the cook would prepare him a coddled egg or a light custard. According to Dr. Wade, he was well enough to eat and must be encouraged to do so.

The cook, Mrs. Crozier, had quite an array of suitable dishes either already prepared or easy to make even as Hester waited. She offered beef tea, eggs, steamed fish, bread-and-butter pudding, baked custard or cold chicken.

"How is he, miss?" she asked with concern in her face.

"He seems very poorly still," Hester answered honestly. "But we should keep every hope. Perhaps you know which dishes he likes?"

The cook's face brightened a little. "Oh, yes, miss, I certainly do. Very fond o' cold saddle o' mutton, he is, or jugged hare."

"As soon as he's ready for that, I'll let you know." Hester took the coddled egg and the custard.

She found him in a changed mood. He seemed very ready to allow her to assist him to sit up and take more than half the food prepared for him, in spite of the fact that to move at all obviously caused him considerable pain. He gasped and sweat broke out on his face. He seemed at once clammy and cold, and for a little while nauseous as well.

She did all she could for him but it was very little. She was forced to stand by helplessly while he fought waves of pain, his eyes on her face, filled with desperation and a plea for any comfort at all, any relief. She reached out and held the ends of his fingers below the bandages, regardless of the bruising and the broken, scabbed skin, and gripped him as she would were he slipping away from her literally.

His fingers clung so hard she felt as if she too would be bruised when at last he let go.

Half an hour passed in silence, then finally he began to relax a

45

little. The sweat was running off his brow and standing in beads on his lip, but his shoulders lay easy on the pillow and his fingers unclenched. She was able to slip her hand out of his grasp and move away to wring the cloth again and bathe his face.

He smiled at her. It was just a small curving of the lips, a softening of his eyes, but it was real.

She smiled back and felt a tightness in her throat. It was a glimpse of the man he must have been before this terrible thing had happened to him.

Rhys did not knock the bell for her during the night; nevertheless, she woke twice of her own accord and went in to see how he was. On the first occasion she found him sleeping fitfully. She waited a few moments, then crept out again without disturbing him.

The second time he was awake, and he heard her the moment she pushed the door. He was lying staring towards her. She had not brought a candle, using only the light from the embers of the fire. The room was colder. His eyes looked hollow in the shadows.

She smiled at him.

"I think it's time I stoked the fire again," she said quietly. "It's nearly out."

He nodded very slightly and then watched her as she crossed the room and took away the guard and bent to riddle the dead ash through the basket and very gently pile more small pieces of coal on what was left, then wait until it caught in a fragile flame.

"It's coming," she said for no reason other than a sense of communication. She looked around and saw him still watching her. "Are you cold?" she asked.

He nodded, but it was halfhearted, his expression rueful. She gathered he was only a very little chilly.

She waited until the flames were stronger, then put on more coals, piling them high enough to last until morning.

She went back to the bed and looked at him more closely, trying to read in his expression what he wanted or needed. He did not seem in physical pain any more than before, but there was an urgency in his eyes, a tension around his mouth. Did he want her to stay or to go? If she asked him, would it be too clumsy, too direct? She must be delicate. He had been hurt so badly. What had happened to him? What had he seen?

"Would you like a little milk and arrowroot?" she suggested. He nodded immediately.

"I'll be back in a few minutes," she promised.

She returned nearly a quarter of an hour later. It was farther to the kitchen than she had remembered, and it had taken longer to bring the cooking range to a reasonable heat. But the ingredients were fresh and she had a handsome blue-and-white porcelain mug filled with steaming milk, just the right temperature to drink, and the arrowroot in it would be soothing. She propped the pillows behind him and held the mug to his lips. He drank its contents with a smile, his eyes steady on hers.

When he was finished she was not sure whether he wanted her to stay or not, to speak or remain silent. What should she say? Usually she would have asked a patient about himself, led him to talk to her. But anything with Rhys would be utterly one-sided. She could only guess from his expression whether her words interested or bored, encouraged or caused further pain.

In the end she said nothing.

She took the empty cup from him. "Are you ready to sleep?" she asked.

He shook his head slowly but decisively. He wanted her to stay.

"You have some very interesting books." She glanced towards the shelf. "Do you like to be read to?"

He thought for a moment, then nodded. She should choose something far removed from his present life, and it must be something without violence. Nothing must remind him of his own experience. And yet it must not be tedious either.

She went over to the shelf and tried to make out the titles in the firelight, which was now considerable. "How about a history of Byzantium?" she suggested.

47

He nodded again, and she returned with the book in her hand. "I'll have to light the gas," she said.

He agreed, and for three quarters of an hour she read quietly to him about the colorful and devious history of that great center of empire, its customs and its people, its intrigues and struggles for power. He fell asleep reluctantly, and she closed the book, marking the page with a taper from the box by the fire, put out the light again, and tiptoed back to her room with a feeling of something close to elation.

There was not a great deal Hester could do for her patient beyond making sure he was as comfortable as possible, that his bedroom was clean and that the bandages on his more minor wounds were changed as often as was consistent with healing. Eating was difficult for him and seemed to cause him immediate distress. Obviously his internal injuries affected his ability to accept and digest food. It was distressing, and yet she knew that if he did not take nourishment he would waste away, his organs would cease to function and he would damage them irreparably. Fluid was vital.

She brought him milk and arrowroot again, beef tea, and a little dry, very thin toast, then half an hour later, more egg custard. It was not without pain that he ate, but he did retain what she gave him.

Dr. Wade came in the late morning. He looked anxious, his face pinched, his eyes shadowed. He himself was limping and in some pain from a fall from his horse over the previous weekend. He came upstairs almost immediately, meeting Hester on the landing.

"How is he, Miss Latterly? I fear it is a wretched job I've given you. I'm truly sorry."

"Please don't apologize, Dr. Wade," she responded sincerely. "I don't wish to have only the easy cases. . . ."

His face softened. "I'm very grateful for that. I had heard well of you, it seems with good reason. Nevertheless, it must be disturbing when there is so little you can do, anyone can do, to help." He frowned and his voice dropped. He stared at the floor. "I've known the family for years, Miss Latterly, ever since I came out of the navy—"

"The navy?" She was caught by surprise. It was something she had not even imagined. "I'm sorry . . . I have no right to . . ."

He smiled suddenly, illuminating his features and changing his appearance entirely. "I was a naval surgeon twenty years ago. Some of the men I tended had served with Nelson." His eyes met hers, bright with memory, seeing in his mind another age, another world. "One old sailor, whose leg I amputated after a cannon had broken loose and pinned him to the bulk-head, had served in the victory at Trafalgar." His voice was thick with concentration. "I don't suppose there is another woman I know to whom I could say that and she would have some idea of what it means. But you have seen battle, you have watched the courage amid horror, the heart and the strength, the endurance through pain and in the face of death. I think we share something that the people around us can never know. I am extremely grateful that you are nursing poor Rhys and will be here to support Sylvestra through what can only be a dreadful ordeal for her."

He did not say so in words, but she saw in his eyes that he was preparing her for the fact that Rhys might not recover. She steeled herself.

"I shall do everything I can," she promised, meeting his gaze steadily.

"I'm sure you will." He nodded. "I have no doubt of it whatever. Now . . . I will see him. Alone. I am sure you understand. He is a proud man . . . young . . . sensitive. I have wounds to tend, dressings which must be changed."

"Of course. If I can be of assistance, just ring the bell."

"Thank you, thank you, Miss Latterly."

In the afternoon Hester left Rhys to rest and spent a little time with Sylvestra in the withdrawing room. It was crowded with furniture, as was the rest of the house, but warm and surprisingly comfortable—to the body, if not to the eye.

The house was very quiet. Tragedy seemed to have settled over it with peculiar loneliness. She could hear only the flames in the fireplace and the driving of rain against the windows. There were no sounds of servants' feet across the hallway, or whispers or laughter as there were in most houses.

Sylvestra asked after Rhys, but it was merely to make conversation. She had been in to see him twice during the day; the second time she had stayed for a painful half hour, trying to think of something to say to him, recalling happiness in the distant past, when he was still a child, and half promising that such peace and joy would come again. She had not mentioned Leighton Duff. Perhaps that was natural. The shock and wound of his loss were far too new, and she certainly would not wish to remind Rhys of it.

In the silences between them, Hester looked around the room for something to prompt a conversation. Again she was unsure whether speech was wanted or not. She was conscious of a painful isolation in the woman who sat a few feet away from her, a polite smile on her face, her eyes distant. Hester did not know if it was loneliness or simply a private dignity of grief.

Hester saw among a group of photographs one of a young woman with dark eyes and level brows and a nose too strong to be pretty, but her mouth was beautiful. She bore a marked resemblance to Rhys, and the gown she was wearing, the top half of which was very clear in the picture, was of very modern style, not more than a year or two old.

"What an interesting face," Hester remarked, hoping she was not touching on another tragedy.

Sylvestra smiled and there was pride in it.

"That is my daughter Amalia."

Hester wondered where she was and how soon she could be there to help and support her mother. Surely no family duty could be more important?

The answer came immediately, again with a lift of pride and shadow of puzzlement.

"She is in India. Both my daughters are there. Constance is married to a captain in the army. She had the most terrible time during the Mutiny, three years ago. She writes often, telling us about life there." She looked not at Hester but into the dancing flames of the fire. "She says things can never be the same again. She used to love it, even when it was most boring for many of the wives. During the heat of the summer the women would all go up to the hill stations, you know?" It was a rhetorical question. She did not expect Hester to have any knowledge of such things. She had forgotten Hester had been an army nurse, or perhaps she did not understand what that really meant. It was another world from hers.

"They can never trust now as they used to. It has all changed," she went on. "The violence was unimaginable, the torture, the massacres." She shook her head. "But of course they can't come home. It is their duty to remain." She said it without bitterness or the slightest resentment. Duty was a strength and a reason for life, as well as its most rigid boundary.

"I understand," Hester said quickly. She did. Her mind flew back to officers she had known in the Crimea, men, clever ones and foolish ones, to whom duty was as simple as a flame. At no matter what cost, personal or public, even when it was painful or ridiculous, they would never think of doing other than what was expected of them. At times she could have shouted at them, or even lashed out at them physically, through sheer frustration at their rigidity, at the sometimes unnecessary and terrible sacrifices. But she never ceased to admire it in them, whether at its noblest or its most futile—or both together.

Sylvestra must have caught something in Hester's voice, a depth of answering emotion. She turned to look at her and for the first time smiled.

"Amalia is in India too, but her husband is in the Colonial Service, and she takes a great interest in the native peoples." There was pride in her face, and amazement for a way of life she could hardly imagine. "She has friends among the women. Sometimes I worry that she is very rash. I fear she intrudes where Westerners are not wanted, thinking she will alter things for the good, when in truth she may only do damage. I have written advising her, but she was never good at accepting counsel. Hugo is a nice young man, but too busy with his own tasks to pay sufficient attention to Amalia, I think."

Hester's imagination pictured a rather stuffy man shuffling

51

papers on a desk while the spirited, more adventurous Amalia explored forbidden territories.

"I'm sorry they are not closer, to be with you at this time," Hester said gently. She knew it would be months before any letters from Sylvestra with the news of Leighton's death could travel around the Cape of Good Hope and reach India, and the answers return to England. No wonder Sylvestra was so terribly alone.

Mourning was always a time for family closeness. Outsiders, no matter how excellent their friendship, felt intrusive and did not know what to say.

"Yes . . ." Sylvestra agreed, almost as if speaking to herself. "I would dearly like their company, especially Amalia. She is always so . . . positive." She shivered a little, in spite of the warmth of the room, the heavy curtains drawn across the windows against the rain and the dark, the empty tea tray with the remains of crumpets and butter. "I don't know what to expect . . . the police again, I suppose. More questions for which I have no answers."

Hester knew, but it was kinder not to reply. Answers would be found, ugly things uncovered, even if only because they were private, and perhaps foolish or shabby. They would not necessarily include finding the man who had murdered Leighton Duff.

Again Rhys ate only beef tea and a little dry toast. Hester read to him for a while, and he fell asleep early. Hester herself did not put out her light until after midnight, and awoke again in the dark with a ripple of horror going over her like an icy draft. The bell had not fallen, yet she rose immediately and went through to Rhys's room.

The fire was still burning well and the flames cast plenty of light. Rhys was half sitting against the pillows, his eyes wide open and filled with blind, unspeakable terror. His face was drenched in sweat. His lips were stretched back over his teeth. His throat convulsed over and over again, and he seemed unable to draw breath except in gasps between each soundless

52

scream. His splinted hands were held up near his face to ward off the terror his mind saw.

"Rhys!" she cried, going towards him quickly.

He did not hear her. He was still asleep, isolated in some terrible world of his own.

"Rhys!" she repeated more loudly. "Wake up! Wake up— you are safe at home!"

Still his mouth was working in the fearful screams which racked his body. He could not see or hear Hester; he was in a narrow alley somewhere in St. Giles, seeing agony and murder.

"Rhys!" Now she shouted peremptorily and put out her hand to touch his wrist. She was prepared for him to strike at her, seeing her as part of the attack. "Stop it! You are at home! You are safe!" She closed her hand over his wrist and shook him. His body was rigid, muscles locked. His nightshirt was wet through with sweat. "Wake up!" she shouted at him. "You must wake up!"

He started to shake violently, moving the whole bed back and forth. Then slowly he crumpled up and silent sobs shuddered through him, tears running down his face, the breath dragging in his throat.

She did not even think about it; she sat on the bed and reached out her arms and held him, touching his thick hair gently, smoothing it off his brow, following the line of it on the nape of his neck.

She sat there for a length of time she did not measure. It could have been as long as an hour.

Then, at last, gently she let him go and eased herself away to stand up. She must change the damp and crumpled linen and make sure that in his distress he had not torn or moved any of his bandages.

"I'm going to fetch clean sheets," she said quietly. She did not want him to think she was simply walking away. "I'll be back in a moment or two."

She returned to find him staring at the door, waiting for her. She put the linen down on the chair and moved over to help him onto one side of the bed so she could begin changing it around him. This was never an easy task, but he was too ill to get out of the bed altogether and sit in a chair. She was uncertain what internal injuries might be strained, or what wounds Dr. Wade had seen and she had not, which might be broken open.

It took her some time. He was obviously in considerable pain and she had to be patient, working around him, smoothing and straightening, rolling up and unfolding again. At last the bed was remade and he lay exhausted. But his nightshirt had to be changed as well. The one he was wearing was soiled not only with sweat but with spots of blood. She longed to redress the larger wounds, to make sure they were properly covered, but Dr. Wade had forbidden her to touch them in case removal of the gauze should tear the healing tissue.

She held out the clean nightshirt.

He stared at it in her hands. Suddenly his eyes were defensive again, the trust was gone. Unconsciously he pressed backwards into the pillows behind him.

She picked up the light top quilt and spread it over him from waist to feet. She smiled at him very slightly, and guardedly, cautiously, he allowed her to pull his nightshirt up and off over his head. It hurt his shoulders to raise his arms, but he gritted his teeth and did not hesitate. She replaced the soiled shirt with the clean one and, fumbling guardedly under the sheets, pushed it down to cover him. Very carefully she smoothed the sheet and blankets again, and at last he relaxed.

She restoked the fire, then sat down in the chair and waited until he should fall asleep.

In the morning she was tired and extremely stiff herself. She never got used to sleeping in a chair, for all the times she had done it.

She told Sylvestra about the incident, but briefly, without the true horror of pain she had witnessed. It was only in order to make sure that Dr. Wade did indeed come, and not perhaps feel that Rhys was recovering and another patient might need him more.

"I must go to him," Sylvestra said immediately, her face

pinched with anguish. "I feel so . . . useless! I don't know what to say or do to help him! I don't know what happened!" She stared at Hester as if believing the nurse could supply an answer.

There had never been an answer, not to Rhys, or to all the other young men who had seen atrocities more than they could bear, except that time and love can heal at least a part of the pain.

"Don't try to talk about what happened," Hester advised. "All the help you can give is simply to be there."

But when Sylvestra came into the bedroom Rhys turned away. He refused to look at her. She sat on the edge of the bed, putting out her hand to touch his arm where it lay on the coverlet, and he snatched it away, then when she reached after him again he lashed out at her, catching her hand with his splints, hurting both her and himself.

Sylvestra gave a little cry of distress, not for the physical pain, but the rebuff. She sat motionless, not knowing what to do.

Rhys turned his head and kept his face away from her.

She looked at Hester.

Hester had no idea why he had acted with such sudden cruelty. It was impossible even to guess wherever it lay—his recent injury, a feeling of guilt that perhaps he should have been able to save his father or, if not, that he should also have died. She knew of men whose shame at their own survival when their comrades had perished was beyond any reason or comfort to console. It was unreachable, and attempts in words by those who could never truly understand only highlighted the gulf between them, the utter loneliness.

But none of that would touch the hurt in Sylvestra.

"Come downstairs," Hester said quietly. "We'll let him rest, at least until the doctor comes."

"But . . ."

Hester shook her head. Rhys was still lying motionless and stiff. Persuasion would not help.

Reluctantly, Sylvestra rose and followed Hester out and

across the corridor and landing and downstairs again. She did not say anything. She was closed in a world of her own confusion.

Shortly after luncheon the maid announced that the man from the police was there again.

"Will you stay?" Sylvestra asked quickly. "I should prefer it."

"Are you sure?" Hester was surprised. Usually people chose to keep such invasions of their privacy from as many people as possible.

"Yes." Sylvestra was quite decisive. "Yes. If he has anything to tell us, it will be easier for Rhys if you know it also. I . . ." It was not necessary to say how frightened she was for him, it was only too plain in her face.

Evan was shown in. He looked cold and unhappy. The maid had taken his hat and outer coat, but his trouser legs were wet at the bottoms, his boots were soaked, and his cheeks glistened with splashes of rain. It had been some time since Hester had last seen him, but they had shared many experiences, both of triumph and of fear and pain, and she had always liked him. There was a gentleness and honesty in him which she admired. And he was sometimes more perceptive than Monk gave him credit for. Now it was discreet to behave as if they were strangers.

Sylvestra introduced them, and Evan made no reference to past acquaintance.

"How is Mr. Duff?" he asked.

"He is very ill," Sylvestra said quickly. "He has not spoken, if that is what you are hoping. I am afraid I know nothing further."

"I'm sorry." His face crumpled a little. It was highly expressive, mirroring his thoughts and feelings more than he wished. He was a trifle thin, with bright hazel eyes and an aquiline nose, rather too long. His words came from sympathy, not annoyance.

"Have you . . . learned anything?" she asked. She was

56

breathing rather quickly and her hands were held tightly together on her lap, fingers clenched around each other.

"Very little, Mrs. Duff," he replied. "If anyone saw what happened, they are not willing to say so. It is not an area where the police are liked. People live on the fringes of the law and have too much to hide to come forward voluntarily."

"I see." She heard what he said, but it was a world beyond her knowledge or comprehension.

He looked at her high-boned, severe and oddly beautiful face, and did not try to explain, although he must have understood.

Hester guessed the question he wanted to ask and why he found it difficult to frame it without offending. Also it was more than possible she had no idea whatever of the truthful answer. Why would a man of Leighton Duff's standing go to such an area? To gamble illegally, to borrow money, to sell or pawn his belongings, to buy something stolen or forged, or to meet a prostitute. He could tell his wife none of these things. Even if it were something as comparatively praiseworthy as to help a friend in trouble, he still would not be likely to share it with her. Such difficulties were private, between men, not for the knowledge of women.

Evan decided to be blunt, which did not surprise Hester. It was the nature she knew in him.

"Mrs. Duff, have you any idea why your husband should go to an area like St. Giles . . . at night?"

"I . . . I know nothing about St. Giles." It was an evasion, a gaining of more time to think.

He could not afford to be put off.

"It is an area of extreme poverty and crime both petty and serious," he explained. "The streets are narrow and dirty and dangerous. The sewage runs down the middle. The doorways are full of drunken and sleeping beggars . . . sometimes they are even dead, especially this time of the year, when they die of cold and hunger very easily, particularly those who are ill anyway. Tuberculosis is rife . . ."

Her face twisted with revulsion, and perhaps pity also, but

57

her horror was too great to tell. She did not wish to know such things, for many reasons. It jarred her past happiness; it frightened and revolted her. It threatened the present. The mere knowledge of it contaminated her thoughts.

"More children die under six than survive," he went on. "Most of them have rickets. Many of the women work in sweatshops and factories, but a great number practice a little prostitution on the side—to make ends meet, to feed their children."

He had gone too far. It was a picture she could not bear.

"No . . ." she said huskily. "I can only imagine that he must have been lost."

He showed a streak of ruthlessness that would have been characteristic of Monk.

"On foot?" He raised his eyebrows. "Did he often walk around parts of London at night where he did not know the way, Mrs. Duff?"

"Of course not!" she responded too quickly.

"Where did he say he was going?" he persisted.

She was very pale, her eyes bright and defensive.

"He did not say, specifically," she answered him. "But I believe he went out after my son. They had had words about Rhys's behavior. I was not in the room, but I heard raised voices. Rhys had left in anger. We had both believed that he had gone to his own room upstairs." She was sitting very upright, her shoulders high and stiff, her hands folded. "Then when my husband went up to resume the discussion, he discovered he was absent, and he was very angry. He went out also . . . I believe to try to find him. Before you ask me, I do not know where Rhys went or where Leighton did find him . . . which obviously he did. Perhaps that was how they became hurt?"

"Perhaps," Evan agreed. "It is not unusual for a young man to frequent some questionable places, ma'am. If he is not squandering money, or paying attentions to another man's wife, it is generally not taken very seriously. Was your husband strict in his moral views?"

She looked confused. To judge from her expression, it was a question she had never considered.

"He was not . . . rigid . . . or self-righteous, if that is what you mean." Her eyebrows rose, her eyes widened. "I don't think he was ever . . . unfair. He did not expect Rhys to be . . . abstinent. It was not really a . . . a quarrel. If I gave that impression, I did not mean to. I did not overhear their words, simply their voices. It may even have been something else altogether." She bit her lip. "Perhaps Rhys was seeing a woman who was . . . married? Leighton would not have told me. He could have wished to spare me. . . ."

"That may be the case," Evan conceded. "It would explain a great deal. If her husband confronted them, violence might have followed."

Sylvestra shuddered and looked away towards the fire. "To commit murder? What kind of a woman can she be? Would it not have taken several men . . . to . . . to do such terrible things?"

"Yes . . . it would," he agreed quietly. "But perhaps there were several . . . a father or a brother, or both."

She put her hands up to cover her face. "If that is true, then he was wrong—very wrong—but he did not deserve a punishment like this! And my husband did not deserve any punishment at all. It was not his fault!" Unconsciously, she ran her slender fingers through her hair, dislodging a pin, letting a long, black strand of hair fall. "No wonder Rhys will not face me." She looked up at him. "How do I answer it? How do I learn to forgive him for it . . . and teach him to forgive himself?"

Hester put her hand on Sylvestra's shoulder. "First by not supposing it is true until we know," she said firmly. "It may not be the case." Although looking across at Evan, and remembering the scene in the bedroom during the night and today when Sylvestra had been there, she found it very easy to believe they had guessed correctly.

Sylvestra sat up slowly, her face white.

Evan rose to his feet. "Perhaps Miss Latterly will take me up to see Mr. Duff. I know he cannot speak, but he may be able to answer with a nod or a shake of his head."

Sylvestra hesitated. She was not yet ready to face even the questions, let alone the answers Rhys might give. Nor was she ready to return to the scene where only a short while ago she had witnessed such a sudden and vicious side of her son. Hester saw it in her eyes; she read it easily because she shared the fear.

"Mr. Duff?" Evan prompted.

"He is unwell," Sylvestra said, staring back at him.

"He is," Hester reinforced. "He had a most difficult night. I cannot allow you to press him, Sergeant."

Evan looked at Hester questioningly. He must have seen some of her feelings, the memories of Rhys cowering against the pillow as his mind relived something unspeakable, so terrible he could not say it in words . . . any words at all.

"I will not press him," he promised, his voice dropping. "But he may wish to tell me. We must give him the opportunity. We need to know the truth. It may be, Mrs. Duff, that he needs to know it also."

"Do you think so?" She looked at him skeptically. "No vengeance, or justice, is going to change my husband's death or Rhys's injuries. It will help some distant concept of what is fair, and I am not sure how much I care about that."

Hester thought for a moment Evan was going to argue, but he said nothing, simply standing back and waiting for her to lead the way.

Upstairs, Rhys was lying quietly, splinted hands on the covers, his expression peaceful, as if he were nearly asleep. He turned his head as he heard them. He looked guarded but not frightened or unduly wary.

"I'm sorry to trouble you again, Mr. Duff," Evan began before even Hester or Sylvestra could speak. "But investigation has taken me very little further forward. I know you cannot speak yet, but if I ask you a few questions, you can indicate yes or no to me."

Rhys stared back at him, almost unblinkingly.

Hester found herself gritting her teeth, her hands sticky. She knew Evan had no choice but to press. Rhys was the only one who knew the truth, but she also knew that it could cost him more than even his mother could guess, let alone Evan, who stood there looking so gentle and capable of pain himself.

"When you went out that evening," Evan began, "did you meet anyone you knew, a friend?"

A shadow of a smile touched Rhys's mouth, bitter and hurt. He did not move.

"I've asked the wrong question." Evan was undeterred. "Did you go in order to meet a friend? Had you made an arrangement?"

Rhys shook his head.

"No," Evan acknowledged. "Did you meet someone by chance?"

Rhys moved his shoulder a little; it was almost a shrug.

"A friend?"

This time it was definite denial.

"Someone you do not like? An enemy?"

Again the shrug, this time angry, impatient.

"Did you go straight to St. Giles?"

Rhys nodded very slowly, as if he had trouble remembering.

"Had you been there before?" Evan asked, lowering his voice.

Rhys nodded, his eyes unwavering.

"Did you know your father was going there also?"

Rhys stiffened, his body tightening till the muscles seemed locked.

"Did you?" Evan repeated.

Rhys cringed back into the pillow, wincing as the movement hurt him. He tried to speak, his mouth forming the words, his throat striving, but no sounds came. He started to tremble. He could not get his breath and gasped, the air dragging and catching in his throat.

Sylvestra bent forward. "Stop it!" she commanded Evan. "Leave him alone." She placed herself between them as if Evan were offering some physical threat. She swiveled to face Rhys, but he cowered away from her too, as if he could not distinguish the difference.

Sylvestra's face was ashen. She struggled for something to

61

say to him, but it was beyond her reason or even her emotion to reach. She was baffled, frightened and hurt.

"You must both leave," Hester said firmly. "Please! Now!" As if assuming their obedience, she turned to Rhys, who was shuddering violently and sounded in danger of choking. "Stop it," she said to him loudly and clearly. "Nobody is going to hurt you now. Don't try to say anything. . . . Just breathe in and out steadily. Very steadily. Do as I tell you."

She heard the door close as Evan and Sylvestra left.

Gradually, Rhys's hysteria subsided. He began to breathe regularly. The scraping sound in his throat eased and he trembled instead of shaking.

"Keep on breathing slowly," she told him. "Gently. In, out. In, out." She smiled at him.

Warily, shakily, he smiled back.

"Now I am going to get you a little hot milk and a herbal draught to make you feel better. You need to rest."

Fear darkened his eyes again.

"No one will come in."

It was no comfort.

Then she thought perhaps she understood. He was afraid of dreams. The horror lay within him.

"You don't need to sleep. Just lie there quietly. It won't make you sleep."

He relaxed, his eyes searching hers, trying to make her understand.

But he did sleep, for several hours, and she sat beside him, watching, ready to waken him if he showed signs of distress.

Corriden Wade came in the late afternoon. He looked anxious when Hester told him of Rhys's distress and of the nightmare which had produced such prolonged pain and hysteria. His face creased with sharp concern, his own physical discomfort from the fall from his horse forgotten.

"It is most worrying, Miss Latterly. I shall go up and examine him. This is not a good turn of events."

She made to follow him.

"No," he said abruptly, holding his hand up as if physically to prevent her. "I will see him alone. He has obviously been profoundly disturbed by what has happened. In his best interest, to keep him from further hysteria, I shall examine him without the possible embarrassment of a stranger, and a woman, present." He smiled very briefly, merely a flicker, more of communication than any lift of mood. He was obviously deeply distressed by what had happened. "I have known Rhys since he was a child," he explained to her. "I knew his father well, God rest his soul, and my sister is a long-standing and dear friend of Sylvestra. No doubt she will call in the near future and offer whatever help or comfort she may . . ."

"That would be good—" Hester began.

"Yes, of course," he cut her off. "I must see my patient, Miss Latterly. It seems his condition might have taken a turn for the worse. It may be necessary to keep him sedated for a while, so he does not further injure himself in his turmoil of mind . . ."

She reached out to touch his arm. "But he is afraid of sleep, Doctor! That is when he dreams—"

"Miss Latterly, I know very well that you have his interests at heart." His voice was quite quiet, almost gentle, but there was no mistaking the iron in his will. "But his injuries are severe, more severe than you are aware of. I cannot risk his becoming agitated again and perhaps tearing them open. The results could be fatal." He stared at her earnestly. "This is not the kind of violence either you or I are accustomed to dealing with. We know war and its heroes, which, God knows, are horrible enough. This is the trial of a different kind of strength. We must protect him from himself, at least for a while. In a few weeks he may be better; we can only hope."

There was nothing she could do but acquiesce.

"Thank you." His face softened. "I am sure we shall work together excellently. We have much in common, tests of endurance and judgment we have both passed." He smiled briefly, a look of pain and uncertainty, then turned and continued up the stairs.

Hester and Sylvestra waited in the withdrawing room. They sat on either side of the fire, stiff-backed, upright, speaking only occasionally in stifled, jerky sentences.

"I have known Corriden Wade for years," Sylvestra said suddenly. "He was an excellent friend of my husband's. Leighton trusted him absolutely. He will do everything for Rhys that is possible."

"Of course. I have heard of him. His reputation is excellent. Very high."

"Is it? Yes. Yes, of course it is."

Minutes ticked by. The coals settled in the fire. Neither of them moved to ring the bell for the maid to add more.

"His sister . . . Eglantyne, is a dear friend of mine."

"Yes. He told me. He said she may call upon you soon."

"I hope so. Did he say that?"

"Yes."

"Should you be . . . with him?"

"No. He said it would be better if he went alone. Less disturbing."

"Will it?"

"I don't know."

More minutes ticked by. Hester decided to rebuild the fire herself.

Corriden Wade returned, his face grim.

"How is he?" Sylvestra demanded, her voice tight and high with fear. She rose to her feet without being aware of it.

"He is very ill, my dear," he replied quietly. "But I have every hope that he will recover. He must have as much rest as possible. Do not permit him to be disturbed again. He can tell the police nothing. He must not be harassed as he was today. Any reminder of the terrible events which he undoubtedly both saw and suffered will make him considerably worse. They may even cause a complete relapse. That is hardly to be wondered at."

He looked at Hester. "We must protect him, Miss Latterly. I trust you to do that. I shall leave you some powders to give him in warm milk—or beef tea, should he prefer it—which will help him to sleep deeply and without dreams." He frowned. "And I must insist absolutely that you do not speak of his ordeal or bring it to his mind in any way. He is not able to recall anything of it without the most terrible distress. That is natural

64

to a young man of any decency or sensitivity whatever. I imagine you or I would feel exactly the same."

Hester had no doubt that what he said was true. She had seen it only too vividly herself.

"Of course," she agreed. "Thank you. I shall be glad to see him find some ease and some rest that is without trouble."

He smiled at her. His face was charming, full of warmth.

"I am sure you shall, Miss Latterly. He is fortunate to have you with him. I shall continue to call every day, but do not hesitate to send for me more often if you should need me." He turned to Sylvestra. "I believe Eglantyne will come tomorrow—if she may? May I tell her you will receive her?"

At last Sylvestra too relaxed a little, a faint smile touching her lips.

"Please do. Thank you, Corriden. I cannot imagine how we would have survived this without your kindness and your skill."

He looked vaguely uncomfortable. "I wish . . . I wish it were not necessary. This is all . . . tragic . . . quite tragic." He straightened up. "I shall call again tomorrow, my dear. Until then, have courage. We shall do all we can, Miss Latterly and I."

MONK *SAT ALONE* in the large chair in his rooms in Fitzroy Street. He was unaware of Evan's case or of Hester's involvement with one of the victims. He had not seen Hester for more than two weeks, and it was high to the front of his mind that he did not wish to see her in the immediate future. His participation in Rathbone's slander case had taken him to the Continent, both to Venice and to the small German principality of Felzburg. It had given him a taste of an entirely different life of glamour, wealth and idleness, laughter and superficiality, which he had found highly seductive. There were also elements not unfamiliar to him. The experience had awoken memories of his distant past, before he had joined the police. He had struggled hard to catch them more firmly, and failed. Like all the rest of his past, it was lost but for a few glimpses now and then, sudden windows opening, showing only a little, and then closing again and leaving him more confused than before.

He had fallen in love with Evelyn von Seidlitz. At least he thought it was love. It was certainly delicious, exciting, filling his mind and very definitely quickening his pulse. He had been hurt, but not as profoundly surprised as he should have been, to discover she was shallow and, under the surface charm and wit, thoroughly selfish. By the end of the matter he had longed for Hester's leaner, harder virtues, her honesty, her love of courage and truth. Even her morality and frequently self-righteous opinions had a kind of cleanness to them, like a sweet, cold wind after heat and a cloud of flies.

He leaned forward and picked up the poker to move the coals. He prodded at them viciously. He did not wish to think of Hester. She was arbitrary, arrogant and at times pompous, a fault he had hitherto thought entirely a masculine one. He could not afford to be vulnerable to such thoughts.

He had no case of interest at present, which added to his dark mood. There were petty thefts to deal with, usually either a servant who was tragically easy to apprehend or a house-breaker who was almost impossible, appearing as he did out of the massed tens of thousands in the slums and disappearing into them again within the space of an hour.

But such cases were better than no work at all. He could always go and see if there was any information Rathbone wanted, but that was a last resort, as a matter of pride. He liked Rathbone. They had shared many causes and dangers together. They had worked with every ounce of imagination, courage and intelligence for too many common purposes not to know a certain strength in each other which demanded admiration. And because they had shared both triumph and failure, they had a bond of friendship.

But there was also an irritation between them, a difference which rankled too often, pride and judgments which clashed rather than complemented. And there was always Hester. She both drew them together and kept them apart.

But he preferred not to think about Hester, especially in relation to Rathbone.

He was pleased when the doorbell rang and a minute later a woman came in. She was in early middle age, but handsome in a full-blown, obvious way. Her mouth was too large, but sensuously shaped, her eyes were magnificent, her bones rather too well padded with flesh. Her figure was definitely buxom. Her clothes were dark and plain, of indifferent quality, but there was an air about her which at once proclaimed a confidence, even a brashness. She was neither a lady nor one who associated with ladies.

"Are you William Monk?" she asked before he had time to

67

speak. "Yes, I can see you are." She looked him up and down very candidly. "Yer've changed. Can't say what, exac'ly, but yer different. Point is . . . are yer still any good?"

"Yes, I am extremely good!" he replied warily. It seemed she knew him, but he had no idea who she was, except what he could deduce from her appearance.

She gave a sharp laugh. "Mebbe you 'aven't changed that much! Still gives yerself airs." The amusement died out of her face and it became hard and cautious. "I want ter 'ire yer. I can pay."

It was not likely to be work he would enjoy, but he was not in a position to refuse. He could at least listen to her. It was unlikely she would have domestic problems. That sort of thing she would be more than capable of dealing with herself.

"Me name's Vida 'Opgood," she said. "In case yer don' remember."

He did not remember, but it was plain she knew him from the past, before the accident. He was reminded of his vulnerability.

"What is your difficulty, Mrs. Hopgood?" He indicated the large chair on the far side of the fire, and when she had made herself comfortable, he sat down opposite her.

She glanced at the burning coals, then around at the very agreeable room with its landscape pictures, heavy curtains and old but good-quality furniture, all of it supplied by Monk's patroness, Lady Callandra Daviot, from the surplus in her country house. But Vida Hopgood did not need to know that.

"Done well fer yerself," she said ungrudgingly. "Yer din't never marry good, or yer wouldn't be grubbin' around wi' other folks' troubles. Besides, yer wasn't the marryin' sort. Too cussed. Only ever wanted the kind o' wives as'd never 'ave yer. So I guess yer in't lorst none o' yer cleverness. That's why I come. This'll take it all, and then maybe more. But we gotter know. We gotter put a stop ter it."

"To what, Mrs. Hopgood?"

"Me 'usband, Tom, 'e runs a fact'ry, makin' shirts and the like . . ."

Monk knew what the sweatshops of the East End were like,

huge, airless places, suffocating in summer, bitterly cold in winter, where a hundred or more women might sit from before dawn until nearly midnight sewing shirts, gloves, handkerchiefs, petticoats, for barely enough to feed one of them, let alone the family which might depend on them. If someone had stolen from Tom Hopgood, Monk for one was not going to look for him.

She saw his expression.

"Wear nice shirts still, do yer?"

He looked at her sharply.

" 'Course yer do!" She answered her own question with a surprising viciousness twisting her mouth. "And what do yer pay for 'em, eh? Wanner pay more? Wot d'yer think tailors and outfitters pay us for 'em, eh? If we put up our prices, we lose the business. An' 'oo'll that 'elp? Gents 'oo like smart shirts'll buy 'em the cheapest they can get. Can't pay more'n I can, can I?"

He was stung. "I presume you aren't looking for me to alter the tailoring economy?"

Her face registered her scorn, but it was not personal, nor was it her principle emotion, far more urgent was the reason she had come. She chose not to quarrel with him. The reason she had come to him at all, defying the natural barrier between them, was a mark of how grave the matter was to her.

Her eyes narrowed. " 'Ere! W'os the matter wiv yer? Yer look diff'rent. Yer don' remember me, do yer?"

Would she believe a lie? And did it matter?

She was staring at him. "W'y d'yer leave the rozzers, then? D'yer get caught doin' summink as yer shouldn't 'a?"

"No. I quarreled with my supervisor."

She gave a sharp laugh. "So mebbe yer 'aven't changed that much arter all! But yer don't look like yer used ter . . . 'arder, but not so cocky. Come down a bit, 'aven't yer." It was a statement, not a question. " 'In't got the power yer used ter 'ave, not w'en yer was slingin' yer weight around Seven Dials 'afore."

He said nothing.

She looked at him even more closely, leaning a fraction

forward. She was a very handsome woman. There was a vitality in her which was impossible to ignore.

"W'y don't yer remember me? Yer should."

"I had an accident. I don't remember a lot of things."

"Jeez!" She let out her breath slowly. "In't that the truth? Well, I never . . ." She was too angry even to swear. "That's a turn up if yer like. So yer startin' over from the bottom." She gave a little laugh. "No better 'n the rest o' us, then. Well, I'll pay yer, if yer earns it."

"I am better than the rest, Mrs. Hopgood," he said, staring at her levelly. "I've forgotten a few things, a few people, but I haven't lost my brains or my will. Why have you come to me?"

"We can get by . . . most of us," she replied levelly. "One way an' another. Least we could, until this started 'appinin'."

"What started happening?"

"Rape, Mr. Monk," she answered, meeting his eyes unflinchingly and with an ice-hard anger.

He was startled. Of all the possibilities which had flickered through his mind, that had not been one of them.

"Rape?" He repeated the word with incredulity.

"Some o' our girls is gettin' raped in the streets." Now there was nothing in her but hurt, a blind confusion because she did not see the enemy. For once she could not fight her own battle.

It could have been a ridiculous subject. She was not speaking of respectable women in some pleasant area, but of sweatshop workers who eked out a living laboring around the clock, then going home to one room in a tenement, perhaps shared with half a dozen other people of all ages and both sexes. Crime and violence were a way of life with them. For her to have come to him, an ex-policeman, seeking to pay him to help her, she must be speaking of something quite outside the ordinary.

"Tell me about it," he said simply.

She had already broken the first barrier. This was the second. He was listening; there was no mockery and no laughter in his eyes.

"First orff I din't think nothink to it," she began. "Jus' one woman lookin' a bit battered. 'Appens. 'Appens lots o' times. 'Usband gets a bit drunker 'n usual. We often gets women inter

70

the shop wif a black eye, or worse. Specially on a Monday. But then the whisper goes around she's been done mòre than that. Still I take no notice. In't nuffink ter do wif me if she's got a bad man. There's enough of 'em 'round."

He did not interrupt. Her voice was tighter and there was pain in it.

"Then there were another woman, one 'oo's 'usband's sick, too sick ter beat 'er. Then there's a third, an' by now I wanna know wot in 'ell's goin' on." She winced. "Some of 'em in't more'n children. Ter cut it short, Mr. Monk, these women is gettin' raped an' beat up. I gets the 'ole story. I makes 'em come in an sit down in me parlor, one by one, an' I gets it out of 'em. I'll tell you wot they tol' me."

"You had better put it in order for me, Mrs. Hopgood. It will save time."

"'Course! Wot did you think I were gonna do? Tell it yer like they tol' me? We'd be 'ere all ruddy night. In't got all night, even if you 'as. I spec yer charge by the hour. Mos' folks do."

"I'll charge by the day. But only after I've taken the case . . . if I do."

Her face hardened. "Wot yer want from me . . . more money?"

He saw the fear behind her defiance. For all her brashness and the show of bravado she put on to impress, she was frightened and hurt and angry. This was not one of the familiar troubles she had faced all her life, this was something she did not know how to deal with.

"No," he interrupted as she was about to go on. "I won't say I can help you if I can't. Tell me what you learned. I'm listening."

She was partly mollified. She settled back into the chair again, rearranging her skirts slightly around her extremely handsome figure.

"Some of our respectable women's fallen on 'ard times and thinks they'd never sell theirselves, no matter wot," she continued. "Thinks they'd starve before they'd go onter the streets. But it's surprisin' 'ow quick yer can change yer mind when yer

71

kids is starvin' an' sick. Yer 'ears 'em cryin', cold an' 'ungry long enough, an' yer'd sell yerself ter the devil if 'e paid yer in bread an' coal for the fire, or a blanket, or a pair o' boots. Martyrin' yerself is one thing, seein' yer kids die is diff'rent."

Monk did not argue. His knowledge of that was deeper than any individual memory; it was something of the flesh and bone.

"It began easy," she went on, her voice thick with disgust. "First just a bloke 'ere an' there wot wouldn't pay. It 'appens. There's always cheats in life. In't much yer can do but cut yer losses."

He nodded.

"I wouldn't 'a thought nuffink o' that." She shrugged, still watching him narrowly, judging his reactions. "Then one o' the women comes in all bruised an' bashed around, like she bin beat up proper. Like I said, at first I took it as 'er man 'ad beat 'er. Wouldn't 'a blamed 'er if she'd stuck 'im wif a shiv fer that. But she said as it'd bin two men wot'd bin customers. She'd picked 'em up in the street an' gone fer a quick one in a dark alley, an' then they'd beat 'er. Took 'er by force, even though she were willin', like." She bit her full lip. "There's always them as likes ter be a bit rough, but this were real beatin'. It in't the same, not jus' a few bruises, like, but real 'urt."

He waited. He knew from her eyes that there was more. One rape of a prostitute was merely a misfortune. She must know as well as he did that, ugly and unjust as it was, there was nothing that could be done about it.

"She weren't the only one," she went on again. "It 'appened again, 'nother woman, then another. It got worse each time. There's bin seven now, Mr. Monk, that I know of, an' the last one she were beat till she were senseless. 'Er nose an' 'er jaw were broke an' she lorst five teeth. No one else don't care. The rozzers in't goin' ter 'elp. They reckon as women wot sells theirselves deserves wot they get." Her body was clenched tight under the dark fabric. "But nobody don't deserve ter get beat like that. It in't safe fer 'em ter earn the extra bit wot they

72

needs. We gotter find 'oo's doin' this, an' that's wot we need you fer, Mr. Monk. We'll pay yer."

He sat without replying for several moments. If what she said was true, then he also suspected that a little natural justice was planned. He had no objection to that. They both knew it was unlikely the police would take much action against a man who was raping prostitutes. Society considered that a woman who sold her body had little or no rights to withdraw the goods on offer or to object if she were treated like a commodity, not a person. She had voluntarily removed herself from the category of decent women. She was an affront to society by her mere existence. The authorities weren't going to exert themselves to protect a virtue which in their opinion did not exist.

The coals subsided in the hearth with a shower of sparks. It was beginning to rain outside.

And there were the uglier, dark emotions. The men who used such women despised them and despised that part of themselves which needed them. It was a vulnerability at best, at worst a shame. Or perhaps the worst was the fact that they had a weakness which these women were aware of. For once they had lost the control they had in ordinary, daily life, and the very people they most despised were the ones who saw it and knew it in all its intimacy. Was a man ever so open to ridicule as when he paid a woman he regarded with contempt for the use of her body to relieve the needs of his own? She saw him not only with his body naked, but part of his soul as well.

He would hate her for that. And he would certainly not care to be reminded of her existence, except when he could condemn her immorality and say how much he desired to be rid of her and her kind. To labor to protect her from the foreseeable ills of her chosen trade was unthinkable.

The police would never seriously try to eradicate prostitution. Apart from the fact that it would be impossible, they knew its value, and that half of respectable society would be horrified if they were to succeed. Prostitutes were like sewers, not to be discussed in the withdrawing room—or at all, for that matter— but vital to the health and order of society.

Monk felt a deep swell of the same anger that Vida Hopgood felt. And when he was angry he did not forgive.

"Yes," he said, staring at her levelly. "I'll take the case. Pay me enough to live on and I'll do what I can to find the man . . . or men . . . who are doing this. I'll need to see the women. They must tell me the truth. I can't do anything on lies."

There was a gleam of triumph in her eyes. She had won her first battle.

"I'll find him for you, if I can," he added. "I can't say the police will prosecute. You know as well as I do what the chances of that are."

She gave an explosive laugh, full of derision.

"What you do after that is your own affair," he said, knowing what it could mean. "But I can't tell you anything until I'm sure."

She drew breath to argue, then saw his face and knew it would be pointless.

"I'll tell you nothing," he repeated, "until I know. That's the bargain."

She put out her hand.

He took it and she gripped him with extraordinary strength.

She waited in the room beside the fire while Monk changed his clothes to old ones, both because he would not soil those he valued and for the very practical purpose of passing largely unnoticed in the areas to which he was going. Then he accompanied Vida Hopgood to Seven Dials.

She took him to her home, a surprisingly well furnished set of rooms above the sweatshop where eighty-three women sat by gaslight, heads bent over their needles, backs aching, eyes straining to see.

Vida also changed her clothes, leaving Monk in her parlor while she did so. Her husband was in the shop below, seeing no one slacked, talked to her neighbor or pocketed anything that was not hers.

Monk stared around the room. It was overfurnished. There was hardly a space on the heavily patterned wallpaper which was not covered by a picture or a framed sampler of embroidery. Table surfaces were decorated with dried flowers, china ornaments, stuffed birds under glass, more pictures. But in spite of the crowding, and the predominance of red, the whole effect was one of comfort and even a kind of harmony. Whoever lived there cared about it. There had been happiness, a certain pride in it, not to show off or impress others but for its own sake. There was something in Vida Hopgood which he could like. He wished he could remember their previous association. It was a burden to him that he could not, but he knew from too many attempts to trace other memories, more important ones, that the harder he sought, the more elusive they were, the more distorted. It was a disadvantage he had learned to live with most of the time; only on occasion was he sharply brought to realize its dangers when someone hated him and he had no idea why. It was an unusual burden that did not afflict most people, not to know who your friends or enemies were.

Vida returned in plainer, shabbier clothes and set straight about the business in hand. She had no intention of socializing with him. It was a temporary truce, and for all her humor, as a former policeman he was still the "enemy." She would not forget it, even if he might.

"I'll take yer ter see Nellie first," she said, patting her skirt and straightening her shoulders. "There in't no use yer goin' alone. She won't speak to yer if I don' tell 'er ter. Can't blame 'er." She stared at him standing still in the comfortable room. "Well, come on then! I know it's snowin' but a bit o' water won't 'urt yer!"

Biting back his retort, he followed her out into the ice-swept street and hurried to keep pace with her. She moved surprisingly rapidly, her boots tapping sharply on the cobbles, her back straight, her eyes ahead. She had given her orders and assumed that if he wanted to be paid, he would obey them.

She turned abruptly along an alley, head down into the flurries of snow, hand up instinctively to keep her hat on. Even there she was going to maintain her superior status by wearing a hat rather than a shawl to protect her from the elements. She stopped at one of the many doors and banged on it sharply. After several moments it was opened by a plump young woman with a pretty face when she smiled, showing gapped and stained teeth.

"I wanna see Nellie," Vida said bluntly. "Tell 'er Mrs. 'Opgood's 'ere. I got Monk. She'll know 'oo I mean."

Monk felt a stab of fear that his name was so well known, even to this woman of the streets he had never heard of. He could not even recall having been to Seven Dials at all, let alone the faces of individual people. His disadvantage was acute.

The girl heard the tone of command in Vida's voice and went off obediently to fetch Nellie. She did not invite them in, but left them standing in the freezing alley. Vida took the invitation as given and pushed the door open. Monk followed.

Inside was cold also, but mercifully out of the wind and now-thickening snow. The walls were damp in the corridor and smelled of mold, and from the pervading odor of excrement, the midden was not far away, and probably overflowing. Vida pushed on the second door, and it swung open into a room with a good-sized bed in it, rumpled and obviously lately used, but relatively clean, and with several blankets and quilts on it. Monk presumed it was a place of business as well as rest.

There was a young woman standing in the farther corner, waiting for them. Her face was marred by yellowing bruises and a severely cut brow, the scar of which was still healing and would never knit evenly. Monk needed no other evidence to tell him the woman had been badly beaten. He could not imagine an accident likely to cause such harm.

"You tell this geezer 'ere wot 'appened to yer, Nellie," Vida ordered.

" 'E's a rozzer," Nellie said incredulously, looking at Monk with intense dislike.

"No 'e in't," Vida contradicted. " 'E used ter be. They threw 'im out. Now 'e works fer 'ooever pays him. An' terday, we do. 'E's goin' ter find 'oo's beatin' the 'ell out o' the girls 'round 'ere, so we can put an end ter it."

"Oh yeah?" Nellie said derisively. " 'An 'ow's 'e gonna do that, eh? W'y should 'e care?"

" 'E probably don't care," Vida said sharply, impatient with

76

Nellie's stupidity. "But 'e 'as ter eat, same as the rest of us. 'E'll do wot 'e's paid ter do. Wot we do with the bastard after 'e finds 'im in't 'is business."

Nellie still hesitated.

"Look, Nellie"—Vida was fast losing her temper—"you may be one o' them daft bitches wot likes bein' beaten ter 'ell and back, Gawd knows!" She put her hands on her ample hips. "But do yer like bein' too scared to go out in the streets ter earn yerself a little extra, eh? Yer wanna live on wot yer get stitchin' shirts, do yer? That's enough for yer, is it?"

Grudgingly, Nellie saw the point. She turned to Monk, her face puckered with dislike.

"Tell me what happened, and where," Monk instructed her. "Start by telling me where you were and what time it was, or as near as you know."

"It were three weeks ago but a day," she answered, sucking her broken tooth. "A Tuesday night. I were in Fetter Lane. I'd just said good-bye ter a gent 'oo'd walked north again. I turned back ter come 'ome, an' I saw another gent, dressed in a good coat, 'eavy, an' wif a tall 'at on. 'E looked like money, an' 'e were 'angin' around like 'e wanted someone. So I went up ter 'im an' spoke nice. Thinkin' like 'e might fancy me." She stopped, waiting for Monk's reaction.

"And did he?" he asked.

"Yeah. 'E said 'e did. Only w'en 'e started, although I were willin', 'e gets real rough an' starts knockin' me around. Afore I can let out a yell, there's another geezer there an' all. An' 'e lights inter me." She touched her eye gingerly. " 'It me, 'e did. 'It me real 'ard. Bloody near knocked me out. Then 'e an' the first geezer 'olds me an' takes me, one after the other. Then one o' them, by now I dunno which one, me 'ead's fair singin' an' I'm 'alf senseless wi' pain, 'e 'its me again an' knocks me teef aht. Laughin', they is, like madmen. I tell yer, I were scared sick."

Looking at her face it was only too easy to believe. She was white at the memory.

"Can you tell me anything about them?" Monk asked. "Anything at all, a smell, a voice, a feel of cloth?"

"Wot?"

"Smell," he repeated. "Can you remember any smell? They were close to you."

"Like wot?" She looked puzzled.

"Anything. Think." He tried not to sound sharp with her. Was she being intentionally stupid? "Men work in different places," he prompted. "Some with horses, some with leather, some with fish or wool or bales of hemp. Did you smell salt? Sweat? Whiskey?"

She was silent.

"Well?" Vida snapped. "Think back! Wot's the matter with yer? Don't yer want these bastards found?"

"Yeah! I'm thinkin'," Nellie protested. "They didn't neither o' them smell o' none o' them things. One o' them smelled o' some drink, real strong, but it in't one I ever drunk. 'Orrible, it were."

"Cloth," Monk went on. "Did you feel the cloth of their clothes? Was it quality or reworked? Thick or thin?"

"Warm," she said without hesitation, thinking of the only thing which would have mattered to her. "Wouldn't mind a coat like that meself. Cost more'n I make in a month, an' then some."

"Clean shaven or bearded?"

"I din't look!"

"Feel! You must have felt their faces. Think!"

"No beard. Clean shaven . . . I s'pose. Mebbe side-whiskers." She gave a grunt of scorn. "Could 'a bin any o' thousands!" Her voice was harsh with disillusion, as if for a moment she had hoped. "Yer in't never goin' ter find 'em. Yer a liar takin' 'er money, an' she's a fool fer givin' it yer."

"You watch yer tongue, Nellie West!" Vida said sharply. "You in't so smart yer can get along on yer own, an' don't yer forget it! Keep civil, if yer knows wot's good for yer."

"What time of night was it?" Monk asked the last thing he thought would be of any use from her.

"Why?" she sneered. "Narrers it down, does it? Know 'oo it is then, do yer?"

"It may help. But if you'd prefer to protect them, we'll ask

78

elsewhere. I understand you are not the only woman to be beaten." He turned for the door, leaving Vida to come after him. He heard her swear at Nellie carefully and viciously, without repeating herself.

The second woman to whom Vida led him was very different. They met her trudging home after a long day in the sweatshop. It was still snowing, although the cobbles were too wet for it to stick. The woman was perhaps thirty-five, although from the stoop of her shoulders she could have been fifty. Her face was puffy and her skin pale, but she had pretty eyes and her hair had a thick, natural curl. With a little spirit, a little laughter, she would still be attractive. She stopped when she recognized Vida. Her expression was not fearful or unfriendly. It said much of Vida's character that as the wife of the sweatshop owner she could still command a certain friendship in such a woman.

" 'Ello, Betty," Vida said briskly. "This 'ere's Monk. 'E's gonner 'elp us with them bastards wot've bin beatin' up women 'round 'ere."

There was a flicker of hope in Betty's eyes so brief it could have been no more than imagined.

"Yeah?" she said without interest. "Then wot? The rozzers is gonna arrest 'em, an' the judge is gonna bang 'em up in the Coldbath Fields? Or maybe they're goin' ter Newgate an' the rope, eh?" She gave a dry, almost soundless laugh.

Vida fell into step beside her, leaving Monk to walk a couple of paces behind. They turned the corner, passing a gin mill with drunken women on the doorstep, insensible of the cold.

" 'Ow's Bert?" Vida asked.

"Drunk," Betty answered. " 'Ow else?"

"An' yer kids?"

"Billy 'as the croup, Maisie coughs summink terrible. Others is a'right." They had reached her door and she went to push it open just as two small boys came running around the corner of the alley from the opposite direction, shouting and laughing. They both had sticks which they slashed around as if they were swords. One of the boys lunged and the other one yelled out, then crumpled up and pretended to be dying in agony, rolling around on the wet cobbles, his face alight with glee. The other one hopped up and down, crowing his victory. Seemingly, it was his turn, and he was going to savor every ounce of it.

Betty smiled patiently. The rags they wore, a mixture of hand-me-downs and clothes unpicked and restitched from others, could hardly get any filthier.

Monk found his shoulders relaxing a little at the sound of children's laughter. It was a touch of humanity in the gray drudgery around him.

Betty led the way into a tenement very like the one in which Nellie West lived. Betty apparently occupied two rooms at the back. A middle-aged man lay in a stupor half in a chair, half on the floor. She ignored him. The room was cluttered with the furniture of living, a lopsided table, the stuffed chair in which the man lay, two wooden chairs, one with a patched seat, a whisk broom and half a dozen assorted rags. The sound of children's voices, and someone coughing, came through the thin walls from the other room. The two boys were still fighting in the corridor.

Vida ignored them all and concentrated on Betty.

"Tell 'im wot 'appened to yer." She jerked her head at Monk to indicate who she meant. The other man was apparently too deep in his stupor to be aware of them.

"I'nt nuffink much ter tell," Betty said resignedly. "I got beat. It still 'urts, but nobody can't do nothin' about it. Thought o' carryin' a shiv meself, but in't worth it. If I stick the bastards, I'll only get topped fer murder. Anyway, don' s'pose they'll come 'ere again."

"Yeah?" Vida said, her voice thick with derision. "Count on that, would yer? Don' mind goin' out in the streets again, takin' yer chances? 'Appy about that, are yer? Yer din't 'ear wot 'appened ter Nellie West, ner Clarrie Drover, ner Dot MacRae? Ner them others wot got raped or beat? Some o' them's only kids. They damn near killed 'Etty Barker, poor little cow."

Betty looked shaken. "I thought that were 'er man wot done that. 'E drinks rotten, an' 'e don' know wot 'e does 'alf

80

the time." She glanced towards the recumbent figure in the corner, and Monk guessed she was only too familiar with the predicament.

"No, it weren't 'im," Vida said bleakly. "George in't that bad. 'E's all wind an' water. 'E don' really do 'er that bad. She jus' likes ter mouth orff. It were a geezer she picked up, an' 'e punched 'er summink rotten an' then kicked 'er, after 'e took 'er. She's all tore, an' still bleedin'. Yer sure yer 'appy ter go out there lookin', are yer?"

Betty stared at her. "Then I'll stay 'ome," she said between clenched teeth. "Or I'll go up the 'Aymarket."

"Don't be a bloody fool!" Vida spat back contemptuously. "You in't 'Aymarket quality, an' yer knows it. Nor 'd they let yer jus' wander up there an' butt in, an' yer knows that too."

"Then I'll 'ave ter stay 'ome an' make do, won't I?" Betty retaliated, her cheeks a dull pink.

Vida stared at the sleeping man in the corner, unutterable scorn in her face. "An' 'e's gonna feed yer kids, is 'e? Grow up, Betty. Yer'll be out there again, rape or no rape, an' yer knows it as well as I do. Answer Monk's questions. We're gonna get these sods. Work together an' we can."

Betty was too tired to argue. Just that moment, Vida was a worse threat than hunger or violence. She turned to Monk resignedly.

He asked her the same questions he had asked Nellie West, and received roughly the same answers. She had been out in the street to earn a little extra money. It had been a thin week for her husband—she referred to him loosely by that term. He had tried hard, but because of the weather there was nothing. Winters were always hard, especially at the fish market where he often picked up a little work. They had had a fight, over nothing in particular. He had hit her, blackening her eye and pulling out a handful of her hair. She had hit him over the head with an empty gin bottle, knocking him out. It had broken, and she had cut her hand picking up the pieces before the children could tread on them and cut their feet.

It was after that that she had gone to look for a spot of trade to make up the money. She had earned seventeen and sixpence,

81

quite a tidy sum, and was looking to improve on it, when three men had approached her, two from in front, one from behind, and after no more than a few moments' verbal abuse, one of them had held her while the other two had raped her, one after the other. She was left badly bruised, one shoulder wrenched and her knees and elbows grazed and bleeding. She had been too frightened to go out again for three weeks after that, or even to allow George anywhere near her. In fact, the thought of going out again made her nearly sick with fear—although hunger drove her past the door eventually.

Monk questioned her closely for anything she could remember of them. They had abused her verbally. What were their voices like?

"They spoke proper . . . like gents. Weren't from around 'ere!" There was no doubt in her at all.

"Old or young?"

"Dunno. Din't see. Can't tell from a voice."

"Clean shaven or bearded?"

"Clean . . . I think! Don' remember no whiskers. Least . . . I don' think so."

"What kind of clothes?"

"Dunno."

"Do you remember anything else? A smell, words, a name, anything at all?"

"Dunno." Her eyes clouded. "Smell? Wot yer mean? They din't smell o' nuffink."

"No drink?"

"Not as I can think of. No . . . din't smell o' nuffink at all."

"Not soap?" Then instantly he wished he had not said it. He was putting the suggestion into her mind.

"Soap? Yeah, I s'pose so. Funny, like . . . diff'rent."

Did she know what cleanliness smelled like? Perhaps it would be odd to her, an absence rather than a presence. It did not tell him anything more than Nellie West had, but it reinforced the same picture: two or three men coming into the area from somewhere else and becoming increasingly violent in their appetites. They apparently knew enough to pick on the women alone—not the professional prostitutes, who might have pimps to protect them, but the amateurs, the women who only took to the streets occasionally, in times of need.

It was dark when they left, and the snow was beginning to stick. The few unbroken street lamps reflected glittering shards of light on the running gutters. But Vida had no intention of stopping. This was when they would find the women at home, and apart from the fact that they might not speak in the company of their colleagues, she was not going to lose good work-time by asking the questions when they should be unpicking or cutting or stitching. The practicalities must be observed. Also it crossed Monk's mind that perhaps Mr. Hopgood was not aware of her campaign, and that indirectly he was paying for it. He might very well not feel as personally about the issue as she did.

Monk caught up with her as she strode purposefully around the corner into another one of the multitudinous alleyways of Seven Dials, crossed a courtyard with a well and pump in it. A drunk lounged in one doorway, a couple kissed in another, the girl giggling happily, the youth whispering something inaudible to her. Monk wondered at their absorption in each other, that they seemed oblivious of the wind and the snow.

Behind a lighted window someone raised a jug of ale, and candlelight fell on a woman's bright hair. The sound of laughter was quick and clear. Past them and across a main thoroughfare an old woman was selling sandwiches and a running patterer finished up his tale of lust and mayhem and began to jog along the pavement to another, warmer spot to entertain a new crowd with stories, news and general invention.

The next victim of violence was Clarrie Drover. She was almost sixteen, the eldest of a family whose parents were both missing or dead. She looked after six younger brothers and sisters, earning what she could one way or another. Monk did not enquire. They sat in one large room all together while she told Vida what had happened to her in a breathless voice which whistled through a broken front tooth. One sister, about a year and a half younger, nursed her left arm in front of her, as if her chest and stomach hurt her, and she listened to all Clarrie said, nodding her head now and then.

In the dim light of one candle, Vida's face was a mask of fury and compassion, her wide mouth set, her eyes brilliant.

It was very much the same story. The two eldest girls had been out, earning a little extra money. It was obviously the way the next girl, now almost ten, would also feed and clothe herself and her younger siblings in a year or less. Now she was busy nursing a child of about two or three, rocking him back and forwards absently as she listened.

These two children were not visibly hurt as badly as the older women Monk had seen, but their fear was deeper, and perhaps their need of the money greater. There were seven to feed, and no one else to care. Monk found the anger so deep in his soul that, whether Vida Hopgood paid him or not, he had every intention of finding the men who had done this and seeing them dealt with as harshly as the law allowed. And if the law did not care, then there would be others who would.

He questioned them carefully and gently, but on every detail. What could they remember? Where did it happen? What time? Was anything said? What about voices? What were the men wearing? Feel of fabric, feel of skin, bearded or shaven? What did they smell like, drunken or sober, salt, tar, fish, rope, soot? The older girl looked blank. All her answers confirmed the previous stories but added nothing. All either of them clearly recalled now was the pain and the overriding terror, the smell of the wet street, the open gutter down the middle, the feel of cobbles hard in their backs, the red-hot pain, first inside their bodies, then outside, bruising, pummeling. Then afterwards they had lain in the dark as the cold ate into them, and at last there had been voices, they had been lifted, and there had been the slow return of sensation and more pain.

Now they were hungry, there was hardly any food left, no coal or even wood, and they were too frightened to go out, but the time was coming when they would have to or starve inside. Monk fished in his pocket and left two coins on the table, saying nothing but seeing their eyes go to them.

"Well?" Vida demanded when they were out on the street again, facing into the wind, heads down. There was a thin rime of ice on the stones and the snow was lying over it. It looked eerie in the gloom, reflecting back the distant street lamps with a pale blur against the black of the roofs and walls and the dense, lightless sky. It was slippery and dangerous underfoot.

Monk shoved his hands deeper into his pockets and hunched his coat around him. His body was rigid with anger, and it was making him even colder.

"Two or three men are beating and raping working women," he answered bitterly. "They're not local men, but they could be from anywhere else. They're not laborers, but they could be clerks, shopkeepers, traders or gentlemen. They could be soldiers on leave or sailors ashore. They didn't even have to be the same men each time, although they probably are."

"Fat lot o' use that is," she spat at him. "We bloody know that much. I in't paying yer ter tell me wot me own sense can see. I thought you were supposed to be the best rozzer in the force. Leastways you always acted like you was." Her voice was high and sharp with not only disgust but fear. The emotion had torn through her. She had trusted him, and he had let her down. She had nowhere else to turn.

"Did you expect me to solve it tonight?" he asked sarcastically. "One evening, and I'm supposed to come up with names or proof? You don't want a detective, you want a magician."

She stopped and faced him. For a moment she was about to come back with something equally vicious. It was instinct to fight back. Then reality asserted itself. Her body sagged. He could only see the outline of it in the dim light and the falling snow. They were twenty yards from the nearest lamp.

"Can yer 'elp or not, Monk? I in't got no time ter play games with yer."

An old man shuffled past them carrying a sack, muttering to himself.

"I think so," Monk answered her. "They didn't materialize out of the ground. They came here somehow, probably a hansom. They hung around before they attacked these women. They may have had a drink or two. Somebody saw them. Somebody drove them here and drove them away again. There were either two or three of them. Men looking for women don't usually go around in twos and threes. Someone will remember."

"An yer'll make 'em talk," she said with a downwards fall in her voice, as if memory was bitter, and there was pain and regret in it.

How did she know so much about him? Was it all repute, and if so, of what? They were in the borders of his area when he had been on the force. Or had they known each other well before, better than she had implied? Another case, another time? What was it she knew of him and he did not know of himself? She knew he was clever and ruthless . . . and she did not like him, but she respected his ability. In a perverse way she trusted him. And she believed he could work in Seven Dials.

Far more than if she had been some decent, wealthy woman, he wanted to succeed for her. It was mainly because of the rage in him against the brutality of these men, the injustice of it all, their lives and the lives of these women; but it was also pride. He would show her he was still the man he had been in the past. He had lost none of his skills . . . only his memory. Everything else was the same—even better. Runcorn might not know that . . .

The thought of Runcorn brought him up sharply. Runcorn had been his superior, but never felt it. He was always aware of Monk treading on his heels; Monk being better dressed, quicker witted, sharper tongued; Monk always waiting to catch him out.

Was that memory speaking to him or only what he had deduced from Runcorn's attitude after the accident?

This was Runcorn's area. When he had the evidence it would be Runcorn he would have to take it to.

"Yes . . ." he said aloud. "It might be hard to find where they come from . . . but easier to find where they went. They'd be dirty after rolling on the cobbles with the women, fighting. One or two of them might have been marked. Those women fought . . . enough at least to scratch or bite." His mind was picturing shadowy figures only, but some things he knew. "They'd be elated, touched with both victory and fear. They'd done a monstrous thing. Some echo of that would be there in their manner. Some cabby, somewhere, will have noticed. He would know where he took them, because it would be out of the area."

"Said you was a clever sod." She let out her breath in a sigh of relief. "Nah there's one more for yer ter see. Dot MacRae. She's married legal, but 'er 'usband's useless. Consumptive, poor devil. Can't do nothin'. Coughin' 'is lungs up. She gotta work, an' shirt stitchin' don't do it."

Monk did not argue, nor did he need it explained to him. Somewhere in his memory was burned such knowledge. He walked beside her in the thickening snow. Other people were hurrying by, heads down, occasionally calling out a greeting or even a joke. Two men staggered out of a public house, supporting each other as far as the gutter, then collapsed, cursing, but without anger. A beggar wrapped his coat tighter around himself and settled down in a doorway. Within moments another man joined him. They would be warmer together than separate.

Dot MacRae told them essentially what they had already heard. She was older than the others, maybe forty, but still handsome. Her face had character and there was courage in her eyes. There was also a helpless anger. She was trapped and she knew it. She did not expect either help or pity. She told Monk quite simply what had happened some two and a half weeks before, when she had been attacked by two men approaching her from opposite sides of a courtyard. Yes, she was quite certain it had been only two men. One of them had held her down while the other had raped her, then when she had fought back, they had both beaten and kicked her, leaving her almost senseless on the ground.

She had been found and helped home by Percy, a beggar who frequently slept in a doorway in the area. He had seen there was something badly wrong and done all he could to assist her. He had wanted to report it to someone, but who was there? Who cared if a woman who sold her body was beaten a little or taken by force?

Vida did not comment, but again her feeling was evident in her face.

Monk asked questions about time and place, anything Dot could remember which would differentiate these men from any others.

She had not seen them clearly; they had been no more than shapes, weight, pain in the darkness. She had been aware of an overwhelming sense of rage in them, and then afterwards excitement, even elation.

Monk walked away through the snow so blind with anger he was almost oblivious of being cold. He had left Vida Hopgood at the corner of her street and then turned to leave Seven Dials and head back towards the open thoroughfares, the lights and the traffic of the main areas of the city. Later he would find a hansom and ride the rest of the way to his rooms in Fitzroy Street. Now he needed to think and to feel the quick exercise of muscles, pour his energy into movement, and smart under the sting of ice on his face.

This helpless rage at injustice was familiar. It was an old pain, dating far back before the accident, into the times he only caught glimpses of when some emotion, or some half-caught sight or smell, carried him back. He knew the real source of it. The man who had been his guide and mentor when he had newly come south from Northumberland, bound to make his fortune in London, the man who had taken him in, taught him so much not only about merchant banking and the uses of money but about cultured life, about society and how to be a gentleman, had been ruined by injustice. Monk had done everything he could to help him, and it had not been enough. He had suffered that same feeling of frustration then, pacing the streets racking his brain for ideas, believing the answer was beyond his reach, but only just.

He had learned a lot since then. His character had become harder, his mind faster, more agile, more patient to wait his chance, less tolerant of stupidity, less afraid of either success or failure.

The snow was settling on his collar and seeping down his neck. He was shuddering with cold. Other people were dim forms in the gloom. In the streets the gutters were running over. He could smell the stench of middens and sour drains.

There was a pattern in these rapes. The violence was the same . . . and always unnecessary. They were not seeking unwilling women. God help them, they were only too willing. These were not professional prostitutes. They were desperate women who worked honestly when they could and went to do the streets only when hunger drove them.

Why not the professional prostitutes? Because they had men who looked after them. They were merchandise, too valuable to risk. If anyone was going to beat them, disfigure them, reduce their value, it would be the pimps, the "owners," and it would be for a specific reason, probably punishment for thieving, for individual enterprise instead of returning their takings to their masters.

Monk had already ruled out a rival trying to take over a territory. These women did not share their takings with anyone. They certainly did not threaten any regular prostitute's living. Anyway, a pimp would beat, but he would not rape. This had none of the marks of an underworld crime. There was no profit in it. People who lived on the edge of survival did not waste energy and resources on pointless violence time after time.

He turned a corner and the wind was bitter and stung his skin, making his eyes water. He wanted to go home, weigh what he had heard and plan a strategy. But these crimes had happened at night. Night was the time when he should look for other witnesses, cabdrivers who had picked up fares and taken them from the edge of Seven Dials back westwards. It was less than honest to go to his own warm rooms, to hot food and a clean bed, and tell himself he was trying to find the man who had done these senseless and bestial things.

He stopped off at a public house and had a hot pie and a glass of stout and felt at least fortified, if not comforted. He thought of scraping a conversation with some of the other patrons, or with the landlord, and decided against it. He did not yet want to be known as an agent of enquiry. Word would spread rapidly enough. Let Vida do the more obvious asking. She belonged there and would be respected, probably even told the truth.

He worked until long after midnight, trudging the streets on the edges of Seven Dials, generally to the west and north, towards Oxford Street and Regent Street, speaking to cabby after cabby, always asking the same questions. The very last began as they all had.

"Where to, guv?"

"Home . . . Fitzroy Street," Monk replied, still standing on the pavement.

"Right."

"Often work this patch?"

"Yeah, why?"

"Sorry to take you so far out of your way." He put his foot on the step, taking his time.

The cabby gave a sharp laugh. "That's wot I'm 'ere fer. Jus' 'round the corner in't no good ter me."

"Take a few trips north and west, do you?"

"Some. Are yer gettin' in or not?"

"Yes," Monk answered without doing so. "Do you remember taking a couple of gentlemen from this area, probably about this time of night or later, who were a bit roughed up, maybe wet, maybe scratched or bruised, back up west?"

"Why? Wot's it to yer if I did? I take lots o' gents ter lots o' places. 'Ere, 'oo are yer, an' w'y d'yer wanna know fer?"

"Some of the local women around here have been beaten, pretty badly," Monk replied. "And I think it was by men from somewhere else, probably west, well-dressed men who came down here for a little sport and took it too far. I'd like to find them."

"Would yer!" The cabby was hesitating, weighing the advantages and disadvantages of cooperation. "W'y? Them women belong to yer, do they?"

"I'm bein' paid for it," Monk said honestly. "It's worth it to someone to have it stopped."

" 'Oo? Some pimp? Look, I in't standin' 'ere all night answering damn silly questions for yer, less you pays, right?"

Monk fished in his pocket and brought out half a crown. He held it where the cabby could see it, but did not yet offer it.

"For Vida Hopgood, whose husband owns the shop where

they work. She doesn't approve of rape. I take it you don't care?"

The cabby swore, his voice angry. " 'Oo the 'ell are you ter tell me I don' care, yer bleedin' toff from up west yerself? Them bastards come down 'ere an' took a woman, an' used 'er like dirt, then go ridin' back 'ome like they'd bin on a day's outin' in the city!" He spat with terse contempt.

Monk handed him the half crown and he bit it automatically.

"So where did you pick them up, and where did you take them?" Monk asked.

"Pick 'em up Brick Lane," the cabby replied. "An' took 'em up ter Portman Square. 'Nother time took 'em ter Eaton Square. Don't mean ter say that's where they lives. You in't got a cat in 'ell's chance o' finding 'em. And wot if yer do? 'Oo d'yer think's gonna believe some poor bitch from Seven Dials agin' a toff from up west? They'll say she's sellin' 'erself, so wot's wrong if 'e's a bit rough? 'E's bought and paid for it, in't 'e? They don't give decent women much of a chance wot's bin raped. Wot chance 'as an 'ore got?"

"Not much," Monk said miserably. "But there are other ways, if the law will do nothing."

"Yeah?" The cabby's voice lifted in a moment's hope. "Like wot? Top the bastard yerself? Yer'd only get strung up for it, in the end. Rozzers'll never let murder of a gent go. They won't upset theirselves too much over it if some 'ore from down 'ere gets bashed over the 'ead an' dies of it. 'Appens all the time. But let some gent get a shiv in 'is gut an' all 'ell'll get loose. There'll be rozzers up an' dahn every street. I tell yer, it in't worth it. We'll all pay, mark my words."

"I was thinking of something a little subtler," Monk replied with a tight, wolfish smile.

"Yeah? Like wot?" But the cabby was listening now, leaning sideways over his box, peering at Monk in the lamp-light through the snow.

"Like making sure everyone knows about it," Monk replied. "Making it a news item, with details."

"They don't care!" The cabby's disappointment was palpable. " 'Is friends'll all think it's clever. Wot's one 'ore ter them?"

"His friends might not care," Monk replied savagely. "But his wife will. His parents-in-law will, especially his mother-in-law!"

The cabby blasphemed under his breath.

"And maybe his investors, or his society friends' wives, the mothers of the girls his sons hope to marry, or of the men his daughters do," Monk continued.

"Or'ight. Or'ight," the cabby said. "I un'erstand yer. Wot yer wanna know? I don' know 'oo they was. I wouldn't know 'em now if yer marched 'em in front o' me. But then I don' s'pose I'd know you temorrer, an' these geezers kep' their faces away. I jus' thought it were 'cos they fancied they were too good ter talk ter the likes o' me. Jus' give orders—"

"What orders?" Monk said quickly.

"Drive 'em north an' drop 'em in Portman Square. They said they'd walk 'ome from there. Careful sods, eh? I di'n think nothin' of it then. They don't even 'ave ter live near Portman Square. Could've got another 'ansom from there ter w'erever they lives. Could be anyplace."

"It's a start."

"Go on! Even the bleedin' rozzers couldn't find 'em from that."

"Maybe, but they've been here a dozen times or more. There'll be a common factor somewhere, and if there is, I'll find it," Monk said in a low, bitter voice. "I'll ask all the other cabbies, people on the street, and there are plenty of those. Someone saw them, someone will know. They'll make a mistake. They will already have made one, maybe several."

The cabby shivered, and it was only partly the snow. He looked at Monk's face.

"Like a bleedin' wolf, you are. I'm ruddy glad you in't after me! Now, if you wanna go 'ome, get in me cab and get on with it. If yer plannin' on standin' 'ere all night, yer'll do it wivout me, or me 'orse, poor critter."

Monk climbed in and sat down, too cold to relax, and was jolted steadily towards Fitzroy Street and a warm bed.

The following morning he woke aching, his head throbbing. He was in a foul mood, and he had no right to be. He had a home, food, clothing and a kind of safety. He hurt only because he had slept with his body still knotted with the anger he felt over what he had heard.

He shaved and dressed, ate breakfast, and went to the police station where he used to work, before he had finally and irrevocably quarreled with Runcorn and been obliged to leave. It had not been so long ago, roughly two years. He was still remembered with clarity—and very mixed emotions. There were those who were afraid of him, still half expecting some criticism or jibe at the quality of their work, their dedication or their intelligence. Sometimes it had been just, too often it had not.

He wanted to catch John Evan before he went out on whatever case concerned him now. Evan was the one friend Monk could count on. He had come to the station after the accident. They had worked together on the Grey case, unraveling it step by step, at the same time exposing Monk's own fears and his terrible vulnerability, and in the end the truth which could now be thought of only with a shudder, and a dark shadow of guilt. Evan knew him as well as anyone, except Hester.

That thought surprised him by its sharpness. He had not intended to allow Hester into his mind. That relationship was entirely different. Most of it had been brought about by circumstances rather than inclination. She was supremely irritating at times. Beyond her skill, her intelligence and undoubtedly her courage, there was so much that he found intensely annoying. Anyway, she was not involved in this case. He had no need to think about her now. He should find Evan. That was important and most urgent. It could happen again. Another woman could be beaten and raped, perhaps murdered this time. There was a pattern in the crimes. They had become steadily more violent. Perhaps they would not end until one of the women was dead, or more than one.

Evan saw him immediately, sitting in his small office, little more than a large cupboard, big enough for a stack of drawers and two hard-backed chairs and a tiny table for writing. Evan himself looked tired. There were shadows under his hazel eyes and his hair was longer than usual, flopping forward in a heavy, fair brown wave.

Monk came straight to the point. He knew better than to waste a policeman's time.

"I've got a case in Seven Dials," he began. "The edge of that's your area. You might know something about it, and I might be able to help."

"Seven Dials?" Evan's eyebrows rose. "What is it? Who in Seven Dials calls in a private agent? For that matter, who has anything to steal?" There was no unkindness in his face, just a weary knowledge of how things were.

"Not theft," Monk replied. "Rape, and then unnecessary violence, beatings."

Evan winced. "Domestic? Don't suppose we can touch that. How could anybody prove it? It's hard enough to prove rape in a decent suburban area. You know as well as I do, society tends to think that if a woman gets raped, then she must somehow have deserved it. People don't want to think it happens to the innocent . . . that way it won't happen to them."

"Yes, of course I know that." Monk's temper was short and his head still throbbed. "But whether a woman deserves to be raped or not, she doesn't deserve to be beaten, to have her teeth knocked out or her ribs broken. She doesn't deserve to be knocked to the ground by two men at once, then punched and kicked."

Evan flinched as if he had seen it as Monk described. "No, of course she doesn't," he agreed, looking at Monk steadily. "But violence, theft, hunger and cold are part of life in a score of areas across London, along with filth and disease. You know that as well as I do. St. Giles, Aldgate, Seven Dials, Bermondsey, Friar's Mount, Bluegate Fields, the Devil's Acre, and a dozen others. You didn't answer my question . . . was it domestic?"

"No. It was men from outside the area, well-bred, well-off men, coming into Seven Dials for a little sport." He heard the anger in his voice as he said it, and saw it mirrored in Evan's face.

"What evidence have you?" Evan asked, watching him

carefully. "Any chance at all of ever finding them, let alone proving it was them and that it was a crime, not simply the indulgence of a particularly disgusting appetite?"

Monk drew breath to say that of course he had, and then let it out in a sigh. All he had was word of mouth from women no court would believe, even if they could be persuaded to testify, and that in itself was dubious.

"I'm sorry," Evan said quietly, his face tight and bleak with regret. "It isn't worth pressing. Even if we found them, there'd be nothing we could do. It's sickening, but you know it as well as I do."

Monk wanted to shout, to swear over and over until he ran out of words, but it would achieve nothing and only make his own weakness the more apparent.

Evan looked at him with understanding.

"I've got a miserable case myself."

Monk was not interested, but friendship compelled him to pretend he was. Evan deserved at least that much of him, probably more.

"Have you? What is it?"

"Murder and assault in St. Giles. Poor devil might have been better if he'd been murdered too, instead of left beaten to within an inch of his life, and now so badly shocked or terrified he can't speak . . . at all."

"St. Giles?" Monk was surprised. It was another area no better than Seven Dials, and only a few thousand yards away, if that. "Why are you bothering with it?" he asked wryly. "What chance have you of solving that either?"

Evan shrugged. "I don't know . . . probably not much. But I have to try, because the dead man was from Ebury Street, considerable money and social standing."

Monk raised his eyebrows. "What the devil was he doing in St. Giles?"

"They," Evan corrected. "So far I have very little idea. The widow doesn't know . . . and probably doesn't want to, poor woman. I have nothing to follow, except the obvious. He went to satisfy some appetite, either for women or other excitement, which he couldn't at home."

"And the one still alive?" Monk asked.

"His son. It appeared they had something of a quarrel, or at least a heated disagreement, before the son left, and then the father went after him."

"Ugly," Monk said succinctly. He stood up. "If I get any ideas, I'll tell you. But I doubt I will."

Evan smiled resignedly and picked up the pen again to resume what he had been writing when Monk came in.

Monk left without looking to right or left. He did not want to bump into Runcorn. He was feeling angry and frustrated enough. The last thing he desired was a past superior with a grudge, and now all the advantages. He must return to Seven Dials, and to Vida Hopgood and her women. There was going to be no help from outside. Whatever was to be done, it rested with him alone.

4

THE EVENING AFTER Corriden Wade had left, Hester went upstairs to see Rhys for the last time before settling him for the night. She found him lying half curled over on the bed, his face turned into the pillow, his eyes wide. If he had been anyone else she would have talked to him, tried to learn—if not directly, at least indirectly—what troubled him. But Rhys still had no way of communicating except by agreement or disagreement with whatever she asked him. She had to guess, to fumble with all the myriad possibilities, and try to frame her questions so he could answer yes or no. It was such a crude instrument to try to find so subtle and terrible a pain. It was like trying to operate on living flesh using an ax.

Yet sometimes words were too precise. She did not even know what it was that hurt him at this moment. It could be fear of what the future held, or simply fear of sleep that night and the dreams and memories it would bring. It could be grief for his father, guilt because he was alive and his father was dead—or, more deeply, because his father had followed him out of the house, and perhaps if he had not he would still be alive. Or it could be the mixture of anger and grief which afflicts someone who has parted with a loved one for the last time in a quarrel and it is too late for all the things that remain unsaid.

It might be no more than the weariness of physical pain and the fear of endless days stretching ahead when it would not ever stop. Would he spend the rest of his life there, locked in silence and this terrible isolation?

Or was memory returning with its terror and pain and help-lessness relived?

She wanted to touch him. It was the most immediate form of communication. It did not need to say anything. There were no queries in it, no clumsiness of wrong guesses, simply a nearness.

But she remembered how he had snatched himself away from his mother. She did not know him well enough, and he might consider it an intrusion, a familiarity to which she had no right, an advantage she took only because he was ill and dependent upon her.

In the end she simply spoke her mind.

"Rhys . . ."

He did not move.

"Rhys . . . shall I stay for a while, or would you rather be alone?"

He turned very slowly and stared at her, his eyes wide and dark.

She tried to read them, to feel what emotion, what need, was filling his mind and tearing at him till he could neither bear it nor loose it in words. Forgetting her resolve, from her own need she reached out and touched him, laying her hand on his arm above the splints and bandaging.

He did not flinch.

She smiled slightly.

He opened his mouth. His throat tightened, but no sound came. He breathed more rapidly, swallowing. He had to gasp to stop choking, but still there was no voice, no word.

She put her hand up to his lips. "It's all right. Wait a little. Give it time to heal. Is . . . is there something in particular you want to say?"

Nothing. His eyes were full of dread and misery.

She waited, struggling to understand.

Slowly his eyes filled with tears and he shook his head.

She brushed his dark hair from his brow. "Are you ready to go to sleep?"

He shook his head.

"Shall I find something to read to you?"

He nodded.

She went to the bookshelf. Should she even try to censor out anything which might give him pain, remind him of his condition or reawaken memory? Might it not end in being more conspicuous by its very absence?

She picked up a translation of the *Iliad*. It would be full of battles and deaths, but the language would be beautiful, and it would be alive with imagery and light, epic loves, gods and goddesses, ancient cities and wine-dark seas . . . a world of the mind away from the alleys of St. Giles.

She sat in the chair beside his bed and he lay still and listened to her, his eyes never leaving her face. Eleven o'clock came and went, midnight, one o'clock, and at last he fell asleep. She marked the place and closed the book, tiptoeing out and to her own room, where she lay down on the bed and fell asleep herself, still fully clothed.

She awoke late and still tired, but she had slept better than any night since she came to Ebury Street. She went immediately to Rhys and found him restless but not yet ready to wake sufficiently to take breakfast.

Downstairs she met Sylvestra, who came across the hall as soon as she saw Hester, her face tense with anxiety.

"How is he? Has he spoken yet?" She closed her eyes, impatient with herself. "I'm sorry. I swore I would not ask that. Dr. Wade says I must be patient . . . but . . ." She stopped.

"Of course it is difficult," Hester assured her. "Every day seems like a week. But we sat reading till very late last night, and he seems to have slept well. He was much more at ease."

Some of the tension slipped out of Sylvestra's body; her shoulders lowered a little and she attempted to smile.

"Come into the dining room. I'm sure you have not breakfasted yet. Neither have I."

"Thank you." Hester accepted not only because it was a request from her employer but because she hoped that gradually she might learn a little more about Rhys, and thus be able to be of more comfort to him. Comfort of mind was about all she could offer him, apart from helping him to eat, to stay clean and attend to his immediate personal wants. So far Dr. Wade had not permitted her to change any dressings but the most superficial, and Rhys's greatest injuries were internal, where no one could reach them.

The dining room was pleasantly furnished, but like the rest of the house, in too heavy a style for Hester's taste. The table and sideboard were Elizabethan oak, solid and powerful, an immense weight of wood. The carved chairs at each end of the table had high backs and ornate armrests. There were no mirrors, which might have given more light and impression of space. The curtains were wine-and-pink brocade, tied back with tasseled cords and splayed wide to show their richness and the burgundy-colored lining. The walls were hung with a dozen or more pictures.

But the room was extremely comfortable. The chairs were padded on their seats and the fire blazed up in the inglenook hearth, filling the room with warmth.

Sylvestra did not wish to eat. She picked at a piece of toast, undecided whether to have Dundee marmalade or apricot preserves. She poured a cup of tea and sipped it before it was cool enough.

Hester wondered what kind of a man Leighton Duff had been, how they had met and what had happened in the relationship during its twenty-five or so years. What friends had Sylvestra to help her in her grief? They would all have been at the funeral, but that had been almost immediate, in the few days when Rhys had been in the hospital and before Hester had arrived. Now the formal acknowledgments of death were over and Sylvestra was left alone to face the empty days afterwards.

Apparently Dr. Wade's sister was one who was eager to call as soon as she could and he himself seemed to be more than merely a professional acquaintance.

"Have you always lived here?" Hester asked.

"Yes," Sylvestra replied, looking up quickly as if she too were grateful for something to say but had simply not known how to begin. "Yes, ever since I was married."

"It's extremely comfortable."

"Yes . . ." Sylvestra answered automatically, as if it were the expected thing to say and she did it as she had always done. It no longer had meaning. The poverty and hour-to-hour dangers of St. Giles were farther away than the quarrels and the gods of the *Iliad*, because they were beyond the horizons of the imagination. Sylvestra recalled herself. "Yes it is. I suppose I have become so accustomed to it I forget. You must have had very different experiences, Miss Latterly. I admire your courage and sense of duty in going to the Crimea. My daughter Amalia would particularly have liked to meet you. I believe you would have liked her also. She has a most enquiring mind, and the courage to follow her dreams."

"A superb quality," Hester said sincerely. "You have many reasons to be most proud of her."

Sylvestra smiled. "Yes . . . thank you, of course, thank you. Miss Latterly . . ."

"Yes?"

"Does Rhys remember what happened to him?"

"I don't know. Usually people do, but not always. I have a friend who had an accident and was struck on the head. He has only the vaguest flashes of his life before that day. At times a sight or a sound, a smell, will recall something to him, but only fragments. He has to piece it together as well as he can and leave the rest. He has re-created a good life for himself." She abandoned the pretense of eating. "But Rhys was not struck on the head. He knows he's home, he knows you. It is simply that night he may not recall, and perhaps that is best. There are some memories we cannot bear. To forget is nature's way of helping us keep our sanity. It is a way for the mind to heal, when natural forgetting would be impossible."

Sylvestra stared at her plate. "The police are going to try to make him remember. They need to know who attacked him and who murdered my husband." She looked up. "What if he can't bear to remember, Miss Latterly? What if they force him, show him evidence, bring a witness or whatever, and make him relive it? Will it break his mind? Can't you stop that? Isn't there a way we can protect him? There has to be!"

"Yes, of course," Hester said before she really thought. Her mind was filled with memories of Rhys trying desperately to speak, of his eyes wide with horror, of his sweat-soaked body as he struggled in nightmare, rigid with terror, his throat contracted in a silent scream and pain ripping through him, and no one heard, no one came. "He is far too ill to be harassed, and I am sure Dr. Wade will tell them so. Anyway, since he cannot speak or write, there is little he can do except to indicate yes or no. They will have to solve this case by other means."

"I don't know how!" Sylvestra's voice rose in desperation. "I cannot help them. All they asked me were useless questions about what Leighton was wearing and when he went out. None of that is going to achieve anything."

"What would help?" Hester poured her cold tea into the slop basin and reached for the pot, politely offering it to Sylvestra as well. At Sylvestra's nod, she refilled both cups.

"I wish I knew," Sylvestra said almost under her breath. "I've racked my brain to think what Leighton would have been doing in a place like that, and all I can imagine is that he went after Rhys. He was . . . he was very angry when he left home, far angrier than I told that young man from the police. It seems so disloyal to discuss family quarrels with strangers."

Hester knew she meant not so much strangers as people from a different social order, as she must consider Evan to be. She would not know his father was a minister of the church, and he had chosen police work from a sense of dedication to justice, not because it was his natural place in society.

"Of course," she agreed. "It is painful to admit, even to oneself, of a quarrel which cannot now be repaired. One has to set it amid the rest of the relationship and see it as merely a part, only by mischance the last part. It was probably far less important than it seems. Had Mr. Duff lived they would surely have made up their differences." She did not leave it exactly a question.

Sylvestra sipped her fresh tea. "They were quite unlike each other. Rhys is the youngest. Leighton said I indulged him. Perhaps I did. I . . . I felt I understood him so well." Her face puckered with hurt. "Now it looks as if I didn't understand him at all. And my failure may have cost my husband his life. . . ." Her fingers gripped the cup so tightly Hester was afraid she would break it and spill the hot liquid over herself, even cut her hands on the shards.

"Don't torture yourself with that, when you don't know if it is true," she urged. "Perhaps you can think of something which may help the police learn why they went to St. Giles. It may stem from something that happened some time before that evening. It is a fearful place. They must have had a very compelling reason. Could it have been on someone else's account? A friend in trouble?"

Sylvestra looked up at her quickly, her eyes bright. "That would make some sense of it, wouldn't it?"

"Yes. Who are Rhys's friends? Who might he care about sufficiently to go to such a place to help? Perhaps someone who had borrowed money. It can happen . . . a gambling debt a young man dared not tell his family about, or a girl of dubious reputation."

Sylvestra smiled; the smile was full of fear, but there was self-mastery in it also. "That sounds like Rhys himself, I'm afraid. He tended to find respectable young ladies rather boring. That was the principal reason he quarreled with his father. He felt it unfair that Constance and Amalia were able to travel to India to have all manner of exotic experiences, and he was required to remain at home and study, and marry well and then go into the family business."

"What was Mr. Duff's business?" Hester felt considerable sympathy with Rhys. All his will and passion, all his dreams, seemed to lie in the Middle East, and he was required to remain in London while his elder sisters had the adventures not only of the mind, but of the body as well.

"He was in law," Sylvestra replied. "Conveyancing, property. He was the senior partner. He had offices in Birmingham and Manchester as well as the City."

Highly respectable, Hester thought, but hardly the stuff of dreams. At least the family would presumably still have some means. Finances would not be an additional cause for anxiety. She imagined Rhys had been expected to go to university and then follow in his father's footsteps in the company, probably a junior partnership to begin with, leading to rapid promotion.

His whole future was built ahead of him, and rigidly defined. Naturally, it required that he make at the very least a suitable marriage, at best a fortunate one. She could feel the net drawing tight, as if it had been around her also. It was a life tens of thousands would have been only too grateful for.

She tried to imagine Leighton Duff and his hopes for his son, his anger and frustration that Rhys was ungrateful, blind to his good fortune.

"He must have been a very talented man," she said, again to fill the silence.

"He was," Sylvestra agreed with a distant smile. "He was immensely respected. The number of people who regarded his opinion was extraordinary. He could perceive both opportunities and dangers that others, some very skilled and learned men, did not."

To Hester it only made his journey into St. Giles the harder to understand. She had no sense of his personality, apart from an ambition for his son and perhaps a lack of wisdom in his approach to pressing it. But then she had not known Rhys before the attack. Perhaps he had been very willful, wasting his time when he should have been studying. Maybe he had chosen poorly in his friends, especially his female ones. He could well have been a son overindulged by his mother, refusing to grow up and accept adult responsibility. Leighton Duff might have had every reason to be exasperated with him. It would not be the first time a mother had overprotected a boy and thereby achieved the very last thing she intended: left him unfit for any kind of lasting happiness, but instead a permanent dependent, and an inadequate husband in his turn.

Sylvestra was lost in her own thoughts, remembering a kinder past.

"Leighton could be very dashing," she said thoughtfully. "He used to ride over hurdles when he was younger. He was terribly good at it. He didn't keep horses himself, but many friends wanted him to ride for them. He won very often, because he had the courage . . . and, of course, the skill. I used to love to watch him, even though I was terrified he would fall. At that speed it can be extremely dangerous."

104

Hester tried to picture it. It was profoundly at odds with the rather staid man she had envisioned in her mind, the dry lawyer drawing up deeds for property. How foolish it was to judge a person by a few facts, when there were so many other things to know. Perhaps the law offices were only a small part of him, a practical side which provided for the family life, and perhaps also the money for the adventure and imagination of his truer self. It could be from their father that Constance and Amalia had inherited their courage and their dreams.

"I suppose he had to give it up as he got older," Hester said thoughtfully.

Sylvestra smiled. "Yes, I'm afraid so. He realized it when a friend of ours had a very bad fall. Leighton was so upset for him. He was crippled. Oh, he learned to walk again, after about six months, but it was only with pain, and he was no longer able to practice his profession. He was a surgeon, and he could not hold his hands steadily enough. It was very tragic. He was only forty-three."

Hester did not reply. She thought of a man whose life had been dedicated to one art, losing it in a moment's fall from a horse, not even doing anything necessary, simply a race. What regret would follow, what self-blame for the hardship to his family.

"Leighton helped him a great deal," Sylvestra went on. "He managed to sell some property for him and invest the money so he was provided for, at least with some income for his family."

Hester smiled quickly, in acknowledgment that she had heard and appreciated it.

Sylvestra's face darkened again. "Do you think Rhys may have gone into that dreadful area searching for a friend in trouble?" she asked.

"It seems possible."

"I shall have to ask Arthur Kynaston. Perhaps he will come to see Rhys when he is a little better. He might like that."

"We can ask him in a day or two. Is he fond of Rhys?"

"Oh yes. Arthur is the son of one of Leighton's closest friends, the headmaster of Rowntrees—that is an excellent boys' school near here." Her face softened for a moment and

105

her voice lifted with enthusiasm. "Joel Kynaston was a brilliant scholar, and he chose to dedicate his life to teaching boys the love of learning, especially the classics. That is where Rhys learned his Latin and Greek, and his love of history and ancient cultures. It is one of the greatest gifts a young person can receive. Or any age of person, I suppose."

"Of course," Hester agreed.

"Arthur is Rhys's age," Sylvestra went on. "His elder brother, Marmaduke—they call him Duke—is also a friend. He is a little . . . wilder, perhaps? Clever people sometimes are, and Duke is very talented. I know Leighton thought him head-strong. He is now at Oxford studying classics, like his father. Of course, he is still home for Christmas. They both must be terribly grieved by this."

Hester finished her toast and drank the last of her tea. At least she knew a little more about Rhys. It did not explain what had happened to him, but it offered a few possibilities.

Nothing she had learned prepared her for what happened that afternoon when Sylvestra came into the bedroom for the third time that day. Rhys had had a very light luncheon and then fallen asleep. He was in some physical pain. Lying in more or less one position was making him very stiff and his bruises were healing only slowly. It was impossible to know what injuries were causing pain, swelling or even bleeding within him. He was very uncomfortable, and after Hester had given him a sedative herbal drink with something to ease him at least a little, he fell into a light sleep.

He woke when Sylvestra came in.

She went over and sat in the chair next to him.

"How are you, my dear?" she said softly. "Are you rested?"

He stared at her. Hester was standing at the end of the bed and saw the pain and the darkness in his eyes.

Sylvestra put out her hand and stroked him gently on the bare arm above his splints and plasters.

"Every day will be a little better, Rhys," she said just above a whisper, her voice dry with emotion. "It will pass, and you will heal."

He looked at her steadily, then slowly his lips curled back from his teeth in a cold glare of utter contempt.

Sylvestra looked as if she had been struck. Her hand remained on his arm, but as if frozen. She was too stunned to move.

"Rhys . . . ?"

A savage hatred filled his face, as if, had he the strength, he would have lashed out at her physically, wounding, gouging, delighting in pain.

"Rhys . . ." She opened her mouth to continue, but she had no words. She withdrew her hand as if it had been injured, holding it protectively.

His face softened; the violence crumpled out of it, leaving him limp and bruised.

She reached out to him again, instant to forgive.

He looked at her, measuring her feelings, waiting; then he lifted his other hand and hit her, jarring the splints. It must have been agony to his broken bones and he went gray with the shock of it, but he did not move his eyes from hers.

Her eyes filled with tears and she stood up, now truly physically hurt, although it was nothing compared with the pain of confusion and rejection and helplessness within. She walked slowly to the door and out of the room.

Rhys's lips curled in a slow, vicious, satisfied smile, and he swung his face back to look at Hester.

Hester was cold inside, as if she had swallowed ice.

"That was horrible," she said clearly. "You have belittled yourself."

He stared at her, confusion filling his face, and surprise. Whatever he had expected of her it was not that.

She was too repelled and too aware of Sylvestra's grief to guard her words. She felt a kind of horror she had never known before, a mixture of pity and fear and a sense of something so dark she could not even stumble towards it in imagination.

"That was a cruel and pointless thing to do," she went on. "I'm disgusted with you!"

Anger blazed in his eyes, and the smile came back to his mouth, still twisted, as if in self-mockery.

She turned away.

She heard him bang his hand on the sheet. It must have hurt; it would jar the broken bones even further. It was his only way of attracting attention, unless he knocked the bell off, and when he did that others might hear, especially Sylvestra if she had not yet gone downstairs.

She turned back.

He was trying desperately to speak. His head jerked, his lips moved and his throat convulsed as he fought to make a sound. Nothing came, only a gasping for breath as he choked and gagged and then choked again.

She went to him and put her arm around him, lifting him a little so he could breathe more easily.

"Stop it!" she ordered. "Stop it! That won't help you to speak. Just breathe slowly. In . . . out. In . . . out. That's better. Again. Slowly." She sat holding him up until his breathing was regular, under control, then she let him lie back on the pillows. She regarded him dispassionately, until she saw the tears on his cheeks and the despair in his eyes. He seemed oblivious of his hands, lying on the cover with the splints broken and crooked, carrying the bones awry. It must have been agonizing, and yet the pain of emotion inside him was so much greater he seemed to not even feel the pain in his hands.

What in God's name had happened to him in St. Giles? What memory tore inside him with such unbearable horror?

"I'll rebandage your hands," she said more gently. "You can't leave them like that. The bones may even have been moved."

He blinked, but made no move of disagreement.

"It's going to hurt," she warned.

He smiled and made a little snort, letting out his breath sharply.

It took her nearly three quarters of an hour to take the bandages off both hands, examine the broken fingers and the bruised and swollen flesh, lacerated across the knuckles, realign the bones, all the time aware of the hideous pain it must be causing him, and then resplint and rebandage his hands. It was really a surgeon's job, and perhaps Corriden Wade would be angry with her for doing it herself, instead of calling him, but he was due to come tomorrow, and she was perfectly capable. She had certainly set enough bones before. She could not leave Rhys like that while she sent a messenger out to Wade's house to look for him. At this time he might very well be out at dinner, or even the theater.

Afterwards Rhys was exhausted. His face was gray with pain and his clothes were soaked with sweat.

"I'll change the bed," she said matter-of-factly. "You can't sleep in that. Then I'll get you a draft to ease the pain of it and help you to rest. Maybe you'll think twice before hitting anyone again?"

He bit his lip and stared at her. He looked rueful, but it was far less than an apology. It was too complicated to express without words, perhaps even with them.

She helped him to the far side of the bed, half supporting his weight; he was dizzy and weak with pain. She eased him down. She took off the rumpled sheets, marked with spots of blood, and put on clean ones. Then she helped him change into a fresh nightshirt and held him steady while he half rolled back to the center of the bed and she straightened the covers over him.

"I'll be back in a few moments with the draft for pain," she told him. "Don't move until I return."

He nodded obediently.

It took her nearly a quarter of an hour to mix up the strongest dose she dared give him from Dr. Wade's medicine. It should be enough to help him sleep at least half of the night. Anything strong enough to deaden the pain of his hands might kill him. It was the best she could do. She offered it to him and held it while he drank.

He made a face.

"I know it's bitter," she agreed. "I brought a little peppermint to take the taste away."

He looked at her gravely, then very slowly he smiled. It was thanks; there was nothing else in it, no cruelty, no satisfaction. He was powerless to explain.

She pushed the hair back off his brow.

"Good night," she said quietly. "If you need me, you have only to knock the bell."

He raised his eyebrows.

"Yes, of course I'll come," she promised.

This time the smile was a little wider, then he turned away suddenly, and his eyes filled with tears.

She went out quietly, bitterly aware that she was leaving him alone with his horror and his silence. The draft would give him at least a little rest.

The doctor called the following morning. It was a dark day, the sky heavy-laden with snow and an icy wind whistling in the eaves. He came in with skin whipped ruddy by the cold and rubbing his hands to get the circulation back after sitting still in his carriage.

Sylvestra was relieved to see him and came out of the morning room immediately when she heard his voice in the hall. Hester was on the stairs and could not help observing his quick effort to smile at her, and her relief. She went to him eagerly and he took her hands in his, nodding while he spoke to her. The conversation was brief, then he came straight up to Hester. He took her arm and led her away from the banister edge and towards the more private center of the landing.

"It is not good news," he said very quietly, as if aware of Sylvestra still below them. "You gave him the powders I left?"

"Yes, in the strongest dose you prescribed. It provided him some ease."

"Yes." He nodded. He looked cold, anxious and very tired, as if he too had slept little. Perhaps he had been up all night with other patients. Below them in the hall Sylvestra's footsteps faded towards the withdrawing room.

"I wish I knew what to do to help him, but I confess I am working blindly." Wade looked at Hester with a regretful smile. "This is very different from the orlop deck on which I trained." He gave a dry little laugh. "There everything was so quick. Men were carried in and laid on the canvas. Each waited his turn, first brought in, first seen. It was a matter of searching

110

for musket balls, splinters of wood—teak splinters are poisonous, did you know that, Miss Latterly?"

"No."

"Of course not. I don't suppose you have them in the army. But then in the navy we didn't have men trodden on or dragged by horses. I expect you did?"

"Yes."

"But we are both used to cannon fire, saber slashes and musket shot, and fever . . ." His eyes were bright with remembered agony. "God, the fevers! Yellow Jack, scurvy, malaria . . ."

"Cholera, typhoid and gangrene," she responded, the past hideously clear for an instant.

"Gangrene," he agreed, his gaze unwavering from hers. "Dear God, I saw some courage. I imagine you could match me, instance for instance?"

"I believe so." She did not want to see the white faces again, the broken bodies and the fever and deaths, but it gave her a pride like a burning pain inside to have been part of it and to be able to share it with this man who understood as a mere reader and listener never could.

"What can we do for Rhys?" she asked.

He drew in his breath and let it go in a sigh. "Keep him as quiet and as comfortable as we can. The internal bruising will subside in time, I believe, unless there is more damage done than we know. His external wounds are healing, but it is very early yet." He looked very grave and his voice dropped even lower, belying his words. "He is young, and was strong and in good health. The flesh will knit, but it will take time. It must still cause him severe pain. It is to be expected, and there is nothing to do but endure. You can relieve him to some extent with the powders I have left. I will redress his wounds each time I call, and make sure they are uninfected. There is little suppuration, and no sign of gangrene, so far. I shall be most careful."

"I was obliged to rebandage his hands last night. I'm sorry." She was reluctant to tell him about the unpleasant incident with Sylvestra.

111

"Oh?" He looked wary, the concern in his eyes deepening, but she saw no anger, no censure of her. "I think you had better tell me what happened, Miss Latterly. I am sensitive to your wish to protect your patient's confidentiality, but I have known Rhys a long time. I am already aware of some of his characteristics."

Briefly, omitting detail, she told him of the encounter with Sylvestra.

"I see," he said quietly. He turned away so she could not see his face. "It is not hopeful. Please do not encourage Mrs. Duff to expect . . . Miss Latterly, I confess I do not know what to say. One should never abandon any effort, try all one can, whatever the odds." He hesitated before going on, as if it cost him an effort to master his feelings. "I have seen miracles of recovery. I have also seen a great many men die. Perhaps it is better to say nothing, if you can do that, living here in the house?"

"I can try. Do you think he will regain his speech?"

He swung around to face her, his eyes narrow and dark, unreadable.

"I have no idea. But you must keep the police from harassing him. If they do, and they send him into another hysteria, it could kill him." His voice was brittle and urgent. She heard the same note of fear in it that she saw in his eyes and mouth. "I don't know what happened, or what he did, but I do know that the memory is unbearable to him. If you want to save his sanity, you will guard him with every spark of courage and intelligence you have from the police attempts to make him relive it with their questions. For him to do so could very well tip him over the abyss into madness from which he might never return. I have no doubt that if anyone is equal to that, you are."

"Thank you," she said simply. It was a compliment she would treasure, because it was from a man who used no idle words.

He nodded. "Now I will go and see him. If you will be good enough to ensure we are uninterrupted. I must examine not only his hands but his other wounds to see he has not torn

112

any of the newly healing skin. Thank you for your care, Miss Latterly."

The following day Rhys received his first visitor since the incident. It was early in the afternoon. The day was considerably brighter. Snow was lying on the roofs and it reflected back from a windy sky and the pale sunlight of short, winter days.

Hester was upstairs when the doorbell rang and Wharmby showed in a woman of unusual appearance. She was of average height and fair, unremarkable coloring, but her features were strong, decidedly asymmetrical and yet possessed of an extraordinary air of inner resolution and calm. She was certainly not beautiful, yet one gained from her a sense of well-being which was almost more attractive.

"Good afternoon, Mrs. Kynaston," Wharmby said with evident pleasure. He looked at the youth who had followed her. His hair and skin were as fair as hers, but his features were quite different. His face was thin, his features finer and more aquiline, his eyes clear light blue. It was a face of humor and dreams, and perhaps a certain loneliness. "Good afternoon, Mr. Arthur."

"Good afternoon," Mrs. Kynaston replied. She was wearing dark browns and blacks, as became one visiting a house in mourning. Her clothes were well cut but somehow devoid of individual style. It seemed evident it did not matter to her. She allowed Wharmby to take her cloak and then to conduct her into the withdrawing room, where apparently Sylvestra was expecting her. Arthur followed a pace behind.

Wharmby came up the stairs.

"Miss Latterly, young Mr. Kynaston is a great friend of Mr. Rhys's. He has asked if he may visit. Is that possible, do you think?"

"I shall ask Mr. Rhys if he wishes to see him," Hester replied. "If he does, I would like to see Mr. Kynaston first. It is imperative he does not say or do anything which would cause distress. Dr. Wade is adamant on that."

"Of course. I understand." He stood waiting while she went to enquire.

Rhys was lying staring at the ceiling, his eyes half closed.

Hester stood in the doorway. "Arthur Kynaston is here. He would like to visit you, if you are feeling well enough. If you aren't, all you have to do is let me know. I shall see he is not offended."

Rhys's eyes opened wide. She thought she saw eagerness in them, then a sudden doubt, perhaps embarrassment.

She waited.

He was obviously uncertain. He was lonely, frightened, vulnerable, ashamed of his helplessness and perhaps of what he had not done to save his father. Maybe, like many soldiers she had known, the sheer fact that he had survived was a reproach to him, when someone else had not. Had he really been a coward, or did he only fear he had been? Did he even remember with any clarity, any approximation to fact?

"If you see him, shall I leave you alone?" she asked.

A shadow crossed his face.

"Shall I stay and see that we talk of pleasant things, interesting things?"

Slowly he smiled.

She turned and went out to tell Wharmby.

Arthur Kynaston came up the stairs slowly, his fair face creased in concern.

"Are you the nurse?" he asked when he stood in front of her.

"Yes. My name is Hester Latterly."

"May I see him?"

"Yes. But I must warn you, Mr. Kynaston, he is very ill. I expect you have already been told that he cannot speak."

"But he will be able to . . . soon? I mean, it will come back, won't it?"

"I don't know. For now he cannot, but he can nod or shake his head. And he likes to be spoken to."

"What can I say?" He looked confused and a little afraid. He was very young, perhaps seventeen.

"Anything, except to mention what happened in St. Giles or the death of his father."

"Oh God! I mean . . . he does know, doesn't he? Someone has told him?"

"Yes. But he was there. We don't know what happened, but the shock of it seems to be what has robbed him of speech. Talk about anything else. You must have interests. Do you study? What do you hope to do?"

"Classics," he replied without hesitation. "Rhys loves the ancient stories, even more than I do. We'd love to go to Greece or Turkey."

She smiled and stood aside. There was no need to say that he had answered his own question. He knew it.

As soon as he saw Arthur, Rhys's face lit up, then instantly was shadowed by self-consciousness. He was in bed, helpless, unable even to welcome him.

If Arthur Kynaston had any idea of such things, he hid it superbly. He walked in as if it were the way they naturally met. He sat down in the chair beside the bed, ignoring Hester, facing Rhys.

"I suppose you've got rather more time to read than you can use?" he said ruefully. "I'll see if I can find a few new books for you. I've just been reading something fascinating. Trust me to get there years after everyone else, but I've got this book about Egypt, by an Italian called Belzoni. It was written nearly forty years ago, 1822 to be exact. It's all about the discovery of ancient tombs in Egypt and Nubia." He could not help his face's tightening with enthusiasm. "It's marvelous! I'm convinced there must be much more there, if only we knew where to look." He leaned forward. "I haven't told Papa yet. But although I keep saying I'll study the classics, actually I think I might like to be an Egyptologist. In fact, I'm pretty sure I would."

In the doorway, Hester already felt herself relaxing.

Rhys stared at Arthur, his eyes wide with fascination.

"I must tell you about some of the stuff they've found," Arthur went on. "I tried to tell Duke, but you know him. He wasn't even remotely interested. No imagination. Sees time like a series of little rooms, all without windows. If you are in today, then that's all that exists. I see it all as a vast whole. Any day is as important and as real as any other. Don't you think so?"

Rhys smiled and nodded.

"Can I tell you about this?" Arthur asked. "Do you mind? I've been longing to tell someone. Papa would be furious with me for wasting time. Mama would just listen with half her mind and then forget it. Duke thinks I'm a fool. But you're a captive audience . . ." He blushed hotly. "Sorry . . . that was a wretched thing to say. I wish I'd bitten my tongue!"

Rhys smiled with sudden brilliance. It changed his whole face, lighting it with an extraordinary charm. It was a warmth Hester had never had a chance to see.

"Thanks," Arthur said with a little shake of his head. "What I mean is, I know you'll understand." And he proceeded to describe the discoveries Belzoni had made in Egypt, his voice rising with eagerness, his hands moving quickly to outline them in the air.

Hester slipped out silently. She was perfectly confident that Arthur Kynaston would cause Rhys no unnecessary harm. If he reminded him of other times, of life and vigor, that was unavoidable. He would think of those things anyway. If he made the occasional clumsy reference, that was bound to happen too. They were still best left alone.

Downstairs, the maid Janet told her that Mrs. Duff would be pleased if she would join her in the withdrawing room for tea.

It was a courtesy, and one that Hester had not expected. She was not a servant in the house, but neither was she a guest. Perhaps Sylvestra wished her to know as much as possible about family friends in order to be able to help Rhys, to explain the rage in him. She must feel a consuming loneliness, and Hester was the only bridge between herself and her son, except Corriden Wade, and he was there only briefly.

She was introduced and Fidelis Kynaston betrayed no surprise at accepting her as part of both the afternoon's visit and the conversation.

"Is he . . . ?" Sylvestra began nervously.

Hester answered with a smile which must have shown her pleasure. "They are having an excellent time," she answered with confidence. "Mr. Kynaston is describing the discoveries along the Nile by a Signore Belzoni, and they are both

116

enjoying it greatly. I admit I too was much interested. I think when I have spare time, I shall purchase the book myself."

Sylvestra gave a sigh of relief and her whole body eased, the muscles of her shoulders and back unknotting, the silk of her dress ceasing to strain. She turned to Fidelis.

"Thank you so much for coming. It is not always easy to visit people who are ill or bereaved. One never knows what to say. . . ."

"My dear, what kind of a friend would one be if the moment one was needed, one chose to be somewhere else? I have never seen you adopt that course," Fidelis assured, leaning forward.

Sylvestra shrugged. "There has been so little . . ."

"Nothing like this," Fidelis agreed. "But there has been unpleasantness, even if largely unspoken, and you have felt it, and been there with companionship."

Sylvestra smiled her acknowledgment.

The conversation became general, of trivial current events, family affairs. Sylvestra recounted the latest letters from Amalia in India, of course still unaware of events in London. She wrote of the poverty she saw, and particularly of the disease and lack of clean water, a subject which seemed to trouble her greatly. Hester was drawn in sufficiently for good manners. Then Fidelis asked her about her experiences in the Crimea. Her interest seemed quite genuine.

"It must feel very strange to you to come home to England after the danger and responsibility of your position out there," she said with a puckered brow.

"It was difficult to alter the attitude of one's mind," Hester admitted with massive understatement. She had found it utterly impossible. One month she was dealing with dying men, terrible injuries, decisions that affected lives, then a month later she was required to behave like an obedient and grateful dependent, to have no more opinions upon anything more important or controversial than a hemline or a pudding.

Fidelis smiled and there was a flash of amusement in her eyes as if she had some awareness of what the truth might be.

"Have you met Dr. Wade? Yes, of course you have. He served in the navy for many years, you know? I imagine you

117

will have a certain amount in common with him. He is a most remarkable man. He has great strength, both of purpose and of character."

Hester recalled Corriden Wade's face as he had stood on the landing talking to her about the sailors he had known, the men who had fought with Nelson, who had seen the great sea battles which had turned the tide of history fifty-five years before, when England stood alone against the massive armies of Napoleon, allied with Spain, and the fate of Europe was in the balance. She had seen the fire of imagination in his eyes, the knowledge of what it had meant, and the cost in lives and pain. She had heard in the timbre of his voice his admiration for the dedication and the sacrifice of those men.

"Yes," she said with surprising vehemence. "Yes he is. He was telling me something of his experiences."

"I know my husband admired him very much," Sylvestra remarked. "He had known him for close to twenty years. Of course, not so well to begin with. That would be before he came ashore." There was a pensiveness in her face for a moment, as though she had thought of something else, something she did not understand. Then it passed and she turned to Fidelis. "It is strange to think how much of a person's life you cannot share, even though you see him every day and discuss all sorts of things with him, have a home and family in common, even a destiny shared. And yet the parts which formed so much of what he thinks and feels and believes all happened in places you have never been to, and were unlike all you have experienced yourself."

"I suppose it is," Fidelis said slowly, her fair brows furrowed very slightly. "There is so much one observes but will never understand. We see what appears to be the same events, and yet when we speak about them afterwards they are quite different, as if we were not discussing the same thing at all. I used to wonder if it was memory, now I know it is quite different perception in the first place. I suppose that is part of growing up." She smiled very slightly at her own foolishness. "You realize that people do not necessarily feel or think as you do yourself. Some things cannot be communicated."

118

"Can't they?" Sylvestra challenged. "Surely that is what speech is for?"

"Words are only labels," Fidelis replied, taking the thoughts Hester felt would be too bold of her to express them herself. "A way of describing an idea. If you do not know what the idea is, then the label does not tell you."

Sylvestra was plainly puzzled.

"I remember Joel trying to explain some Greek or Arabic ideas to me," Fidelis attempted to clarify. "I did not understand, because we do not have such a concept in our culture." She smiled ruefully. "In the end all he could do was use their word for it. It did not help in the slightest. I still had no idea what it was." She looked at Hester. "Can you tell me what it is like to watch a young soldier die of cholera in Scutari, or see the wagonloads of mangled bodies come in from Sebastopol, or Balaclava, some of them dying of hunger and cold? I mean, can you tell me so that I will feel what you felt?"

"No." The bare word was enough. Hester looked at this woman with the extraordinary face far more closely than before. At first she had seemed simply another well-bred wife of a successful man, come to offer her sympathy to a friend bereaved. In what had begun as an afternoon's trivial conversation, she had touched on one of the mysteries of loneliness and misunderstanding that underlay so many incomplete relationships. Hester saw in Sylvestra's eyes the sudden flare of her own incomprehension. Perhaps the chasm between Rhys and herself was more than his loss of speech? Maybe words would not have conveyed what had really happened to him anyway?

And what of Leighton Duff? How well had Sylvestra known him? Hester could see that thought reflected in his widow's dark eyes even now.

Fidelis was watching Sylvestra too, her lopsided face touched with concern. How much had she been told, or had she guessed, of that night? Had she any idea of why Leighton Duff had gone to St. Giles?

"No," Hester broke the silence. "I think there must always be experiences we can share only imperfectly."

Fidelis smiled briefly, the shadow again behind her eyes.

119

"The wisest thing, my dear, is to accept a certain blindness and not either to blame yourself or to blame others too much. You must succeed by your own terms, not anyone else's."

It was a curious remark, and Hester had the fleeting impression that it was made with some deeper meaning which Sylvestra would understand. She was not sure if it referred to Rhys or to Leighton Duff, or simply to some generality of their lives which was relevant to this new and consuming misery. Whatever it was, Fidelis Kynaston wished Sylvestra to believe she understood it.

Their tea was cold and the tiny sandwiches eaten when Arthur Kynaston returned, looking slightly flushed but far less tense than when he had gone up.

"How is he?" his mother asked before Sylvestra could speak.

"He seems in good spirits," he replied hastily. He was too young, too clear-faced, to lie well. He had obviously been profoundly shaken but was trying to conceal it from Sylvestra. "I'm sure when his cuts and bruises have healed, he'll feel a different man. He was really quite interested in Belzoni. I promised to bring him some drawings—if that's all right?"

"Of course," Sylvestra said quickly. "Yes . . . yes, please do." She seemed relieved. At last something was returning to normal; it was a moment when things were back to the sanity, the wholeness, of the past.

Fidelis rose to her feet and put a hand on her son's arm. "That would be most kind. Now I think we should allow Mrs. Duff a little time to herself." She turned and bade Hester goodbye, then looked at Sylvestra. "If there is anything whatever I can do, my dear, you have only to let me know. If you wish to talk, I am always ready to listen—and then forget . . . selectively. I have an excellent ability to forget."

"There are so many things I would like to forget," Sylvestra replied almost under her breath. "I can't forget what I don't understand. Ridiculous, isn't it? You would think that would be the easiest. Why St. Giles? That is what the police keep asking me and I cannot answer them."

"You probably never will," Fidelis said wryly. "You might

be best advised, happiest, if you do not guess." She kissed Sylvestra lightly on each cheek and then took her leave, Arthur a few steps behind her.

Hester offered no comment, and Sylvestra did not raise the matter. Hester had been present as a courtesy, and she was owed no confidences. They both went up to see if Rhys was still in the good spirits Arthur had described, and found him lying half asleep and apparently at as much ease as was possible in his pain.

That evening Eglantyne Wade called. It was the first time she had come since the funeral, no doubt knowing how ill Rhys was and not wishing to intrude. Hester was curious to see what kind of woman Dr. Wade's sister might be. Hester hoped she would prove to be not unlike him, a woman of courage, imagination and individuality, perhaps not unlike Fidelis Kynaston.

In the event, she proved to be far prettier, or far more conventional in appearance, and Hester felt a stab of disappointment. It was totally unreasonable. Why should his sister have any of his intelligence or inner courage of the spirit? Her own brother, Charles, was nothing at all like her. He was kind, in his own way, honest, and infinitely predictable.

She replied politely to Sylvestra's introduction, searching Miss Wade's face for some sign of inner fire, and not finding it. All she met was a bland, blue stare which seemed without thought, or any but the mildest interest. Even Sylvestra's remark on Hester's service in the Crimea provoked no surprise but the usual murmur of respect which mention of Scutari and Sebastopol always earned. It seemed as if Eglantyne Wade were not even truly listening.

Sylvestra had promised Hester that she might have the evening free to do as she pleased. She had even suggested that Hester might like to go out somewhere, visit friends or relatives. Since Oliver Rathbone had asked that if she were permitted an evening's respite from her new case she would use it to dine with him, she had sent a note to his office at midday. By late afternoon she received the reply that he would be honored if she would allow him to send a carriage for her that they might dine together. Therefore at seven she waited in the hall, dressed in her one really good gown, and felt a distinct ripple of excitement when the doorbell rang and Wharmby informed her that it was for her.

It was a bitter night, a rime of ice on the cobbles, steam rising from the horses' flanks, and the wreaths of fog curling around the lamps and drifting in choking clammy patches. Smoke and soot hung heavy in the air above, blotting out the stars, and a daggerlike wind scythed down the tunnels made by the high house walls on either side of the street.

She had dined at Rathbone's home before, but with Monk also present, and to discuss a case and their strategy to fight it. She had also dined with Rathbone several times at his father's house in Primrose Hill, but she had gathered from the invitation that this was to be in some public place, as was only proper if they were not to be accompanied by any other person.

The cab drew up at a very handsome inn, and the footman immediately opened the door and offered his hand to assist her to alight. She was shown into a small alcove off the main dining room where Rathbone was waiting.

He turned from the mantel, where he had been standing in front of the fire. He was formally dressed in black with icy white shirt front, the light from the chandelier catching his fair hair. He smiled and watched her come in until she was in the center of the room, and the door closed behind her, before he came forward. He took her hands in his.

Her dress was gray-blue, severely cut, but she knew it flattered her eyes and her strong, intelligent face. Frills had always looked absurd on her, out of style with her character.

"Thank you for coming in such extreme haste," he said warmly. "It is a most ungentlemanly way of snatching an opportunity to see you purely for pleasure, and not some wretched business, either of yours or of mine. I am happy to say that all my current cases are merely matters of litigation and require no detecting at all."

She was not sure if that was an allusion to Monk or simply a statement that for once they had no cause for their meeting but each other's company. It was an extraordinary departure for him. He had always been so guarded in the past, so very private where anything personal was concerned.

"And mine has no trial that would interest you," she replied with an answering smile. "In fact, I fear probably no trial at all." She withdrew her hands and he let her go. He walked back slowly towards the chairs near the fire and indicated for her to sit on one, before he sat on the other. It was a delightful room, comfortable and private without being too intimate for decorum. Anyone might come or go at any moment, and they could hear the chatter and laughter, and the clink of china, in another room very close. The fire burned hotly in the grate and there was a pleasant glow from the pink and plum shades of the furniture. Light gleamed on the polished wood of a side table. A main table was set with linen, crystal and silver for two.

"Do you want a trial?" he asked with amusement. His eyes were extraordinarily dark, and he watched her intently.

She had thought she would find his attention disconcerting, but although perhaps it was, it was also unquestionably pleasant, even if it made her skin a little warm and very slightly disturbed her concentration. In a subtle way it was like being touched.

"I would very much like the offenders caught and punished," she said vehemently. "It is one of the worst cases I have seen. Often I think I can see some sort of reason for things, but this seems to be simply the most bestial violence."

"What happened?"

"A young man and his father were attacked in St. Giles and appallingly beaten. The father died; the young man, whom I am nursing, is very badly injured and cannot speak." Her voice dropped unintentionally. "I have watched him have nightmares when it is quite obvious he is reliving the attack. He is agonized with terror, hysterical, trying over and over to scream, but his voice won't come. He is in great physical pain, but the anguish in his mind is even worse."

"I'm sorry," he said, regarding her gravely. "It must be very difficult for you to watch. Can you help him at all?"

"A little . . . I hope."

He smiled across at her, the warmth in his eyes praise

123

enough. Then his brow puckered. "What were they doing in St. Giles? If they can afford a private nurse for him, they don't sound like residents, or even visitors, of such a place."

"Oh, they aren't," she said quickly. "They live in Ebury Street. Mr. Duff was a senior solicitor in property conveyancing. I have no idea what they were doing in St. Giles. That is one of the problems the police are trying to solve. It is John Evan, by the way. I feel odd behaving as if I do not know him."

"But it is best, I'm sure," he agreed. "I'm sorry you have such a distressing case." The servant had left a decanter of wine, and Rathbone offered it to her, and when she accepted, poured a glass full and passed it to her. He raised his own glass to his lips in an unspoken toast. "I suppose many of your cases are trying, one way or another?"

She had not thought of it in that light. "Yes . . . I suppose they are. Either the person is very ill, and to watch suffering is hard, or he is not, and then I feel I am not challenged enough, not really necessary." She smiled suddenly—with real laughter this time. "I'm impossible to please!"

He stared at the light reflecting through the wine in the glass. "Are you sure you want to continue nursing? In an ideal situation, if you did not have to provide for yourself, would you not rather work for hospital reform, as you originally intended?"

She found herself sitting very still, suddenly aware of the crackling of the fire and the sharp edges of the crystal on the glass in her hands. He was not looking at her. Perhaps there was no deeper meaning behind what he had said? No . . . of course there wasn't. She was being ridiculous. The warmth of the room and the glow of the wine were addling her wits.

"I haven't thought about it," she replied, trying to sound light and casual. "I fear reform will be a very slow process, and I have not the influence necessary to make anyone listen to me."

He looked up, his eyes gentle and almost black in the candlelight.

Instantly she could have bitten her tongue out. It sounded exactly as if she were angling for the greater influence he had obliquely referred to . . . perhaps . . . or perhaps not. It was the last thing she had meant. It was not only crass, it was clumsily done. She could feel the color burning up her cheeks.

She rose to her feet and turned away. She must say something quickly, but it must be the right thing. Haste might even make it worse. It was so easy to talk too much.

He had risen when she did and now he was behind her, closer than when they were sitting. She was sharply aware of him.

"I don't really have that kind of skill," she said very measuredly. "Miss Nightingale has. She is a brilliant administrator and arguer. She can make a point so that people have to concede she is correct, and she never gives up. . . ."

"Do you?" he said with laughter in his voice. She could hear it, but she did not look around.

"No, of course I don't." There were too many shared memories for that to need an answer. They had fought battles together against lies and violence, mystery, fear, ignorance. They had faced all kinds of darkness and found their way through to at least what justice there was left, if not necessarily any resolution of tragedy. The one thing they had never done was give up.

She swung around to face him now. He was only a yard away, but she was confident of what she was going to say. She even smiled back at him.

"I have learned a few tricks of a good soldier. I like to choose my own battlefield and my own weapons."

"Bravo," he said, answering softly, his eyes studying her face.

She stood still for a moment, then moved to the table and sat in one of the chairs, her skirts draped unusually dramatically. She felt elegant, even feminine, although she had never seemed to herself stronger or more alive.

He hesitated, looking down at her for several moments.

She was aware of him, and yet now she was not uncomfortable.

The servant came in and announced the first course of the meal.

Rathbone accepted, and it was brought and dished.

Hester smiled across at him. She felt a little fluttering inside, but curiously warm, excited.

"What cases are you engaged in that need no detection?" she asked. For a second Monk came to her mind, and the fact that Rathbone had chosen issues where he did not use him. Could it be intentional? Or was that a shabby thought?

As if he too had seen Monk's face in his inner vision, Rathbone looked down at the plate.

"A society paternity suit," he said with a half smile. "There is really very little to prove. It is an exercise in diplomacy." He raised his eyes to hers and again they were brilliant with inner laughter. "I am endeavoring to judge discretion to the precise degree of knowing how much pressure I can exert before there will be war. If I succeed, you will never hear anything about it. There will simply be a great exchange of money." He shrugged. "If I fail, there will be the biggest scandal since . . ." He took a deep breath and his expression became rueful, self-mocking.

"Since Princess Gisela," she finished for him.

They both laughed. Their laughter was crowded with memories, mostly of the appalling risk he had taken and her fear for him, her efforts and ultimately her success in saving at least the truth, if not unmixed honor, from the issue. He had been vindicated, that was probably the best that could be said, and the truth, or at least a good deal of it, had been laid bare. But there had been a vast number of people who would have preferred not to know, not to be obliged to know.

"And will you win?" she asked him.

"Yes," he replied firmly. "This I will win . . ." He hesitated.

Suddenly she did not want him to say whatever it was that was on his tongue.

"How is your father?" she asked.

"Very well." His voice dropped a little. "He has just returned from a trip to Leipzig, where he met a number of interesting people and, I gather, sat up half of every night talking with them about mathematics and philosophy. All very German. He enjoyed it immensely."

She found herself smiling. She liked Henry Rathbone more each time she saw him. She had been happy the evenings she had spent in his house in Primrose Hill with its doors which

126

opened onto the long lawn, the apple trees at the far end, the honeysuckle hedge and the orchard beyond. She remembered walking once with Oliver across the grass in the dark. They had spoken of other things, not connected with any case, personal things, hopes and beliefs. The moment did not seem so very far away. It was the same feeling of trust, of companionable ease. And yet there was something different now, an added quality between them which sharpened as if on the brink of some decision. She was not sure if she wanted it, or if perhaps she was not ready.

"I am glad he is well. It is a long time since I traveled anywhere."

"Where would you like to go?"

She thought instantly of Venice, and then remembered Monk had been there so very recently with Evelyn von Seidlitz. It was the last place she wanted now. She looked up at him and saw the understanding of it in his eyes, and what might have been a flash of sadness, an awareness of some kind of loss or pain.

It cut her. She wanted to eradicate it.

"Egypt!" she said with a lift of enthusiasm. "I have just been hearing about Signore Belzoni's discoveries . . . a trifle late, I know. But I should love to go up the Nile. Wouldn't you?" Oh God. She had done it again . . . been far too forthright—and desperately clumsy. There was no retracting it. Again she felt the tide of color hot in her face.

This time Rathbone laughed outright. "Hester, my dear, don't ever change. Sometimes you are so unknown to me I cannot possibly guess what you will say or do next. At others you are as transparent as the spring sunlight. Tell me, who is Signore Belzoni, and what did he discover?"

Haltingly at first, she did so, struggling to recall what Arthur Kynaston had said, and then as Rathbone asked her more questions, the conversation flowered again and the unease vanished.

It was nearly midnight when his carriage stopped in Ebury Street to return her home. The fog had cleared and it was a cloudless night, dry and bitterly cold. He alighted to help her down, offering his hand, steadying her on the icy cobbles with the other.

"Thank you," she said, meaning it as far more than a mere politeness. It had been an island of warmth, both physical and of a deeper inward quality, a few hours when all manner of pain and struggle had been forgotten. They had talked of wonderful things, shared excitement, laughter and imagination. "Thank you, Oliver."

He leaned forward, his hand tightening over hers and pulling her a little closer. He kissed her lips softly, gently, but without the slightest hesitation. She could not have pulled back, even if for an instant she had wanted to. It was an amazingly sweet and comfortable feeling, and as she was going up the steps, knowing he was standing in the street watching her, she could feel the happiness of it run through her, filling her whole being.

5

E*VAN FOUND* the Duff case increasingly baffling. He had had an artist draw likenesses of both Leighton and Rhys Duff, and he and Shotts had taken them around the area of St. Giles to see if anyone recognized them. Surely two men, a generation apart, would of themselves be something noticeable. They had tried pawnbrokers, brothels and bawdy houses, inns and lodging rooms, gambling dens, gin mills, even the attics high on the rooftops under the skylights where forgers worked, and the massive cellars below, where fencers of stolen goods stored their merchandise. No one showed the slightest recognition. Not even promise of reward could elicit anything worth having.

"Mebbe it were the first time they came?" Shotts said dismally, pulling his collar up against the falling snow. It was nearly dark. They were walking, heads down into the wind, leaving St. Giles behind them and turning north towards Regent Street and the traffic and lights again. "I dunno 'oo else ter ask."

"Do you think they are lying?" Evan said thoughtfully. "It would be natural enough, since Duff was murdered. No one wants to get involved with murder."

"No." Shotts nimbly avoided a puddle. A vegetable cart rattled by them, its driver hunched under half a blanket, the snow beginning to settle on the brim of his high black hat. "I know when at least some o' them weasels is lyin'. Mebbe they did come 'ere by accident—got lorst."

Evan did not bother to give a reply. The suggestion was not worthy of one.

They crossed George Street. The snow was falling faster, settling white on some of the roofs, but the pavements were still wet and black, showing broken reflections of the gaslights and the carriage lamps as the horses passed by at a brisk trot, eager to get home.

"Maybe they don't recognize them because we are asking the wrong questions," Evan mused, half to himself.

"Yeah?" Shotts kept pace with him easily. "What are the right ones, then?"

"I don't know. Perhaps Rhys went there with friends his own age. After all, one doesn't usually go whoring with one's father. Maybe that is what put people off, the older man."

"Mebbe," Shotts said doubtfully. "Want me ter try?"

"Yes . . . unless you can think of something better. I'm going to the station. It's time I reported to Mr. Runcorn."

Shotts grinned. "Sooner you'n me, sir. 'E won't be 'appy. I'll get summink ter eat, then I'll go an' try again."

Runcorn was a tall, well-built man with a lean face and very steady blue eyes. His nose was long and his cheeks a little hollow, but in his youth he had been good-looking, and now he was an imposing figure. He could have been even more so, had he the confidence to bear himself with greater ease. He sat in his office behind his large leather-inlaid desk and surveyed Evan with wariness.

"Well?"

"The Leighton Duff case, sir," Evan replied, still standing. "I am afraid we do not seem to be progressing. We can find no one in St. Giles who ever saw either of the two men before—"

"Or will admit to it," Runcorn agreed.

"Shotts believes them," Evan said defensively, aware that Runcorn thought he was too soft. It was partly his vague, unspecific anger at a young man of Evan's background choosing to come into the police force. He could not understand it. Evan was a gentleman, something Runcorn both admired and resented. He could have chosen all sorts of occupations if he had not the brains or the inclination to go to university and follow one of the professions. If he needed to make his living, then he could quite easily have gone into a bank or a trading house of some description.

Evan had not explained to Runcorn that a country parson with an ailing wife and several daughters to marry off could not afford expensive tuition for his only son. One did not discuss such things. Anyway, the police force interested him. He had begun idealistically. He had not a suit of armor or a white horse, he had a quick mind and good brown boots. Some of the romance had gone, but the energy and the desire had not. He had that much at least in common with Monk.

"Does he?" Runcorn said grimly. "Then you'd better get back to the family. Widow, and the son who was there and can't speak, that right?"

"Yes sir."

"What's she like, the widow?" Runcorn's eyes opened wider. "Could it be a conspiracy of some sort? Son got in the way, perhaps? Wasn't meant to be there and had to be silenced?"

"Conspiracy?" Evan was astonished. "Between whom?"

"That's for you to find out," Runcorn said testily. "Use your imagination. Is she handsome?"

"Yes . . . very, in an unusual sort of way . . ."

"What do you mean, unusual? What's wrong with her? How old is she? How old was he?"

Evan found himself resenting the implications.

"She's very dark, sort of Spanish looking. There's nothing wrong with her, it's just . . . unusual."

"How old?" Runcorn repeated.

"About forty, I should think." The thought had never occurred to him until Runcorn had mentioned it, but it should have. It was obvious enough, now that it was there. The whole crime might have nothing to do with St. Giles, which might have been no more than a suitable place. It could as easily have been any other slum, any alley or yard in a dozen such areas, just somewhere to leave a body where it would be believed to be an attack by ruffians. It was sickening. Of course, Rhys was never meant to have been there; his presence was mischance. Leighton Duff had followed him and been caught up with . . . but that did not need to be true either. He had only Sylvestra's word for that. The two men could have gone out at any time, separately or together, for any reason. He must consider it independently before he accepted it to be the truth. Now he was angry with himself. Monk would never have made such an elementary mistake.

Runcorn let out his breath in a sigh. "You should have thought of that, Evan," he said. "You think everybody who speaks well belongs in your country vicarage."

Evan opened his mouth and then closed it again. Runcorn's remark was unfair, but it sprang not from fact, or not primarily, but from his own complex feelings about gentlemen and about Evan himself. At least some of it stemmed from Runcorn's long relationship with Monk and the rivalry between them, the years of unease, of accumulated offenses which Monk could not remember and Runcorn never forgot. Evan did not know the origin of it, but he had seen the clash of ideals and natures when he first came, after Monk's accident, and he had been there when the final and blazing quarrel had severed the tie and Monk had found himself out of the police force. Like every other man in the station, he was aware of the emotions. He had been Monk's friend, therefore he could never truly be trusted by Runcorn, and never liked without there always being a reservation.

"So what have you got?" Runcorn asked abruptly. Evan's silence bothered him. He did not understand him; he did not know what he was thinking.

"Very little," Evan answered ruefully. "Leighton Duff died somewhere about three in the morning, according to Dr. Riley. Could have been earlier or later. He was beaten and kicked to death, no weapon used except fists and boots. Young Rhys Duff was almost as badly beaten, but he survived."

"I know that! Evidence, man!" Runcorn said impatiently, curling his fist on the desktop. "What evidence have you? Facts, objects, statements, witnesses who can be believed."

"No witnesses to anything, except finding the bodies," Evan

replied stiffly. There were moments when he wished he had Monk's speed of mind to retaliate, but he did not want the ordinary man on the beat to fear him, only respect him. "No one admits to having seen either man, separately or together, in St. Giles."

"Cabbies," Runcorn said, his eyebrows raised. "They didn't walk there."

"We're trying. Nothing so far."

"You haven't got very much." Runcorn's face was plainly marked with contempt. "You'd better have another look at the family. Look at the widow. Don't let elegance blind you. Maybe the son knows his mother's nature, and that's why he's so horrified that he cannot speak."

Evan thought of Rhys's expression as he had looked at Sylvestra, of his flinching from her when she moved to touch him. It was a repellent thought.

"I'm going to do that," he said reluctantly. "I'm going to look into his friends and associates more closely. He may have been seeing a woman in that area, perhaps a married woman, and her male relatives may have taken offense at his treatment of her."

Runcorn let out a sigh. "Possible," he concluded. "What about the father? Why attack him?"

"Because he was a witness to the scene, of course," Evan replied with a lift of satisfaction.

Runcorn looked at him sharply.

"And another thing, sir," Evan went on. "Monk has been hired to look into a series of very violent rapes across in Seven Dials."

Runcorn's blue eyes narrowed. "Then he's more of a fool than I took him for. If ever there were a profitless exercise, that is it."

"Have we any reports that might help?"

"Help Monk?" Runcorn said with disbelief.

"Help solve the crime, sir," Evan answered with only a hint of sarcasm.

"I can solve it for you now!" Runcorn stood up. He was at least three inches taller than Evan, and considerably more

133

solid. "How many were there? Half a dozen?" He ticked off on his fingers. "One was a drunken husband. One was a pimp taking his revenge for a little liberty turned license. At least two were dissatisfied clients, probably too drunk. One was an amateur who changed her mind and wanted more money when it was too late. And probably one was drunk herself and fell over and can't remember what happened."

"I disagree, sir," Evan said coldly. "I think Monk can tell the difference between a woman who was raped and beaten and one who fell over because she was drunk."

Runcorn glared at Evan. He was standing beside the bookshelf of morocco-bound volumes in a variety of profound subjects, including philosophy.

Evan had used Monk's name and the memory of his skill, quicker, sharper than Runcorn's, on purpose. He was angry and it was the easiest weapon. But even as he did it, he wondered what had started the enmity between the two. Had it really been no more than a difference of character or beliefs?

"If Monk thinks he can prove rape of half a dozen part-time prostitutes in Seven Dials, he's lost the wits he used to have," Runcorn said with a flush of satisfaction under his anger. "I knew he'd come to nothing after he left here. Private agent of enquiry, indeed! He's no good for anything but a policeman, and now he's no good even for that." His eyes were bright with satisfaction and there was a half smile on his lips. "He's come right down in the world, hasn't he, our Monk, if he's reduced to running after prostitutes in Seven Dials. Who's going to pay him?"

Evan felt a tight, hard knot of rage inside him.

"Presumably someone who cares just as much about poor women as rich ones," he said with his teeth clenched. "And who doesn't believe it will do them any good appealing to the police."

"Someone who's got more money than brains, Sergeant Evan," Runcorn retorted, a flush of anger blotching his cheeks. "And if Monk were an honest man, and not a desperate one trying to scrape any living he can, no matter at whose expense, then he'd have told them there's nothing he can do." He jerked

134

one hand dismissively. "He'll never find who did it, if anything was done. And if he did find them, who's to prove it was rape and not a willing one that got a bit rough? And even supposing all of that, what's a court going to do? When was a man ever hanged or jailed for taking a woman who sells her body anyway? And at the end of it all, what difference would it make to Seven Dials?"

"What difference is one death more or less to London?" Evan demanded, leaning towards him, his voice thick. "Not much—unless it's yours—then it makes all the difference in the world."

"Stay with what you can do something about, Sergeant," Runcorn said wearily. "Let Monk worry about rape and Seven Dials if he wants to. Perhaps he has nothing else, poor devil. You have. You're a policeman, with a duty. Go and find out who murdered Leighton Duff, and why. Then bring me proof of it. There'd be some point in that."

"Yes sir." Evan replied so sharply it was almost one word, then swiveled on his heel and went out of the room, the anger burning inside him.

The following morning when he set out for Ebury Street he was still turning over in his mind his conversation with Runcorn. Of course Runcorn was right to consider the possibility that Sylvestra was at the heart of it. She was a woman of more than beauty; there was a gravity, a mystery about her, an air of something different and undiscovered which was far more intriguing than mere perfection of form or coloring. It was something which might fascinate for a lifetime and last even when the years had laid their mark on physical loveliness.

Evan should have thought of it himself, and it had never crossed his mind.

He walked part of the way. It was not an unpleasant morning, and his mind worked more clearly if he exerted some effort of body. He strode along the pavement in the crisp air, frost sharpened. There were rims of white along the roofs where the snow had remained, and curls of smoke rose from chimneys almost straight up. At the edge of Hyde Park the bare trees were black against a white sky, the flat winter light seeming almost shadowless.

He must learn a great deal more about Leighton Duff: What manner of man had he been? Could this, after all, be a crime of passion or jealousy, and not a random robbery at all? Had Rhys's presence there simply been the most appalling mischance?

And how much of what Sylvestra said was the truth? Were her grief and confusion for her son, and not for her husband at all? Evan must learn very much more of her life, her friends, especially those who were men, and who might possibly now court a fascinating and quite comfortably situated widow. Dr. Wade was the first and most apparent place to begin.

It was a thought which repelled him, and he shivered as he crossed Buckingham Palace Road, running the last few steps to get out of the way of a carriage turning from the mews off Stafford Place. It went past him at a smart clip, harness jingling, horses' hooves loud on the stones, their breath steaming in the icy air.

The other questions which lay unresolved at the back of his mind concerned his relationship with Runcorn. There were many occasions when he saw a side of him he almost liked, at least a side he could understand and feel for. Runcorn's aspirations to better himself were such as any man might have, most particularly one from a very ordinary background, a good-looking man whose education was unremarkable, but where intelligence and ability were greater than his opportunities would allow. He had chosen the police as a career where avenues were open for him to exercise his natural gifts, and he had done so with great success. He was not a gentleman born, nor had he the daring and the confidence to bluff his way, as Monk had. He lacked the grace, the quick-wittedness, or the model from whom to learn. Evan thought that very possibly he had received little encouragement from whatever family he possessed. They might see him as being ashamed of his roots, and resent him accordingly.

And he had never married. There must be a story to that. Evan wondered if it were financial. Many men felt they could not afford a home fit for a wife and the almost certain family which would follow. Or had it been emotional, a woman who had refused him, or perhaps who had died young, and he had not loved again? Probably Evan would never know, but the possibilities lent a greater humanity to a man whose temper and whose weakness he saw, as well as his competence and his strengths.

He stood on the curb waiting for the traffic to ease so he could cross the corner at Grosvenor Street. A newspaper seller was calling out headlines about the controversial book published last year by Charles Darwin. A leading bishop had expressed horror and condemnation. Liberal and progressive thinkers disagreed with him and labeled him reactionary and diehard. The murder in St. Giles was forgotten. There was a brazier on the corner and a man selling roasted chestnuts and warming his hands at the fire.

There was congestion at the junction of Eccleston Street and Belgrave Road. Two draymen were in a heated discussion. Evan could hear their raised voices from where he stood. The traffic all ground to a halt, and he went across the street, dodging fresh horse droppings, pungent in the cold air. He was a short block from Ebury Street.

The worst of Runcorn, the times he descended into spite, were when Monk's name—or, by implication, his achievements—were mentioned. There was a shadow between them far deeper than the few clashes Evan had witnessed or the final quarrel when Monk had left, simultaneously with Runcorn's dismissing him.

Monk no longer understood it. It was gone with all the rest of his past, returning only in glimpses and unconnected fragments, leaving him to guess, and fear the rest. Evan would almost certainly never know, but it was there in his mind when he saw the weakness and the vulnerability in Runcorn.

He reached Ebury Street and knocked on the door of number thirty-four. He was met by the maid, Janet, who smiled at him a slight uncertainly, as if she liked him but knew his errand only too painfully. She showed him into the morning room and

137

asked him to wait while she discovered if Mrs. Duff would see him.

However, when the door opened it was Hester who came in quickly, closing it behind her. She was wearing blue, her hair was dressed a little less severely than usual, and she looked flushed, but with vitality rather than fever or any embarrassment. He had always liked her, but now he thought perhaps she was also prettier than he had realized before, softer, more openly feminine. That was another thing he wondered about, why Monk quarreled with her so much. He would be the last man on earth to admit it, but perhaps that was exactly why he could not afford, he did not dare, to see her as she really was.

"Good morning, Hester," he said informally, echoing his thoughts rather than his usual manners.

"Good morning, John," she answered with a smile, a touch of amusement in it as well as friendship.

"How is Mr. Duff?"

The laughter vanished from her eyes, and even the light in her face seemed to fade.

"He is very poorly still. He has the most dreadful nightmares. He had another again last night. I don't even know how to help him."

"There is no question he saw what happened to his father," he said regretfully. "If only he could tell us."

"He can't," she said instantly.

"I know he can't speak, but—"

"No! You can't ask him," she interrupted. "In fact, it would be better if you did not even see him. Really—I am not being obstructive. I would like to know who murdered Leighton Duff, and also did this to Rhys, as much as you would. But his recovery has to be my chief concern." She looked at him earnestly. "It has to be, John, regardless of anything else. I could not conceal a crime, or knowingly tell you anything that was not true, but I cannot allow you to cause him the distress—and the real damage it may do—if you try in any way at all to bring back to his mind what he saw and felt. And if you had witnessed his nightmares as I have, you would not argue with me." Her eyes were dark with her own distress, her face

138

pinched with it, and he knew her well enough to read in her expression far more than she said.

"And Dr. Wade has forbidden it," she added. "He has seen his injuries and knows the damage further hysteria on his part might cause. His wounds could be torn open so easily were he to wrench his body around or move suddenly or violently."

"I understand," he conceded, trying not to imagine too vividly the horror and the pain, and finding it hideously real. "I came principally to report to Mrs. Duff."

Her eyes widened. "Have you found something?" She remained curiously still, and for a moment he thought she was afraid of the answer.

"No." That was not totally true. She had not asked him openly, but had he been honest to the question which was understood between them, he would have said he had new suspicions about Sylvestra. He had returned not because of a discovery but a realization. "I wish there were new facts," he went on. "It's only a matter of trying better to understand the old ones."

"I can't help you," she said quietly. "I'm not even sure whether I want you to find the truth. I have no idea what it is, except that Rhys cannot bear it."

He smiled at her, and all the memory of past tragedies and horrors they had known was there with its emotion, for an instant shared.

Then the door opened and Sylvestra came in. She looked at Hester with dark eyebrows lifted in question.

"Miss Latterly says that Mr. Duff is not well enough to be spoken to," Evan explained. "I am sorry. I had hoped he was better for his own sake, as well as for the truth."

"No . . . he's not," Sylvestra said quickly, relief filling her face, and a softening of gratitude towards Hester. "I'm afraid he still cannot help."

"Perhaps you can, Mrs. Duff." Evan was not going to allow her to close him out. "Since I cannot speak with Mr. Duff, I shall have to speak with his friends. Some of them may know something which can tell us why he went to St. Giles and whom he knew there."

Hester went out silently.

"I doubt it," Sylvestra said almost before Evan had finished speaking, then seemed to regret her haste, not as having said something untrue but as being tactically mistaken. "I mean . . . at least I don't think so. If they did, surely they would have come forward by now. Arthur Kynaston was here yesterday. If he or his brother had known anything at all, they would surely have told us."

"If they realize the relevance," Evan said persuasively, as if he had not thought she was being evasive. "Where may I find them?"

"Oh . . . the Kynastons live in Lowndes Square, number seventeen."

"Thank you. I daresay they can tell me of any other friends whose company they kept from time to time." He made his tone casual. "Who would know your husband in his leisure hours, Mrs. Duff? I mean, who else might frequent the same clubs or have the same hobbies or interests?"

She said nothing, staring at him with wide, black eyes. He tried to read in them what she was thinking, and failed completely. She was different from any woman he had seen before. There was a composure to her, a mystery, which filled his mind even when he had thought he was concentrating on something else, some utterly different aspect of the case. He would never understand her until he knew a great deal more about Leighton Duff, what manner of man he had been: brave or cowardly, kind or cruel, honest or deceitful, loving or cold. Had he had wit, charm, gentleness, imagination? Had she loved him, or had it been a marriage of convenience, workable but without passion? Had there even been friendship in it, or trust?

"Mrs. Duff?"

"I suppose Dr. Wade, and Mr. Kynaston principally," she replied. "There are many others, of course. I think he had interests in common with Mr. Milton, in his law partnership, and Mr. Hodge. He spoke of a James Wellingham once or twice, and he wrote to a Mr. Phillips quite regularly."

"I'll speak with them. Perhaps I may see the letters?" He

140

had no idea what possible use they could be, but he must try everything.

"Of course." She seemed perfectly at ease with the idea. If she had a lover, he did not lie in that direction. He could not help thinking again of Corriden Wade.

He spent a profitless morning reading agreeable but essentially tedious correspondence from Mr. Phillips, largely on the subject of archery. He left and went to the law office of Cullingford, Duff and Partners, where he learned that Leighton Duff had been a brilliant man in his chosen career and the driving force behind the success of the concern. His rise from junior to effective leader had been almost without hindrance. Everyone spoke well of his ability and was concerned for the continued preeminence of the company in its field now that he was no longer with them.

If there was envy or personal malice Evan did not see it. Perhaps he was too easily persuaded. Possibly he lacked Monk's sharper, harder mind, but he saw in the replies of Leighton Duff's associates nothing more sinister than respect for a colleague, a decent observance for the etiquette of speaking no ill of the dead, and a lively fear for their own future prosperity. Apparently they had not been socially acquainted, and none of them claimed to know the widow. Evan could catch them in no evasion, let alone untruth.

He left feeling he had wasted his time. All he had learned had confirmed his earlier picture of Leighton Duff as a clever, hardworking and eminently, almost boringly, decent man. The side of his character which took him to St. Giles, for whatever reason, was perfectly hidden from his partners in the law. If they suspected anything, they did not allow Evan to see it.

But then if a gentleman took occasional release for his natural carnal appetites, it was certainly not a matter to be displayed before the vulgar and the inquisitive, and Evan knew that in their minds the police would fall into both those categories.

It was after four o'clock and already dusk, with the lamplighters hurrying to the last few before it was too late, when Evan arrived at the home of Joel Kynaston, friend of Leighton

Duff and headmaster of the excellent school at which Rhys had obtained his education. He did not live on the school premises but in a fine Georgian house about a quarter of a mile away.

The door was opened by a rather short butler, straightening to stand up to every fraction of his height.

"Yes sir?" He must be used to parents of pupils turning up at unexpected hours. He showed no surprise at all, except perhaps at Evan's comparative youth as he stepped into the light.

"Good afternoon. My name is John Evan. I would very much appreciate speaking confidentially with Mr. Kynaston. It is in regard to the recent tragic death of Mr. Leighton Duff." He did not give his rank or occupation.

"Indeed, sir," the butler said without expression. "I shall enquire if Mr. Kynaston is at home. If you will be so good as to wait."

It was the customary polite fiction. Kynaston would have expected someone to call. It was surely inevitable. He would be prepared in his mind. If he had anything relevant he was willing to say, he would have sought out Evan himself.

Evan looked around the hallway where he had been left. It was elegant, a trifle cold in its lack of personal touches. The umbrella stand held only sticks and umbrellas of one character, one length. Such ornaments as there were, were all of finely wrought brass, possibly Arabic, beautiful but lacking the variety of objects collected by a family over a period of years. Even the pictures on the walls spoke of one taste. Either Kynaston and his wife were remarkably alike in their choices or one person's character prevailed over the other's.

But the man who came out of the double oak doors of the withdrawing room was not more than twenty-two or -three. He was handsome, if a little undershot of jaw, with fair hair which curled attractively and bold, direct blue eyes.

"I'm Duke Kynaston, Mr. Evan," he said coolly, stopping in the middle of the polished floor. "My father is not at home yet. I am not sure when he will be. Naturally we wish to be of any assistance to the police that we can, but I fear there is nothing we know about the matter. Would you not be better pursuing

142

your enquiries in St. Giles? That is where it happened, is it not?"

"Yes it is," Evan replied, trying to sum up the young man, make a judgment as to his nature. He wondered how close he had been to Rhys Duff. There was an arrogance in his face, a hint of self-indulgence about the mouth, which made it easy to imagine that if Rhys had indeed gone whoring in St. Giles, Duke Kynaston might well have been his companion. Had he been there that night? At the dark edges of Evan's mind, something he did not even want to allow into his conscious thought, was the knowledge of Monk's case, the rapes of poverty-stricken women, amateur prostitutes. But that had been in Seven Dials, beyond Aldwich. Was it just conceivable that Rhys and his companions had been responsible for that, and had this time met their match, a woman who had a brother or a husband who was not as drunk as they had supposed? Possibly even a vigilante group of their own? That would explain the violence of the reprisal. And Leighton Duff had feared as much and had followed his son, and he had been the one who had paid the ultimate price, dying to save his son's life?

Little wonder Rhys had nightmares and could not speak. It would be a memory no man could live with.

Evan looked at the young Duke Kynaston's rather supercilious face, with the consciousness of youth, strength, and money so plain in it. But there were no bruises, even healed ones fading, no cuts or scratches except one faint scar on his cheek. It would have been no more than a nick of the razor such as any young man might make.

"So what is it you imagine we can tell you?" Duke said a little impatiently.

"St. Giles is a large area—" Evan began.

"Not very," Duke contradicted. "Square mile or so."

"So you know it?" Evan said with a smile.

Duke flushed. "I know *of* it, Mr. Evan. That is not the same thing." But his annoyance betrayed that he perceived it was.

"Then you will know that it is densely populated," Evan continued, "with people who are most unlikely to offer us any assistance. There is a great deal of poverty there, and crime. It

143

is not a natural place for gentlemen to go. It is crowded, dirty and dangerous."

"So I have heard."

"You have never been there?"

"Never. As you said, it is not a place any gentleman would wish to be." Duke smiled more widely. "If I were to go searching cheap entertainment, I would choose the Haymarket. I had imagined Rhys would do the same, but possibly I was wrong."

"He has never been to the Haymarket with you?" Evan asked mildly.

For the first time Duke hesitated.

"I hardly think my pleasures are any of your concern, Mr. Evan. But no, I have not been with Rhys to the Haymarket, or anywhere else, for at least a year. I have no idea what he was doing in St. Giles." He stared back at Evan with steady, defiant eyes.

Evan would have liked to disbelieve him, but he thought it was literally true, even if there was an implicit lie embedded in it somewhere. It was pointless to press him on the subject. He was obviously not willing to offer anything, and Evan had no weapon with which to draw him out against his will. His only tactic was to bide his time and look as if he were content with it.

"Unfortunate," Evan said blandly. "It would have made our task shorter. But no doubt we shall find those who do. It will take more work, more disruption to others, and I daresay more investigation of private lives, but there is no help for it."

Duke looked at him narrowly. Evan was not sure if he imagined it, but there seemed a flicker of unease.

"If you want to wait in the morning room, there may be a newspaper there, or something," Duke said abruptly. "It's that way." He indicated the door to his left, Evan's right. "I expect when Papa comes home he'll see you. Not that I imagine he can tell you anything either, but he did teach Rhys at school."

"Do you imagine Rhys might have confided in him?"

Duke gave him a look of such incredible contempt no answer was necessary.

Evan accepted the invitation and went to the cold and very uncomfortable morning room. The fire had long since gone out and he was too chilly to sit. He walked back and forth, half looking at the books on the shelf, noticing a number of classical titles, Tacitus, Sallust, Juvenal, Caesar, Cicero and Pliny in the original Latin, translations of Terence and Plautus, the poems of Catullus, and on the shelf above, the travels of Herodotus and Thucydides' history of the Peloponnesian war. They were hardly the reading a waiting guest would choose. He wondered what manner of person usually sat there.

What he really wanted was to ask Kynaston about Sylvestra Duff. He wanted to know if she had a lover, if she was the sort of woman to seize her own desires even at the expense of someone else's life. Had she the strength of will, the courage, the blind, passionate selfishness? But how did you say that to anyone? How did you elicit it from him without his wish?

Not by pacing the floor alone in a cold room, thinking about it. He wished he had Monk's skill. Monk might have known how to proceed.

He went to the fireplace and pulled the bell rope. When the maid answered he asked if he could see Mrs. Kynaston. The maid promised to enquire.

He had no picture in his mind, but still Fidelis Kynaston surprised him. He would have said at a glance that she was plain. She was certainly over forty, nearer to forty-five, and yet he found himself drawn to her immediately. There was a composure in her, an inner certainty which was integrity.

"Good evening, Mr. Evan." She came in and closed the door. She had fair hair which was fading a little at the temples, and she wore a dark gray dress of simple cut, without ornament except for a very beautiful cameo brooch, heightened by its solitary presence. The physical resemblance to her son was plain, and yet her personality was so utterly different she seemed nothing like him at all. There was no antagonism in her eyes, no contempt, only amusement and patience.

"Good evening, Mrs. Kynaston," he said quickly. "I am sorry to disturb you, but I need your help, if you are able to give it, in endeavoring to learn what happened to Rhys Duff and his

145

father. I cannot question him. As you may know, he cannot speak and is too ill to be distressed by having the subject even mentioned to him. I dislike raising it with Mrs. Duff more than I am obliged to, and I think she is too deeply shocked at present to recall a great deal."

"I am not sure what I know, Mr. Evan," she answered with a frown. "The imagination answers why Rhys may have gone to such an area. Young men do. They frequently have more curiosity and appetite than either sense or good taste."

He was surprised at her candor, and it must have shown in his expression.

She smiled, a lopsided gesture because of the extraordinariness of her face.

"I have sons, and I had brothers, Mr. Evan. Also, my husband is the principal of a school for boys. I should indeed have my eyes closed were I to be unaware of such things."

"Did you not find it difficult to believe that Rhys would go there?"

"No. He was an average young man, with all the usual desires to flout convention as he thought his parents considered it, and yet to do exactly what all young men have always done."

"His father before him?" he asked.

Her eyebrows rose. "Probably. If you are asking me if I know, then the answer is that I do not. There are many things a wise woman chooses not to know, unless the knowledge is forced upon her, and most men do not force it."

He hesitated. Was she referring to the use of prostitutes, or something else as well? There was a shadow in her eyes, a darkness in her voice. She had looked at the world clearly and seen much unpleasantness. He was quite sure she had known pain and accepted it as inevitable, her own no less than that of others. Could it be to do with her son Duke? Might he have a great deal to do with the younger, more impressionable, Rhys's behavior? Duke was the kind of youth others wanted to impress—and to emulate.

"But nevertheless, you guess?" he said quietly.

"That is not the same, Mr. Evan. What you only guess you

can always deny to yourself. The element of uncertainty is enough. But before you ask: no, I do not know what happened to Rhys or to his father. I can only assume Rhys fell in with bad company, and poor Leighton was so concerned for him that in this instance he followed him, perhaps in an attempt to persuade Rhys to leave, and in the ensuing fight, Leighton was killed and Rhys injured. It is tragic. With a little more consideration, less pride and stubbornness, it need not have happened."

"Is this guess based on your knowledge of the character of Mr. Duff?"

She was still standing, perhaps also too cold to sit.

"Yes."

"You knew him quite well?"

"Yes, I did. I have known Mrs. Duff for years. Mr. Duff and my husband were close friends. My husband is profoundly grieved at his death. It has made him quite unwell. He took a severe chill, and I am sure the distress has hindered his recovery."

"I'm sorry," Evan said automatically. "Tell me something about Mr. Duff. It may help me to learn the truth."

She had an ability to stand in one place without looking awkward or moving her hands unnecessarily. She was a woman of peculiar grace.

"He was a very sober man, of deep intelligence," she answered thoughtfully. "He took his responsibilities to heart. He knew a large number of people depended upon his skills and his hard work." She made a small gesture of her hands. "Not merely his family, of course, but also all those whose futures lay in the prosperity of his company. And you will understand, he dealt with valuable properties and large amounts of money almost daily." A flicker crossed her face; her eyes lightened as if a new thought had occurred to her. "I think that is one of the reasons Joel, my husband, found him so easy to speak with. They both understood the burden of responsibility for others, of being trusted without question. It is an extraordinary thing, Mr. Evan, to have people place their confidence in you, not only in your skills but in your honor, and

147

take it for granted that you will do for them all that they require."

"Yes . . ." he said slowly, thinking that he too was on occasion treated with that kind of blind faith. It was a remarkable compliment, but it was also a burden when one realized the possibilities of failure.

She was still lost in her thoughts. "My husband is the final judge in so many issues," she went on, not looking at Evan but at some inner memories of her own. "The decisions upon a boy's academic education—and, perhaps even more, his moral education—can affect the rest of his life. In fact, I suppose when you speak of the boys who will one day lead our nation, the politicians, inventors, writers, and artists of the future, then it may affect us all. No wonder these decisions have to be made with care, and with much searching of conscience, and with absolute selflessness. There can be no evasions into simplicity. The cost of error may never be recovered."

"Did he have a sense of humor?" The words were out before Evan realized how inappropriate they were.

"I beg your pardon?"

It was too late to withdraw. "Did Mr. Duff have a sense of humor?" He felt the blush creep up his face.

"No . . ." She stared back at him in what seemed like a moment's complete understanding, too fragile for words. Then it was gone. "Not that I saw. But he loved music. He played the pianoforte very well, you know? He liked good music, especially Beethoven and occasionally Bach."

Evan was forming no picture of him, certainly nothing to explain what he had been doing in St. Giles, except following a wayward and disappointing son whose taste in pleasures he did not understand, and perhaps whose appetites frightened him, knowing the danger to which they could lead—disease being not the least of them. Evan would not ask this woman the questions whose answers he needed, but he would ask Joel Kynaston: he must.

It was another half hour of largely meaningless but pleasant conversation before the butler came back to say that Mr.

Kynaston had returned and would see Evan in his study. Evan thanked Fidelis and followed where he was directed.

The study was obviously a room for use. The fire blazed in a large hearth, glinting on wrought brass shovel and tongs and gleaming on the fender. Evan was shivering with cold, and the warmth enveloped him like a welcome blanket. The walls were decorated with glass-fronted bookcases and pictures of country domestic scenes. The oak desk was massive and there were three piles of books and papers on it.

Joel Kynaston sat behind the desk looking at Evan curiously. It was impossible to tell his height, but he gave the impression of being slight. His face was keen, nose a trifle pinched, mouth highly individual. It was not a countenance one would forget, nor easily overlook. His intelligence was inescapable, as was his consciousness of authority.

"Come in, Mr. Evan," he said with a slight nod. He did not rise, immediately establishing their relative status. "How may I be of service to you? If I had known anything about poor Leighton Duff's death I should already have told you, naturally. Although I have been ill with a fever and spent the last few days in my bed. However, today I am better, and I cannot lie at home any longer."

"I'm sorry for your illness, sir," Evan responded.

"Thank you." Kynaston waved to the chair opposite. "Do sit down. Now, tell me what you think I can do to be of assistance."

Evan accepted, finding the chair less comfortable than it looked, although he would have sat on boards to stay near the warmth. He was obliged to sit upright rather than relax.

"I believe you have known Rhys Duff since he was a boy, sir," he began, making a statement rather than a question.

Kynaston frowned very slightly, drawing his brows together. "Yes?"

"Does it surprise you that he should be in an area like St. Giles?"

Kynaston drew in a deep breath and let it out slowly. "No. I regret to say that it does not. He was always wayward, and lately his choice of company caused his father some concern."

"Why? I mean, for what specific reason?"

149

Kynaston stared at him. Several reactions flickered across his face. He had highly expressive features. They showed amazement, disdain, sadness, and something else not so easily read, a darker thing, a sense of tragedy, or perhaps evil.

"What exactly do you mean, Mr. Evan?"

"Was it the immorality of it?" Evan expanded. "The fear of disease, of scandal or disgrace, of losing the favor of some respectable young lady? Or the knowledge that it might lead him to physical danger or greater depravity?"

Kynaston hesitated so long Evan thought he was not going to answer. When finally he did speak, his voice was low, very careful, very precise, and he held his strong, bony hands in front of him, clutched tightly together.

"I should imagine all of those things, Mr. Evan. A man is uniquely responsible for the character of his son. There cannot be many experiences in human existence more harrowing than witnessing your own child, the bearer of your name and your heritage, your immortality, treading a downward path into weakness, corruption of the mind and of the body." He looked at Evan's surprise. His eyebrows rose. "Not that I am suggesting Rhys was depraved. There was a predisposition to weakness in him which required greater discipline than perhaps he received. That is all. It is common among the young, especially an only boy in a family. Leighton Duff was concerned. Tragically, it now appears that he had grave cause."

"You believe Mr. Duff followed Rhys into St. Giles, and they were both attacked as a result of something that happened because they were there?"

"Don't you? It seems a tragically apparent explanation."

"You don't believe Mr. Duff would have gone alone otherwise? You knew him well, I believe?"

"Very well," Kynaston said decisively. "I am perfectly certain he would not. Why in heaven's name should he? He had everything to lose and nothing of any conceivable value to gain." He smiled very slightly, a fleeting, bitter humor, swallowed instantly in the reality of loss. "I hope you catch whoever is responsible, sir, but I have no sensible hope that you will. If Rhys had a liaison with some woman of the area, or something worse"—his mouth twisted very slightly in distaste—"then I doubt you will discover it now. Those involved will hardly come forward, and I imagine the denizens of that world will protect their own rather than ally with the forces of law."

What he said was true. Evan had to admit it. He thanked him and rose to take his leave. He would speak to Dr. Corriden Wade, but he did not expect to learn much from him that would be of any value.

Wade was tired, at the end of a long and harrowing day, when he allowed Evan into his library. There were dark shadows under the doctor's eyes and he walked across the room ahead of Evan as if his back and legs hurt him.

"Of course I will tell you what I can, Sergeant," he said, turning and settling in one of the comfortable chairs by the embers of the fire and gesturing towards the other chair for Evan. "But I fear it will not be anything you do not already know. And I cannot permit you to question Rhys Duff. He is in a very poor state of health, and any distress, which you cannot help but cause him, could precipitate a crisis. I cannot tell what injuries may have been caused to his inner organs by the treatment he received."

"I understand," Evan replied quickly. The memory returned to him with sharp pity of Rhys lying in the alley, of his own horror when he had realized he was still alive, still capable of immeasurable pain. Nor could he ever rid his mind of the horror in Rhys's eyes when he had regained his senses and first tried to speak, and found he could not. "I had no intention of asking to see him. I hoped you might tell me more about both Rhys and his father. It may help to learn what happened."

Wade sighed. "Presumably they were attacked, robbed and beaten by thieves," he said unhappily. Sadness and gravity were equal in his face. "Does it matter now why they went to St. Giles? Have you the least real hope of catching whoever it was or of proving anything? I have little experience of St. Giles in particular, but I spent several years in the navy. I have seen some rough areas, places where there is desperate poverty, where disease and death are commonplace and a child is fortunate to reach its sixth birthday—and more fortunate still to reach manhood. Few have an honest trade which earns them sufficient to live. Fewer still can read or write. This is, then, a way of life. Violence is easy, the first resort, not the last."

He was looking at Evan intently, his dark eyes narrowed. "I would have thought you were familiar with such places also, but perhaps you are too young. Were you born in the city, Sergeant?"

"No, in the country . . ."

Wade smiled. He had excellent teeth. "Then perhaps you still have something to learn about the human battle for survival and how men turn upon each other when there is too little space, too little food, too little air, and no hope or strength of belief to change it. Despair breeds rage, Mr. Evan, and a desire to retaliate against a world in which there is no apparent justice. It is to be expected."

"I do expect it, sir," Evan replied. "And I would have imagined a man of Mr. Leighton Duff's intelligence and experience of the world to have expected it also—indeed, to have foreseen it."

Wade stared at him. He looked extremely tired. There was little color in his face and his body slumped as though he had no strength left and his muscles hurt him.

"I imagine he knew it as well as we do," he said bleakly. "He must have gone in after Rhys. You have only seen Rhys as he is now, Mr. Evan, a victim of violence, a man confused and in pain, and extremely frightened." He pushed out his lower lip. "He is not always so. Before this . . . incident . . . he was a young man of considerable bravado and appetite, and with much of youth's belief in its own superiority, invincibility, and insensitivity to the feelings of others. He had the average capacity to be cruel and to enjoy a certain power." His mouth tightened. "I make no judgments, and God knows, I would cure him of all of this if I could, but it is not impossible he was involved with a woman of that area and exercised certain desires without regard to their consequences upon others. She may have belonged to someone else. He may even have been rougher than was acceptable. Perhaps she had family who . . ." He did not bother to finish; it was unnecessary.

Evan frowned, searching his way through crowding possibilities.

"Dr. Wade, are you saying that you have observed a streak of cruelty or violence in Rhys Duff before this incident?"

Wade hesitated. "No, Sergeant, I am not," he said finally. "I am saying that I knew Leighton Duff for close to twenty years, and I cannot conceive of any reason why he should go to an area like St. Giles, except to try to reason with his son and prevent him from committing some act of folly from which he could not extricate himself. In the light of what has happened, I can only believe that he was right."

"Did he speak to you of such fears, Dr. Wade?"

"You must know, Sergeant, that I cannot answer you." Wade's voice was grave and heavy, but there was no anger in it. "I understand that it is your duty to ask. You must understand that it is my duty to refuse to answer."

"Yes," Evan agreed with a sigh. "Yes, of course I do. I do not think I need to trouble you further, at least not tonight. Thank you for your time."

"You are welcome, Sergeant."

Evan stood up and went to the door.

"Sergeant."

He turned. "Yes sir?"

"I think your case may be insoluble. Please try to consider Mrs. Duff's feelings as much as you can. Do not pursue tragic and sordid details of her son's life which cannot help you and which she will have to live with, as well as with her grief. I cannot promise you that Rhys will recover. He may not."

"Do you mean his speech or his life?"

"Both."

"I see. Thank you for your kindness. Good night, Dr. Wade."

"Good night, Sergeant."

Evan left with a deep grief inside him. He went out into the dark street. The fog had descended since he had gone inside and now he could barely see four or five yards in front of him. The gas lamps were no more than blurs in the gloom in front of and behind him. Beyond that the fog was a dense wall. The sound of traffic was muffled, wheels almost silent, hooves a dull sound on stone, eaten by the fog as soon as they touched. Carriage lamps lurched towards him, passed and disappeared.

He walked with his collar up and his hat pulled forward over his brow. The air was wet and clung to his skin, smelling of soot. He thought of the people of St. Giles on a night like this, the ones huddled together, a dozen to a room, cold and hungry. And he thought of those outside in doorways, without even shelter.

What had happened to Rhys Duff? Why had he thrown away everything he had—warmth, home, love, opportunity of achievement, respect of his father—to chase after some appetite which would end in destroying him?

Evan thought of his own youth, of his mother's kitchen full of herbs and vegetables and the smell of baking. There was always soup on the stove all winter long. His sisters were noisy, laughing, quarreling, gossiping. Their pretty clothes were all over the place, their dolls, and later their books and letters, paintbrushes and embroidery.

He had sat for hours in his father's study talking about all manner of things with him, mostly ideas, values, old stories of love and adventure, courage, sacrifice and reward. How would his father have explained this? What meaning and hope could he have found in it? How could he equate it with the God he preached of every Sunday in the church amid its great trees and humble gravestones where the village had buried its dead for seven hundred years and laid flowers on quiet graves?

Evan felt no anger, no bitterness, only confusion.

The following morning he met Shotts back in the alley in St. Giles and started over again in the search for witnesses, evidence, anything which would lead to the truth. He could not disown the possibility that Sylvestra Duff had had some part in her husband's death. It was an ugly thought, but now that it had entered his mind, he saw more that upheld it, at least sufficiently to warrant its investigation.

Was it that knowledge which had horrified Rhys so much he

154

could not speak? Was it at the core of his apparent chill now towards his mother? Was that burden the one which tormented him and kept him silent?

Who was the man? Was he implicated or merely the unknowing motive? Was it Corriden Wade, and did Rhys know that?

Or was it as the doctor had implied: Rhys's own weakness had taken him to St. Giles, and his father, in desperation for him, had followed, interrupted him, and been killed for his trouble?

Which led to the other dreadful question: What hand had Rhys in his father's death? A witness . . . or more?

"Have you got those pictures?" he asked Shotts.

"What? Oh, yeah." Shotts took out of his pocket two drawings, one of Rhys, as close as the artist could estimate, removing the present bruises; the other of Leighton Duff, necessarily poorer, less accurate, made from a portrait in the Duffs' hall. But they were sufficient to give a very lively impression of how each man must have appeared in life.

"Have you found nothing more?" Evan pressed. "Peddlers, street traders or cabbies? Someone must have seen them."

Shotts bit his lip. "Nobody wants ter 'ave seen 'em," he said candidly.

"What about women?" Evan went on. "If they were here for women, someone must know them."

"Not for sure," Shotts argued. "Quick fumble in an alley or a doorway. 'Oo cares about faces?"

Evan shivered. It was bitterly cold, and he felt the chill eating inside him as well as numbing his face, his hands and his feet. It was beginning to rain again, and the broken eaves were dripping steadily. The gutters overflowed.

"Would have thought women would be careful about familiarity in the street these days. I hear there have been several bad rapes of dolly mops and amateur prostitutes lately," Evan remarked.

"Yeah," Shotts said with a frown. "I 'eard that too. But it's over Seven Dials way, not 'ere."

"Who did you hear it from?" Evan asked.

There was a moment's silence.

"What?"

"Who did you hear it from?" Evan repeated.

"Oh . . . runnin' patterer," Shotts said casually. "One of 'is stories. I know some o' them tales is 'alf nonsense, but I reckoned as there was a grain o' truth in it."

"Yes . . ." Evan agreed. "Unfortunately, there is. Is that all you found?"

"Yeah. Least about the father. Got a few likely visits o' the son, women 'oo think they 'ad 'im. But none's fer sure. They don't take no notice o' faces, even if they see 'em. 'Ow many young men d'yer suppose there are 'oo are tall, a bit on the thin side, an' wi' dark 'air?"

"Not so many who come from Ebury Street to take their pleasures in St. Giles," Evan answered dryly.

Shotts did not say anything further. Together they trudged from one wretched bawdy house to another with the pictures, asking questions, pressing, wheedling, sometimes threatening. Evan learned a considerable respect for Shotts's skills. He seemed to know instinctively how to treat each person in order to obtain the most cooperation. And he knew surprisingly many people, some with what looked like a quite genuine camaraderie. A few jokes were exchanged. He asked after children by name and was answered as if his concern were believed.

"I hadn't realized you knew the area so well," Evan mentioned as they stopped and bought pies from a peddler on the corner of a main thoroughfare. The pies were hot and pungent with onions. As long as he did not think too hard as to what the other contents might be, they were most enjoyable. They provided a little highly welcome warmth inside as the day became even colder and the fine rain turned to sleet.

"Me job," Shotts replied, biting into the pasty and not looking at Evan. "Couldn't do it proper if I din' know the streets an' the people."

He seemed reluctant to talk about it; possibly he was unused to praise and his modesty made him uncomfortable. Evan did not pursue it.

156

They continued on their fruitless quest. Everything was negative or uncertain. No one recognized Leighton Duff, they were all adamant in that, but half a dozen thought perhaps they had seen Rhys, then again perhaps not. No one mentioned the violence in Seven Dials. It could have been another world.

They also tried the regular street peddlers, beggars—the occasional pawnbroker or innkeeper. Two beggars had seen someone answering Rhys's description on half a dozen occasions, they thought . . . possibly.

It was the running patterer, a thin, light-boned man with straggly black hair and wide blue eyes, who gave the answer which most surprised and disturbed Evan. When he had been shown the pictures, he was quite certain he had seen Leighton Duff once before, on the very outskirts of St. Giles, alone and apparently looking for someone, but he had not spoken to him. He had seen him talking to a woman he knew to be a prostitute. He appeared to be asking her something, and when she had denied it, he had walked away and left her. The patterer was certain of it. He answered without a moment's hesitation and looked for no reward. He was also certain he had seen Rhys on several occasions.

"How do you know it was this man?" Evan said doubtfully, trying to keep a sense of victory at last from overtaking him. Not that it was a victory of much. It was indication, not proof of anything, and even then only what he had assumed. "There must be lots of young men hanging around in the shadows in an area like this."

"I saw 'im under the lights," the patterer responded. "Faces is me business, least it's part of it. I 'member 'is eyes partic'lar. Not like most folks'. Big, black almost. 'E looked lorst."

"Lost?"

"Yeah, like 'e weren't sure wot 'e wanted nor which way ter go. Kind o' miserable."

"That can't be unusual around here."

" 'E don' belong around 'ere. I knows most 'oo belongs 'ere. Don' I, Mr. Shotts?"

Shotts looked startled. "Yeah . . . yeah, I s'pose you would."

"But you go Seven Dials way as well." Evan remembered

what Shotts had said about the patterer's telling him of Monk's case. "Have you seen him there too?" It was a remote chance, but one he should not overlook.

"Me?" The patterer looked surprised, his blue eyes staring at Evan. "I don' go ter Seven Dials. This is me patch."

"But you know what happens there." He should not give up too easily, and there was an uncertainty at the back of his mind.

"Sorry, guv, no idea. Yer'd 'ave ter ask some o' them wot works there. Try Jimmy Morrison. 'E knows Seven Dials."

"You don't know about violence in Seven Dials towards women?"

The patterer gave a sharp, derisive laugh. "Wot, yer mean diff'rent from always?"

"Yes."

"Dunno. Wot is it?"

"Rape and beatings of factory women."

The patterer's face wrinkled in disgust. Evan could not believe he had already known. Why had Shotts lied? It was a small thing, very small, but what was the point of it? It was out of the character he knew of the man, and disturbing.

"You told me he knew," he said as soon as they were a dozen yards away.

Shotts did not look at him. "Must 'a bin someone else," he replied dismissively.

"Don't you write down who tells you what?" Evan pressed. "It makes a lot of difference. Did you ever speak to him before on this case?"

Shotts turned into the wind and his answer was half lost.

" 'Course I did. Said so, didn't I?"

Evan let the matter rest, but he knew he had been lied to, and it troubled him. His instinct was to like Shotts and to respect his abilities. There was something he did not know. The question was, was it something important?

He saw Monk that evening. Monk had left a note for him at the police station, and he was happy to spend an hour or two over a good meal in a public house and indulge in a little conversation.

158

Monk was in a dour mood. His case was going badly, but he had considerable sympathy for Evan.

"You think it could be the widow?" he asked, his eyes level and curious. The slight smile on his lips expressed his understanding of Evan's reluctance to accept such a thing. He knew Evan too well, and his affection for him did not prevent his amusement and slight derision at his friend's optimism in human nature.

"I think it was probably just what it looked like," Evan replied gloomily. "Rhys was a young man who had been indulged by his mother and whose father had great expectations of him which he possibly could not live up to—and did not want to. He indulged a selfish and possibly cruel streak in his character. His father went after him to try to stop him, perhaps to warn of the dangers, and somehow they became involved in a fight with others. The father died. The son was severely injured physically, and so horrified by what he saw that now he cannot even speak."

Monk cut into the thick, light suet crust of his steak-and-kidney pudding.

"The question is," he said with his mouth full, "were they both attacked by the denizens of St. Giles, or did Rhys kill his own father in a quarrel?"

"Or did Sylvestra Duff have a lover, and did he either do it himself or have someone else do it?" Evan asked.

"Who is he? Samson?" Monk raised his eyebrows.

"What?"

"He took on two men at once, killed one and left the other senseless, and walked away from the scene himself," Monk pointed out.

"Then there was more than one," Evan argued. "He hired somebody, two people, and it was coincidence Rhys was there. He was following Leighton Duff, and happened to come on him when he had found Rhys."

"Or else Rhys was in it with his mother." Monk swallowed and took a mouthful of his stout. "Have you any way of looking into that?" He ignored Evan's expression of distaste.

"Hester's there. She's nursing Rhys," Evan replied. He saw

the emotion cross Monk's face, the momentary flicker, the light and then the shadow. He knew something of what Monk felt for her, even though he did not understand the reasons for its complexity. He had seen the trust between them. Hester had fought for Monk when no one else would. She had also quarreled with Monk when, at least to Evan, it made no sense at all. But he knew the dark areas of Monk's heart prevented him from committing himself as Evan would have. Half memories and fears of what he did not know made it impossible for him. What Evan did not know was whether it was fear for Hester and the hurt he might cause her in that part of himself which lay secret, or simply fear for himself and his own vulnerability if he allowed her to know him so well, to become even more important to him, and to understand it himself.

Nothing in Monk's behavior let him know. He thought perhaps Hester did not know either.

Monk was halfway through his meal.

"She won't tell you," he said, looking at his plate.

"I know that," Evan replied. "I'm not placing her in the position of asking."

Monk looked up at him quickly, then down again.

"Made any advance in your case?" Evan asked.

Monk's expression darkened, the skin on his face tight with the anger inside him.

"Two or three men came into Seven Dials quite regularly, usually a Tuesday or Thursday, about ten in the evening up until two or three in the morning. As far as I can tell they were not drunk, nor did they go into any public houses or brothels. No one seems to have seen their faces clearly. One was of above average height, the other two ordinary, one a little heavier than the other. I've found cabbies who have taken them back to Portman Square, Eaton Square . . ."

"They're miles apart!" Evan exclaimed. "Well, a good distance."

"I know," Monk said. "They've also been taken to Cardigan Place, Belgrave Square and Wimpole Street. I am perfectly aware that they may live in three different areas, or more likely very simply have changed cabs. I don't need you to tell me the obvious. What I need is for the police to care that over a dozen women have been beaten, some of them badly injured, and could have been dead, for all these animals cared. What I need is a little sense of outrage for the poor as well as the inhabitants of Ebury Street, a little blind justice, instead of justice that looks so damned carefully at the size and shape of your pockets and the cut of your coat before it decides whether to bother with you or not."

"That's unfair," Evan replied, staring back at Monk with equal anger. "We have only so much time, so many men, which you know as well as I do. And even if we find them, what good would it do? Who's going to prosecute them? It will never get to court, and you know that too." He leaned forward, elbows on the table. "What are you hoping for, Monk? Private vengeance? You'd better be damned sure you are right."

"I shall be," Monk said between his teeth. "I shall have the proof before I act."

"And then what—murder?" Evan demanded. "You have no right to take the law into your own hands or to put it in the hands of men you know will take it for themselves. The law belongs to all of us, or we are none of us safe."

"Safe!" Monk exploded. "Tell that to the women in Seven Dials! You're talking about theory . . . I'm dealing with fact!"

Evan stood his ground. "If you find these men and tell whoever has hired you, and they commit murder, that will be fact enough."

"So what is your alternative?" Monk said.

"I haven't one," Evan admitted. "I don't know."

6

As HE HAD TOLD Evan, Monk was having peripheral success in finding the men responsible for the rapes and violence in Seven Dials. He was still not sure if there were generally three or only two. No cabby could reliably describe three men at any one time. Everything that was said was imprecise, vague, little more than an impression: hunched figures in the fog and cold of the winter night, voices in the darkness, orders given for a destination, shadows moving in and out, a sudden shift in weight in the cab. One driver was almost certain that a third person had got out at an intersection where he had been obliged to stop because of the traffic.

Another had said one of his fares had been limping badly. One had been wet as though he had rolled in a gutter or fallen in a water butt. One, caught briefly in the coachlight, had had a bloody face.

There was nothing to prove any of them were the men Monk was looking for.

On Sunday, when he knew he would find her at home, he told Vida Hopgood as much. They were seated in her red parlor in front of a very healthy fire and sipping dark brown tea with so strong a flavor he was glad of a sticky sweet bun to moderate it a little.

"Yer sayin' yer beat?" she asked contemptuously, but he heard the note of disappointment in her and saw the shadow cross her eyes. She was angry, but her shoulders sagged beneath the burden of hope lost.

162

"No I'm not!" he responded sharply. "I'm telling you what I know so far. I promised I'd do that, if you remember?"

"Yeah . . ." she agreed grudgingly, but she was sitting up a little straighter. She looked at him with narrowed eyes. "Yer do believe they was raped, don't yer?"

"Yes I do," he said without doubt. "Not necessarily all by the same men, but at least eight of them probably were, and three of them I think may be provable."

"Mebbe?" she said guardedly. "Wot use's 'mebbe'? Wot about the others? 'Oo done them, then?"

"I don't know, and it doesn't matter. If we prove two or three, that will be enough, won't it?"

"Yeah. Yeah, it'll do fine." She stared at him, defying him to ask her what she planned to do about it.

He had not intended to ask. He was angry enough not to care.

"I'd like to speak to more women." He took another sip of the bitter tea. The flavor was appalling, but it did have an invigorating effect.

"Wot fer?" She was suspicious.

"There are gaps in times, weeks when I know of no one attacked. Is that true?"

She sat in thought for several minutes.

"Well?" Monk asked.

"No, it in't. Yer could try Bella Green. Din't wanna bring 'er inter it, but if I 'ave ter, then I will."

"Why not?"

"Geez! Why the 'ell der yer care? Because 'er man's an ol' soljer an' it'll cut 'im up summink terrible ter know as she bin beat, an' 'e couldn't 'elp 'er, let alone that she goes aht ter earn wot 'e can't that way. Poor sod lorst 'is leg at the Battle o' the 'Alma. In't good fer much now. 'Urt bad, 'e were. Never bin the same since 'e come back."

He did not let his emotion show.

"Any others?"

She offered him more tea, and he declined.

"Any others?" he repeated.

"Yer could try Maggie Arkwright. Yer prob'ly won't believe

163

a word wot she says, but that don' mean it in't true . . . sometimes, anyway."

"Why would she lie to me about that?"

" 'Cos 'er geezer's a thief, professional like, an' she'll never tell a rozzer the truth, on principle." She looked at him with wry humor. "An' if yer thinks as yer can kid 'er yer in't, yer dafter 'n I took yer fer."

"Take me to them."

"I in't got time nor money ter waste. Yer doin' anythin' 'cept keepin' bread in yer belly, an' yer pride?" Her voice rose. "Yer any damn use at all? Or yer gonna tell me in a monf's time that yer dunno 'oo done it, any more 'n yer do now, eh?"

"I'm going to find who did it," he said without even a shadow of humor or agreeability. "If you won't pay, then I'll do it myself. The information will be mine." He looked at her with cold clarity, so she could not possibly mistake him.

"Or'ight," she said at length, her voice very low, very quiet. "I'll take yer ter Bella an' ter Maggie. Get up then. Don' sit all day usin' up me fire."

He did not bother to reply, but rose and followed her out, putting his coat back on as they went through the door into the street, where it was nearly dark and the fog was thicker. It caught in his throat, damp, cold and sour with the taste of soot and old smoke.

They walked in silence, their footsteps without echo, sound swallowed instantly. It was a little after five o'clock. There were many other people on the streets, some idling in doorways, having lost heart in begging or seeing no prospects. Others still waited hopefully, peddling matches, bootlaces and similar odds and ends. Some went briskly about business, legal or illegal. Pickpockets and cutpurses loitered in the shadows and disappeared again, soft-footed. Monk knew better than to carry anything of value.

As he followed Vida Hopgood along the narrow alleys, staying close to the walls, memory hovered at the edge of his mind, fleeting impressions of having been somewhere worse than this, of urgent danger and violence. He passed a window, half filled with straw and paper, ridiculous as a barrier against the cold. He turned as if thinking he knew what he would see, but it was only a blur of yellow faces in the candlelight, a bearded man, a fat woman, and others equally meaningless to him.

Who had he expected? His only feeling was of danger, and that he must hurry. Others were depending upon him. He thought of narrow passages, crawling on hands and knees through tunnels, and the knowledge all the time that he could fall headfirst into the abyss of the sewers below and drown. It was a favorite trick of the thieves and forgers who hid in the great festering tenements of the Holy Land, seven or eight acres between St. Giles and St. Georges. They would lead a pursuer along a deliberate track through alleys and up and down stairs. There were trapdoors to cellars leading one to another for hundreds of yards. A man might emerge half a mile away, or he might wait and stick a knife into his pursuer's throat, or open up a trap to a cesspool. The police went there only armed, and in numbers, and even then rarely. If a man disappeared into the rookeries he might not be seen again for a year. It hid its own, and trespassers went there at their peril.

How long ago had that been? Stunning Joe's public house had gone. He knew that much. He had passed the corner where it used to be. At least he thought he knew it. The Holy Land itself had certainly opened up. The worst of the creaking tenements were gone, collapsed and rebuilt. The criminal strongholds had crumbled, their power dissipated.

Where had the memory come from, and how far back was it? Ten years, fifteen? When he and Runcorn had both been new and inexperienced, they had fought there side by side, guarding each other's backs. It had been a comradeship. There had been trust.

When had it gone? Gradually, a dozen, a score of small issues, a parting of the paths of choice, or one sudden ugly incident?

He could not remember.

He followed Vida Hopgood across a small yard with a well in it, under an archway and then across a surprisingly busy street and into another alley. It was bone-achingly cold, the fog an icy shroud. He racked his brain, and there was nothing there at all, only the present, his anger with Runcorn now, his contempt for him, and the knowledge that Runcorn hated him, that the hate was deep and bitter and that it governed him. Even when it was against his own interest, his dignity and all that he wanted to be, the hate was so passionate in him he could not control it. It consumed his judgment.

" 'Ere! Wot's the matter wiv yer?" Vida's voice cut across his thoughts, dragging him back to Seven Dials and the rape of the sweatshop women.

"Nothing!" he said sharply. "Is this Bella Green's?"

" 'Course it is. Wot the 'ell d'yer think we're 'ere fer?" She banged on the rickety door and shouted Bella's name.

It was several minutes before the door was answered by a girl somewhere between twelve and fifteen. Her long hair was curling and knotted, but her face was clean and she had nice teeth.

Vida asked for Bella Green.

"Me ma's busy," the girl replied. "She'll be back in a w'ile. You wanna wait?"

"Yeah." Vida was not going to be put off, even had Monk allowed it.

But they were not permitted in. The child had obviously been warned about strangers. She slammed the fragile door and Monk and Vida were left on the step in the cold.

"The gin mill," Vida said immediately, taking no offense. "She'll 'a gorn ter get Jimmy a bottle. Dulls the pain, poor sod."

Monk did not bother to enquire whether the pain was physical or the bleak despair of the mind. The difference was academic; the burden of living with either was the same.

Vida's guess was right. Inside the noise and filth of the gin shop, the sound of laughter, the shards of broken glass and the women huddled together for warmth and the comfort of living flesh rather than the cold stones, they found Bella Green. She was coming towards them cradling a bottle in her arms, holding it as if it were a child. It was a few moments' oblivion for her husband, a man she must have seen answer his country's

166

call whole and full of courage and hope, and received back again broken in body and fast sinking in mind as he looked at the long, hopeless years ahead, and daily pain.

Beside her a woman wept and sank slowly to the floor in the maudlin self-pity of gin drunkenness.

Bella saw Vida Hopgood and her tired face showed surprise—and something that might have been embarrassment.

"Need ter see yer, Bella," Vida said, ignoring the gin as if she had not seen it. "Din' wanner. Know yer busy wi' yer own troubles, but need yer 'elp."

"Me 'elp!" Bella could not grasp it. "Fer wot?"

Vida turned and went out into the street, stepping over a woman fallen on the cobbles, insensible to the cold. Monk followed, knowing the uselessness of trying to pick anyone up. At least on the ground a person could fall no farther. The woman would be colder, wetter, but less bruised.

They walked quickly back to the door where Monk and Vida had knocked. Bella went straight in. It was cold and the damp had seeped through the walls. The air inside smelled sour, but there were two rooms, which was more than some people had. The second had a small black stove in it, and it gave off a faint warmth. Sitting beside it was a man with one leg. His empty trouser hung flat over the edge of his chair, fastened up with a pin. He was clean shaven, his hair combed, but his skin was so pale it seemed gray, and there were dark shadows around his blue eyes.

Monk was reminded of Hester with a jolt so sharp it caught his breath. How many men like this must she have known, have nursed, have seen when they were carried in from the battlefield, still stunned with horror and disbelief, not yet understanding what had happened to them, what lay ahead, only wondering if they would survive, hanging on to life with the grim, brave desperation that had brought them so far.

She had helped them during the worst days and nights. She had dressed the appalling wounds, encouraged them, bullied them into fighting back, into hanging on when there seemed no point, no hope. As she had done to Monk at the end of the Grey case. He had wanted to give up then. Why waste energy and

167

hope and pain on a battle you could not win? It was exhausting, futile. It had not even dignity.

But she had refused to give up on him, on the struggle. Perhaps she was used to going on, enduring, keeping up the work, the sense of purpose, the outward calm, even when it seemed utterly useless. How could exhausted men fight against absurd odds, survive the pain and the loss, support their fellows, except if the women who nursed them showed the same courage and blind pointless faith?

Or perhaps faith was never pointless. Maybe faith itself was the point? Or courage?

But he had not meant to think of Hester. He had promised himself he would not. It left an emptiness inside him, a sense of loss which pervaded everything else, spoiling his concentration, darkening his mood. He needed his energy to think of details he was storing in his mind about the violence in Seven Dials. These women had no help but that which Vida Hopgood could wring from him. They deserved his best.

He must forget the man slumped in the chair, waiting with desperation for the few hours' release the gin would give him, and concentrate on the woman. Perhaps it could even be done without the man's realizing his wife had been raped. Monk could word it so it sounded like a simple assault. There was a great difference between what one thought one knew, privately, never acknowledging directly, and what one was forced to admit, to hear spoken, known by others where it could never after be forgotten.

"How many men were there?" he asked quietly.

She knew what he was referring to; the understanding and the fear were plain in her eyes.

"Three."

"Are you sure?"

"Yeah. First there was two, then a third one came. I din't see where from."

"Where was it?"

"The yard orff Foundry Lane."

"What time?"

"About two, near as I can remember." Her voice was very

168

low; never once did she look sideways at her husband. Perhaps she wanted to pretend he was not there, that he did not know.

"Do you remember anything about them? Height, build, clothes, smell, voices?"

She thought for several minutes before she replied. Monk began to feel a lift of hope. Perhaps that was foolish.

"One o' them smelled like summink odd," she said slowly. "Like gin, on'y it weren't gin. Kind o' . . . sharper, cleaner, like."

"Tar? Creosote?" he guessed, as much to keep her mind on it as in hope of defining it quickly.

"Nah . . . cleaner 'n that. I know tar. An' I know creosote. Weren't paint nor nuffink. Anyway, 'e weren't a laborer, 'cos 'is 'ands was all smooth . . . smoother 'n mine."

"A gentleman . . ."

"Yeah."

Vida gave an ugly snort expressive of her opinion.

"Anything else?" Monk pressed. "Fabric of clothes, height, build? Hair thick or thin, whiskers?"

"No w'iskers." Bella's face was white as she recalled, her eyes dark and hollow. She was speaking in little more than a whisper. "One o' them was taller than the others. One were thin, one 'eavier. The thin one were terrible angry, like there were a rage eatin' 'im up inside. I reckon as mebbe 'e were one o' them lunatics from down Lime'ouse way wot eats them Chinese drugs an' goes mad."

"Opium doesn't make you violent like that," Monk replied. "They usually go off into dreams of oblivion, lying on beds in rooms full of smoke, not wandering around alleys"—he stopped just before using the word raping—"attacking people. Opium eating is a very solitary pursuit, in mind if not in body. These men seemed to work together, didn't they?"

"Yeah . . . yeah, they did." Her face tightened with bitterness. "I'd 'a thought wot they did ter me were summink a man'd do by 'isself."

"But they didn't?"

"Nah . . . proud o' theirselves, they was." Her voice sank

169

even lower. "One o' them laughed. I'll remember that till the day I die, I will. Laughed, 'e did, just afore 'e 'it me."

Monk shivered, and it was more than the cold of the room.

"Were they old men or young men?" he asked her.

"I dunno. Mebbe young. They was smooth, no whiskers, no . . ." She touched her own cheek. "Nuffink rough."

Young men out to savor first blood, Monk thought to himself, tasting violence and intoxicated with the rush of power; young men inadequate to make their mark in their own world, finding the helpless where they could control everything, inflict their will with no one to deny them, humiliate instead of being humiliated.

Was that what had happened to Evan's young man? Had he and one or two of his friends come to St. Giles in search of excitement, some thrill of power unavailable to them in their own world, and then violence had for once met with superior resistance? Had his father followed him this time, only to meet with the same punishment?

Or had the fight been primarily between father and son?

It was possible, but he had no proof at all. If it was so, then at least one of the perpetrators had met with a terrible vengeance already, and Vida Hopgood need seek no more.

He thanked Bella Green and glanced across to see if it was worth speaking to her husband. It was impossible to tell from his eyes if he had been listening. Monk spoke to him anyway.

"Thank you for giving us your time. Good day to you."

The man opened his eyes with a sudden flash of clarity but he did not answer.

Bella showed them out. The child was nowhere to be seen, possibly in the other room. Bella did not speak again either. She hesitated, as if to ask for hope, but perhaps as if to thank Monk. It was in her eyes, a moment's softness. But she remained silent, and they went out into the street and were swallowed instantly by the ever-thickening fog, now yellow and sour with smoke, catching in the throat, settling as ice on the cobbles.

"Well?" Vida demanded.

"I'll tell you when I'm ready," Monk retorted. He wanted to

170

stride out—he was too angry to walk slowly to keep pace with her, and too cold—but he did not know where he was or where he was going. He was forced against his will to wait for her.

The next house they went to was a trifle warmer. They came out of the now-freezing fog into a room where a potbellied stove smelled of stale soot but gave off quite a comforting heat. Maggie Arkwright was plump and comfortable, black-haired, ruddy skinned. It was easy to understand that she might do very well at her part-time profession. There was a good humor about her, even a look of health which was attractive. Glancing around at the room, with two soft chairs, a table with all four of its original legs, a stool, and a wooden chest with three folded blankets, Monk wondered if the things in it had been bought with the proceeds of her trade.

Then he remembered that Vida had said her husband was a petty thief, and he realized that might be the source of their relative prosperity. The man came in a moment after them. His face was genial, eyes lost in wrinkles of general goodwill, but his head was close shaved in what Monk knew was a "terrier crop," a prison haircut. He had probably been out no more than a week or ten days. Presumably she kept the household going when he was accepting Her Majesty's hospitality in Millwall or the Coldbath Fields.

There was a burst of laughter from the next room, an old woman's high cackle, and the giggling of children. It was a sound of hilarity, unguarded and carefree.

"Wot yer want?" Maggie asked civilly, but with eyes wary on Monk's face. He had an air of authority about him she did not trust.

Vida explained, and bit by bit Monk drew from Maggie the story of the attack upon her. It was one of the earliest, and seemed to be far less vicious than more recent ones. The account was colorful, and he thought very possibly embellished a trifle for his benefit. It was of no practical value, except that it told him of yet another victim, one Vida had not known of. Maggie told Monk where to find her, but said to go the next day. She would be drunk at present and no use to him at all.

Maggie laughed as she said it, a sound rich with mocking pleasure but little unkindness.

When Monk found the woman, she was at her stall selling all kinds of household goods, pots, dishes, pails, the occasional picture or ornament, candlesticks, here and there a jug or ewer. Some of them were of moderate value. She was not young, maybe in her late thirties or early forties, it was hard to tell. Her bones were good, as if she had been handsome in her youth, but her skin was clouded by too much gin, too little clean air and water, and a lifetime's ingrained grime.

She looked at Monk as a prospective customer, mildly interested, never giving up hope. To lose interest was to lose money, and to lose money was death.

"Are you Sarah Blaine?" he asked, although she fitted Maggie's description of her and she was in the right place. It was rarely a person allowed their place to be taken, even for a day.

" 'Oo wants ter know?" she said carefully. Then her eyes widened and filled with unmistakable loathing, a deep and bitter remembrance. She drew in her breath and let it out in a hiss between her teeth. "Geez! 'Oped I'd never see yer again, yer bastard! Thought yer was dead. 'Eard yer was, in '56. Went out an' shouted the 'ole o' the Grinnin' Rat ter a free drink on it. Danced an' sang songs, we did. Danced on yer grave, Monk, only yer wasn't in it! Wot 'appened? Devil din't want yer? Too much, even fer 'is belly, was yer?"

Monk was stunned. She knew him. It was impossible to deny. And why not? He had not changed.

Had had no idea who she was or what their relationship had been, except what was obvious, which was that she hated him, more than simply because he was police, but from some individual or personal cause.

"I was injured," he replied with the literal truth. "Not killed."

"Yeah? Wot a shame," she said laconically. "Never mind, better luck next time." The brilliance of her eyes and the curl of her lip made her meaning obvious. "Well, none o' this lot's 'ot, so naff orff! I'nt nuffink 'ere for yer. An' I i'nt tellin' yer nuffink abaht nobody."

He debated whether or not to tell her he was no longer with the police, or if it would be useful for her to believe he was. It lent him power, a certain authority, the loss of which still hurt him.

"The only people I want to know about are the men who raped and beat you in Steven's Alley a couple of weeks ago." He watched her face and was gratified to see the total amazement in it, making it blank of all other expression for a moment.

"I dunno wot yer talkin' abaht," she said at length, her jaw set hard, her eyes flat and still filled with hatred. "Nobody never raped me. Yer wrong again. Damn sure o' yerself, y'are. Come down 'ere in yer fancy kit like yer was Lord Muck, flingin' yer weight arahnd, an' yer knows nuffink!"

He knew she was lying. It was nothing he could define, not a matter of intelligence but an instinct. He was met with disbelief and contempt.

"I overestimated you," he said witheringly. "Thought you had more loyalty to your own." It was the one quality he was certain she would value.

He was right; she flinched as if he had struck her.

"Yer not one o' me own, any more 'n them rats in that pile o' dirt over there. Mebbe you should go an' try one o' them, eh? Yer want loyalty ter yer own . . . they might speak to yer, if yer ask 'em pretty, like." She laughed loudly at her own joke, but there was a brittle edge to it. She was afraid of something, and as he looked at her, sitting huddled in her gray-black shawl, shoulders hunched, hair blowing across her face in the icy air, the more the conviction hardened in him that it was him she feared.

Why? He posed no possible threat to her.

The answer had to lie in the past, whatever it was that had brought them together before and which had made her rejoice when she had believed him dead.

He raised his eyebrows sarcastically.

"You think so? Would they be able to describe the men who

beat you . . . and all the other women, the poor devils that work in the sweatshop all day and then go out in the streets a few hours in the night to try to get a little extra to feed their children? Would they tell me how many there were, if they were old or young, what their voices were like, which way they came from and which way they went . . . after they beat sixteen-year-old Clarrie Drover and broke her younger sister's arm?"

He had achieved his effect. She looked hurt and surprised. The pain in her was real. For a moment her anger against him was forgotten and it was aimed against these men, the world of injustice which allowed such a thing, the whole monstrosity of the fear and the misery she saw closing in on her and her kind, and the certainty that there was no redress and no vengeance.

He was the only living thing within her immediate reach, the only one to share the hurt.

"So wadda you care, yer bloody jackal. Filth, that's all you are." Her voice was hoarse with bitterness and the knowledge of her own helplessness, even to hurt him beyond a mere scratch to the skin, nothing like the jagged wound which was killing her. She hated him for it with all the passion of futility. "Filth! Livin' orff other folk's sins . . . if we don't sin, you in't worth nothin' at all. Shovel the gutters, you do—clean out other folk's middens—that's all you are. Can't tell yer from the muck." There was a gleam of satisfaction in her face at the simile.

It was not worth retaliating.

"There is no need to be frightened of me; I'm not after stolen candlesticks or teapots—"

"I in't afraid o' yer!" she said, fear sharp in her eyes, hating him the more because she knew he saw it as certainly as he had before.

"I'm not with the police," he went on, ignoring her interruptions. "I'm working privately, for Vida Hopgood. She's paying me, and she doesn't give a damn where your goods come from or go to. She wants the rapes stopped, and the beatings."

She stared at him, trying to read truth in his face.

"Who beat you, Sarah?"

"I dunno, yer eejut!" she said furiously. "If'n I knew, don't yer think I'd 'a got somebody ter cut 'is throat fer 'im, the bastard?"

"It was only one man?" he said with surprise.

"No, it were two. Least I think so. It were black as a witch's 'eart an' I couldn't see nuffink. Ha! Should say black as a rozzer's 'eart, shou'n't I? 'Ceptin' 'oo knows if a rozzer's got an 'eart? Mebbe we should get one an' cut 'im open, jus ter see, like?"

"What if he does, and it's just as red as yours?" he asked.

She spat.

"Tell me what happened," he persisted. "Maybe it will help me to find these men."

"An' wot if yer do? 'Oo cares? 'Oo'll do anyfin' abaht it?" she said derisively.

"Wouldn't you, if you knew who they were?" he asked.

It was enough. She told him all she could remember, drawn from her a piece at a time and, he thought, largely honest. It was of little use, except that she also remembered the strange smell, sharp, alcoholic, and yet unlike anything she could name.

He left, walking into the wind, turning over in his mind what she had said, but against his will more and more preoccupied, wondering what he had done in the past to earn the intensity of her hatred.

In the evening, on impulse, he decided to go and see Hester. He did not give himself a reason. There was not any. He had already decided to keep her from his mind while he was on this case. There was nothing to say to her, nothing to pursue or to discuss. He knew where she was because Evan had told him. He had mentioned the name Duff and Ebury Street. It was not very difficult, therefore, to find himself on the front step of the correct house.

He explained to the maid who answered the door that he was acquainted with Miss Latterly and would be obliged if he might visit with her if she could be spared for a few minutes. The answer from Mrs. Sylvestra Duff was most gracious. She was to be at home herself, and if Miss Latterly cared to, she might spend the entire evening away from Ebury Street. She had worked extremely hard lately and would be most welcome to a complete respite and change of scene, if she so desired.

Monk thanked her with the feeling of something close to alarm. It seemed Mrs. Duff had assumed more about the relationship than was founded in fact. He did not want to spend all evening with her. He had nothing to say. In fact, now that he was there, he was not sure he wanted to see her at all. But to say so now would make him look absurd, a complete coward. It could be interpreted all sorts of ways, none of them to his advantage.

Hester seemed ages in coming. Perhaps she had no desire to see him either. Why? Had she taken offense at something? She had been very brittle lately. She had made some waspish remarks about his conduct in the slander case, especially his trip to the Continent. It was as if she were jealous of Evelyn von Seidlitz, which was idiotic. His temporary fascination with Evelyn did not affect their friendship, unless she forced it to.

He was pacing back and forth across the morning room while he waited, nine steps one way, nine steps back.

Evelyn von Seidlitz could never be the friend Hester was. She was beautiful, certainly, but she was also as shallow as a puddle, innately selfish. That was the kind of ugliness which touched the soul. Whereas Hester—with her angular shoulders and keen face, eyes far too direct, tongue too honest—had no charm at all, but a kind of beauty like a sweet wind off the sea, or light breaking on an upland when you can see from horizon to horizon, as it had in his youth on the great hills of Northumberland. It was in the blood and the bone, and one never grew tired of it. It healed the petty wounds and laid a clean hand on the heart, gently.

There was a noise in the hall.

He swung around to face it just as she came through the door. She was dressed in dark gray with a white lace collar. She looked very smart, very feminine, as if she had made a special effort for the occasion. He felt panic rise up inside him. This was not a social call, certainly the last thing from a romantic one. What on earth had Mrs. Duff told her?

176

"I only came for a moment," he said hastily. "I did not wish to interrupt you."

The color burned up her cheeks.

"Quite well, thank you," she said sarcastically. "And you?"

"Tired, chasing an exhausting and unhopeful case," he answered. "It will be difficult to solve, even harder to prove, and I am not optimistic the law will prosecute it even should I succeed. Am I interrupting you?"

She closed the door and leaned against the handle.

"If you were I should not have come. The maid is perfectly capable of carrying a message."

She might look less businesslike than usual, but she had absolutely no feminine charm. No other woman would have spoken to him like that.

"You have no idea how to be gracious, have you?" he criticized.

Her eyes widened. "Is that what you came for, someone to be gracious to you?"

"I would hardly have come here, would I?"

She ignored him. "What would you like me to say? That I am sure you know what you are doing and your skill will triumph in the end? That a just cause is well fought, win or lose?" Her eyebrows rose. "The honor is in the battle, not the victory? I'm not a soldier. I have seen too much of the cost of ill-planned battles, and the price of loss."

"Yes, we all know you would have fought a better war than Lord Raglan if the War Office had had the good sense to put you in charge instead."

"If they had picked someone at random off the street, they would have," she rejoined. Then her face softened a little. "What is your battle?"

"I would rather tell you somewhere more comfortable and more private," he replied. "Would you like to dine?"

If it was a surprise, she hid it very well . . . too well. Perhaps it was what she had expected. It was not what he had intended to say. But to retreat now would make it even worse. It would draw attention to it—and to his feelings about it. He could not

177

even pretend he thought she was busy; Mrs. Duff had told him she was not.

"Thank you," she said with an aplomb he had not expected. She seemed very cool about it. She turned and opened the door, leading the way out into the hall. She asked the footman for her cloak, and then together she and Monk went outside to the bitter evening, again dimmed by fog, the street lamps vague moons haloed by drifting ice, the footpaths slippery.

It took just under ten minutes to find a hansom and climb into it. He gave directions to an inn he knew quite well. He would not take her to an expensive place, in case she misunderstood his intent, but to take her to a cheap one would find her thinking he could not afford better, and possibly even offering to pay.

"What is your battle?" she repeated when they were sitting side by side in the cold as the cab lurched forward, then settled into a steadier pace. It was miserably cold, even inside. There was very little to see, just gloom broken by hazes of light, sudden breaks in the mist when outlines were sharp, a carriage lamp, a horse's head and forequarters, the high, black silhouette of a hansom driver, and then the shroud of fog closed in again.

"At first, just women being cheated in Seven Dials," he answered. "To begin with it was no more than using a prostitute and refusing to pay . . ."

"Don't they have pimps and madams to help prevent that?" she asked.

He winced, but then he should have expected her to know such things. She had hardly been sheltered from many truths.

"These were amateurs," he explained. "Mostly women who worked in factories and sweatshops during the day and just needed a little more now and again."

"I see."

"Then they were raped. Now it has escalated until they are being beaten . . . increasingly violently."

She said nothing.

He glanced sideways at her as they passed close to another carriage; the light from the lamps caught her face. He saw the

178

pity and anger in it, and suddenly his loneliness vanished. All the times of resentment and irritation and self-protectiveness telescoped into the causes they had shared, and disappeared, leaving only the understanding. He went on to describe to her his efforts to elicit some facts about the men, and about his questioning of the cabbies and street vendors in order to learn where they had come from.

They arrived at the hostelry where he planned to eat. They alighted, paid the driver, and went in. He was barely aware of the street, or the noise and warmth once they were inside. He ordered without realizing he had done it for both of them, and she made a very slight face, but she did not interrupt, except to ask for clarification as he omitted a point or was vague on an issue.

"I'm going to find them," he finished with hard, relentless commitment. "Whether Vida Hopgood pays me for it or not. I'll stop them, and I'll make damned sure everyone like them knows they've paid the price, whether it's the justice of the law or of the streets." He waited, half expecting her to argue with him, to preach the sanctity of keeping the civilized law, of the descent into barbarism if it were abandoned, whatever the cause or the provocation.

But she sat in thoughtful silence for several minutes before she replied.

The room around them swirled with the clatter of crockery, the sounds of voices and laughter. The smells of food and ale and damp wool filled the air. Light glinted on glass and was reflected on faces, white shirt fronts and the white of plates.

"The young man I'm nursing was beaten, nearly to death, in St. Giles," she said at last. "His father did die." She looked across at him. "Are you sure enough you can get the right man? If you make a mistake, there can be no undoing it. The law will try them, there will have to be proof, weighed and measured, and someone to speak in their defense. If it is the streets, then it will simply be execution. Are you prepared to be accuser, defender, and jury . . . and to let the victims judge?"

"What if the alternative is freedom?" he asked. "Not only freedom to enjoy all the pleasures and rewards of life, without

179

hindrance or answerability for wrong, but the freedom to go on committing it, creating new victims, on and on, until someone is murdered, maybe one of the young ones, twelve or fourteen, too weak to fight back at all?" He stared at her, meeting her clear eyes. "I am involved. I am the jury, whatever I decide. Omission is a judgment as well. To walk away, to pass on the other side, is as much a decision."

"I know," she agreed. "Justice may be blindfolded, but the law is not. It sees when and whom it chooses, because it is administered by those who see when and whom they choose." She was still frowning.

He broached the subject which was hanging unspoken between them. He knew it, and he thought perhaps she did also. With anyone else, he would have let the moment pass. It was too delicate and had all the possibilities of being too painful as well. With Hester, to have thought it was almost the same as to have spoken it to her.

"Are you sure it cannot be your young man and his father, or his friends? Tell me about him. . . ."

Again she waited several moments before she replied. At the next table an old man broke into a fit of coughing. Beyond him a woman laughed; they could hear her but not see her. It was a high, braying sound. The room was getting warmer all the time.

"No, I'm not sure," she said so quietly he had to lean forward to hear her, ignoring the last of his food. "Evan is investigating the case. I assume you know that. He has not been able to find out what they were doing in St. Giles. It is hardly likely to be anything admirable." She hesitated, unhappiness profound in her face. "I don't think I believe he would do such a thing, not willingly, not intentionally . . ."

"But you are not sure?" he said quickly.

Her eyes searched his face, longing to find some comfort there and failing.

"No . . . I'm not sure. There is a cruelty in him which is very ugly to see. I don't know why. It seems directed largely at his mother. . . ."

"I'm sorry." Without thinking he reached forward and put

his hand over hers where it lay on the table. He felt the slenderness of her bones, a strong hand, but so slight his own covered it.

"It doesn't have to be anything to do with this," she said slowly, and he thought it was more to convince herself than him. "It's just . . . it could be . . . because he cannot speak. He's alone. . . ." She looked at Monk with an intensity that made her oblivious of the room around her or anything else. "He's utterly alone. We don't know what happened to him, and he can't tell us. We guess, we talk to each other, we work at the possibilities, and he can't even tell us where we are wrong, where it is ludicrous or unjust. I can't imagine being more helpless."

He was torn whether to say what was in his mind or not. She looked so hurt, so involved with the pain she saw.

But this was Hester, not a woman he needed to protect, gentle and vulnerable, used only to the feminine things of life. She had already known the worst, worse than he had.

"Your pity for him now does not alter what he may have done before," he answered her.

She drew her hand away.

He felt vaguely hurt, as if she had withdrawn something of herself. She was so independent. She did not need anyone. She could give, but she could not take.

"I know," she said quietly.

"No, you don't." He was answering his own thoughts. She did not know how arrogant she was, how so much of her giving was a form of taking; whereas if she had taken, it would have been a gift.

"Yes, I do!" She was angry now, defensive. "I just don't think it was Rhys. I know him. You don't."

"And your judgment is clear, of course?" he challenged, sitting back in his chair. "You could not be biased, just a trifle?"

A couple passed by them, the woman's skirt brushing Hester's chair.

"That's a stupid remark." Her voice was sharp, her face flushed. "You're saying that if you know something about a thing, then you are biased and your judgment is no good,

181

whereas if you know nothing, your mind is clear and so your judgment is fine. If you know nothing, your mind isn't clear, it's empty. By that standard we could do away with juries, simply ask someone who's never heard of the case, and they will give you a perfect, unbiased decision!"

"You don't think perhaps it could be a good idea to know something about the victims as well?" he said sarcastically. "Or even the crimes? Or is all that irrelevant?"

"You've just told me what the crimes are, and the victims," she pointed out, her voice rising. "And yes, in a way it is irrelevant in judging Rhys. The horror of a crime has nothing to do with whether a particular person is guilty or not. That is elementary. It only has to do with the punishment. Why are you pretending you don't know that?"

"And liking somebody, or pitying them, has nothing to do with guilt or innocence," he responded, his voice louder also. "Why are you pretending you've forgotten that? It doesn't matter how much you care, Hester, you can't change what has already happened."

A man at the next table turned to look at them.

"Don't be so patronizing," she said furiously. "I know that. Don't you care anymore that you find the truth? Are you so keen to take someone back to Vida Hopgood and prove you can do it that you'll take anyone, right or wrong?"

He was hurt. It was as if she had suddenly and without warning kicked him. He was determined she should not know it.

"I'll find the truth, comfortable or uncomfortable," he said coldly. "If it is someone we can all be happy to dislike and rejoice in his punishment, so much the easier." His voice dropped, the emotion tighter. "But if it is someone we like and pity, and his punishment will tear us apart along with him, that won't make me turn the other way and pretend it is not so. If you think the world is divided into those who are good and those who are bad, you are worse than a fool, you are a moral imbecile, refusing to grow up—"

She stood up.

"Would you be so kind as to find me a hansom so I may

return to Ebury Street? If not, I imagine I can find one for myself."

He rose also and bowed his head sarcastically, remembering their meeting earlier. "I am delighted you enjoyed your dinner," he replied cuttingly. "It was my pleasure."

She blushed with annoyance, but he saw the flash of acknowledgment in her eyes.

They went out in silence into the now dense fog in the street. It was bitterly cold, the freezing air catching in the nose and throat. The traffic was forced to a walk and it took him several minutes to find a hansom. He climbed in and they sat side by side in rigid silence all the way back to Ebury Street. She refused to speak, and he had nothing he wanted to say to her. There were hundreds of things in his mind, but he was prepared to share none of them, not now.

They parted with a simple exchange of "Good night," and he rode on to Fitzroy Street, cold, angry and alone.

In the morning he returned yet again to Seven Dials and his pursuit of witnesses who might have seen anything to do with the attacks, most particularly anyone who was a frequent visitor to the area. He had already exhausted the cabbies and was now trying street peddlers, beggars and vagrants. His pockets were full of all the small change he could afford. People often spoke more readily for some slight reward. It was his own money, not Vida's.

The first three people he approached knew nothing. The fourth was a seller of meat pies, hot and savory smelling but probably made mostly of offal and other castoffs. He bought one, and overpaid, but without intention of eating it. He held it in his hand while talking to the man. There was a wind that morning. The fog had lifted, but it was intensely cold. The cobbles were slippery with ice. As he stood there the pie became more and more tempting and he was less inclined to consider what was in it.

"Seen or heard anything about two or three strangers roaming around at night?" he said casually. "Gentlemen from up west?"

"Yeah," the peddler replied without surprise. "They bin beatin' the 'ell out o' some o' our women, poor cows. W'y d'yer wanna know, eh? In't rozzers' bus'ness." He looked at Monk with steady dislike. "Want 'em for summink else, do yer?"

"No, I want them for that. Isn't that enough for you?"

The man's scorn was open. "Yeah? An' yer gonna 'ave 'em up for it, are yer? Don' give me that muck. Since w'en did yer sort give a toss wot 'appened ter the likes o' us? I know you, yer evil bastard. Yer don't even care fer yer own, never mind us poor sods."

Monk looked at the man's eyes and could not deny the recognition in them. He was not speaking of police in general, this was personal. Should he ask, capture some tangible fact of the past? Would it be the truth? Would it help? Would it tell him something he would rather not have known, ugly, incomplete, and without explanation?

Probably. But perhaps imagination alone was worse.

"What do you mean, 'not even my own'?" The instant he had said it, he wished he had not.

The man gave a grunt of disgust.

A woman in a black shawl came past and bought two pies.

"I seen yer shaft yer own," the peddler answered when she had gone. "Left 'im 'angin' out ter dry, like a proper fool, yer did."

Monk's stomach turned cold and a little fluttery. It was what he had feared.

"How do you know?" he argued.

"Saw 'is face, an' seen yours." The peddler sold another pie and fished for change for a threepenny piece. " 'E weren't 'spectin' it. Caught 'im proper, poor sod."

"How? What did I do?"

"Wot's the matter wiv yer?" The man looked at him incredulously. "Want the pleasure of it twice, do yer? I dunno. Jus' know yer came 'ere tergether, an' yer done 'im some'ow. 'E trusted yer, an' finished up in the muck. I guess it's 'is own fault. 'E should 'a knowed better. It were writ in yer face. I wouldn't 'a trusted yer far as I can spit!"

184

It was ugly and direct, and it was probably the truth. He would like to think the man lied, find some way out of it, but he knew there was no hope. He felt cold inside in his stomach, in his chest.

"What about these men you've seen?" he asked, his voice sounding hollow. "Don't you want them stopped?"

The man's face darkened. " 'Course I do . . . an' we'll do it . . . without your 'elp."

"Haven't done a very good job so far," Monk pointed out. "I'm not with the police anymore. I'm working for Vida Hopgood . . . in this. Anything I find out, I tell her."

The man's disbelief was plain.

"Why? P'lice threw yer out, did they? Good. Guess that fella got the best o' yer in the end." He smiled, showing yellow teeth. "So there's some justice arter all."

"You don't know what happened between us," Monk said defensively. "You don't know what he did to me first." It sounded childish even as he said it, but it could not be taken back. Very little ever could.

The man smiled. "Agin you? I reckon as yer a first-class swine, but I'd back yer ter win agin anyone."

Monk felt a shiver of apprehension, and perhaps pride as well, perverse, hurting pride, a salvage from the wreck of other things.

"Then help me to find these men. You know what they've done. Let Vida Hopgood learn who they are and stop them."

"Yeah . . . right." The man's face eased, the anger melting. "I s'pose if anyone can find them it's you. I dunno much, or I'd 'a done 'em myself."

"Have you seen them, or anyone who could be them?"

" 'Ow do I know? I seen lots o' geezers wot don't belong 'ere, but usual yer knows wot they're 'ere for. Reg'lar brothels, or gamblin', or ter 'ock summink as they daren't 'ock closer ter 'ome."

"Describe them," Monk demanded. "I don't care about the others. Tell me all you saw of these men, where and when, how many, how dressed, anything else you know . . ."

The man thought carefully for a few moments before giving

185

his answer. His description established what Monk had already heard regarding build, and that there were three men on several occasions, on others only two. The one new fact the peddler added was that he had seen them meet on the outskirts of Seven Dials, as if they had arrived from different directions, but he had only ever seen them leave together.

Monk could no longer avoid putting his theory to the test. He would much rather not have, because he was afraid it was true and he did not wish it to be. Hester was being foolish about it, of course, but he did not wish her to be hurt, and she would be when she was forced to accept that Rhys Duff had been one of the rapists.

It took him all day, moving from one gray and bitter street to another, asking, cajoling, threatening, but by dusk he had found others who had seen the men immediately after one of the attacks, and only a mere fifty yards from the place. They had been disheveled, staggering a little, and one of them had been marked with blood, as his face was caught for a moment in the glare of a passing hansom's carriage lights.

It was not what he wanted. It was bringing him inevitably closer to a tragedy he was now almost certain would involve Rhys Duff, but he still felt a kind of elation, a surge inside him of the knowledge of power, the taste of victory. He was turning a corner into a wider street, stepping off the narrow pavement, avoiding the gutter, when he remembered doing exactly the same before, with the same surge of knowledge that he had won.

Then it had been Runcorn. He did not know what about, but there had been men who had told him something he needed to know, and they had been afraid of him, as they were now. It was an unpleasant knowledge to look back on, the guarded eyes, the hatred in them and the defeat because he was stronger, cleverer, and they knew it. But he could not remember it hurting them. It was only now, in retrospect, that he doubted he had been wholly right.

He shivered and increased his pace. There was no going back.

He had enough now to go to Runcorn. It should be a police matter. That would protect Vida Hopgood, forestall the mob

186

justice Hester was afraid of. This way there would be a trial, and proof.

He found a cab and gave the address of the police station. Runcorn would have to listen. There was too much to ignore.

"Beatings?" Runcorn said skeptically, sitting back in his chair and staring up at Monk. "Sounds domestic. You know better than to bring that to us. Most women withdraw the complaints. Anyway, a man is entitled to hit his wife to chastise her, within reason." His lip curled in a mixture of irritation and amusement. "It's not like you to waste your time on lost causes. Never saw you as a man to tilt at windmills . . ." He left the sentence hanging in the air, a wealth of unspoken meaning in it. "You have changed. Had to come down a bit, have you?" He tipped his chair back a trifle. "Take on the cases of the poor and desperate . . ."

"Victims of beating and rape are often desperate," Monk said with as much control of his temper as he was able, but he heard the anger coming through his voice.

Runcorn responded immediately. It woke memories of a score of old quarrels. They were replaying so many past scenes: Runcorn's anxiety, stubbornness, provocation; Monk's anger and contempt, and quicker tongue. For an instant, for Monk it was as if he were removed from himself, a spectator seeing two men imprisoned in reenacting the same pointless tragedy over and over again.

"I told you before," Runcorn said, sitting forward, banging the chair legs down, leaning his elbows on his desk. "You'll never prove some men got violent with a prostitute. She's already sold herself, Monk. You may not approve of it." He wrinkled his long nose as if imitating Monk, although there had been no scorn in Monk's voice or in his mind. "You may find it an immoral and contemptible way to make a living, but we'll never get rid of it. It may offend your susceptibilities, but I assure you, a great many men you might call gentlemen, or might aspire to join, with your social airs and graces, a great many of them go to the Haymarket, and even to places

187

like Seven Dials, and make use of women they pay for the privilege."

Monk opened his mouth to argue, but Runcorn plowed on, talking over him deliberately.

"Maybe you would like to think differently, but it's time you looked at some of your gentry as they really are." He jabbed his finger at the desk. "They like to marry their wives for social nicety, to wear on their arms when they dine and dance with their equals. They like to have a cool and proper wife." He kept on jabbing his finger, his face sneering. "A virtuous woman who doesn't know anything about the pleasures of the flesh, to be the mother of their children, the guardian of all that's safe and good and uplifting and morally clean. But when it comes to their appetites, they want a woman who doesn't know them personally, doesn't expect anything of them except payment for services rendered, and who won't be horrified if they exhibit a few tastes that would disgust and terrify their gentle wives. They want the freedom to be any damned thing they like. And that can include a great deal you may not approve of, Monk."

Monk leaned over the desk towards him, his jaw tight, spitting the words through his teeth.

"If a man wants a wife he won't satisfy and can't enjoy, that's his misfortune," he retorted. "And his hypocrisy . . . and hers. But it is not a crime. But if he joins with two of his friends and comes to Seven Dials and then rapes and beats the sweatshop women who practice a little prostitution on the side . . . that is a crime. I intend to stop it before it becomes murder as well."

Runcorn's face was dark with anger and surprise, but this time it was Monk who overrode him, still leaning forward, looking down on him. Runcorn's earlier advantage of being seated while Monk stood was now the opposite, he refused to move back. They were less than two feet away from each other.

"I thought you had the courage and the sense of your own duty to the law to have felt the same," Monk went on. "I expected you to ask for my information and be glad to take it.

What you think of me doesn't matter . . ." He snapped his fingers in the air with a sharp sound. "Aren't you man enough to forget it for as long as it takes to catch these men who rape and beat women, and even girls, for their 'pleasure,' as you put it? Or do you hate me enough to sacrifice your honor just to be able to deny me this? Have you really lost that much of yourself?"

"Lost?" Runcorn's face was a dull purple, and he leaned even closer. "I haven't lost anything, Monk. I have a job. I have a home. I have men who respect me . . . some of them even like me . . . which is more than you could ever say. I haven't lost any of that." His eyes were brilliant, accusing and triumphant, but his voice was rising higher and there was a sharpness that betrayed old wounds between them which none of this could heal. There was no ease on his face, no peace with himself.

Monk felt his own body rigid. Runcorn had struck home with his words, and they both knew it.

"Is that your answer?" he said very quietly, stepping back. "I tell you that women are being raped and beaten in an area in which you are responsible for the law, and you reply by rehearsing old quarrels with me as a justification for looking the other way? You may have the job, the money for it, and the liking of some of your juniors . . . do you think you have any claim to their respect—or anyone's—if they heard you say this? I had forgotten why I despised you . . . but you remind me. You are a coward, and you put your personal, petty dislikes before honor."

He straightened up, squaring his shoulders. "I shall go back and tell Mrs. Hopgood that I told you I had evidence and wanted to share it with you; but you were so intent on having your personal revenge on me, you would not look at it. It will get out, Runcorn. Don't imagine this is between you and me, because it isn't. Our dislike for each other is petty and dishonorable. These women are being injured, maybe the next one will be killed, and it will be our fault, because we couldn't work together to stop these men—"

Runcorn rose to his feet, his skin sweating, white around the lips.

"Don't you dare tell me how to do my job! And don't try coercing me with threats! Bring me one piece of evidence I can use in a court and I'll arrest any man it points to! So far you've told me nothing that means a thing. And I'm not wasting men until I know there's a probable crime and some chance of prosecution. One decent woman who's been raped, Monk. One woman who will give evidence I can use . . ."

"Who are you trying?" Monk retaliated. "The man or the woman, the rapist or the victim?"

"Both," Runcorn said, suddenly lowering his voice. "I have to deal with reality. Have you forgotten that, or are you just pretending you have because that is easier? Gives you a high moral note, but it's hypocrisy, and you know it."

Monk did know it. It infuriated him. He hated it with all the passion of which he was capable. There were times when he hated people, almost all people, for their willing blindness. It was injustice, burning, callous, self-righteous injustice.

"Have you got anything, Monk?" Runcorn asked, this time quietly and seriously.

Still standing, Monk told him everything he knew and how he knew it. He told him the victims he had spoken to, collating it all chronologically, showing how the attacks had increased in violence, each time the injuries worse and more viciously given. He told Runcorn how he had traced the men to specific hansom drivers, times and places. He gave him the most consistent physical descriptions.

"All right," Runcorn said at last. "I agree crimes have been committed. I don't doubt that. I wish I could do something about it. But set your outrage aside for long enough to let your brain think clearly, Monk. You know the law. When did you ever see a gentleman convicted of rape? Juries are made up of property owners. You can't be a juror if you're not. They are all men . . . obviously. Can you imagine any jury in the land convicting one of their own of raping a series of prostitutes from Seven Dials? You would put the women through a terrible ordeal . . . for nothing."

Monk did not speak.

"Find out who they are, if you can, by all means," Runcorn

went on. "And tell your client. But if she provokes the local men into attacking those responsible, even killing them, then we still step in. Murder's another thing. We'll have to go on with it until we find them. Is that what you want?"

Runcorn was right. It was choking to have to concede it.

"I'll find out who they are," Monk said almost under his breath. "And I'll prove it . . . not to Vida Hopgood or to you. I'll prove it to their own bloody society. I'll see them ruined!" And with that he turned on his heel and went out of the door.

It was dark and snowing outside, but he barely noticed. His rage was blazing too hotly for mere ice in the wind to temper it.

7

RHYS PROGRESSED only very slowly. Dr. Wade pronounced himself satisfied with the way in which his external wounds were healing. He came out of Rhys's room looking grave but not more concerned than when Hester had shown him in. As always, he had chosen to see Rhys alone. Bearing in mind the site of some of the injuries, and a young man's natural modesty, it was easy to understand why. Hester was not as impersonal a nurse to him as she had been to the men in the hospitals of the Crimea. There were so many of them she had had no time to become a friend to any one, except in brief moments of extremity. With Rhys she was far more than merely someone who attended to his needs. They spent hours together; she talked to him, read to him, sometimes they laughed. She knew his family and his friends, like Arthur Kynaston, and now also Arthur's brother, Duke, a young man she found less attractive.

"Satisfactory, Miss Latterly," Wade said with a very slight smile. "He seems to be responding well, although I do not wish to give false encouragement. He is certainly not recovered yet. You must still care for him with the greatest skill you possess."

His brows drew together and he looked at her intensely. "And I cannot impress upon you too strongly how important it is that he should not be disturbed or caused anxiety, fear or other turbulence of spirit that can be avoided. You must not permit that young policeman, or any other, to force him to attempt a recollection of what happened the night of his injury.

192

I hope you understand that. I imagine you do. I feel that you are very fully aware of his pain and would do anything, even place yourself at risk, to protect him." He looked very slightly self-conscious, a faint color on his cheeks. "I have a high opinion of you, Miss Latterly."

She felt a warmth inside her. Simple praise from a colleague for whom she had a supreme regard was sweeter than the greatest extravagance from someone who did not know precisely what it meant.

"Thank you, Dr. Wade," she said quietly. "I shall endeavor not to give you cause ever to think otherwise."

He smiled suddenly, as if for an instant he forgot the care and unhappiness which had brought them together.

"I have no doubt of you," he replied, then bowed very slightly and walked past her and down the stairs to where Sylvestra would be waiting for him in the withdrawing room.

Early in the afternoon Hester tried to spin out small domestic tasks, getting smears out of Rhys's nightshirt where one of his bandages had been pulled crooked and blood from the still-open wound had seeped through; mending a pillowcase before the tiny tear became worse; sorting the books in the bedroom into some specific order. There was a knock on the door, and when she answered it the maid informed her that a gentleman had called to see her and had been shown to the housekeeper's sitting room.

"Who is he?" Hester asked with surprise. Her immediate thought was that it was Monk, then she realized how unlikely that was. It had come to her mind only because some thought of him was so close under the surface of her consciousness. It would be Evan, come to see if he could enlist her help in solving the mystery of Rhys's injuries, at least in learning something more about the family and the relationship between father and son. It was absurd to feel this sudden sinking of disappointment. She would not know what to say to Monk anyway.

Nor did she know what to say to Evan. Her duty lay to the truth, but she did not know if she wanted to learn it. Her professional loyalty, and her emotions, were toward Rhys. And she was employed by Sylvestra; that required of her some kind of honesty.

She thanked the maid and finished what she was doing, then went downstairs and through the green baize door, along the passage to the housekeeper's sitting room. She went in without knocking.

She stopped abruptly. It was Monk who stood in the middle of the floor, slim and graceful in his perfectly cut coat. He looked short-tempered and impatient.

She closed the door behind her.

"How is your patient?" he asked. His expression was one of interest.

Was it politeness, or did he have a reason to care? Or was it simply something to say?

"Dr. Wade tells me he is recovering fairly well but still far from healed," she replied a trifle stiffly. She was angry with herself for the elation she felt because it was him and not Evan. There was nothing to be pleased about. It would only be another pointless quarrel.

"Haven't you got an opinion of your own?" He raised his eyebrows. He sounded critical.

"Of course I have," she retorted. "Do you think it is likely to be of more use to you than the doctor's?"

"Hardly . . ."

"So I imagined. That is why I gave you the doctor's."

He took a breath and then let it out quickly.

"And he still does not speak?"

"No."

"Or communicate in any other way?"

"If you mean in words, no. He cannot hold a pen to write. The bones in his hands are far from healed yet. I assume from your persistence that your interest is professional? I don't know why. Do you imagine he witnessed your attackers in Seven Dials, or that he knows who the assailants were?"

He put his hands in his pockets and looked down at the floor, then up at her. His expression softened, the guardedness slipped away from it.

"I would like to think he had nothing to do with them what-

194

ever." His eyes met hers, steady and clear, jolting her suddenly with memory of how well they knew each other, what losses and victories they had shared. "Are you sure that is so?"

"Yes," she said immediately, then knew from his look, and from her own inner honesty, that it was not so. "No—not absolutely." She tried again. "I don't know what happened, except that it was very dreadful, so dreadful it has rendered him speechless."

"Is that genuine . . . ? I mean to ask that truly." He looked apologetic, unwilling to hurt. "If you say it is so, I will accept it."

She came farther into the room, standing closer to him. The fire in the small, carefully blacked grate burned briskly, and there were two chairs near it, but she ignored them, and so did he.

"Yes," she said with complete certainty this time. "If you had seen him in nightmare, trying desperately to cry out, you would know it as I do."

His face reflected his acceptance, but there was a sadness in it also which frightened her. It was a tenderness, something she did not often see in him, an unguarded emotion.

"Have you found evidence?" she asked, her voice catching. "Do you know something about it?"

"No." His expression did not change. "But the suggestions are increasing."

"What? What suggestions?"

"I'm sorry, Hester. I wish it were not so."

"What suggestions?" Her voice was rising a little higher. It was mostly fear for Rhys, but also it was the gentleness in Monk's eyes. It was too fragile to grasp, too precious to break, like a perfect reflection in water—touch it and it shatters. "What have you learned?"

"That the three men who attacked these women were gentlemen, well dressed, arriving in cabs, sometimes together, sometimes separately, leaving in a hansom, nearly always together."

"That's nothing to do with Rhys!" She knew she was interrupting and that he would not have mentioned it had he no

195

more than that. She just found it impossible to hear him out, the thought hurt so much. She could see he knew that, and that he hated doing it. The warmth in his eyes she would hoard up like a memory of joy, a sweet light in darkness.

"One of them was tall and slender," he went on.

The description fitted Rhys. They both knew it.

"The other two were of average height, one stockier, the other rather thin," he went on quietly.

The coals settled in the fire and neither of them noticed. There were footsteps down the corridor outside, but they passed without stopping.

Monk had not seen Arthur and Duke Kynaston, but Hester had. Glimpsed hastily, hurrying in a dark street, it could very well be them. A coldness filled her. She tried to shut it out, but memory was vivid of the cruelty in Rhys's eyes, the sense of power as he had hurt Sylvestra, his smile afterwards, his relish in it. It had not happened only once, a mistake, an aberration. He exulted in his power to hurt. She had tried not to believe it, but in Monk's presence it was impossible. She could be furious with him, she could despise elements in him, she could disagree violently; but she could not intentionally harm him, and she could not lie. To build that barrier between them would be unbearable, like denying part of herself. The protection must be emotional, self-chosen, not to divide them but merely to cover from a pain too real.

He moved towards her. He was so close she could smell the damp wool of his coat where the rain had caught his collar.

"I'm sorry," he said quietly. "I can't turn aside because he's injured now or because he is your patient. If he had been alone, perhaps I could, but there are the other two."

"I can't believe Arthur Kynaston was involved." She met his eyes. "I would have to see proof that could not be argued. I would have to hear him admit it. Duke I do not know about."

"It could have been Rhys, Duke and someone else," he pointed out.

"Then why is Leighton Duff dead and Duke Kynaston unhurt?"

He put out a hand as if to touch her, then let it fall.

"Because Leighton Duff guessed there was something profoundly wrong, and he followed them and challenged his son,"
he answered gravely, a pucker between his brows. "The one
with whom he was most concerned, the one for whom he
cared. And Rhys lost his temper, perhaps high on whiskey,
fueled by guilt and fear and a belief in his own power. The
others ran off. The result is what Evan found . . . two men who
began a fight and couldn't stop it, short of the death of one of
them and the near-mortal injury of the other."

She shook her head, but it was to close out the vision,
to defend herself from it, not because she could deny its
possibility.

This time he did put his hands on her shoulders, very gently,
not to hold her, simply to touch.

She stared at the floor, refusing to look up at him.

"And perhaps some men of the area, husbands or lovers of
the last victim, brothers, or even friends, caught up with them.
They had stopped running for too long . . . and it was they who
beat them both. Rhys cannot tell us . . . even if he wanted to."

There was nothing to say. The impulse was to deny it, and
that was pointless.

"I don't know any way to find out," she said defensively.

"I know." He smiled very slightly. "And if you did, you
wouldn't . . . until you had to know, for yourself. You would
have to prove him innocent . . . and when you proved him
guilty, you would say nothing, and I would know anyway."

She raised her eyes quickly. "No, you wouldn't. Not if I
chose to conceal it."

He hesitated, then stepped back half a pace.

"I would know," he repeated. "Why? Would you defend
him for it? I should take you to see these women, beaten by
poverty, dirt, ignorance, and now beaten by three young
gentlemen who are bored by their comfortable lives and want
a little more dangerous entertainment, something to make the
heart beat a trifle faster and bring the blood to the head." His
voice was hard in his throat with outrage, a deep and abiding
hurt he felt for the injured. "Some of them are no more than
children. At their age you were in the schoolroom wearing a

pinafore and doing your sums, and your most urgent distress was being forced to eat your rice pudding." He was exaggerating and he knew it, but it hardly mattered. The essence was real. "You wouldn't defend that, Hester . . . you couldn't. You have more honor, more imagination than that."

She turned away. "Of course I do. But you haven't seen Rhys's pain now. Judgment is fine when you only know one side. It is much harder when you know the offender, and, like him, feel his pain too."

He stood close behind her. "I was not concerned with ease, only what was right. Sometimes we cannot have both. I know some people don't understand that, or accept it, but you do. You have always been able to face the truth, no matter what it was. You will do it this time."

There was certainty in his voice, no doubt at all. She was Hester, reliable, strong, virtuous Hester. No need to protect her from pain or danger. No need even to worry about her.

She wanted to lash out angrily at him for taking her for granted. She was exactly like anybody else inside, like any other woman. She ached to be protected sometimes, to be cherished and have ugliness and danger warded off by someone else, not because he thought she could not bear it but because he did not wish her hurt.

But she could not possibly say that to him . . . not to Monk, of all people. To be worth anything at all, it had to be offered freely. It must be his wish, even his need. If she had been one of the fragile, warm, feminine women he so admired, he would have done it instinctively.

What could she say? She was so angry and confused and hurt, words tumbled over each other in her mind, and all of them were useless, only betraying what she felt, which was the last thing she wished him to know. She could protect herself at least as much as that.

"Of course," she said stiffly, her voice thick in her throat. "There is little point in doing anything else, is there?" She moved another step away from him, her shoulders rigid, as if she would flinch were he to touch her. "I imagine I shall endure whatever it is. I shall have no alternative."

"You're angry," he said with a lift of surprise.

"Nonsense!" He was missing the point entirely. It had nothing to do with Rhys Duff or who had beaten the women. It was his assumption that she could be treated like another man, that she could and should always look after herself. She could. But that was not the point either.

"Hester!"

She had her back to him but he sounded patient and reasonable. It was like vinegar on the wound.

"Hester, I'm not choosing it to be Rhys. I'll look for any other possibility as well."

"I know you will."

Now he was puzzled. "Then what the devil more do you want of me? I cannot alter what happened, nor will I settle for less than the truth. I can't save Rhys from himself, and I can't save his mother . . . if that is what you want."

She swung around.

"It isn't what I want! And I don't expect anything of you. Heavens above! I've known you long enough now to be precisely aware of what I shall get from you." The words poured out of her, and even as she heard them, she wished she had kept silent, not made herself so obvious and so vulnerable. He would read her plainly now. He would hardly be able to help it.

He was dumbfounded and annoyed. His face showed the only too familiar marks of temper. A veil came over his eyes, the gentleness hidden.

"Then our conversation seems to be pointless," he said grimly. "We understand each other perfectly, and there is no more to be said." He gave a little gesture, rather less than a bow. "Thank you for sparing your time. Good day." He walked out, leaving her miserable and equally angry.

Later in the afternoon Arthur Kynaston called again, this time accompanied by his elder brother, Duke. Hester saw them as they crossed the hall from the library to go upstairs.

"Good afternoon, Miss Latterly," Arthur said cheerfully. He glanced down at the book she was carrying. "Is that one for Rhys? How is he?"

Duke was behind him, a larger and stronger version of his brother, heavier shouldered. He had walked in with more grace, something of a swagger. His face was broader boned, more traditionally handsome but perhaps less individual. He had the same soft, wavy hair with a touch of auburn in it. He was now regarding Hester with impatience. It was not she they had come to see.

Arthur turned around. "Oh, Duke, this is Miss Latterly, who is looking after Rhys."

"Good," Duke said abruptly. "We'll carry the book up for you." He held out his hand for it. It was rather more a demand than an offer.

Hester felt an instant dislike for him. If these were indeed the young men Monk was looking for, then he was responsible not only for the brutal attacks on the women but for the ruin of his brother and of Rhys.

"Thank you, Mr. Kynaston," she replied coldly, making an immediate change of mind. "It is not for Rhys; I intend reading it myself."

He looked at it. "It is a history of the Ottoman Empire," he said with a slight smile.

"A most interesting people," she observed. "Last time I was in Istanbul I found much of great beauty. I should like to know more about it. They were a generous people in many respects, with a culture of great subtlety and complexity." It was also cruel beyond her understanding, but that was irrelevant just now.

Duke looked taken aback. It was not the reply he had expected, but he regained his composure rapidly.

"Is there much call for domestic servants in Istanbul? I would have thought most people would have employed natives, especially for fetching and carrying."

"I imagine they do." She answered him without looking at Arthur. "I was too busy to think of such things. I left my own lady's maid in London. I did not think it was any place for her, and it was quite unfair to ask her to go." She smiled back at him. "I have always believed consideration for one's servants is the mark of the gentleman . . . or lady, as the case may be. Don't you agree?"

"You had a lady's maid?" he said incredulously. "Whatever for?"

"If you ask your mother, Mr. Kynaston, I am sure she will acquaint you with the duties of a lady's maid," she answered, tucking the book under her arm. "They are many and varied, and I am sure you do not wish to keep Mr. Duff waiting." And before he could find a reply to that, she smiled charmingly at Arthur and went up the stairs ahead of them, her temper still seething.

An hour later there was a knock on her door, and when she opened it, Arthur Kynaston was standing on the threshold.

"I'm sorry," he apologized. "He can be awfully rude. There's no excuse for him. May I come in and speak with you?"

"Of course." She could not have refused him anyway, and Monk was right, she would search for the truth, however much against her will, hoping with every step that it would prove Rhys innocent, but compelled to know it anyway. "Please come in."

"Thank you." He glanced around in curiosity, then blushed. "I wanted to ask you if Rhys really is getting better, and if . . ." His brows furrowed and his eyes darkened. "If he's going to speak again. Is he, Miss Latterly?"

Instantly she wondered if it was fear she saw in him. What was it Rhys would say if he could speak? Was that why Duke Kynaston was there, to see if Rhys was any danger to him . . . and perhaps to ensure that he was not? Should she leave them alone with him? He could not even cry out. He was utterly at their mercy.

No, that was a hideous thought. And nonsense. If anything happened to him while they were there, they would certainly be blamed for it. There was no way they could explain or escape. They must know that as surely as she did. Was Duke alone with him now? Instinctively she turned towards the connecting door.

"What is it?" Arthur asked quickly.

"Oh." She turned back to him, forcing herself to smile. Was she virtually alone with a young man who had raped and beaten a dozen or more women, and were there two more only the thickness of the door away? She should be frightened, not for them but of them . . . for herself. She collected her wits. "I wish I could give you more hope, Mr. Kynaston . . ." She must protect Rhys. "But there is no sign at all. I am so sorry."

He looked stricken, as if she had destroyed a hope in him.

"What happened to him?" he said, shaking his head a little. "How was he hurt that he can't speak? Why can't Dr. Wade do anything for him? Is it something broken? It should heal then, shouldn't it?"

He looked as if he cared intensely. She found it almost impossible to believe his wide stare concealed guilt.

"It is not physical." She answered with the truth before weighing if it was the wisest thing to do. Now she could not stop. "Whatever he saw that night was so fearful it has affected his mind."

Arthur's eyes brightened. "So he could regain his speech any day?"

What should she say? What was best for Rhys?

Arthur was watching her, the anxiety clouding over his face again.

"Couldn't he?" he repeated.

"It is possible," she said cautiously. "But don't expect it yet. It can take a long time."

"It's awful!" He shoved his hands deep in his pockets. "Rhys used to be such fun, you know?" He looked at her earnestly, willing her to understand. "We did all kinds of things together, he and I . . . and Duke some of the time. Rhys had a great sense of adventure. He could be terribly brave—and make us all laugh." His face was full of distress. "Can you think of anything worse than having hundreds of things to say and lying alone not able to say a single one of them? Thinking of something funny and not being able to share it? What's the point of a joke if you can't tell it to people and watch their faces as they grasp it? You can't share anything beautiful, or awful, or even ask for help, or say you are hungry or scared rigid." He

202

shook his head a little. "How do you even know what he wants? You might be giving him rice pudding when he's asking for bread and butter."

"It is not as bad as that," she said gently, although in essence it was true. Rhys could not share his real pain or terror. "I can ask him questions, and he can answer with a nod or a shake. I'm getting quite good at guessing what he would like."

"It's hardly the same, though, is it?" he said with a sudden touch of bitterness. "Will he ever be able to ride a horse again, or race one? Will he dance or be able to play cards? He used to be so quick with cards. He could shuffle them faster than anyone else. It made Duke furious, because he couldn't match it. Can't you do anything to help, Miss Latterly? It's awful standing by like this and simply watching him. I feel so . . . useless."

"You are not useless," she assured him. "Your visits are greatly encouraging. Friendship always helps."

His smile came and vanished in a moment. "Then I suppose I'll go back and talk to him a while. Thank you."

But he did not remain as long as usual, and when Hester went in to see Rhys after Arthur and Duke had left, she found him staring at the ceiling, his eyes thoughtful, his lips pursed in an expression of withdrawn unhappiness she had come to know well. She could only guess what had disturbed him. She did not want to ask; it might only make things worse. Perhaps seeing Duke Kynaston, less tactful than his brother, had reminded him of the past when they had all been virile, a little reckless, thinking themselves capable of anything. The other two still were. Rhys entertained them lying silently on a bed. He could not even offer wit or interest.

Or was it memory of an appalling secret they all shared?

He turned slowly to look at her. His eyes were curious, but cold, defensive.

"Do you want to see Duke Kynaston again if he comes?" she asked. "If you had rather not, I can have him turned away. I can think of a reason."

He stared at her without giving any indication that he had heard.

"You don't seem to like him as much as you do Arthur."

This time his face filled with expression: humor, irritation, impatience and then resignation. He sat up an inch or two and took a deep breath. His lips moved.

She leaned towards him, only a little, not enough to embarrass him if he failed.

He let out his breath and tried again. His mouth formed the words, but she could not read them. His throat tightened. His eyes were fixed desperately on her.

She placed her hand on his arm, above the bandages, tightening her fingers to grip him.

"Is it something about Duke Kynaston?" she asked him.

He hesitated only a moment, then shook his head, his eyes full of loneliness and confusion. There was something he ached to tell her, and the harder he tried, the more his helplessness thwarted him.

She could not walk away. She must guess, she must take the risk, in spite of what Dr. Wade had said. This frustration was hurting him.

"Is it to do with the night you were hurt?"

Very slowly he nodded, as if now he was uncertain whether to go on or not.

"Do you know what happened?" she said very quietly.

His eyes filled with tears and he turned his head away from her, pulling his arm roughly out of her grip.

Should she ask him directly? What would it do to him? Would forcing him to remember and answer to someone else shock him as violently as Dr. Wade had warned her? Could she undo any of the harm to him if it did?

He was still turned away from her, motionless. She could no longer see his face to guess what he was feeling.

Dr. Wade cared for him deeply, but he was not a soft or cowardly man. He had seen too much suffering for that, faced danger and hardships himself. He admired courage and that inner strength which survives. Her judgment of him answered her question. She must obey his instructions; in fact, they had been quite unequivocal commands.

"Do you want to tell me about something?" she asked.

He turned back slowly. His eyes were bright and hurt. He shook his head.

"You would just like to be able to talk?"

He nodded.

"Would you like to be alone?"

He shook his head.

"Shall I stay?"

He nodded.

In the evening Rhys was exhausted and slept very early. Hester sat by the fire opposite Sylvestra. There was no sound in the room but the rain beating on the windows, the fire flickering in the hearth, and the occasional settling of the coals. Sylvestra was embroidering, her needle weaving in and out of the linen, occasionally flashing silver as it caught the light.

Hester was idle. There was no mending to do and she had no one to whom she owed a letter. Nor was she in the mood to write. Lady Callandra Daviot, the only person to whom she might have considered confiding her feelings, was on a trip to Spain and moving from place to place. There was no address where Hester could be certain of catching her.

Sylvestra looked up at her.

"I think the rain is turning to snow again," she said with a sigh. "Rhys was planning to go to Amsterdam in February. He used to be very good at skating. He had all the grace and courage one needs. He was even better than his father. Of course, he was taller. I don't know if that makes any difference."

"No, neither do I," Hester answered quickly. "He may recover, you know."

Sylvestra's face was wide-eyed, tense in the soft light from the gas lamps and the fire.

"Please do not be kind to me, Miss Latterly. I think perhaps I am ready to hear the truth." A very faint smile touched her face and was gone. "I received a letter from Amalia this morning. She writes about such conditions in India it makes me feel very feeble to be sitting here before the fire with everything a person could need for their physical comfort and safety,

205

and still to imagine I have something to complain about. You must have known many soldiers, Miss Latterly?"

"Yes . . ."

"And their wives?"

"Yes. I knew several." She wondered why Sylvestra asked.

"Amalia has told me something of the mutiny in India," Sylvestra went on. "Of course, that was three years ago now, I know, but it seems as if things will be changed forever by it. More and more white women are being sent over there to keep their husbands company. Amalia says that it is to keep the soldiers apart from the native Indians, so they can never trust and be taken unaware like that again. Do you suppose she is right?"

"I should think it very likely," Hester replied candidly. She did not know a great deal about the circumstances of the Indian Mutiny. It had occurred too close to the end of the war in the Crimea, when she was deeply concerned with the tragic death of both her parents, with finding a means of supporting herself, and with accommodating to the dramatically different way of life afforded to her when she returned to England.

Attempting to adapt to the life of a single woman rather past the best age for marriage, not possessed of the sort of family connections to make her sought after, nor the money to provide for herself or a handsome dowry, and unfortunately not of great natural beauty or winning ways, had made the task extremely difficult. She was also not of a docile disposition.

She had read the fearful stories and heard accounts of starvation and massacre, but she had not known anyone who had been affected personally.

"It is hard to imagine such atrocity," Sylvestra said thoughtfully. "I am beginning to realize how very little I know. It is disturbing . . ." She hesitated, her hands idle, the linen held up but quite still. "And yet there is something not unlike exhilaration in it also. Amalia wrote to me of the most extraordinary incident." She shook her head, her face troubled, eyes far away. "It seems that the siege of Cawnpore was particularly brutal. The women and children were starved for three weeks, then the survivors were taken to the river and placed upon boats, where the native soldiers—sepoys, I believe they are called—

fell upon them. Those hundred and twenty-five or so who still survived even that were taken to a building known as the Bibighar, and after a further eighteen days were slaughtered— by butchers brought in from the bazaar for the purpose."

Hester did not interrupt.

"It seems when the Highland Regiment relieved Cawnpore, they found the hacked-up bodies and exacted a fearful revenge, killing every one of the sepoys there. What I wanted to mention was the tale Amalia wrote me of one soldier's wife, named Bridget Widdowson, who during the siege was sent to guard eleven mutineers, because at that time there were no men available. This she accomplished perfectly, marching up and down in front of them all day, terrifying them immobile, and it was only when she was finally relieved by a regular soldier that they all escaped. Is that not remarkable?"

"Indeed it is," Hester agreed wholeheartedly. She saw the wonder and the amazed admiration in Sylvestra's eyes. There was something stirring in her which was going to find the loneliness of this house without her husband, the restrictions of society widowhood and her enforced idleness as a kind of imprisonment. Rhys's dependency would only add to it, in time. "But the heat and the endemic disease are things I should find very trying," she said to counter it.

"Would you?" It was a genuine question, not an idle remark. "Why did you go out to the Crimea, Miss Latterly?"

Hester was startled.

"Oh, forgive me," Sylvestra apologized immediately. "That was an intrusive question. You may have had all manner of private reasons which are none of my concern. I do beg your pardon."

Hester knew what she was thinking. She laughed outright. "It was not a broken affair of the heart, I promise you. I wanted the adventure, the freedom to use such brains and talents as I have where I would be sufficiently needed that necessity would remove prejudices against women's initiative."

"I imagine you succeeded?" There was vivid interest in Sylvestra's face.

Hester smiled. "Most assuredly."

"My husband would have admired that," Sylvestra said with certainty. "He loved courage and the fire to be different, inventive." She looked rueful. "I sometimes wonder if he would have liked to have gone somewhere like India, or perhaps Africa. Amalia's letters would thrill him, but I had a feeling they also awoke a restlessness in him, even a kind of envy. He would have loved new frontiers, the challenge of discovery, the chance of great leadership. He was an outstanding man, Miss Latterly. He had a most remarkable mind. Amalia gets her courage from him, and Constance too."

"And Rhys?" Hester said quietly.

The shadow returned to Sylvestra's face. "Yes . . . Rhys too. He wanted so much for Rhys. Is it terrible of me to say that there is a kind of way in which I am glad he did not live to see this? . . . Rhys so ill, unable to speak . . . and so . . . so changed." She shook her head a little. "It would have hurt him beyond bearing." She stared down at her hands. "Then I wish with all my heart that Leighton could have lived longer, and they could have grown closer together. Now it is too late. Rhys will never know his father man-to-man, never appreciate his qualities as I did."

Hester thought of Monk's vision of what had happened in the dark alley in St. Giles. She hoped with an overwhelming fierceness that it was not true. It was hideous. For Sylvestra it would be more than she could live through and keep her sanity.

"You will have to tell him," Hester said aloud. "There will be a great deal you can say to make his father's true character and skills real to him. He will need your company as he recovers, and your encouragement."

"Do you think so?" Sylvestra asked quickly, hope and doubt in her eyes. "At the moment he seems to find even my presence distressing. There is much anger inside him, Miss Latterly. Do you understand it?"

Hester did not, and it frightened her with its underlying cruelty. She had seen that exultancy in the power to hurt a number of times, and it chilled her even more than Monk's words.

"I daresay it is only the frustration of not being able to speak," she lied. "And of course the physical pain."

208

"Yes . . . yes, I suppose so." Sylvestra picked up her embroidery again and resumed stitching.

The maid came in and banked up the fire, taking the coal bucket away with her to refill it.

The following evening Fidelis Kynaston called again, as she had promised she would, and Sylvestra urged Hester to take time away from Ebury Street and do as she pleased, perhaps visit with friends. She had accepted with pleasure, most particularly because Oliver Rathbone had again invited her to dine with him and to attend the theater, if she cared to.

Normally clothes were of less interest to her than to most women, but that evening she wished she had a wardrobe full of gowns to choose from, all selected for their ability to flatter, to soften the line of shoulder and bosom, to give color and light to the complexion and depth to the eyes. Since she had already worn her best gown on the previous occasion, she was reduced to wearing a dark green which was over three years old—and really a great deal more severe than she would have chosen had she any other available to her. Still, she must make the best of what she had and then think about it no more. She dressed her hair softly. It was straight and unwilling to fall into the prescribed coils and loops, but it was thick, and there was a nice sheen on it. Her skin had not sufficient color, but pinching it now would serve no purpose by the time she arrived at the theater, and in a hansom it would hardly matter.

And indeed when Rathbone came for her and she was unintentionally a few minutes late, thought of appearance lingered only a moment before it vanished in the pleasure of seeing him, and a quickening of her pulse as she recalled their last parting and the touch of his lips upon hers.

"Good evening, Oliver," she said breathlessly as she almost tripped on the last stair and hurried across the hall to where he stood a few feet from a surprised butler. He looked startlingly elegant to be calling for the hired nurse, and was quite obviously a gentleman.

He smiled back at her, exchanged some pleasantries, then escorted her out to the waiting hansom.

The evening was cold but quite dry, and for once there was no fog and a clear view of a three-quarter moon over the rooftops. They rode in companionable conversation about totally trivial matters—the weather, political gossip, a smattering of foreign news—until they reached the theater and alighted. He had chosen a play of wit and good humor, something for a social occasion rather than to challenge the mind or harrow the emotions.

They stepped inside and were instantly engulfed in a tide of colors and light and the hubbub of chatter as women swirled past, huge skirts brushing one another, faces eager to greet some old acquaintance or to pursue some new one.

It was the social life Hester had been accustomed to before she went to the Crimea, when she was at home in her father's house and it was everyone's very natural assumption that she would meet an eligible young man and marry, one hoped within a year or two at most. That had only been six years before, but it seemed like a lifetime. Now it was alien, and she had lost the skills.

"Good evening, Sir Oliver!" A large lady bore down on them enthusiastically. "How charming to see you again. I had quite feared we had lost the pleasure of your company. You do know my sister, Mrs. Maybury, don't you!" It was a statement, not a question. "May I introduce you to her daughter, my niece, Miss Mariella Maybury?"

"How do you do, Miss Maybury." Rathbone bowed to the young woman with practiced ease. "I am delighted to make your acquaintance. I hope you will enjoy the play. It is said to be most entertaining. Mrs. Trowbridge, may I introduce to you Miss Hester Latterly." He offered no further explanation, but put his hand on Hester's elbow as if making some affirmation that she was not a mere acquaintance but a friend towards whom he felt a sense of pride and even closeness.

"How do you do, Miss Latterly," Mrs. Trowbridge said with ill-concealed surprise. Her rather thin eyebrows rose as if she were about to add something further, but whatever it was eluded her.

"How do you do, Mrs. Trowbridge," Hester answered politely, a little trickle of warmth bubbling inside her. "Miss Maybury."

Mrs. Trowbridge fixed Hester with a baleful eye. "Have you known Sir Oliver long, Miss Latterly?" she asked sweetly.

Hester was about to reply truthfully but Rathbone spoke first.

"We have been acquainted for several years," he said with an air of satisfaction. "But I feel we are better friends now than ever before. Sometimes I think the best affections grow slowly, through shared beliefs and battles fought side by side . . . don't you?"

Miss Maybury looked lost.

Mrs. Trowbridge caught her breath. "Indeed." She nodded. "Especially family friendships. Are you a family friend, Miss Latterly?"

"I know Sir Oliver's father, and I like him enormously," Hester answered, again with the truth.

Mrs. Trowbridge murmured something inaudible.

Rathbone bowed and offered his arm to Hester, leading her away towards another group of people, most of them men in their middle years and obviously well-to-do. He introduced Hester to them one by one, each time without explanation.

By the time they had taken their seats and the curtain had risen on the first act, Hester's mind was whirling. She had seen the speculation in their eyes. Rathbone knew precisely what he was doing.

Now she sat beside him in the box and could not help glancing away from the stage to watch what expression she could read in his face in the reflected lights. He seemed at ease—if anything, a trifle amused. A very slight smile touched his lips and the skin across his cheeks was perfectly smooth. Then she glanced down at his hands and saw they were constantly moving, only slightly, but as if he found himself unable to keep them still. He was nervous about something.

She turned back to the stage, her heart beating so she felt she could almost hear it. She watched the actors and heard all their words, but a moment later could not have recalled anything of it. She thought of the first time she had come to the theater with

211

Rathbone. Then she had said far more, probably too much, expressing her opinions on the things she felt most passionate about. He had been courteous, he always would be, his own dignity would forbid anything else. But she had been aware of the coolness in him, always a certain distance, as if he wanted to be sure his friends did not assume too much about his regard for her, or that their relationship to each other was more than slight. His conventionality deplored her outspokenness, as if it admired her courage and fought in different ways for the same end.

But since then he had defended Zorah Rostova and nearly ruined his career. He had learned in an acutely real way the boundaries of judgment and intolerance of his own profession, and how quickly society could reverse its loyalties when certain borders were crossed. Compassion and belief did not excuse. He had spoken from conviction and without weighing the results first. Suddenly he and Hester were on the same side of the gulf which had separated them before.

Was that what he was aware of and which at once alarmed and exhilarated him?

She turned to look at him again and found he was also looking at her. She had remembered how dark his eyes were, in spite of his fair brown hair, but still she was startled at their warmth. She smiled, then swallowed and turned back to the stage. She must pretend she was interested, that at least she knew what was going on. She had not the faintest idea. She could not even have identified the hero or the villain, presuming there was one.

When the interval came she found she was ridiculously self-conscious.

"Are you enjoying it?" he asked as he followed behind her up to the foyer, where refreshments were served.

"Yes, thank you," she answered, hoping he would not press her as to the plot.

"And if I told you I have not been paying close attention to it, that my mind was elsewhere, could you tell me what I have missed?" he said gently. "So I may understand the second act."

She thought quickly. She must concentrate on what he was

saying, not on what he might mean—or might not! She must not leap to conclusions and perhaps embarrass them both. Then she would never be able to resume their friendship. It would be over, even if neither of them acknowledged it, and that would hurt. She realized with surprise how very much it would hurt.

She looked at him with a smile, quite a casual one, but not so slight as to appear cool or studied.

"Have you a case which troubles you, a new one?"

Would he retreat into that excuse, or was it the truth anyway? She had left the way open for him.

"No," he said quite directly. "I suppose in a sense it has to do with law, but it was most certainly not the legal aspect of it which was on my mind."

This time she did not look at him. "The legal aspect of what?"

"Of what concerns me." He put his hand on her back to guide her through the throng of people, and she felt the warmth of it ripple through her. It was a safe feeling, disturbingly comfortable. Why should comfort disturb her? That was ridiculous.

Because it would be so easy to get used to. The gentleness, the sweetness of it was overwhelmingly tempting. It was like coming into sunlight and suddenly realizing how chilled you had been.

"Hester?"

"Yes?"

"Perhaps this is not really the best place, but . . ."

Before he could finish what he was about to say, he was accosted by a large man with sweeping silver hair and an avuncular manner.

"My goodness, Rathbone, you are miles away, man! I swear I have seen you pass half a dozen acquaintances as if you were unaware of their existence. Do I credit that to your charming companion or a particularly challenging case? You do seem to select the very devil of the lot of them."

Rathbone blinked slightly. It was something very few situations had ever caused him to do.

"To my companion, of course," he replied without hesitation.

"Hester, may I introduce Mr. Justice Charles? Miss Hester Latterly."

"Ah!" Charles said with satisfaction. "Now I recognize you, ma'am. You are the remarkable young lady who uncovered such damning evidence in the Rostova case. In the Crimea, weren't you? Extraordinary! How the world is changing. Not actually sure I care for it, but no choice, I suppose. Make the best of it, eh?"

At another time she would have challenged him as to what he meant. Did he disapprove of women having the opportunity to make such a contribution as Florence Nightingale had? Their freedom? Their use of knowledge and authority, and the power it gave them, even if only temporarily? Such an attitude infuriated her. It was antiquated, blind, rooted in privilege and ignorance. It was worse than unjust, it was dangerous. It was precisely that sort of blinkered idiocy which had kept inadequate men in charge of the battles in the Crimea and cost countless men their lives.

She drew in her breath to begin the assault, then remembered Rathbone standing so close to her he was actually touching her elbow, and she let out her breath in a sigh. It would embarrass him dreadfully, even if in truth he half agreed with her.

"I am afraid we are all in that situation, sir," she said sweetly. "There is a good deal I am quite certain I do not care for, but I have not yet found a way of altering it."

"Not for want of seeking," Rathbone said dryly when they had bidden Mr. Justice Charles good-evening and moved a few yards away. "You were remarkably tactful to him. I expected you to take him thoroughly to task for his old-fashioned views."

"Do you think it would have changed his mind one iota?" she asked, looking at him with wide eyes.

"No, my dear, I don't," he said with a smile, on the verge of laughter. "But that is the first time I have seen such a consideration halt you."

"Then perhaps the world really is changing?" she suggested.

"Please do not allow it to change too much," he said with a

214

gentleness that amazed her. "I appreciate the tact—it has its place—but I should not like you to become like everyone else. I really care for you very much exactly as you are." He put his hand on hers lightly. "Even if at times it alarms me. Perhaps it is good to be disturbed now and again? One can become complacent."

"I have never thought of you as complacent."

"Yes, you have. But I assure you that you would be wrong if you thought so now. I have never been less comfortable or less certain of myself in my life."

Suddenly she was not certain either. Confusion made her think of Monk. She liked Rathbone immensely. There was something in him which was uniquely valuable. Monk was elusive, unyielding, at times arbitrary and cold. But she could not turn away from him. She did not wish Rathbone to say anything which would require an answer.

Her heart was quieter again. She smiled and put up her hand to touch his cheek.

"Then let us forget yesterday and tomorrow, and simply be certain that this evening is an island of friendship, and of a trust of which there is no doubt at all. I have no idea what the play is about either, but since the audience is laughing every few moments, I expect it is just as witty as they say."

He took a deep breath and smiled back at her. There was a look in his face of sudden ease. He took her hand and moved it softly to his lips.

"I should enjoy that enormously."

When Dr. Wade called the next day he was accompanied by his sister, Eglantyne, who expressed the same concern for Sylvestra as before, coming to her with a kind of silent understanding which Hester now appreciated more than on the previous occasion. Then it had seemed as if she were at a loss for what to say. Looking at her more closely, it now appeared instead to be a knowledge that no words would serve any purpose; they might end in belittling what was too large for everyday speech.

When Sylvestra and Eglantyne had gone together into the

withdrawing room, Hester looked at Corriden Wade. He was quite obviously tired and the strain was showing in the lines of weariness around his mouth and eyes. There was no longer the same energy in his bearing.

"Can I help you at all, Dr. Wade?" she asked gravely. "Surely there must be something I can do to lessen the burden upon you? I imagine you have many other patients, both in hospital and in their homes." She searched his eyes. "When did you last take any thought for yourself?"

He stared at her as if for a moment he was not sure what she meant.

"Dr. Wade?"

He smiled, and his face altered completely. The dejection and anxiety vanished, although nothing could mask the tiredness in him.

"How generous of you, Miss Latterly," he said quietly. "I apologize for allowing my own feelings to be so obvious. It is not a quality I intend, or admire. I admit, this case does trouble me deeply. As you have no doubt observed, both my sister and I are very fond of the whole family." A shadow of pain crossed his eyes, and the surprise of it was naked to see. "I still find it hard to accept that Leighton . . . Mr. Duff . . . is dead. I had known him for years. We had shared . . . a great deal. That it should all end"—he took a deep breath—"like this . . . is appalling. Rhys is much more than a patient to me. I know . . ." He made a slight gesture with his hands. "I know a good doctor, or a good nurse, should not allow himself or herself to become personally involved with any patient. It can affect their judgment to offer the best care possible. Relatives can lend sympathy and grief, moral support and love. They look to us to provide the best professional treatment, not emotion. I know all this as well as anyone. Still, I cannot help being moved by Rhys's plight."

"And I too," she confessed. "I don't think anyone expects us not to care. How could we dedicate our time to helping the sick and injured if we did not care?"

He looked at her closely for several moments.

"You are a remarkable woman, Miss Latterly. And of course

216

you are right. I shall go up and see Rhys. Perhaps you will keep the ladies company and . . ."

"Yes?" She was now used to his pattern of seeing Rhys alone, and no longer questioned it.

"Please, do not offer them too much encouragement. I do not know if he is progressing as well as I had hoped. His outer wounds are healing, but he seems to have no energy, no will to recover. I detect very little returning strength, and that disturbs me. Can you tell me if I have missed something, Miss Latterly?"

"No . . . no, I wish I could, but I also have wished he would develop more desire to sit up longer, even get into a chair for a while. He is still very weak and not able to take as much food as I had expected."

He sighed. "Perhaps we hope too much. But guard your words, Miss Latterly, or we may unintentionally cause even more pain." And with an inclination of his head, he went up the stairs past her and disappeared across the landing.

Hester went to the withdrawing room and knocked on the door. She had a fear of interrupting a moment that could be confidential. However, she was invited in immediately and with apparently genuine pleasure.

"Do come in, Miss Latterly," Eglantyne said warmly. "Mrs. Duff was telling me about Constance's letters from India. It sounds extraordinarily beautiful, in spite of the heat and the disease. Sometimes I regret there is so much of the world I shall never see. Of course, my brother has traveled a great deal . . ."

"He was a naval surgeon, wasn't he?" Hester sat in the chair offered her. "He mentioned something of it to me."

Eglantyne's face showed little expression. It was plain that her brother's career did not excite in her either the imagination of danger, personal courage, and desperate conditions or the knowledge of suffering that it did in Hester. But then how could it? Eglantyne Wade had probably never witnessed anything more violent or distressing than a minor carriage accident, the odd broken bone or cut hand. Her grief would be . . . what? Boredom, a sense of life passing by without touching her, of being very little real use to anyone. Almost certainly a loneliness, perhaps a broken romance, a love known and lost, or merely dreamed of. She was pretty—in fact, very pretty—and it seemed she was also kind. But that was not enough to understand a man like Corriden Wade.

Eglantyne avoided Hester's eyes. "Yes, he does speak of it occasionally. He believes very strongly in the power of the navy, and the life at sea, to build character. He says it is nature's way of refining the race. At least I think that is what he said." She seemed uninterested. There was no life in her voice, no lift of understanding or care.

Sylvestra looked at her quickly, as if sensing some emotion, perhaps loneliness, beyond her words.

"Would you like to travel?" Hester asked to fill the silence.

"Sometimes I think so," Eglantyne answered slowly, recalling herself to the polite necessities of conversation. "I am not sure where. Fidelis . . . Mrs. Kynaston . . . speaks of it sometimes. But of course it is only a dream. Still, it is pleasant to read, is it not? I daresay you read a great deal to Rhys?"

The conversation continued for nearly an hour, touching on a dozen things, exploring none of them.

Eventually Corriden Wade returned looking very grave, his face deeply lined, as if he were close to exhaustion. He closed the door behind him and walked across to stand in front of them.

Silently Eglantyne reached out and took Sylvestra's hand, and Sylvestra clung to it until her knuckles shone white with the pressure.

"I am sorry, my dear," he said quietly. "I have to warn you that Rhys is not progressing as well as I would like. As no doubt Miss Latterly will have told you, his outer wounds are healing well. There is no suppuration and certainly no threat of gangrene. But internally we cannot tell. Sometimes there is damage to organs that we have no way of knowing. There is nothing I can do for him except prescribe sedatives to give him as much rest as possible, and bland food that will not cause him pain, and yet will be nourishing and easy to digest."

Sylvestra stared up at him, her face stricken.

"We must wait and hope," Eglantyne said gently, looking from Sylvestra to her brother and back again. "At least he is no worse, and that in itself is something to be thankful for."

Sylvestra attempted to smile, and failed.

"Why does he not speak?" she pleaded. "You said he had not sustained any injury to make him dumb. What is wrong with him, Corriden? Why has he changed so terribly?"

He hesitated. He glanced at his sister, then drew in his breath as if to answer, but remained silent.

"Why?" Sylvestra demanded, her voice rising.

"I don't know," he said helplessly. "I don't know, and my dear, you must brace yourself for the fact that we may never know. Perhaps he will only recover if he can forget it entirely. Begin life again from now onward. And possibly in time that may happen." He turned to Hester, his eyes wide in question.

She could not answer. They were all staring at her, waiting for her to offer some kind of hope. She longed to be able to, and yet if she did, and it proved false, how much harder would it be then? Or was getting through that night and the next day all that mattered at this moment? A step at a time. Don't attempt the entire journey in one leap of thought. It will be enough to cripple you.

"That may well be the case," she agreed aloud. "Time and forgetting may heal his spirit, and his body will follow."

Sylvestra relaxed a little, blinking back tears. Surprisingly, even Corriden Wade seemed to be pleased with her answer.

"Yes, yes." He nodded slightly. "I think you are very wise, Miss Latterly. And of course you have experience with men who were fearfully injured and who must have seen the most terrible sights. We will do all we can to help him forget."

Hester rose to her feet. "I must go up and see if there is anything I can do for him now. Please excuse me."

They murmured assent, and she left the room wishing them good-bye and hurried across the hall and up the stairs. She found Rhys lying hunched up in the bed, the sheets tangled, a bowl of bloodstained bandages left by the door, half covered with a cloth. He was shivering, although the blankets were up around his chest and the fire was burning briskly.

"Shall I change your bed—" she began.

He glared at her with blazing eyes of such rage she stopped in mid-sentence. He looked so savage she thought he might even attempt to strike at her if she came close enough, and he would damage his broken hands again.

What had happened? Had Dr. Wade told him how seriously ill he was? Had he suddenly realized there was a possibility he would not get better? Was this rage his way of concealing a pain he could not bear? She had seen such rage before, only too often.

Or had Dr. Wade examined him and been obliged to hurt him physically in order to look more carefully at his wounds? Were the fury in his eyes and the tearstains on his cheeks from unbearable pain and the humiliation of not having been able to live up to his ideal of courage?

How could she begin to help him?

Perhaps fussing was the last thing he wanted at the moment. Maybe even a rumpled bed, stale and uncomfortable, sheets smeared with blood, was better than the interference of some-body who could not share his pain.

"If you want me, knock the bell," she said quietly, looking to make sure it was still where his fingers could reach it. It was not there. She glanced around. It was across on the tallboy. Dr. Wade had probably moved it because he had wished to use the bedside table for his instruments or the bowl. She replaced it where it usually sat. "It doesn't matter what time it is," she assured him. "I'll come."

He stared at her. He was still furious, still imprisoned in silence. His eyes brimmed over with tears, and he turned away from her.

8

Monk *WALKED BRISKLY* along Brick Lane, head down under the wind which was clearing the last of the fog. He must see Vida Hopgood again before he pursued the case any further. She had the right to know of Runcorn's refusal to involve the police in the case in spite of the mounting proof that there had been a series of crimes of increasing violence. Memory of their encounter still angered him, the more so because part of his mind knew Runcorn was right, and in his place Monk might well have made the same decision. He would not have done it out of indifference, but as a matter of priorities. Runcorn had too few men as it was. They only touched the surface of crime in areas like Seven Dials. It was an easy excuse to ignore people like Vida Hopgood, but it was also unfair to all the countless other victims to put men where they could make no effective difference.

Thinking of it made him angrier still, but it was better than thinking of Hester, which was so natural to him, and at the same time so full of all kinds of discomfort. It was the same kind of temptation as pulling a bandage off a wound to see if it had healed yet, touching the place that hurt in the hope that this time it would not. It always did . . . and he did not learn by experience.

He turned the corner into Butcher's Yard and was suddenly sheltered. He almost slipped where there was ice on the cobbles. He passed a man shouldering a heavy load covered in sacking, probably a carcass. It was quarter past four and the light was fading. In late January the days were short.

He reached Vida Hopgood's door and knocked. He expected her to be in. He had found this a good time to call. He looked forward to the warmth of her fire and, if he were fortunate, a hot cup of tea.

"You again," she said when she saw him. "Still got a face like a pot lion, so I s'pose yer in't found nothin' useful. Come on in, then. Don't stand there lettin' in the cold." She retreated along the passageway, leaving him to close the door and follow her.

He took his coat off and sat down uninvited in front of the fire in the parlor, rubbing his hands together and leaning towards the grate to catch the warmth.

She sat opposite him, her handsome face sharp-eyed, watchful.

"Did yer come 'ere ter warm yerself 'cos yer got no fire at 'ome, or was there summink in particular?"

He was used to her manner. "I put all we have before Runcorn yesterday. He agrees there is plenty of proof of crime but says he won't put police onto it because no court would prosecute, let alone convict." He watched her face for the contempt and the hurt he expected to see.

She looked at him equally carefully, judging his temper. There was a gleam in her eyes, a mixture of anger, humor and cunning.

"I wondered w'en yer was gonna say that. D'yer wanna give it up then, that wot yer mean? Come ter it straight?"

"No, if that was what I meant, I'd have said it. I thought you knew me better."

She smiled with a moment of real amusement.

"Yer a bastard, Monk, but there are times w'en if yer wasn't a rozzer, or I could ferget it . . . which I can't . . . I could almost fancy yer."

He laughed. "I wouldn't dare," he said lightly. "You might suddenly remember, and then where would I be?"

"In bed wi' a shiv in yer back," she said laconically, but there was still a warmth in her eyes, as if the whole idea had an element which pleased her. Then the ease died away. "So wot yer gonna do about these poor cows wot bin raped, then? If yer in't givin' up, wot's left, eh? You gonna find them bastards fer us?"

"I'm going to find them," he said carefully, giving due weight to every word. "What I tell you depends upon what you are going to do about it."

Her face darkened. "Listen, Monk—"

"No, you listen!" he cut across her. "I have no intention of ending up giving evidence at your trial for murder, or of being in the dock beside you as an accessory before the fact. No jury in London is going to believe I didn't know what you would do with the knowledge once I found it for you."

There was confusion in her face for a moment, then contempt. "I'll see yer in't caught up in it," she said witheringly. "Yer don't need ter run scared o' that. Jus' tell us 'oo they are, we'll take care o' the rest. Won't even tell anyone 'ow we found 'em."

"They already know." He ignored the sarcasm, the reasoning, and the excuses.

"I'll tell 'em yer failed," she said with a grin. "We found 'em ourselves. Won't do yer reputation no good, but it'll keep yer from the rope . . . seein' as that's wot yer after, in't it?"

"Stop playing, Vida. When I know who they are, we'll come to some agreement as to what we do about it, and we'll do it my way, or I'll not tell you."

"Got money, 'ave yer?" she said with raised eyebrows. "Can afford ter work fer no pay, all of a sudden? In't wot I 'eard."

"It's not your concern, Vida." He saw from her face she did not believe him. "Maybe I have a rich woman who'll see I don't go hungry or homeless. . . ." It was true. Callandra Daviot would help him, as she had from the beginning, although it was far from in the sense Vida would take from his words.

Her eyes opened wide in amazement, then she began to laugh, a rich, full-throated surge of merriment.

"You!" She chortled. "Yer got yerself a rich woman ter keep yer. That's priceless, that is. I never 'eard anythink so funny in all me life." But she was watching him all the same, and there was belief in her eyes.

"So those are my conditions, Vida," he said with a smile. "I intend to find out who they are, then we bargain as to what we do about it, and what I tell you rests on our agreement."

She pursed her lips and looked at him steadily in silence, weighing up his strength of resolve, his will, his intelligence.

He looked back at her without wavering. He did not know what she knew of him from the past, but he had felt his reputation in Seven Dials keenly enough to be sure she would not judge him lightly.

"Or'ight," she said at last. "I reckon as yer in't gonna let the bastards orff, or yer wouldn't care enough ter catch them whether I paid yer or not. Yer wants 'em fer summink near as much as I do." She stood up and went over to a drawer in a small table and took out two guineas. " 'Ere y'are. That's all until yer come up wi' summink as we can use, Monk. Get on wif it. Jus' 'cos some woman wi' more money 'n sense fancies yer don' mean I want yer clutterin' up me best room 'alf the evenin'." But she smiled as she said it.

Monk thanked her and left. He walked slowly, hands pushed hard into his pockets. The deeper he looked into the case, the more it did seem as if Rhys Duff could be guilty. One thing he had noticed which he had not told Vida Hopgood was that from everything he had been able to establish, there had been no attack since the incident in which Rhys had been injured. They had begun slowly, building up from small unpleasantnesses, gradually escalating until they were assaults so violent as to threaten life. Then suddenly they had stopped altogether. The last of them had happened ten days before.

He crossed an open square and went into the alley on the far side, passing a man selling bootlaces and an old woman with a carpetbag.

Why the ten days? That was a larger space than between the other attacks. What had kept them away for such a length of time? Was there a victim he had missed? To fit in with the pattern there should have been at least two.

Further afield? Rhys had been found in St. Giles. Had he and his friends moved territories, perhaps fearing Seven Dials had become too dangerous for them? That was an answer that fitted with what he knew so far. But he must put it to the test.

He turned and began to walk west again until he came to a thoroughfare and caught a cab. It was not very far. He could have gone all the way on foot in half an hour, but suddenly he was impatient.

He alighted just past the Church of St. Giles itself and strode towards the first lighted hostelry he saw. He went inside and sat down at one of the tables, and after several minutes was served with a mug of stout. Noise surged all around him, the press of bodies, shouts, laughter, people swaying and shoving to get past, calling out to one another greetings, friendly abuse, snippets of gossip and news, little bits of business. There were fencers of stolen goods there, pickpockets, forgers picking up a few likely customers, card sharps and gamblers, pimps.

He watched them all with a growing feeling of familiarity, as if he had been there before, or in a score of places like it. He remembered the way the lamp hung a trifle crookedly, shedding an uneven light on the brass railing above the bar. The line of hooks where customers hung their mugs dipped a little at the far end.

A small man with a withered arm looked at him and shook his head towards his companion, and they both pulled up their collars and went outside into the cold.

A woman laughed overloudly and a man hiccuped.

A fair-haired man with a Scots accent slid into the seat opposite Monk.

"We've no' got anything here for ye, Mr. Monk. Tell me what it is ye're after an' I'll pass the word, but ye know I'd 'a great deal sooner ye did not sit in my house drinkin' yer ale. Aye, we've the odd thief in here, but small folk, no' worth the bother o' a man like yourself."

"Murder is worth my trouble, Jamie," Monk replied very quietly. "And so is rape and the beating of women."

"If ye're talking about those two men that were found in Water Lane, none of us around here know who did that. Young policeman's been all over asking and wasting his time, poor devil. And Constable Shotts, who was born and bred around here, should know better. But why are you here?" His broad, fair face was wary, his crooked nose, broken years ago, and wide, blue eyes gave him a comfortable look which belied his intelligence. "And what's it to do wi' rape?"

"I don't know," Monk replied, taking another drink of his stout. "Have any women been raped around here in the last month or two? I mean ordinary women, women who work in the factories and sweatshops and maybe go on the streets now and then when things get a little tight?"

"Why? What do you care if they have? Po-liss don't give a toss. Though I heard as you're not with the po-liss anymore." A flicker of amusement crossed his face; his lips curled as if he would laugh, but he made no sound.

"You heard truly," Monk replied. He was certain he knew this man. He had spoken his name without thinking. Jamie . . . the rest of it escaped him, but they knew each other well, too well to pretend. It was an uneasy truce, a natural enmity held at bay by a certain common interest and a thread, very fragile, of respect, not unmixed with fear. Jamie—his last name was MacPherson, Monk suddenly recalled—was a brawler, hot-tempered; he carried a grudge and he despised cowardice or self-pity. But he was loyal to his own, and far too intelligent to strike out without a reason or to act against his own interests.

He was smiling now, his eyes bright. "Throw you out, eh? Runcorn. Yer should o' seen that coming, man. Waited a long time to get his own back, that one."

Monk felt a shiver of cold run through him. The man not only knew him, he knew Runcorn also, and he knew more than Monk did of what lay between them. The chatter and laughter washed around him like a breaking sea, leaving him islanded in his own silence, not a part of them but separate, alone. They knew, and he did not.

"Yes," Monk agreed, not knowing what else to say. He had lost control of the conversation, and it was not what he had intended or was used to. "For the time being," he added. He must not let this man think he was no longer a force to fear or respect.

MacPherson's smile widened. "Aye, this is his patch. He'll no' be happy if you take his case from him."

"He isn't interested in it," Monk said quickly. "I'm after the rapists, not the murderer."

"Are they no' the same?"

"No . . . I don't think so . . . at least, one is, I think."

"You're talking daft, man," MacPherson said tartly. "Ye know better than to take me for a fool. Be straight wi' me, an' I'll maybe help ye."

Monk made up his mind on the spur.

"A woman in Seven Dials hired me to find who was raping and beating factory women over there. I've followed the case for three weeks now, and the more I learn, the more I think it may be connected with your murder here."

"Ye just said it was no' the same people." MacPherson's blue eyes narrowed, but he was still listening intently. He might dislike Monk, but he did not despise his intelligence.

"I think the young man who was beaten, but lived, may have been one of the rapists," Monk explained. "The man who died is his father . . ."

"Aye, we all ken that much . . ."

"Who followed him, having learned, or guessed, what he was doing and got caught in the fight, and he was the one who got the worst of it."

MacPherson pursed his lips. "What does the young man say?"

"Nothing whatever. He can't speak."

"Oh, aye? Why's that then?" MacPherson said skeptically.

"Shock. But it's true. I know the nurse who is caring for him." In spite of all he could do to prevent it, the picture of Hester was so vivid in his mind it was as though she were sitting beside him. He knew she would hate what he was doing; she would fight desperately to protect her patient. But she would also understand why he could not leave the truth concealed if there was any way he could uncover it. If it were not Rhys, she would want it known just as passionately.

MacPherson was regarding him closely. "So what is it ye're wanting from me?"

"There have been no attacks or rapes in Seven Dials since the murder," Monk explained. "Or for some short time before. I need to know if they moved to St. Giles."

"Not that I heard," MacPherson said, his brow puckered. "But then that's a thing folk don't talk about easy. Ye'll have to work a little harder for that than just come in here and ask for it."

"I know that. But a little cooperation would cut down the time. There's not much point in going to the brothels; they weren't professional prostitutes, just women in need of a little extra now and then."

MacPherson pushed out his lip, his eyes hot and angry. "No protection," he said aloud. "Easy pickings. If we knew who it was, and they come back to St. Giles, it'll be their last trip. They'll not go home again, an' that's a promise."

"You'll not be the first in the line," Monk said dryly. "But we have to find them before we can do anything about it."

MacPherson looked at him with a bleak smile, showing his teeth. "I know you, Monk. Ye may be a hard bastard, but ye're far too fly to provoke a murder that can be traced back to ye. Ye'll no tell the likes o' me what ye find."

Monk smiled back at him, although it was the last thing he felt like. Every other time he spoke, MacPherson was adding new darkness to Monk's knowledge of himself. Had he really been a man who had led others to believe he could countenance a murder, any murder, so long as it could not be traced to him? Could it conceivably be true?

"I have no intention of allowing you, or Vida Hopgood, to contrive your own revenge for the attacks," he said aloud icily. "If the law won't do it, then there are other ways. These men are not clerks or petty tradesmen with little to lose. They are men of wealth and social position. To ruin them would be far more effective. It would be slower, more painful, and it would be perfectly legal."

MacPherson stared at him.

"Let their own punish them," Monk went on dryly. "They are very good at it indeed . . . believe me. They have refined it to an art."

228

MacPherson pulled a face. "Ye have no' changed, Monk. I should no' have underestimated ye. Ye're an evil devil. I could no' cross ye. I tried to warn Runcorn agin ye, but he was too blind to see it. I'd tell him now to watch his back for getting rid o' ye from the force, but it would no' do any good. Ye'll bide your time, and get him one way or another."

Monk felt cold. Hard as he was, MacPherson thought Monk harder, more ruthless. He felt Runcorn the victim. He did not have the whole story. He did not know Runcorn's social ambitions, his moral vacillation when a decision jeopardized his own career, or how he trimmed and evaded in order to please those in power . . . of any sort. He did not know his small-mindedness, the poverty of his imagination, his sheer cowardice, his meanness of spirit!

But then Monk himself did not know the whole story either.

And the coldest thought of all, which penetrated even into his bones, was whether Monk was responsible for what Runcorn had become. Was it something Monk had done in the past which had warped Runcorn's soul and made him what he was now?

He did not want to know, but perhaps he had to. Imagination would torment him until he did. For now, perhaps it would be useful to allow MacPherson to retain his image of Monk as ruthless, never forgetting a grudge.

"Who do I go to?" he said aloud. "Who knows what's going on in St. Giles?"

MacPherson thought for a moment or two.

"Willie Snaith, for one," he said finally. "And old Bertha for another. But they'll no' speak to ye unless someone takes ye and vouches for ye."

"So I assumed," Monk replied. "Come with me."

"Me?" MacPherson looked indignant. "Walk out on my business? And who's to care for this place if I go attendin' to your affairs for ye?"

Monk took one of Vida's guineas out of his pocket and put it on the table.

MacPherson grunted. "Ye are desperate," he said dryly. "Why? What's it to you if a few miserable women are raped or beaten? Don't tell me any of them mean something to you." He watched Monk's face closely. "There must be more. These bastards cross you somehow? Is that it? Or is it still to do with Runcorn and the po-liss? Trying to show them up, are ye?"

"I've already told you," Monk said waspishly. "It's not a police case."

"Ye're right," MacPherson conceded. "It couldn't be. Not one for putting himself out on a limb, Runcorn. Always safe, always careful. Not like you." He laughed abruptly, then rose to his feet. "All right, then. Come on, and I'll take you to see Willie."

Monk followed immediately.

Outside, both dressed again in heavy overcoats, MacPherson led the way deeper into St. Giles and the old area that had earlier in the century been known as the Holy Land. He did not go by streets and alleys as Evan had done, but through passages sometimes no more than a yard wide. The darkness was sometimes impenetrable. It was wet underfoot. There was a constant sound of dripping water from eaves and gutterings, the rattle and scratch of rodent feet, the creak of rotting timbers. Several times MacPherson stopped and Monk, who could not see him, continued moving and bumped into him.

Eventually they emerged into a yard with a single yellow gas lamp and the light seemed brilliant by comparison. The outlines of timber frames stood sharp and black, brick and plaster work reflecting the glow. The wet cobbles shone.

MacPherson glanced behind him once to make sure Monk was still there, then went across and down a flight of stone steps into a cellar where one tallow candle smoked on a holder made of half an old bottle, but it showed the entrance to a tunnel and MacPherson went in without hesitation.

Monk followed. He had a sharp memory of stomach-knotting, skin-prickling danger, of sudden pain and then oblivion. He knew what it was. It came from the past he dreaded, when he and Runcorn had followed wanted men into areas just like this. Then there had been comradeship between them. There had never been the slightest resentment on his part, he knew that clearly. And he had gone in headfirst without a second's doubt that Runcorn would be there to guard his back. It had been the kind of trust that had been built on experience, time and time again, of never being found wanting.

Now he was following Jamie MacPherson. He could not see him, but he could re-create in his mind exactly his broad shoulders and slight swagger as he walked, a little roll, as if in his youth he had been at sea. He had a pugilist's agility and his fists were always ready. He looked in his middle fifties, his reddish fair hair receding.

How long ago had it been that Monk and Runcorn had worked together there? Twenty years? That would make Monk in his twenties then, young and keen, perhaps too angry still from the injustice to the man who had been his friend and mentor, too ambitious to gain the power for himself which would allow him to right the wrongs.

Hester would have told him he was arrogant, claiming for himself a position in judgment to which he had no right and no qualification. He would never admit it to her, but he winced now for the truth of it.

MacPherson's voice came out of the darkness ahead of him, warning him of the step, and an instant later he nearly fell over it. They were climbing again, and emerged into another cellar, this time with a lighted door at the far side which led into a room, and another. MacPherson banged sharply, once, then four times, and the door was opened by a man whose hair stood up in spikes on his head. His face was full of humor and the hand he held up was missing the third finger.

"Well, bless me if it in't Monk agin," he said cheerfully. "Thought yer was dead. Wot yer doin' 'ere, then?"

"Looking into the rapes over in Seven Dials," MacPherson said, replying before Monk could speak.

Jimmy Snaith's hazel eyes opened wide, still looking at MacPherson. "Yer never tellin' me the rozzers give a toss about that? I don' believe ya. Ya gorn' sorft in the 'ead, Mac? Ya forgot 'oo this is, 'ave ya?"

"He's no' with the po-liss anymore," MacPherson explained, going farther into the room and closing the door to the cellar behind them. "Runcorn got his revenge, it seems, and had him

231

drummed out. He's on his own. And I'd like to know for myself who's been doing this, because it's no' one of us who live here, it's some fancy fellar from up west way, so it is."

"Well, if that don't beat the devil! 'E wot lives longest sees most, as they say. So Monk's workin' fer us, in a fashion. That I'd live ter see the day." He gave a rich chortle of delight. "So wot you want from me, then? I dunno 'oo dun it, or I'd 'a fixed 'im meself."

"I want to know if there were any beatings or rapes of factory women in the last three weeks," Monk replied immediately. "Or in the two weeks before that either."

"No . . ." Snaith said slowly. "Not as I 'eard. 'Ow does that 'elp yer?"

"It doesn't," Monk answered him. "It was not what I was hoping you would say." Then he realized that was not true. It would have indicated a solution, but not the one he wanted. He did not care about Rhys Duff himself, but he knew how it would hurt Hester. That should not matter. The truth was what counted. If Rhys Duff was guilty, then he was one of the most callous and brutal men Monk had ever known of. He was twisted to a depravity from which it would be unimaginable to redeem him. And more immediate than that, although he might recover, in time, there were his companions. He was not guilty alone. Whoever had been with him was still at large, presumably still bent on violence and cruelty. Even if the attack on Rhys had temporarily frightened them, it would not last. Such ingrained sadism did not vanish from the nature in one act, however harsh. The need to hurt would rise again, and be satisfied again.

Snaith was regarding him with growing interest.

"Yer've changed," he observed, nodding his head. "Dunno as I like it. Mebbe I do. Edges 'a gorn. Yer in't so 'ungry no more. Bloody nuisance, yer was. More 'n Runcorn, poor sod. Never 'ad yer nose fer a lie, 'e din't. 'E'd believe yer w'en you'd smell the truth. Looks like yer lorst that, though, eh?"

"Difficult truths take longer," Monk said tensely. "And we all change. You shouldn't discount Runcorn. He's persistent too, just weighs his priorities, that's all."

Snaith grinned. "Eye ter the main chance, that one, I know that, whereas you . . . yer like a dog wi' a bone. Never let go. Cut orff yer 'ead an' yer teeth'd still be fast shut. Bleedin' bastard, y'are! Still, nobody crossed yer twice, not even yer own."

"You said that before." Monk was stung by his helplessness. "Did I do anything to Runcorn he didn't have coming?" He framed the question aggressively, as if he knew the answer, but his stomach knotted as he looked at Snaith's face in the gaslight and waited for the answer. It seemed an age in coming. He could feel the seconds slip by and hear his own heart beating.

MacPherson cleared his throat.

Snaith stared back, his round, hazel eyes shadowed, his face a trifle puckered. Monk knew before he spoke that his reply was the one he feared.

"Yeah, I reckon so. Enemy in front of yer's one thing, be'ind yer's another. I don' know wot yer dun ter 'im, but it fair broke 'im, an' 'e weren't 'spectin' it from yer. Learned me summink abaht yer. Never took yer light arter that. Yer an 'ard bastard, an' that's the truth." He took a breath. "But if yer want the swine wot done them women in Seven Dials, I'll 'elp yer ter that. I in't fussy 'oo I use. Go an' ask Wee Minnie. Ol' Bertha dunno nuthink. Find Wee Minnie an' tell 'er I sent yer."

"She won't believe me," Monk said reasonably.

"Yeah, she will, 'cos less'n I tell yer w'er ter find 'er, yer'll be wand'rin' around the rookeries for the rest o' yer life."

"That's the truth, so it is," MacPherson agreed.

"So tell me," Monk said.

Snaith shook his head. "In't yer never scared, Monk? In't it never entered yer 'ead as we'd cut yer throat an' drop yer in the midden, jus' for ol' times' sake?"

Monk grinned. "Several times, and if you do there is nothing I can do now to stop you. I'm too far into St. Giles to yell for help, even supposing anyone would come. But you're a businessman, at least MacPherson is. You want what I want. You'll wait until I've got it before you do anything to me."

"There are times when I could almost like yer," Snaith said, surprised at himself. "One thing I'll say for yer, yer in't never an 'ypocrite. Got that much on Runcorn, poor sod."

"Thank you," Monk said sarcastically. "Wee Minnie?"

It was a tortuous hour, and Monk got lost three times before he finally slipped through an alley gateway, across a brick yard and up the back steps into a series of rooms which finally ended in the airlessly hot parlor where Wee Minnie sat on a pile of cushions, her wrinkled face in a toothless smile, her gnarled hands clicking knitting needles of bone as she worked on what appeared to be a sock without looking at it.

"So yer got 'ere," she observed with a dry chuckle. "Thought as yer'd got lorst. Yer wanter know about rape, do yer?"

He should have known word would reach her before he did. "Yes."

"There was two. Bad, they was, so bad no one never said nothing."

"I don't understand. If it was bad, surely that was all the more reason to do something, warn people, stay together . . . anything . . ."

She shook her head, her fingers never losing their rhythm.

"Yer gets beat, yer tell people. It in't personal. Yer gets raped bad, it's different."

"How do you know?"

"I know everything." There was satisfaction in her voice. Then suddenly it hardened and her eyes became cruel. "Yer get them bastards! Give 'em ter us an' we'll draw an' quarter 'em, like they did in the old days. Me gran'fer told me abaht it. Yer string 'em up, or by 'ell's door, we will!"

"Can I speak to the women who were raped?"

"Can yer wot?" she said incredulously.

"Can I speak to the women?" he repeated.

She swore under her breath.

"I need to ask them about the men. I have to be sure it was the same ones. They might remember something—a face, a voice, even a name, the feel of fabric, anything."

"It were the same men," she said with absolute certainty.

"Three of 'em. One tall, one 'eavier, an' one on the skinny side."

He tried to keep the sense of victory out of his voice. "What age were they?"

"Age? I dunno. Don't yer know?"

"I believe so. When were these attacks?"

"Wot?"

"Before or after the murder in Water Lane?"

She looked at him with her head a trifle to one side, like a withered old sparrow.

"Afore, o' course. In't bin nuffink since. Wouldn't, would there now?"

"No, I think not."

"That were 'im, then, wot got killed?" she said with satisfaction.

"One of them." He did not bother to correct her error. "I want the other two."

She grinned toothlessly. "You an' a few others."

"Where did they happen, exactly? I need to know. I need to speak to people who might have seen them coming or going, people in the street, traders, beggars, especially cabbies who might have brought them or taken them away afterwards."

"Wot fer?" She was genuinely puzzled; it was plain in her face. "Yer know 'oo it were, don't yer?"

"I think so, but I need to prove it. . . ."

"Wot fer?" she said again. "If yer think as the law'll take any notice, yer daft. An' yer in't daft, not yer worst enemy'd say that o' yer. Other things mebbe."

"Do you want them caught?" he asked. "You imagine after what happened to one of them, they'll come back to St. Giles, for you to knife them and dump them on some midden? It'll be Limehouse, or the Devil's Acre, or Bluegate Fields next time. If we want justice, it will have to be in their territory, and that means with better weapons than yours. It means evidence, proof, not for the law, which, as you say, doesn't care, but for society, which does."

"Abaht prostitutes gettin' raped or beat?" she said, her voice

235

cracking high with disbelief. "Yer've lorst your wits, Monk. It's finally got to yer."

"Society ladies know their men use prostitutes, Minnie," he explained patiently. "They don't like to think other people know it. They certainly don't like to marry their daughters to young men who frequent places like St. Giles to pick up stray women, who could have diseases, and who practice violence against women, extreme violence. What society knows and what it acknowledges can be very different. There are things which privately can be overlooked but publicly are never forgiven or forgotten." He looked at her wrinkled face. "You have loyalties to your own. You understand that. You don't betray the tribe with someone else. Neither do they. These young men have let the side down; they will not be forgiven for that."

"Yer get 'em, Monk," she said slowly, and for the first time her fingers stopped moving on the needles. "Ye're a clever sod, you are. Yer get 'em for us. We'll not ferget yer."

"Where did they happen, the two in St. Giles?"

"Fisher's Walk, the first one, an' Ellicitt's Yard, the second."

"Time?"

"Jus' arter midnight, both times."

"Dates?"

"Three nights afore the murder in Water Lane, an' night afore Christmas Eve."

"Thank you, Minnie. You have been a great help. Are you sure you won't give me the names? It would help to talk to the victims themselves."

"Yeah, I'm sure."

The following day Monk went to Evan and, after a little persuasion, obtained from him copies of the pictures of Rhys Duff and his father. He looked at the faces with curiosity. It was the first time he had seen them, and they were neither as he had pictured them. Leighton Duff had powerful features, a strong, broad nose, clear eyes that were blue or gray from the light in them, and the appearance of keen intelligence. Rhys was utterly different, and it was his face which troubled Monk. It was the face of a dreamer. He should have been a poet or an explorer of ideas. His eyes were dark under winged brows, his nose good, if a trifle long, his mouth sensitive, even vulnerable.

But it was only a drawing, probably made after the incident, and perhaps the artist had allowed his sense of pity to influence his hand.

Monk put the drawings in his pocket, thanked Evan, and set out through a light drizzle towards St. Giles again.

In Fisher's Walk he began asking street traders, peddlers, beggars, anyone who would answer him, if they recognized either of the two men.

It did not take long to find someone who identified Rhys.

"Yeah," he said, scratching his finger at the side of his head and knocking his cap askew. "Yeah, I seen 'im 'angin' around once or twice, mebbe more. Tall, eh? Nice-lookin' gent. Spoke proper, like them up west. Dressed rough, though. Down in 'is luck, I reckon."

"Dressed rough?" Monk said quickly. "What do you mean, exactly?" Had it been Rhys, or only someone who looked a little like him?

"Well, not like a gent," the man replied, looking at Monk earnestly as if he doubted Monk's intelligence. "I know wot gents look like. Overcoat, 'e 'ad, but nuffink special, no fur on the collar, no 'igh 'at, no stick. In fact, no 'at at all, come ter think on it."

"But it was this man? You are sure?"

" 'Course I'm sure! Yer fink I dunno wot I sees, or yer fink I'm a liar, eh?"

"I think it's important you are sure," Monk said carefully. "Someone's life might hang on it."

The man laughed uproariously, his breath coming in gasps between rich, rolling gurgles of merriment.

"Yer a caution, you are! I never 'eard yer was a wit afore. On'y 'eard yer was clever, an' never ter cross yer. Mean bastard, but fair, most o' the time, but one ter give a bloke enough rope ter 'ang 'isself, an' then watch w'ile 'e does it. Pull the trap fer 'im, if e'd done yer wrong."

Monk felt the cold close in on him, penetrating his skin. "I wasn't being funny," he said in a voice that caught in his throat. "I meant depend on it, not hang with a rope."

"Well, if you ain't gonna 'ang them bastards wot raped those women over in Seven Dials, wot yer want 'em for? Ye gonna get 'em orff 'cos they're gents? That in't like yer. I never 'eard from nobody, even yer worst enemy, as yer feared nor favored no one, not for nuffink at all."

"Well, that's something, I suppose. I'm not going to hang them because I can't. I'd be perfectly happy to." He was not sure that that was true. *Happy* might not be the right word, but he could certainly accede to it. He knew Hester would not, but that was irrelevant . . . well, almost.

"It were 'im," the man said, shivering a little as he grew colder standing still on the street corner. "I seen 'im 'ere three, mebbe four times. Always at night."

"Alone, or with others?"

"Wif others, twice. Once by 'isself."

"Who were the others? Describe them. Did you ever see him with women, and what were they like?"

" 'Ang on! 'Ang on! Once 'e were wif an older man, 'eavy-set, dressed very smart, like a gent. 'E were real angry, shouting at 'im—"

"Who was shouting at whom?" Monk interrupted.

"They was shouting at each other, o' course."

Monk produced the picture of Leighton Duff. "Was this him, or could it have been?"

The man studied it for several moments, then shook his head. "I dunno. I don' fink so. W'y? 'Oo is 'e?"

"That doesn't matter. Have you ever seen him, the older man?"

"Not as I knows of. Looks like a few as I seen."

"And the other time? Who was the young man with then?"

"Woman. Young, mebbe sixteen or so. They went together inter an alley. Dunno after that, but I can guess."

"Thank you. I don't suppose you know the name of the woman, or where I can find her?"

"Looked like Fanny Waterman ter me, but that don't mean it were."

Monk could scarcely believe his good fortune. He tried not to let his sense of victory show too much in his voice.

"Where can I find her?"

"Black 'Orse Yard."

Monk knew better than to try for a number. He would have to go there and simply start asking. He paid the man half a crown, a magnificent reward he feared he would regret later, and then set out for Black Horse Yard.

It took him two hours to find Fanny Waterman, and her answers left him totally puzzled. She recognized Rhys without hesitation.

"Yeah. So wot?"

"When?"

"I dunno. Mebbe free or four times. Wot's it to yer?" She was a slight, skinny girl, hardly handsome, but she had a face which reflected intelligence and some humor behind the belligerence, and in different circumstances she could well have had a kind of charm. She was certainly fluent enough with words, and there was a cockiness in her walk and the attitude of her head. There was nothing of self-pity in her. She seemed as curious about Monk as he was about her. "W'y d'yer wanna know, eh? Wot's 'e done to yer? If 'e broke the law, I in't shoppin' 'im."

"He didn't hurt you?"

"'Urt me? Wo's matter wive yer? 'Course 'e din't 'urt me! W'y'd 'e 'urt me?"

"Did he pay you?"

"W'y yer wanna know?" She cocked her head to one side, looking at him out of wide, dark brown eyes. "Like lookin' at fellas, do yer?" There was the beginning of contempt in her voice. "Cost yer."

"No, I don't," he said tartly. "A lot of women have been raped and beaten, mostly in Seven Dials, but some here. I'm after whoever did it."

"Geez," she said in awe. "Well, nobody 'urt me. 'E paid proper an' willin'."

"When was that? Please try to recall."

She thought for a moment.

"Was it before or after Christmas?" he prompted. "New Year?"

"It were between," she said with sudden enlightenment. "Then 'e came again arter New Year. W'y? Can't yer tell me w'y? Ye don' think as it were 'im, do yer?"

"What do you think?"

"Never!" She tilted her head to one side. "Were it? 'Onest?"

"When was the last time you saw him?"

"Dunno. I din' see 'im for a couple o' weeks afore them blokes was done in Water Lane. Rozzers all over the place arter that. In't good for business."

He took out the picture of Leighton Duff. "Did you ever see this man?"

She studied it. "No."

"Are you sure?"

"Yeah. I never seen 'im. 'Oo is 'e? Is 'e the bloke wot got beat ter death?"

"Yes."

"Well, I see'd Rhys, that's 'is name, wi' other gents, but this geezer weren't one of 'em. They was young, like 'im. One were real 'andsome. Called 'isself 'King' or 'Prince' or summink like that. The other were Arfur."

"Duke, perhaps?" Monk felt his pulse beating like a hammer. This was it; this was the three of them seen together and named.

"Yeah . . . that's right! Were he a duke, for real?"

"No. It's just short for 'Marmaduke.' "

"Oh . . . shame. Like ter fink as I'd 'ad a duke. Still, never mind, eh? All the same wif their pants orff." She laughed with genuine humor at the absurdity of pretension.

"And they all paid you?" he pressed one more time.

"Nah . . . that Duke were a nasty piece o' work. 'E'd 'a 'it me if I'd 'a pushed, so I din't. Jus' took wot I could."

"Did he hit you?"

"Nah. I knows w'en ter push me luck an' w'en not ter."

"Did you see him the night of the murder?"

"Nah."

"None of them?"

240

"Nah."

"I see. Thank you." He produced a shilling, all the change he had left, and gave it to her.

He continued in his search. As he was already aware, the word had spread whom he was seeking and why. For once cooperation was less grudgingly given. Once or twice it was even volunteered. He wanted one more piece, if possible. Had there been a victim that night? Had Leighton Duff caught them before they had attacked, or after? Was there any room at all for denial?

If they had been exultant, intoxicated with the excitement of their victory, disheveled, perhaps marked with blood, then there was nothing else left to seek. Evan would have the force of the law behind him when the crime was murder of a respectable member of society rather than the rape of women whom society chose to forget, and with Monk's help he would have proof enough for any court.

It took him another complete day, but at last he found the second victim, a woman in her forties, still pretty in spite of her tiredness and persistent cough. Her cheekbone was broken and she limped badly. She was severely bruised. Yes, they had raped her, but she had not had the strength to fight, and that in itself had seemed to anger them. She was lucky. They had been interrupted.

"Don' tell anyone," she begged. "I'll lose me job."

He wished he could promise her that. He said what he could.

"They went on to commit murder within a few minutes of leaving you," he said grimly. "You won't need to say you were raped. You can swear you were walking along the street and they fell on you . . . that will be good enough."

"Yeah?" She looked doubtful.

"Yes," he said firmly. "Where was it?"

Her voice was husky, her face pale. "Just orff Water Lane."

"Thank you. That will be enough . . . I promise."

It was sufficient. He would have to take it to Evan. He could not conceal it any longer. It was material evidence on the murder of Leighton Duff. If Rhys and his friends had been using prostitutes in St. Giles, which was now inarguable, and it had escalated in violence over the months, then it seemed more than likely that Leighton Duff had found out and had followed Rhys, going to St. Giles just the once. That was borne out by Monk's lack of ability to find anyone who had recognized him. That was ample motive for the quarrel which had followed, the battle which had gone so far it could only end in the death of the one person who knew the truth of what Rhys had done . . . his father. Whether Arthur and Marmaduke Kynaston had been present or not, what part they had played, would have to be proved.

But Monk must go to Evan.

First he would tell Hester. She should not learn it when Evan came to arrest Rhys. He hated having to tell her, but it would be worse if he evaded the issue. As the man in the street who had named Fanny had said, not even his worst enemies had ever accused him of cowardice.

It was late when he arrived at Ebury Street. A sickle moon glittered in a frosty sky and over towards the east the clouds obscured the faint light and promised more snow.

The butler opened the door and said he would enquire whether Miss Latterly was able to receive him. Ten minutes later Monk was in the library beside a very small fire when Hester came in. She looked frightened. She closed the door behind her, her eyes fixed on his face, searching.

"What is it?" she said without preamble. "What has happened?"

She looked so fierce and vulnerable he ached to be able to shield her from the truth, but there was no way. He could lie now, but it would open a chasm between them, and in a few hours, a day or two at most, she would learn it anyway. She would be there and see it. The shock, the sense of betrayal, would only be worse.

"I've found someone who saw Rhys and Arthur and Duke Kynaston together in St. Giles," he said quietly. He heard the regret in his own voice. It sounded harsh, as if his throat hurt. "I'm sorry. I have to take it to Evan."

She swallowed, her face white. "It doesn't prove anything!" She was struggling and they both knew it.

"Don't, Hester," he begged. "Rhys was there with two of his friends. Together they answer the descriptions exactly. If Leighton Duff knew, or suspected, and followed Rhys to argue with him, to try to prevent him from doing it again, then there was plenty of motive to kill him. He may even have found them immediately after they attacked the woman that night. Then they would have no defense."

"It . . . it could have been Duke or . . . Arthur . . ." Her words trailed away. There was no belief in them, or in her eyes.

"Are they injured?" he asked gently, although he knew the answer from her face.

She shook her head minutely. There was nothing to say. She stared at him. The facts closed in like an iron mesh, unbendable, inescapable. Her mind tried every direction, and he watched her do it and fail each time. There was no real hope in her, and gradually even the determination died.

"I'm sorry," he said softly. He thought of adding how much he wished it had not been so, how hard he had looked for other answers, but she knew it already. There was no need for such explanations between them. They understood pain and reality far too well, the dull ache of knowledge that must be faced, the familiarity of pity.

"When will you tell Evan?" she asked when she had mastered the tension in her voice, or almost.

"I shall tell him tomorrow."

"I see."

He did not move. He did not know what to say, there was nothing, and yet he wanted to say something. He wanted to remain with her, at least to share the hurt, even though he could not ease it. Sometimes sharing was all there was left.

"Thank you . . . for telling me first." She smiled a little crookedly. "I think . . ."

"Perhaps I shouldn't have," he said with sudden doubt. "Maybe it would have been easier for you if you had not known? Then your response would have been honest. You would not have had to wait tonight, knowing, when they didn't. I . . ."

She started to shake her head.

243

"I thought honesty was best," he went on. "Perhaps it wasn't. I thought I knew that, now I don't."

"It would have been hard either way," she answered him, meeting his eyes with the same candor as in the past, in their best moments. "If I know, tonight will be hard, and tomorrow. But when Evan does come, then I shall have prepared myself, and I shall have the strength to help, instead of being stunned with my own shock. I shan't be busy trying to deny it, to find arguments or ways to escape. This is best. Please don't doubt it."

He hesitated for an instant, wondering if she were being brave, taking the responsibility to herself to spare his feelings. Then he looked at her again and knew it was not so. There was a kind of understanding in her which bridged the singleness of this incident and was part of all the triumphs and disasters they had ever shared.

He walked over to her and very gently bent forward and kissed her temple above the brow, then laid his cheek against hers, his breath stirring the loose tendrils of her hair.

Then he turned and walked away without looking back. If he did, he might make an error he could never redeem, and he was not yet ready for that.

9

$E_{VAN \ KNEW}$ that Monk had crossed into St. Giles, although, of course, they were on different cases.

"Wot does 'e want?" Shotts said suspiciously as they were walking back towards the station.

"To find out who raped the women in Seven Dials," Evan replied. "It's a problem we can't help."

Shotts swore under his breath and then apologized. "Sorry, guv."

"You don't need to be," Evan said sincerely. His father might have been offended, but that case angered him so profoundly the release of shouting and using language otherwise forbidden seemed very natural. "If anyone can deal with it, it will be Monk," he added.

Shotts gave a snort of derision edged with something which could have been fear. "If 'e catches the bastards I'll lay they'll wish they were never born. I wouldn't want Monk on my back, even if I hadn't done anything wrong."

Evan looked at him curiously. "If you hadn't done anything wrong, would he be on your back?"

Shotts looked at him, hesitated a moment on the edge of confiding, then changed his mind.

" 'Course not," he denied.

It was a lie, at least in intent, and Evan knew it, but it was pointless to pursue. Nor was it the only time Shotts had told him something which he had later learned to be false. There was time unaccounted for, small errors of fact. He glanced sideways at Shotts's stolid face as they crossed the street, avoiding the gutter and the horse droppings awash in the rain, ducked past a coal cart and onto the farther footpath. What else was there that he had not yet learned? Why should Shotts lie to him about anything?

He had a sudden acutely unpleasant feeling of loneliness, as if the ground had given way beneath him and old certainties had vanished without anything to replace them. All around him was gray poverty, people whose lives were bounded by hunger, cold and danger. They were so used to it they could eat and sleep in its midst, laugh and beget children, bury their dead, steal from each other, and practice their trades and their crafts, legal or otherwise. Illegality was probably the least of their problems, except insomuch as it trespassed certain safeguards. The cardinal principle was to survive. If he had spoken to them of his father's notion of a just God, one who loved them, he would have been greeted with utter incomprehension. Even good fairy stories had some relevance to fact, some meaning that a person could understand.

They entered an alley too narrow to walk abreast, and Shotts went first, Evan behind him. It was a shortcut back to the main thoroughfare. They crossed a tanner's yard stinking of hides and went through a gate that was loosely chained and into the footpath.

Evan increased his stride and caught up with Shotts.

"Why did you lie to me?" he said bluntly.

Shotts tripped on the curbstone, then regained his balance and stood still.

"Sir?"

Evan stopped also. "Why did you lie to me?" he repeated, his voice mild, no accusation in it, simply puzzlement and curiosity.

Shotts swallowed. "About what, sir?"

"Lots of things: Where you were last Friday when you told me you were questioning Hattie Burrows. You weren't, because I learned afterwards where she was, and it was not with you.

About Seven Dials and the running patterer, and hearing from him the case Monk was on."

"That . . ." Shotts began. "That was a . . . mistake . . ." He did not look at Evan as he was speaking.

"Have you a bad memory?" Evan enquired politely, in the same tone as he would have asked if Shotts liked sausages.

Shotts was caught. To say he had would make him an unsuitable policeman. Above all, a policeman needed keen observation and an excellent memory. He had already demonstrated these qualities very effectively.

"Well . . . pretty good . . . most of the time . . . sir," he said, compromising rather well.

"You need to have a perfect memory to be a good liar." Evan resumed walking at a level pace, and Shotts kept up, but not looking at him. "Better than yours. Why, Shotts? Do you know something about this murder that you don't want to tell me? Or is it something else altogether that you are hiding?"

Shotts blushed scarlet. He must have felt the heat flush up his face, because he surrendered.

"It's nothing agin the law, sir, I swear it! I would never do nothing agin the law!"

"I'm listening." Evan kept his eyes straight ahead.

"It's a girl, sir, a woman. I were seein' 'er w'en I shouldn't 'ave. It's me only chance, yer see, wi' all the extra duty I been pullin', wi' the murder. I was . . . I was tryin' ter keep 'er fam'ly out o' it. Not that they're in it . . ."

Evan attempted to hide his smile, and only partially succeeded.

"Oh. Why the secrecy?"

"Mr. Runcorn wouldn't approve, sir. I mean ter marry 'er, but I 'aven't saved enough money yet, an' I can't afford ter lose me job."

"Then be a little more efficient with your lying, and Mr. Runcorn won't need to find out. At least be wholehearted in your inventions."

Shotts stared at him.

Evan kept on walking, coming to the crossroad and, after a

247

brief glance to left and right, striding out, leaving Shotts on the curb as a rag-and-bone cart lumbered between them. Now he was smiling widely.

When Evan reached the police station there was a message that Monk wanted to see him and had information to impart relevant to the Leighton Duff case of a nature which would bring to a conclusion the initial part of the enquiry. That was very strong language for Monk, who never exaggerated, and Evan went out again immediately and took a hansom to Fitzroy Street, and knocked on the door of Monk's rooms.

It was some time since he had been there, and he was surprised to see how comfortable they were—in fact, even inviting. He was too intent on his purpose for calling to notice more than peripherally, but he was aware of personal touches. It was not something he would have associated with Monk, it was too restful. There were antimacassars on the chair backs and a palm tree of some sort in a large brass pot. The fire was hot, as if it had been lit for some time. He found he was relaxing, in spite of himself.

"What is it?" he asked as soon as his coat was off and even before he sat in the chair opposite Monk's. "What have you found out? Have you proof?"

"I have witnesses," Monk replied, crossing his legs and leaning back, his eyes on Evan's face. "I have several people who saw Rhys Duff in St. Giles leading up to the murder, and a prostitute he used there on several occasions. It was definitely him. She identified him from the picture you gave me, and she knew him by name, also Arthur and Duke Kynaston. I even have the last victim of rape, attacked just before the murder, only a few yards from Water Lane."

"She identified Rhys Duff?" Evan said incredulously. It was almost too good to be true. How had he and Shotts missed that? Were they really so inferior to Monk? Was Monk's skill, and his ruthlessness, so much greater? Evan looked across at where Monk sat, the firelight red on his lean cheeks and casting shadows across his eyes. It was a strong, clever face, but not insensitive, not without imagination or the possibility of compassion. There was a certain darkness in it now, as if this victory destroyed as well as created. There was so much in him Evan did not understand, but it did not stop him caring. He had never been afraid to commit his friendship.

"No," Monk answered. "She described three men, one tall and fairly slight, one shorter and leaner built, and one of average height and thin. She did not see or remember their faces."

"That could be Rhys Duff and Duke and Arthur Kynaston, but it's not proof," Evan argued. "A decent defense lawyer would tear that apart."

Monk linked his fingers together in a steeple and stared at Evan. "When this defense lawyer you have in mind asks why on earth Rhys Duff should murder his father," he said, "we will be able to say that Rhys was a decent, well-bred young man who, like any other of his age and class, occasionally took his pleasures with a prostitute. Simply because his father was a trifle straitlaced about such things, even a little pompous perhaps, is not cause for anything beyond a quarrel, and perhaps a reduction in his allowance. This provides the answer: Leighton Duff interrupted his son and his friends raping and beating a young woman. He was horrified and appalled. He would not accept it as part of any young man's natural appetites. Therefore he had to be silenced."

Evan followed the reasoning perfectly. A possible motive had been the one thing lacking before. A quarrel was easy to understand, even a few blows struck. But a fight to the death over the issue of using a prostitute was absurd. The issue of a series of rapes of increasing violence, by three of them together, and being caught red-handed, was another matter entirely. It was repellent, and it was criminal. It was also escalating to the degree that sooner or later it would become murder. To imagine three young men, fresh from the victory of violence against a terrified victim, beating to death the one man who threatened their exposure, was sickening but not difficult to believe.

"Yes, I see," he agreed with a sudden sadness. They were hideous crimes, so ugly he should have been overwhelmed

249

with revulsion and a towering anger against the young men who had committed them. Yet what filled his mind was the picture of Rhys as he had seen him on the cobbles, soaked with blood, insensible, and yet still breathing, still just barely alive.

And then leaping to his mind came the sight of him in the hospital bed, his face swollen and blue with bruising as he opened his eyes and tried desperately to speak, choking in horror, gagging, drowning in pain.

Evan felt no sense of victory, not even the usual loosening of tension inside himself that knowledge brought. There was no peace in this. "You had better take me to these witnesses," he said flatly. "I presume they will tell me the same thing? Will they swear in court, do you suppose?" He did not know what he hoped. Even if they would not, nothing could alter the truth of it.

"You can make them," Monk answered with impatience in his voice. "The majesty of the law will persuade them. Once in the witness box they have no reason to lie. That is not your decision anyway."

He was right. There was nothing to argue about.

"Then I'll take it to Runcorn," Evan went on. He smiled with a downward turn of his lips. "He won't be amused that you solved the case."

A curious look crossed Monk's face, a mixture of irony and something which could have been regret, or even a form of guilt. Evan was aware of uncertainty in him, a hesitation, as if there was something else he wanted to talk about, but was unsure how to begin. He was making no move to rise from his comfortable chair.

"I know he refused to pursue the rapes," Evan started. "But with this it's different. No one will bother prosecuting that when there is the murder. That's what we'll charge them with. We will only prove the rapes to establish motive. The ones in Seven Dials will be by implication."

"I know."

Evan was puzzled. Why did Monk's contempt for Runcorn run so deep? Runcorn was pompous at times, but it was his manner of defending himself from the triviality he felt in his life, perhaps the loneliness. He was a man who seemed to know little else but the concern of his work, the value it gave him, even his relationships with others. Evan realized he knew nothing whatever of the man Runcorn was when he left the police station, except that he never spoke of family or other friends, other pastimes. Had Monk ever considered such things?

"Do you still think he should have pressed the cases of rape alone?" he asked, hearing the criticism in his voice.

Monk shrugged. "No." He sounded reluctant. "He was right. It would have put the victims through more of an ordeal than the offenders . . . presuming they would even have testified . . . which they probably wouldn't. I would not ask any woman I cared for to do that. We would be pursuing it far more for our own sense of vengeance than anything to do with the well-being of the women, or even justice. They would suffer and the men would go free. We wouldn't even be able to try them again, even if we eventually found proof, because they would have been vindicated by the law." There was anger in his face, but it was for the situation, not for Runcorn.

"Rape is not a crime for which we have any answer even remotely just or compassionate," he went on. "It strikes at a part of the emotions which we don't exercise honestly, let alone govern with rationality. It is even more primitive than murder. Why is that, Evan? We deny it, excuse it, torture logic and twist facts to pretend it did not happen, that somehow it was the victim's fault and therefore not the crime we named it."

"I don't know," Evan said, even as he was thinking. "It is something to do with violation—"

"For God's sake! It is the woman who is violated!" Monk exploded, his face dark.

"Yes, it is," Evan agreed wryly. "But the violation we get so upset about is our own. Our property has been spoiled. Someone has taken something to which only we have the right. The rape of any woman is a reminder that our own women can also be spoiled that way. It is a very intimate thing."

"So is murder," Monk retorted.

251

"Murder is only your own life." Evan was still thinking aloud. "Rape is the contamination of your posterity, the fountainhead of your immortality, if you look at it that way."

Monk's eyebrows rose. "Do you look at it that way?"

"No. But then I believe in a resurrection of the body." Evan had thought he would apologize to Monk for his faith, but he found himself speaking with a perfectly calm and untroubled voice, as his own father would have done to a parishioner. "I believe in an individual soul which travels through eternity. This life is far from all there is—in fact, it is a minute part, simply an antechamber, a deciding place where we choose the light from the dark, where we come to know what we truly value."

"It's a place of bloody injustice, inequity and waste," Monk said hoarsely. "How can you possibly walk around St. Giles, as you have been doing, and even imagine a God that is worthy of anything but fear or hate? Better for your sanity to think injustice is random and simply do what you can to redress the worst monstrosities."

Evan leaned forward, all the energy of his spirit in his words, fragments half remembered returning to his tongue. "Do you want a just world, where sin is punished immediately and virtue rewarded?"

"Why not?" Monk challenged. "Is there something wrong with that? Food and clothing for everyone, health, intelligence, a chance to succeed?"

"And forgiveness, and pity, and courage?" Evan pressed. "Compassion for others, humility, and faith?"

Monk frowned, the beginning of a doubt in his mind. "You say that as if the answer were not a certainty. Why not? I thought they were the qualities you valued most. Aren't they?"

"Do you value them?"

"Yes! I may not always behave as if I do, but yes, certainly."

"But if the world were always just, and immediately so, then people would choose to be good, not out of compassion or pity, but because it would be idiotic to be anything else," Evan reasoned. "Only a fool would council any act he knew he would be punished for immediately and certainly."

Monk said nothing.

"Courage against what?" Evan went on. "Do the right thing and there can be nothing to fear. Virtue will always be rewarded straightaway. There will be no need for humility or forgiveness either. Justice will take care of everything. For that matter, neither will there be need for pity or generosity, because no one will need it. The remedy for every ill will lie with the sufferer. We would be full of judgment for each other—"

"All right!" Monk cut across him. "You have made your point. Perhaps I would rather accept the world as it is than change it for the one you paint. Although there are times when I find this one almost beyond bearing, not for me, but for some of those I see." He rose to his feet. "Your father would be proud of you. Perhaps you are wasted on a police beat instead of a pulpit." He was frowning. "Do you want me to take you to these witnesses?"

Evan rose also. "Yes, please."

Monk fetched his overcoat and Evan put his back on again, and together they went out into the dark, cold evening, walking side by side towards Tottenham Court Road and a hansom.

Inside, rattling towards St. Giles, Monk spoke again, his voice uncertain, as if he were struggling for words, seizing the opportunity of the temporary blindness of the night to voice some troubling thought.

"Does Runcorn ever speak to you about the past . . . about me?"

Evan could hear the emotion in Monk's voice and knew he was searching for something of which he was afraid.

"Now and then, but very little," he answered as they passed the Whitefields Tabernacle and continued down towards Oxford Street.

"We used to work St. Giles together," Monk went on, staring straight ahead of him. Evan could not see his face, but could judge from the sound of his voice. "Back before they rebuilt any of it. When it was known as the Holy Land."

"It must have been very dangerous," Evan said to fill the silence.

"Yes. We always went in with at least two at a time, usually more."

"He hasn't spoken of it."

"No. He wouldn't." Monk's voice dropped at the end of the sentence, betraying a sense of loss, not for Runcorn's friendship but for whatever it was which had destroyed it. Evan understood what it was that disturbed him, but it was too delicate to speak between them. Monk wanted to know what it had been, but only step by step, so he could withdraw again if it became too ugly. It was his own soul he was exploring, the one territory from which there was no escape, the one enemy which must always be faced, sooner or later, more certain than anything else in life or death.

"He never mentions family," Evan said aloud. "He didn't marry."

"Didn't he . . ." Monk's tone was remote, as if the remark were meaningless, but the tension in his body belied that.

"I think he regrets it," Evan added, remembering casual references made and the momentary grief in Runcorn's face, instantly hidden. There had been a sergeant's wedding anniversary; everyone had wished him well, spoken of their own families. For an instant Evan had seen the pain in Runcorn's eyes, the knowledge of loneliness, of exclusion. He was not a man gifted by his nature or temperament to fill his own emptiness. He would have been happier with someone there, someone to encourage him when he failed, admire him, be grateful for his support, someone with whom he could share his successes.

Had Monk, with his greater inner strength, his natural courage, intentionally or not, robbed Runcorn of that? Monk feared he had blocked Runcorn's professional success, stood in his path, taken credit for some victory that rightly belonged to him. The inner loss was the one Evan feared, the confidence, the hope, the courage to put fate to the test and abide the consequences, that was what nestled cold in Evan's mind. Could one man really rob another of that? Or merely fail to help?

Monk could not bear the silence.

"Did he . . . want to? I mean, was there someone, do you know?"

Evan recalled a fragment of conversation overheard, a name.

"Yes, I think so. But it was several years ago, fifteen or sixteen or more. Her name was Ellen, I think."

"What happened?"

"I don't know."

The cab swung around into Oxford Circus, jolting and lurching as the dense traffic caused it to change course. In a few moments they would be there. After that it would be on foot, all alleys and yards, steps up and down, icy rooms while Monk retraced his questions and Evan made notes for evidence. There was no more time for conversation.

Monk drew in his breath and let out a sigh.

The next afternoon Evan had all he needed. As Monk had told him, it was inescapable. He sent up a message that he wished to see Runcorn, and at five minutes to three he knocked on the office door.

"Come in," Runcorn called from inside.

Evan opened the door, went into the warmth that filled the room from the fire, but the chill that he carried with him did not ease.

"Yes?" Runcorn looked up from the papers he had been reading. "This news had better be definite. I don't want any more feelings. Sometimes you are too soft for your own good, Evan. If you want to be a preacher you should have stayed at home."

"If I had wanted to be a minister, sir, I would have," Evan replied, meeting Runcorn's eyes boldly. He recognized in himself the same shortness of temper he saw in Monk, the same desire to win, the temptation to fight for the sake of it. Runcorn brought out the least admirable traits in him, as he did in Monk.

"Come to the point." Runcorn pursed his lips. "What do you have? I assume we are talking about the murder of Leighton Duff? You are not off on some crusade for Monk?" His eyes were hard, as if part of him actually wanted to catch Evan in the trespass. He wanted to like Evan. Instinctively, he did. And yet Evan's closeness to Monk so often soured it.

"Yes sir." Evan stood to attention, or as nearly as possible for a man of his natural ease. "I have witnesses to Rhys Duff and his two friends using prostitutes in St. Giles. His picture had been recognized by one of the women. I have her statement. She also names him. Rhys is not a common Christian name, sir."

Runcorn leaned forward, the other papers pushed aside.

"Go on . . ."

"I also have testimony from the last victim of rape, sir, on the night of the murder. She describes three men who answer the physical characteristics of Rhys Duff and his two friends, Arthur and Marmaduke Kynaston."

Runcorn let out his breath slowly and sat back, linking his fingers across his stomach.

"Any proof that the Kynaston brothers were involved in the murder? I mean proof, not reasonable supposition. We have to be absolute."

"I know that, sir. And no, no proof. If we can convict Rhys Duff, then the others may follow." It infuriated him to have to allow their freedom until then. Whoever had actually killed Leighton Duff, the other two were guilty of the string of crimes which had precipitated it. If they had run away at the final moment, it was an act of cowardice, not compassion or honor. Decency of any kind at all would have intervened and prevented the ultimate tragedy.

"Can you place them there?" Runcorn questioned sharply.

"I can place them whoring in St. Giles with Rhys, but not that night, not by name. He was with two other men who answer their descriptions. That is all . . . so far. The worst thing is that they neither of them seem to be hurt, which would indicate they were not involved in the last fight with Leighton Duff."

"Well, we're not charging them with rape," Runcorn said decisively. "That is not a possibility, so dismiss it. What we have is evidence that three young men, of whom Rhys Duff was one, have been beating and raping women in St. Giles— specifically, on the night on which Leighton Duff was murdered." Outside in the passage someone's footsteps stopped

256

and then went on. Runcorn did not seem to hear them. "Did Rhys and his father go separately or together, do you know?" he asked.

"Separately, sir. We have cabdrivers' testimony to that."

"Good. So apparently on this occasion Leighton Duff followed his son. Presumably he had cause to suspect what his son was doing. It would be excellent if you could know what that was. The wife may know, but I imagine it will take some skill to elicit it from her." His face did not betray the imagination to conceive of her suffering. Evan hardly dared think of what such knowledge would do to her. He hoped profoundly that she did have some relationship of tenderness with Dr. Wade. She would surely need all his support now.

"But you had better try," Runcorn went on. "Be very careful how you question her, Evan. She will be a vital witness when it comes to trial. You will search the house, of course. You may find clothes with bloodstains from his earlier attacks. You must establish that he was out on every occasion you intend to specify. Don't get caught on details! I imagine if he does not confess to it, and there is a major case, then his mother will employ the best Queen's Counsel she can find in his defense." He compressed his lips. "Although why anyone would wish to take on such a battle, I don't know. If you do your job properly, he cannot win."

Evan said nothing. As far as he was concerned, nobody won.

"What finally led you to it?" Runcorn asked curiously. "Was it just persistence? The right question, eventually?"

"No sir." Evan did not really know why he took such pleasure in being perverse. It was something to do with the air of satisfaction in Runcorn. "Monk found it, actually. He was following his rape cases, and they led him to Rhys Duff."

Runcorn's head jerked up and his face darkened. He seemed on the edge of interrupting, then changed his mind.

"He called me yesterday late afternoon and simply gave me the information," Evan continued. "I checked it myself and spoke to the people, and took their testimony." He looked at Runcorn innocently, as if he had no idea it would annoy him.

"As well for us he was so stubborn about it," he added for good measure. "Otherwise I might still have been pressing Mrs. Duff and looking for a lover."

Runcorn glared at him, a dull pink rising up his cheeks.

"Monk follows his cases for money, Evan," he said between his teeth. "Don't you forget that. You follow yours because you are the servant of justice, without fear or favor, with loyalties to no one but Her Majesty, whose law you represent." He leaned forward over the desk, his elbows on its polished surface. "You think Monk is a hell of a clever fellow, and to a certain level, so he is. But you don't know everything. You don't know everything about him, by a long way. Watch him and learn, by all means, but I warn you, don't make a friend of him. You'll regret it!" Runcorn said that last with a frown, not viciously but as a warning, as though he was afraid of something for Evan, not for himself. A shadow of old sadness crossed his face.

Evan was taken by surprise. Runcorn was speaking against Monk, and he should have been angry with him. Instead, he was aware of something lost, a loneliness, and he felt only sorrow, and perhaps a touch of guilt.

"Don't trust him—" Runcorn added, then stopped abruptly. "I don't suppose you'll believe me." There was anger in his voice, with himself for having spoken so openly, revealing more of his feelings than he intended to, and a thread of self-pity because he did not expect to be believed.

Against his will, Evan did believe him, not because Runcorn said so but because Monk himself feared it. But it was what Monk had been, not necessarily what he was now. And what he was in the future lay within his own grasp.

"I don't disbelieve you, sir," he said aloud. "You haven't told me anything, only to be careful. I imagine you are speaking from some experience of your own, or you would not feel as you do, but I have no idea what it is. Monk has never spoken of it."

Runcorn let out a burst of laughter, hard and almost choking in his throat. It was filled with helplessness and rage and unhappiness which time had never healed.

"He wouldn't. He likes you. He needs you. He may not

know how to be ashamed, but he's sense enough to understand what you would think of him."

Evan did not want to know, he would much rather have kept his ignorance, but he knew Monk himself needed to know.

"For what, sir?"

Runcorn stood up suddenly, pushing his chair back so sharply it teetered on two legs and all but overbalanced. He turned away to the chest of drawers full of files, his back to Evan.

"Go and arrest Rhys Duff for the murder of his father," he ordered. "You did well in the case. I didn't expect you to be able to solve it. You were wise to take advantage of Monk. Use him when you can. Just don't ever let him use you. Don't turn your back on him. Above all, don't trust him. Don't count on him to be behind you when you need him." He swung around, his eyes hard and clear. "I mean that, Evan. I don't want to see you hurt. You're soft, but you're a good man. Think well of him if you want, but never trust him."

Evan hesitated. It was ugly, very ugly, but it was indefinite, all implications and insubstantial pain. There was nothing he could get hold of to prove . . . or disprove . . . nothing to take to Monk for him to retrace his own steps and understand himself.

"Did Monk betray you, sir?" he said aloud, then instantly wished he had not. He did not want to hear any of it. Now it was unavoidable.

Runcorn stared at him.

"Yes, he betrayed me. I trusted him, and he destroyed everything I ever wanted," he replied bitterly. "He saw the trap in front of me, and he watched me walk right into it."

Evan drew in his breath to question how much it was fair to blame Monk for such a thing. Maybe he had not seen the pitfall any more than Runcorn himself had. Or maybe he had assumed Runcorn had seen it also. Then he realized that it was pointless to argue over the letter when the spirit was what drove. In his heart Monk believed himself guilty.

"I see," he said quietly.

Runcorn faced him. "Do you? I doubt it. But I've done all I

can. Go and arrest Rhys Duff. And don't mention anything about the other two men, do you hear me, Evan? I forbid it. You could jeopardize any chance we have of getting them in the future." His eyes betrayed the anger and frustration of his helplessness now. It scalded inside him to see them escape and know it could be forever.

"Yes sir. I understand." He turned and walked out, his mind already made up to take Monk with him when he went to Ebury Street. Monk had solved this case, and his own case too. He deserved to be there.

It was cold and growing dark as Monk, Evan and P.C. Shotts arrived in a cab at Ebury Street. Evan had considered taking the police wagon, and decided against it. Rhys was still too ill to be transported in such a vehicle, if he could be moved at all. The fear that he could not was the reason he had brought Shotts. He expected to leave him to guard Rhys and watch against the extreme event of Sylvestra trying to smuggle Rhys away.

The cab drew up and they alighted. Evan paid the cabby and, pulling his coat collar up, walked ahead of the other two across the pavement. He had never made an arrest which gave him less sense of achievement. In fact, now that his foot was on the step and his hand stretched towards the bell, he admitted he dreaded it. He knew that Monk, a yard behind him, felt the same, but Monk did so for Hester's sake. He had never met Rhys. He had not seen his face. To Monk, Rhys was only the sum of the evidence he had found, and above all the cause of pain in the women he had listened to, whose bruised lives he had witnessed.

The door opened and the butler's face darkened as soon as he recognized Evan.

"Yes sir?" he said guardedly.

"I'm sorry," Evan began, then straightened his shoulders and continued. "But I require to speak to Mrs. Duff. I am aware it may not be convenient, but I have no alternative."

The butler looked beyond him to Monk and Shotts. His face was white.

"What is it, sir? Has there been another . . . incident?"

"No. Nothing further has happened, but we now understand more of what occurred the night of Mr. Duff's death. I am afraid we need to come in."

The butler hesitated only a moment. He had caught the authority in Evan's voice and he knew suddenly the weight of his office.

"Yes sir. If you will please follow me I shall inform Mrs. Duff you are here." He stood back for them to enter. Evan and Monk did so, leaving Shotts outside as previously agreed. He was there only as a precaution. He expected the possibility of remaining all night, until he was relieved by someone else in the morning. His only release lay in Rhys's being deemed sufficiently well to be moved to a place of imprisonment pending his trial.

Inside the hall was warm and bright, a different world from the icy gloom of the street. The butler walked across the hall towards the withdrawing room door.

"Wharmby," Evan said suddenly.

"Yes sir?"

"Perhaps you had better ask Miss Latterly to come downstairs."

"Sir?"

"It might be easier for Mrs. Duff to have someone else present, someone who can offer her some . . . assistance . . ."

Wharmby turned even paler. He swallowed so his throat jerked.

"I'm sorry . . ." Evan repeated.

"What . . . what have you come for, sir?" Wharmby asked.

"To tell Mrs. Duff what we know of how Mr. Duff met his death, and then the duty which follows from that. Tell her we are here, and then please ask Miss Latterly to come."

Wharmby pulled his jacket down and straightened his back, then opened the withdrawing room door.

"Mr. Evan is here to see you, ma'am, and another gentleman with him." He said no more but backed out again, gave Evan one more look, then went to the stairs, leaving them to go in alone.

261

Sylvestra was standing on the carpet in front of the fire. Naturally she was still dressed in black, with her dark hair piled in a great coil on the back of her head and falling to her neck. In the firelight she looked beautiful with her high cheekbones and slender throat.

"Yes, Mr. Evan. What is it?" she asked with a slight surprise arching her brows. She looked beyond him to Monk.

Evan introduced them briefly, without explanation.

"Good evening, Mr. Monk . . ." She did no more than acknowledge him.

"Ma'am." He inclined his head. To have wished her "Good evening" in return would have been a mockery. He closed the door and went farther into the room.

Evan wished there were any way whatever to escape this moment. He was acutely conscious of Monk standing at his shoulder, his mind filled with the cruelty whose results he had seen, the rage smoldering inside him.

"Yes, Mrs. Duff. We have learned a great deal of what happened the night your husband was killed. First I would like to ask you one or two last questions." He ignored the look of astonishment on her face, and Monk shifting from one foot to the other behind him. "Did Mr. Duff express to you, or in any way show, anxiety as to what Mr. Rhys was doing during the evenings he was away from home or the company he was keeping?"

"Yes . . . you know he did. I told you so myself."

"Did he indicate, either in words or by his behavior, that he had learned anything recently which troubled him additionally?"

"No. At least, he said nothing to me. Why?" Her tone was getting sharper. "Will you please be plain with me, Mr. Evan? Have you discovered what my husband was doing in St. Giles, or not? I told you when you first came here that I believed he had followed Rhys to try to reason with him about the type of young woman he was associating with. Are you telling me that is true?" She lifted her chin a little, almost as if challenging him. "That hardly warrants your coming here, with Mr. Monk, at this hour."

262

"We also believe we know how he met his death, Mrs. Duff, and we must act accordingly," Evan replied. He had not intended to be cruel, but he realized that by stretching out what he had to say, he was doing so. A swift blow was better in the end. "We have witnesses who saw Rhys several times in St. Giles, sometimes with others, sometimes alone. One young woman places him there that evening—"

"Obviously he was there that evening, Mr. Evan," Sylvestra cut in. "What you are telling me we already know. It is obvious."

Monk could bear it no longer. He stepped forward into the circle of candlelight from the shadows, his face grim.

"I have been investigating a series of violent rapes, Mrs. Duff. They were committed by three men together. They raped women, sometimes as young as twelve or thirteen years old, then beat them, breaking their bones, kicking them . . . sometimes into insensibility."

Her face registered her horror. She stared at him as if he had risen out of the ground, carrying the stench of terror and pain with him.

"The last of the rapes was committed in St. Giles the night your husband was murdered in the same manner," he said very quietly. "It is impossible to escape the evidence he followed Rhys to St. Giles and caught up with him immediately after the crime was committed. It happened less than fifty yards from the spot where his body was found."

She was ashen pale. "What . . . are . . . you . . . saying?" she whispered.

"We have come to arrest Rhys Duff for the murder of his father, Leighton Duff," Monk answered her. "There is no choice."

"You cannot take him away." It was Hester. Neither of them had heard her come in behind them. "He is too ill to be moved. If you doubt my word, Dr. Wade will attest to it. I have sent a message for him to come immediately." She glanced at Sylvestra. "I thought his presence might be necessary."

"Oh, thank God!" Sylvestra swayed for a moment but regained her composure. "This . . . this is . . . absurd.

Rhys would . . . not . . ." She looked from Evan to Hester. "Could . . . he?"

"I don't know," Hester said gravely, coming right into the room. "But whatever the truth of it is, he cannot be taken away from here tonight, or within the near future. He may be charged, but he is not yet proven guilty of anything. To move him from proper medical care might jeopardize his life, and that cannot be permitted."

"I am aware of his state of health," Evan responded. "If Dr. Wade says he cannot be moved, then I shall leave a constable on duty outside." He turned to Sylvestra. "He will not intrude upon you unless you give him cause to believe you plan to move Mr. Duff yourself. If that should happen, he will naturally arrest him immediately and place him in prison."

Sylvestra was speechless.

"That will not happen." Hester spoke for her. "He will remain here, in Dr. Wade's care . . . and mine."

Sylvestra nodded her assent.

"I will go up to inform him of his situation," Evan said, turning towards the door.

Hester stood in front of him. For a moment he was afraid she was going to try to bar his way physically, but after an instant's hesitation she went to the door ahead of him.

"I shall come with you. He may need some . . . help. I . . ." She met his eyes with both challenge and pleading. "I intend to be there, Sergeant Evan. What you say will cause him great distress, and he is still very weak."

"Of course," he agreed. "I am not trying to cause him harm."

She turned and led the way across the hall. It seemed Monk intended to remain with Sylvestra. Perhaps he thought he could elicit some information from her where Evan had failed. He might be right.

Hester went up the stairs and across the landing, opening the door to Rhys's room, then, as soon as she was inside, standing away so Evan could face the bed.

Rhys was lying on his back, his broken hands on the covers. He was simply staring at the ceiling. He was propped up on

264

sufficient pillows to be able to meet Evan's eyes without discomfort. He looked surprised to see the policeman, but the blue bruising was gone and the swelling had entirely disappeared. He was a handsome young man in an unconventional way: nose a little too long, mouth too sensitive, dark eyes dominating his white face.

Evan was reminded sickeningly of when he had found him. He felt responsible. He had been part of willing him to live, bringing him back from the brink of darkness and into this white light of pain. He should have been able to protect him somehow. It was his duty to find a better answer than this.

"Mr. Duff," he began with a dry mouth. He swallowed and felt worse. "We have traced your movements on the night your father was killed, and on at least three other nights before that. You regularly went to St. Giles, and there used the services of a prostitute—in fact, several prostitutes . . ."

Rhys stared at him. A faint flush colored his cheeks. It embarrassed him that that sort of thing should be mentioned in front of Hester; it was plain in his eyes, in the way he glanced at her and away again.

"On the night in question, a woman was raped and beaten—" Evan stopped. Rhys had gone ashen, almost gray-faced, and his eyes were filled with such horror Evan was afraid he was suffering some kind of seizure.

Hester moved towards him, then stopped.

The room seemed to roar with the silence. The lights flickered. A coal fell in the fire.

"Rhys Duff . . . I am arresting you for the murder of Leighton Duff on the night of January 7, 1860, in Water Lane, St. Giles." It would be a cruel brutality to warn him that anything he said might be used in evidence at his trial. He could say nothing, no defense, no explanation, no denial.

Hester swung in front of Evan and sat on the bed between them, taking Rhys's hands in her own and turning him to look at her.

"Did you do it, Rhys?" she demanded, pulling his arms, hurting him to break the spell.

He looked at her. He made a choking sound in his throat almost like a laugh, the tears spilled over his cheeks and he shook his head, a little at first, then more and more violently till he was thrashing from side to side, still making the desperate, tearing sounds in his throat.

Hester stood up and faced Evan.

"All right, Sergeant, you have fulfilled your duty. Mr. Duff has heard your charge, and he has told you he is not guilty. If you wish to wait for Dr. Wade to confirm that he is too ill to be moved, you may do so downstairs, perhaps in the morning room. Mrs. Duff may also need to be alone . . ."

"It will not be necessary to wait."

Evan swung around to find Corridon Wade behind him looking exhausted, hollow-cheeked but absolutely unflinching.

"Good evening, Dr. Wade."

"Hardly," Wade said dryly. "I have been fearing this would happen, but now that it has, I must inform you officially, in my capacity as Rhys's physician, that he is not well enough to be moved. If you do so you may jeopardize not only his recovery but possibly even his life. And I must remind you that you have made a charge but you have not yet proved it. Before the law he is still an innocent man."

"I know that, Dr. Wade," Evan answered calmly. "I have no intention of forcing the issue. I shall leave a constable on duty outside the house. I came only to inform Mr. Duff of the charge, not to attempt to take him into custody."

Wade relaxed a little. "Good. Good. I'm sorry if I was a little hasty. You must understand it is extremely distressing for me on a personal level, as well as professionally. I have been a friend of the family for many years. I feel their tragedies very keenly."

"I know that," Evan conceded. "I wish my errand were something other."

"I'm sure." Wade nodded, then walked past Evan into the room, glancing at Hester with a look of quick appreciation. "Thank you, Miss Latterly, for your part. I am sure you have been of great strength. I shall remain with Rhys for a while, to make sure the shock of this has not affected him too seriously.

Perhaps you would be good enough to be of what comfort you may to Mrs. Duff. I shall be down very shortly."

"Yes, of course," Hester agreed, and instantly shepherded Evan out of the room and down the stairs.

"I'm sorry, Hester," Evan said, going down behind her. "There really is no alternative. The proof is overwhelming."

"I know," she answered without turning. "William told me." She was stiff, holding herself upright with an effort, as if once she let go she might never find the strength to regain her composure. She crossed the hallway and went into the withdrawing room without knocking.

Inside, Sylvestra was sitting on the sofa near the fire, and Monk was standing in the middle of the carpet. Neither of them had been speaking at that moment.

Sylvestra looked at Hester, her eyes terrified, questioning.

"Dr. Wade is with him," Hester said in answer. "He is distressed, of course, but he is not in any danger. And naturally he will remain here." Her voice dropped. "I asked him if he was guilty, and he shook his head vehemently."

"But . . ." Sylvestra stammered. "But . . ." She looked at Monk, then at Evan, behind Hester.

"That is not helpful, Hester," Monk said sharply.

Sylvestra looked bemused. Her hands moved as if to grasp at something, and closed on air. Her body was rigid and she moved jerkily, increasingly close to hysteria. At this very moment, her need was greater than Rhys's.

Hester went over to her and touched her, taking her arms.

"There is nothing we can do tonight, but in the morning we must plan ahead. The charge has been made. It must be answered, whatever that answer is. Mr. Monk is a private agent of enquiry. There may yet be more to discover, and naturally you will employ the best legal counsel you can. Just now you must keep up your strength. No doubt Dr. Wade will tell his sister, but I will tell Mrs. Kynaston, if you would find that easier."

"I . . . don't know . . ." Sylvestra was shaking violently and her skin was cold where Hester held her.

Evan moved uncomfortably. He should not be witnessing this agony. His task was completed here. This was an intrusion, as it was for Monk. He looked at Hester. She was absorbed in her feelings for Sylvestra. He and Monk barely touched the periphery of her mind.

"Hester . . ." It was Monk who spoke, but hesitantly.

Evan looked at him. Monk's face was filled with pity so profound it stood naked, startling, and it was a moment or two before Evan realized it was for Hester, not the woman who had received such a devastating blow. It was not only pity, there was also in it a burning admiration and a tenderness which betrayed his defenses utterly.

Evan longed for Hester to turn and see it, but she was consumed by her anguish for Sylvestra.

Evan walked towards the door. He was in the hall when he saw Dr. Wade coming down the stairs. The doctor looked haggard, and he still had the trace of a limp remaining from his accident.

"There will be no possibility of your moving him," he said as he neared the bottom. "Whether he will be fit to stand a trial I cannot say."

"We will have to have a medical opinion of more than one man to that," Evan answered him. He looked at Wade's strained expression, the darkness in his eyes and what he thought might even be fear, or the shadow of fear to come.

"Sergeant . . ."

"Yes, Doctor?"

"Have . . ." Wade bit his lip. What he was about to say seemed to hurt him intensely. He struggled with it, hovered on the edge of decision, and finally summoned the strength. "Have you considered the possibility that he is not sane . . . not responsible, as you and I understand the sense?"

So Wade accepted that Rhys was guilty. Was it simply the evidence they had presented? Or did he know something from Rhys himself, some communication, some long knowledge and perception of the boy's nature over the years?

"No man could do what was done to those women, Doctor,

268

and be what you and I understand as sane," Evan replied quickly. "Blame is not for us to decide . . . thank God."

Wade took a deep breath and let it out in a sigh, then nodded his acknowledgment and walked past Evan to the withdrawing room door.

10

AFTER MONK AND EVAN had left, Corriden Wade remained in the withdrawing room, pacing the floor, unable to be still long enough to sit. Sylvestra was motionless, staring into space as if all will and strength within her had died. Hester stood by the fire.

"I'm sorry," Wade said passionately, looking at Sylvestra. "I'm so sorry. I had no conception this would happen . . . it is the most ghastly thing."

Hester stared at him. Had he seen some darkness in Rhys all the time, and feared disaster, but something less than this, less intense, less irretrievable than death? Looking at his face now, cast in deep shadow, his eyes hollow, his cheeks somber with draining emotion and lack of sleep, it would be easy to believe he was seeing the realization of a long-held dread, but something he had been helpless to prevent.

Then another thought occurred to her. Was Corriden Wade the missing link in Evan's chain of evidence? Was it he, perhaps, who had tried to warn Leighton Duff of his son's weakness, his propensity for real vice? Had it been something Wade had said which had made Leighton Duff ultimately piece together all the sharp words, looks, little facts here and there, and realize the terrible truth?

With a shiver of horror she realized she had accepted within herself that Rhys was guilty. She had fought against it so long, and then in a moment had surrendered without even being conscious of it.

Wade stopped pacing and stared down at Sylvestra.

"You must rest, my dear. I shall give you a draft to help you sleep. I am sure Miss Latterly will sit up with Rhys should it be necessary, but I doubt it will. You will need your strength." He turned to Hester. "I am sorry to place so much upon you, but I have no doubt both your courage and your compassion are equal to it."

It was a profound compliment, and gravely given. It was not a time for thanks, only acceptance.

"Of course," she agreed. "Tomorrow we shall begin what is to be done."

He nodded and at last seemed to relax a fraction. Hester believed it prudent to allow him a few moments alone with Sylvestra. His care for her was apparent. Now, of all times, they should be permitted a privacy to reach towards each other through the tragedy which engulfed them.

"I shall go and see how Rhys is now," she said. "Good night." She did not wait for a reply, but turned and went out, closing the door behind her.

Rhys did not call her in the night. Whatever Dr. Wade had given him was sufficient to induce in him not rest but unconsciousness. She had no idea how long he had been awake when she heard the bell fall on the floor.

She rose immediately. It was full daylight. She grasped her shawl and opened the connecting door.

Rhys was lying facing her, his eyes wide and terrified.

She went in and sat on the bed.

"Tell me again, Rhys," she said quietly. "Did you kill your father?"

He shook his head slowly, keeping his eyes on her.

"Not even by accident?" she pressed. "Did you fight with him, not realizing who he was, in the dark?"

He hesitated, then shook his head. His expression was filled with horror, his lips drawn back, his jaw clenched, the muscles of his neck corded with tension inside him.

"Could you see in the alley?" she pressed, the evidence

271

heavy in her mind. "If someone accosted you, attacked you, are you sure you would know who it was?"

He gave a curious little jerk. If he had had the ability to make a sound, it might have been laughter, but bitter, self-hurting. There was some dreadful irony in what he knew, and he could not tell her, even if he would have.

"Could you see?" she asked again.

He stared at her without moving.

There were so many questions. She thought desperately which would be the right one.

"Do you know what happened that night?"

He nodded, still not taking his eyes from hers, although the horror in him was so palpable she could feel coldness creeping through her, and despair so great it consumed and destroyed everything else.

"Rhys . . ." She put her hand on his arm, holding him hard, feeling the muscle and bone beneath her fingers. "I'll help you in any way I can, but I have to know how to. Can you tell me, somehow, what happened? You were there, you saw it. If you want to plead against the charge they are bringing, then you must give them something else to believe."

For seconds he simply gazed back at her, then slowly he closed his eyes and turned away.

"Rhys!"

He shook his head.

She did not know what to think. Whatever had happened, he still could not bear to have anyone know. Even facing arrest, and in time a trial for his life, he would not impart it.

But did he understand that? Did he imagine because Evan had not taken him away that somehow it would not happen?

"Rhys!" she said urgently. "It hasn't gone away, you know. You are under house arrest. It is just the same as being in a public cell or in Newgate. The only reason you are here, not there, is because you are too ill to move. There will be a trial, and if you are found guilty, they will take you to Newgate, no matter how ill you are. They won't care, because they will hang you anyway. . . ." She could not go on. She could not bear it, even though he had not turned back or even opened his eyes.

His body was rigid, tears running under his lids and down his cheeks.

"Rhys," she said softly. "I have to make you realize this is real. You must tell someone the truth to save yourself."

Again he shook his head.

"Did you kill him?" she whispered.

He shook his head again, very little, but quite unmistakably.

"But you know who did?" she persisted.

He turned back very slowly, meeting her eyes. He lay still for seconds. She could hear the sound of distant feet as a maid crossed the landing.

"Do you?" she said again.

He closed his eyes without answering.

She stood up and went out of the room and down the stairs to the withdrawing room, where Sylvestra was moving aimlessly from one idle task to another. A pile of embroidery yarns sat tangled on a small table, linen bunched up near them. A bowl of winter flowers from the hothouse were half arranged, half simply poked into the water. Several letters lay on a salver on the large semicircular table by the wall; two were opened, the others were not.

Sylvestra swung around as soon as she heard the door.

"How is he?" she asked quickly, then bit her lip as though unsure what she wanted the answer to be. "I simply don't know what to do. Leighton was my husband. I owe him . . . everything, not only loyalty but love, respect, decency." Her brow puckered. "How could it have happened? What . . . what changed him? And don't tell me Rhys hasn't changed . . . I've seen the difference in him and it terrifies me!"

She swung away, her hands clenched in front of her. A less controlled woman would have wept or screamed, thrown something just to release the tension inside herself.

"He never used to be like this, Miss Latterly." Her voice was tight in her throat, as if she had difficulty making herself speak. "He was willful at times, thoughtless, like most young people, but there was no cruelty in him. I don't understand it. I thought I was so tired last night I would have slept from exhaustion. I wanted to." She emphasized it fiercely. "I wanted simply to cease to be able to think or feel anything. But I lay awake for hours. I racked my brain trying to understand what had changed him, why he had become so different, when it had begun to happen. I found no answer. It still makes no sense to me." She turned back to Hester, her face bleak and desperate. "Why would anyone want to beat those women? Why rape a woman who is willing anyway? Why would anyone do that? It isn't sane."

"I don't understand either," Hester said candidly. "But obviously it is not appetite, but rather more a desire for power over someone else, a need to hurt and humiliate—" She stopped. Sylvestra was looking at her with amazement, as though she had said something new and almost inconceivable.

"Haven't you ever wanted to punish, not for justice but for anger?" Hester asked her.

"I . . . I suppose so," Sylvestra said slowly. "But that is hardly . . . yes, I suppose I have." She stared at Hester curiously. "Are you saying it is the same thing, hideously magnified?"

"I don't know. I am only trying to imagine."

The fire settled with a shower of sparks.

"You mean it is not appetite . . . but . . . hate?" Sylvestra asked, struggling to understand.

"Perhaps."

"But why would Rhys hate such women? He doesn't even know them."

"Maybe it doesn't matter who it is. Anyone will do, the weaker, the more vulnerable, the better . . ."

"Stop it!" Sylvestra took a shuddering breath. "I'm sorry. It is not your fault. I asked you, and now I do not want to hear the answer." Her hands were twisting around one another. She had scratched herself with her nails but she seemed unaware of it. "Poor Leighton. He must have suspected there was something terribly wrong for ages, and at last he had to put it to the test. And when he followed him, and he knew . . ." She could not finish. They stood there in the quiet, dignified room, two women imagining the same terrible scene in the alley, father and son face-to-face over a horror which had to divide them forever. And then the son had attacked, perhaps out of rage, or

274

guilt, perhaps out of some kind of fear that he would be caught by the law, and he imagined he could escape the consequences if he fought his way out. And they had beaten and punched and kicked at each other until Leighton was dead and Rhys was so badly hurt he lost consciousness and lay there on the stones, soaked with his own blood.

And now it was so terrible to him he could not accept that it was he who had done it. It had been another person, another self, one he did not own.

"We must find a barrister for him," Hester said aloud. "He must have some defense when he comes to trial. Do you have someone you wish?"

"A barrister?" Sylvestra blinked. "Will they really try him? He is too ill. He must be mad, won't they realize that? Corriden will tell them—"

"He is not too mad to stand trial," Hester said with absolute certainty. "Whether insanity will be the best defense or not, I cannot say, but you must find a barrister. Do you have someone?"

Sylvestra seemed to find it difficult to concentrate. Her eyes looked without focus. "A barrister? Mr. Caulfield has always dealt with our affairs. Of course, I have never spoken to him. Leighton handled business, naturally."

"Is he a solicitor?" Hester asked, almost sure of the answer. "You need a barrister for this, someone who will appear in court to represent Rhys. He must be engaged through Mr. Caulfield, but if you do not have any preferences, I am acquainted with Sir Oliver Rathbone. He is the best barrister there is."

"I . . . suppose so . . ." Sylvestra was uncertain. Hester was not sure if it was her shock at the turn of events, or if now she doubted whether she wished to engage an unknown barrister, at unknown expense, to defend Rhys when she feared him guilty. Maybe it was simply too big a decision for her to make alone. She was not used to decision. She had always had her husband to see to such things. He would find and assess the information. His word would be final. She would probably not even be expected to contribute an opinion.

It was up to Hester to see that Rhys was defended. Possibly no one else would.

"I'll speak to Sir Oliver and ask him to come to see you." She chose not to make it a question, so Sylvestra could not so easily refuse. She smiled encouragingly. "Will it be reasonable if I go first thing in the morning?"

Sylvestra drew in her breath, but could not make up her mind.

"Thank you," Hester accepted, her voice gentle, full of an assurance she was far from feeling.

Hester was in Rathbone's office at nine o'clock. She waited until his first client had been and gone, then she was ushered into his office, the clerk advised that the next client should be handsomely entertained and informed that Sir Oliver was regrettably kept by an emergency, which was at least half true.

She did not waste his time with preamble. She was sufficiently conscious of the fact that he had seen her without an appointment, and she was presuming on his regard for her to ask a favor. She hated doing it, the more so since their last encounter, and her belief as to his feelings towards her. Had Rhys's life not depended upon it, she would not have come. Sylvestra's solicitor could have briefed whomever he wished.

"They have arrested Rhys for the murder of his father," she said bluntly. "They have not removed him, of course, because he is too ill, but they will bring him to trial. His mother is at her wits' end, and not in a position or a state of mind to find for him the best barrister for his defense." She stopped, acutely aware of his dark eyes on her and his expression of concern leaping ahead of what she had already told him.

"I think you had better sit down and tell me the facts of the case, so far as you know them." He indicated the chair opposite his desk and moved around to sit at the one behind it. He did not yet reach for the quill to make notes.

She tried to compose her mind so that she could tell him sensibly, in order so that it was comprehensible, and without over-weighing it with emotion.

"Rhys Duff and his father, Leighton Duff, were found in

276

Water Lane, an alley in the area of St. Giles," she started to explain. "Leighton Duff was beaten to death. Rhys was severely injured, in a similar manner, but he survived, although he is unable to speak and both his hands are badly broken, so neither can he hold a pen. That is important, because it means he cannot communicate, except by a nod or a shake of his head."

"That is an added complication," he agreed gravely. "I have read something of the case. It is impossible to pick up a newspaper and not at least be aware of it. What evidence is there that leads the police to presume that Rhys killed his father, rather than the more natural assumption that both of them were attacked, and possibly robbed, by thieves or general ruffians of the area? Do you know?"

"Yes. Monk has found evidence which ties them to the rape cases in Seven Dials—"

"Just a minute," he interrupted, holding up his hand. "You said 'them.' Who are we talking about? And what rape cases in Seven Dials? Is he charged with rape as well?"

She was not being as clear as she had intended after all. She had seen the fractional change in his face when she had mentioned Monk's name, and she felt guilty. What had he seen in her eyes?

She must speak intelligently, in an orderly fashion. She started again.

"Monk was engaged by a woman from Seven Dials to discover who had been first cheating, then, with increasing violence, raping and beating factory women, amateur prostitutes in Seven Dials—" She stopped.

He was frowning. Did he disapprove of Monk or of the women, or did he fear it made Rhys's case even worse?

"What is it?" The words were out before she intended.

"Rape is a very ugly crime," he said quietly. "But it is one, the courts will not pursue . . . for a dozen different reasons, both social . . ." He wrinkled his nose very slightly in a wealth of distaste, subtle and deep. "And legal impossibilities also," he added. "Rape is a difficult crime to prove. Why did Monk

277

pursue it? Whatever else he has forgotten, he must be aware of these things."

"I argued it with him," she said with a very slight smile. "It is not what you fear." She hoped as she was saying it that it was the truth, not merely her wish. "He intended only to expose them to their own society, not to provoke the people of St. Giles to take their revenge."

Rathbone's lips curled in a faint, ironic humor. "That sounds like Monk. A nice irony, using society's hypocrisy to make it punish its own for the very crime it pretends does not exist and will not strengthen the law to judge." He kept his eyes on her face. "But what has this to do with Rhys Duff and the death of his father?"

"For some time Rhys had been keeping company with women of whom his father did not approve, and to the exclusion of suitable young ladies," she explained. "At least that is what his mother believed." She was twisting her hands in her lap without realizing it. "Perhaps, in fact, he had some idea of what Rhys was really doing. Anyway, on that particular evening they quarreled, Rhys left the room, and apparently the house. Leighton Duff left about half an hour afterwards, when he realized that Rhys had gone, and perhaps suspected to where." She looked at him to make sure he was following her explanation.

"Proceed," he directed. "It is all perfectly clear so far."

"One woman was raped and beaten in St. Giles that night," she went on. "Within a few yards of Water Lane. A short time after that, the bodies of Rhys and his father were found in Water Lane itself. Rhys was insensible, and has not spoken since. Leighton Duff was dead."

"And the assumption," he concluded, "is that Leighton Duff caught up with Rhys and his friends while it was still apparent they were the rapists of the woman . . . either they were in the act or they had just completed it. He was furious, endeavored to reason with them or apprehend them, and one, or all of them, attacked him. He drove off the other two quite quickly, but Rhys, knowing he would not escape the matter, fought until he had killed him."

"Yes . . . more or less." It was a terrible admission, and she could not make it easily. Her voice sounded tight and brittle.

"I see." He sat silently for several moments, deep in thought, and she did not interrupt him. He looked up. "Have they anything to link Rhys or his companions—Who are they, do you know?"

"Yes, Arthur and Marmaduke Kynaston. They answer the descriptions given, and one girl, who actually named Rhys, named them also—Arthur and Duke. Marmaduke is known as Duke."

"I see." He nodded very slightly. "Were they injured at the time Rhys was, do you know?"

"Yes, I do know, and no, they do not appear to have been." She realized what he was thinking. "But that only makes them cowards as well."

"I am afraid so. But can anyone place any of the three in Seven Dials or connect them to the earlier rapes?"

"Not so far as I know."

"And is there evidence to prove these rapes are not random, committed by several people? There must be many rapes in London in a week."

"I don't think many are carried out by three men together, answering the descriptions of one tall and slight, one average and one slender, and all three gentlemen, arriving and leaving by hansom," she said bleakly.

He sighed. "You sound as if you believe him guilty, Hester. Do you?"

She did not want to answer. Now that the question was put so bluntly, and she faced Rathbone's clever, subtle gaze, which would not permit evasion and in front of which she could not lie, she must make a decision.

He waited.

"He says he didn't," she answered very slowly, choosing her words. "I am not sure what he remembers. It frightens him, horrifies him. I think maybe when he says that, he is saying what he wishes were true. Perhaps he does not entirely know."

"But you think physically, for whatever reason, he committed the act," he said.

"Yes . . . yes, I think so. I can't avoid it."

"Then what is it you wish me to do?"

"Help him . . . I . . ." Now she realized how much she was being emotional rather than rational, not only regarding Rhys but in her plea to Rathbone as well. Still, she could not turn aside from doing it, even now that she was aware. "Please, Oliver? I don't know how it happened, or why he should have let himself fall into such a desperate situation. I . . . I can't argue anything in mitigation for him . . . I don't know what there is, I just have to believe there is something." She looked at his face with its humor and intelligence, sometimes so cool—and just now, gazing back at her, so gentle.

She forced herself to think of Rhys, his terror, his helplessness.

"Maybe it is not justice I'm asking for, but mercy? He needs someone to speak for him . . ." She gave a painful little laugh. "Even literally. I don't believe he's purely evil. I've spent too many hours with him, close to him. I've watched his pain. If he did these things, there must be some reason, at least some cause . . . I mean . . ."

"You mean insanity," he finished for her.

"No, I don't . . ."

"Yes, you do, my dear." His voice was very patient, trying not to hurt her more than he had to. "A young man doesn't rape and beat women he doesn't know, then murder his father because he found out, if he is anything that ordinary men and women would recognize as sane. Whether the law will make the same nature of distinction I don't know. I very much doubt it." His eyes were filled with sadness. "It is precise as to what insanity is, and the fact that Rhys attacked his father suggests he knew very well that his violence against the women was wrong, which is what the law will view. He knew what he was doing, and that is the crucial factor."

"But there must be something else," she said desperately. "I can't let it go at that. I've watched him too long . . ."

He rose to his feet and came around the desk towards her. "Then let me make arrangements to come and see him for myself—that is, if Mrs. Duff wishes me to represent him . . ."

"He's not underage!" she said hotly, rising also. "It is if he wants you to!"

He smiled with dry, rueful amusement. "My dear Hester, if he cannot speak or write, and has no occupation of his own, he will not only have very little power to defend himself, he will have no financial means."

"His father is—was—wealthy. He will have been left provided for," she protested.

"Not if he killed his father, Hester. You know that as well as I do. If he is convicted of the crime, he cannot inherit."

She was furious. "You mean he cannot have a defense because if he is found guilty he will not be able to pay? That is monstrous." She was so angry she almost choked on the words. "It's . . ."

He put both hands on her shoulders, holding her so firmly she was obliged to face him.

"I did not say that, Hester. I think you know me better than to imagine I work only for money. . . ."

She swallowed. She had cause to be ashamed. She had come to plead with him to take on an impossible case because she believed he would.

"I am sorry."

"But I do work within the law," he finished. "In the circumstances, I shall have to speak first to his mother." His lips twisted with genuine humor. "Although I imagine that with you in the house, and doubtless in charge, I shall find her cooperative."

She blushed. "Thank you, Oliver."

He said nothing, but made a little sound of acquiescence.

It was mid-evening before Rathbone arrived at Ebury Street. Hester had informed Sylvestra of his willingness at least to consider the case, and Sylvestra had been too confused and unhappy to argue. She had consulted her own solicitor, a mild man skilled in the matters of property, inheritance and finance, and totally out of his depth where the criminal law was concerned. He was willing to engage anyone recommended to him who was willing to undertake such an unpromising cause.

"Sir Oliver Rathbone," the butler announced, and Rathbone came into the withdrawing room almost on his heels. He was as elegant as always, with the ease of someone who knows his own power and feels no need to impress.

"How do you do, Mrs. Duff," he said with a very slight smile. "Miss Latterly."

"How do you do, Sir Oliver," Sylvestra replied with a commendable calm she could not have felt. "It is good of you to have come. I am not sure what you can do for my son. Miss Latterly speaks most highly of you, but I fear our situation may be beyond any help. Please do sit down." She indicated the chair opposite and he accepted.

Hester sat on the sofa, a little removed from them, but where she could watch both their faces.

"One does not always know what a defense will be until one begins, Mrs. Duff," Rathbone replied calmly. "May I assume that you wish your son to have any assistance that is possible, in his present tragic circumstances?" He looked at her patiently, gently, as if his words had been a simple question and without pressure.

"Yes . . ." she said slowly. "Yes, of course. I . . ." Her face was composed, but it was plain from the shadows under her eyes and the fine lines of stress around her lips that the effort cost her very dearly. It would be inconceivable that it should not.

Rathbone smiled immediately. "Of course, you cannot yet see what can be done. I admit, neither can I, but that is not unusual. Whatever the truth of the matter may prove to be, we must see that, as much as possible, both justice and mercy are served. That cannot be unless Mr. Duff is represented by someone who will fight as hard for him as if he believed him valuable, capable of hope and of pain, and deserving every opportunity to explain himself."

Sylvestra frowned. "You are already a brilliant advocate for him, Sir Oliver. I could not possibly disagree with anything you have said. No one could." She sat without moving, a touch of immobility in spite of the emotion which must be tearing inside her. It was an extraordinary self-discipline, learned over the years, to have the strength to apply now. "What confuses me is why you should wish to represent my son," she continued. "And it is obvious from your presence here, let alone your words, that you do. I know better than to imagine you are some young man seeking to make a career and a name for himself . . . not that you would choose this case if you were. Nor are you so hungry for business that you would pursue any case at all. Why my son, Sir Oliver?"

Rathbone smiled, and there was a very faint touch of color in his cheeks.

"For Miss Latterly's sake, Mrs. Duff. She feels very strongly for Rhys's plight, regardless of whether he should prove guilty of this or not. She persuaded me that he needs the best defense he can obtain. With your agreement, I shall do all in my power to see that he has it."

Hester felt the blood burn up her own face and she looked away, avoiding Rathbone's eyes, in case he should glance in her direction. She had used his feeling for her, perhaps even misled him, because she was uncertain of her own emotions. She was guilty, but she did not regret it. She would do the same again. If she did not fight for Rhys, there was no one else who could.

Sylvestra relaxed at last, the rigidity easing out of her shoulders.

"Thank you, Sir Oliver, both for your honesty and for your compassion for my son. I fear there will be few others, if any at all, who will feel the same for him. He . . . he will be regarded . . . I think . . . as a monster." She stopped abruptly, unable to go on. The words were too hard, too painfully true, and it was a future which loomed within days, not weeks. It would be the pattern of life from then on. The world would be changed forever.

Hester wanted to argue, just to offer any comfort at all, but it would be a lie, and they all knew it. Anything she said would only belittle the truth and imply that she did not understand.

Rathbone rose to his feet. "It will be my task to see that everything that can be said for him is put as eloquently as possible, Mrs. Duff. Now, I would like to speak to Rhys myself. Perhaps you would allow Miss Latterly to take me upstairs."

Sylvestra rose also, taking a step forward.

Rathbone held up his hand in a very slight gesture.

"If you please, Mrs. Duff, I require to see him in effect alone. What passes between a barrister and his client is privileged and must be confidential. Miss Latterly will be party to it only in her capacity as his nurse, in case he should become distressed and need her. She will be bound by the same absolute rules."

Sylvestra looked taken aback.

"It is necessary," he assured her. "Otherwise I cannot proceed."

Reluctantly she fell back, her face still filled with uncertainty, her eyes moving from Rathbone to Hester.

"I shall see he is not distressed more than is absolutely necessary in order to learn what we must," Hester promised.

"Do you really think . . ." Sylvestra began, then faltered. She was afraid. It was stark in her eyes; she was afraid of the truth. She hesitated on the brink of telling Rathbone not to seek it. She turned to Hester.

Hester smiled at her, pretending she did not understand, and walked to the door.

She led Rathbone upstairs and after a knock on Rhys's door, merely as a courtesy, she led him in.

"Rhys, this is Sir Oliver Rathbone. He is going to speak for you in court."

Rhys stared at her, then at Rathbone. He was lying on his back, propped up on pillows as she had left him, his splinted hands on the covers in front of him. He looked frightened and stiff.

"How do you do," Rathbone said with a smile and an inclination of his head, as if Rhys had replied quite normally. "May I sit down?"

Rhys nodded, then looked at Hester.

"Would you prefer me to leave?" she asked. "I can go next door and you can knock the bell off if you need me."

He shook his head immediately and she could sense his

anxiety, his loneliness, his feeling almost of drowning under the weight of confusion inside him. She retreated to the corner of the room and sat down.

"You must be honest with me," Rathbone began quietly. "Everything you tell me will remain in confidence, if you wish it. I am bound by law not to act other than in your interests, as long as I remain honest myself. I cannot lie, but I can and will keep anything secret, if that is what you wish."

Rhys nodded.

"The same applies to Miss Latterly. That is her bond as well as mine."

Rhys stared at him.

"Do you know what happened the night your father was killed?"

Rhys winced and seemed to shrink within himself, but he did not move his eyes from Rathbone's face, and he nodded slowly.

"Good. I know you can indicate only yes or no. I shall ask you questions and if you can answer them so, then do. If you cannot, then wait, and I shall reword them." He hesitated only a moment. "Did you go with your friends, Arthur and Duke Kynaston, to the area of St. Giles, and when there use the services of prostitutes?"

Rhys bit his lip, and then nodded, a dull flush of pink in his cheeks. His eyes remained steady on Rathbone's face.

"Did you at any time injure any of these women, or fight with them, even accidentally?"

Rhys shook his head violently.

"Did either Arthur or Duke Kynaston do so?"

Rhys remained still.

"Do you know if they did or not?"

Rhys shook his head.

"Did you also go with them to Seven Dials?"

Rhys nodded very slowly, uncertainly.

"You want to add something?" Rathbone asked. "Did you go often?"

Rhys shook his head.

"Only a few times?"

He nodded.

"Did you injure any women there?"

Again Rhys shook his head, sharply, his eyes angry.

"Did your father go with you?"

Rhys's eyes widened in amazement.

"No," Rathbone answered his own question. "But he knew you went, and he did not approve?"

Rhys nodded, a bitter smile twisting his mouth. There was rage in it and hurt and a blazing frustration. He tried to speak, his throat muscles knotting, his head jerking forward.

Hester started up from her chair, then realized she must not interrupt. She might protect him for the moment—and damage him for all the future. Rathbone must learn all he could, however painful.

"Did you quarrel about it?" Rathbone continued.

Rhys nodded slowly.

"Here at home?"

He nodded.

"And when you went to St. Giles the night of his death?"

Again the sharp, violent movement of denial and the jolt forward as if he would laugh, had he the power.

"Did you quarrel about something else?"

Rhys's eyes filled with tears and he banged his broken hands up and down on the bedclothes, his body locked in an inner pain far worse than the sickening jolting of the bones.

Rathbone turned to Hester, his face white.

She moved forward.

"Rhys!" she said sharply. She sat down on the bed and took hold of his wrists, trying to force him to be still, but his muscles were clenched so hard she could not. He was stronger than she had expected, and his whole body was caught in the emotion. "Rhys!" she said again, more urgently. "Stop it! You'll move the bones again. I know you think you don't care, but you do. Please . . ."

He unclenched his muscles slowly, and the tears spilled over his cheeks. He stared at her, then turned away, and she saw only the back of his head.

"Rhys," she said firmly. "Did you kill your father?"

There was a long silence. Neither Hester nor Rathbone moved. Then slowly he turned back to her and shook his head, his eyes intent on her face.

"But you know who did?" she pressed.

This time he refused to answer even by a look.

She turned to Rathbone.

"All right, for now," he conceded, standing up. "I will consider what to do. Try to rest and recover as much as you can. You will need your strength when the time comes. I will do everything I can to help you, that I promise."

Rhys looked at him without blinking and Rathbone looked back for a long moment, then with a slight smile, not of hope but only of a kind of warmth, he turned and left the room.

Outside on the landing, he waited until Hester joined him and closed the door.

"Thank you," she said simply.

"I may have been a little rash," he acknowledged with a tiny shrug, his voice so low she could only just hear him.

Her heart sank. For a moment she had allowed herself to hope. She realized just how much she trusted him, how deep her confidence ran that he could accomplish even the impossible. She had not been fair to lay such a burden on him. She had seen people do it to doctors, and then they had struggled under the weight of impossible hope, and then the despair which followed, and the guilt. Now she had done the same thing to Rathbone because she wanted it so much for Rhys.

"I am sorry," she said humbly. "I know there may not be anything to be done."

"There'll be something," he replied with a tiny frown between his brows, as if he were puzzled. "I am confused by him. I went in persuaded by circumstance and evidence of his guilt. Now that I have spoken to him, I don't know what to think. I am not even sure what other possibilities there are. Why will he not answer as to who killed his father, if it was not him? Why will he not say what they quarreled over? You saw his face when I asked."

She had no suggestions to give. She had lain awake and

racked her brains night after night searching for the same answers herself.

"The only thing I can imagine is that he is defending someone," she said quietly. "And the only people he would defend are his family or close friends. I cannot see Arthur Kynaston doing this, and Rhys's only family here is his mother."

"What do you know of his mother?" he asked, glancing towards the hall below them as he heard footsteps crossing it and fading away in the direction of the baize door through to the servants' quarters. "Is it conceivable she has done something and that Rhys is willing to suffer even this to protect her?"

She hesitated. At first she had thought to deny even the possibility. She could recall far too vividly Rhys's anger with Sylvestra, the joy he had taken in hurting her. Of course, he could not be protecting her. Then she realized that neither love nor guilt were always so clear. It was possible he loved and hated her at the same time, that he knew something which he would never betray, but that he still despised her for it.

"I don't know," she said aloud. "The more I think of it, the less sure I am. But I have no idea what."

He was looking at her closely. "Haven't you?"

"No. Of course not. If I knew I would tell you."

He nodded. "Then if we are to help Rhys, we are going to have to know more than we do now. Since he cannot tell us, and I imagine Mrs. Duff either cannot or will not, we shall have to employ some other means." A flicker of amusement touched his lips. "I know of none better than Monk, if he will consent to it and Mrs. Duff is prepared to agree."

"Surely she cannot refuse?" Hester said, fearing as she spoke that Sylvestra might very well. "I mean . . . unless . . . without suggesting she fears there is something even worse to conceal?"

"I shall frame it so she will find it extremely difficult to refuse," he promised. "I should also like to speak with Arthur and Duke Kynaston. What can you tell me about them?"

"I find it hard to believe Arthur is the chief protagonist in this," she said sincerely. "He has honesty in him, an openness I could not but like. His elder brother Marmaduke is a different matter." She bit her lip. "I should find it far easier to imagine he reacted with violence if challenged or criticized, and certainly if he felt himself in any danger. His words are quick enough to attempt to hurt." Honesty compelled her to go on. "But he has been here to visit Rhys, and he certainly was not involved in a fight of anything like the proportions that killed Leighton Duff and left Rhys like this. I wish I could say that he was."

Rathbone smiled. "I can see that, my dear, and hear it in your voice. Nevertheless, I shall visit them. I must begin somewhere, apart from engaging Monk. Perhaps we had better go and set Mrs. Duff's mind at ease that at least we shall begin and give the battle all we have."

Rathbone did as he had said, and asked Sylvestra's permission to employ someone to learn more of the events with the view to helping Rhys, not simply to find material proof, as the police had done. He phrased his request in such a way she could scarcely refuse him without appearing to wish to abandon Rhys—and to have something of her own to conceal. He also asked her for the address of the Kynaston family, and she explained that Joel Kynaston had known Rhys since childhood and she was certain he would offer any assistance within his power.

After Rathbone had left she turned to Hester, her face pale and tense.

"Is there really anything he can do, Miss Latterly? Or are we simply fighting a battle we must lose, because to do less would be cowardly and a betrayal of courage and the sense of honor we admire? Please answer me honestly. I would rather have truth now. The time for reassuring lies, however well meant, is past. I need to know the truth in order to make the decisions I must."

"I don't know," Hester said honestly. "We can none of us know until the case is heard and concluded. I have seen several trials, many of which have ended far from the way we had expected and believed. Never give up until there is nothing else left to try and it is all over. We are very far from that point now. Believe me, if anyone can mitigate even the worst circumstances, it is Sir Oliver."

Sylvestra's face softened in a smile, sadness touching her eyes.

"You are very fond of him, aren't you." It was barely a question.

Hester felt the heat in her face.

"Yes . . . yes, I have a high regard for him." The words sounded stilted and absurd, so very halfhearted, and Rathbone deserved better than that. But the shadow of Monk was too sharp in her mind to allow Sylvestra to misunderstand, as she seemed willing to do. It was not difficult to comprehend. Love was one sweet and gentle thing, one thing which led on into the future in a world which for Sylvestra was full of darkness and violence and the ending of all the peace and hope she knew.

"I . . ." Hester started again. "I do have a great . . . regard for him."

Sylvestra was too sensitive to probe any further, and Hester excused herself, saying she must go up and see how Rhys was.

She found him lying exactly as she had left him, staring up at the ceiling, eyes wide open. She sat down on the bed.

"We won't give up," she said quietly.

He looked at her, searching her face, then suddenly anger twisted his features and he swung his head away.

She thought of getting up and leaving. Perhaps he would rather be alone. Then she looked at him more closely and saw the despair beneath the anger, and she could not leave. She simply sat and waited, silent and helpless. At least he knew she cared enough to remain.

It was the middle of the evening when Rathbone returned. He was shown into the dining room, where Hester and Sylvestra were picking at dinner, pushing it around the plate in an attempt to eat sufficient not to offend the cook.

Rathbone came in looking grave, and immediately both of them stopped.

"Good evening, Sir Oliver," Sylvestra said huskily. "Have

you . . . learned something? May I offer you something to eat? If you would like to dine . . . I . . ." Her voice trailed off and she stared up at him, too frightened of what he was going to say to continue.

He sat down but declined to eat. "No, I have not learned anything new, Mrs. Duff. I have been to speak to Mr. Kynaston, in the hope that he might shed some light on what has happened. He has known your family for twenty-five years, I believe. I also intend to meet his sons, who were with Rhys in St. Giles. I wanted to form some opinion as to whether we should call them to testify. I imagine the prosecution may do that anyway."

Sylvestra swallowed and seemed almost to choke.

"You speak in the past, Sir Oliver, as if it were no longer true. Do you mean that Joel Kynaston is so . . . so repelled by what Rhys has done, that he will not . . . that what he says will . . . will hurt Rhys?"

"It is not favorable, Mrs. Duff," Rathbone said unhappily. "I tell you because I wonder if there is some reason you are aware of why Mr. Kynaston may have such a view. He expressed the opinion that Rhys has been a poor influence upon his sons, especially the elder, Marmaduke, whom he feels has led a more"—he hesitated, searching for the right word—"libertine life than he would have done without Rhys's example and encouragement."

Hester was amazed. The arrogance in Duke Kynaston had been so apparent, as had the natural assumption of leadership, that it was inconceivable to her that Rhys had influenced him and not the other way around. But then she had not known Rhys before the incident. She hardly knew Duke at present. All she had seen of him was a young man's swagger and bravado, and a considerable rudeness to one he felt his social and intellectual inferior.

She looked at Sylvestra to try to judge the surprise in her face.

"Joel Kynaston is a very strict man," Sylvestra said thoughtfully, staring not at Rathbone but down at her plate. "He believes in great self-discipline, especially among the young. It

291

is the foundation of strong character. It is what courage and honor are built upon, and without it all else may fail, eventually." Her voice was careful, full of long-held, familiar conviction. "I have heard him say so many times. He is much admired for it. It may appear like hardness to others, but in his position, if he were to make exceptions, be seen to be lenient towards one, it would invalidate the principles for which he stands." Her face was intent, but there was a slight frown between her brows, as if she were concentrating on what she was saying and it flowed from memory rather than understanding.

"And he felt Rhys set a poor example?" Rathbone said gently. "Was he not a good student?"

Sylvestra looked surprised. "Yes, he was excellent. But it was not only in academic studies Joel felt passionately—above all, it was moral worth. His school has a very high reputation, and it is largely due to his own example." She looked down at her hands. "Sometimes I think he expected too much of boys, forgetting they cannot have the strength of character one would hope of men. He did not understand the need of youth to discover boundaries for itself. Rhys was . . . an explorer . . . of thought, I mean. At least . . ." She gave up suddenly, her lip trembling. "I am not sure what I do mean." She swallowed and regained control with an intense effort. "I am sorry. I know my husband had a deep respect for Joel Kynaston. He believed him a most remarkable man." She hurried on, as if she feared interruption. "I should not be surprised that Joel feels his death profoundly and cannot forgive anyone who was involved in causing it. I am sorry, Sir Oliver, but you will have to look elsewhere for anyone to help us."

Before Rathbone could answer her, the door opened and Corriden Wade came in. He looked deeply concerned, his face was gaunt as if he had slept little, and there was a tension in him which was apparent even before he spoke. He looked at Rathbone with surprise and some anxiety.

Sylvestra stood up immediately and went over to Wade, relief and expectation in her eyes.

"Corriden, this is Sir Oliver Rathbone, whom I have engaged to defend Rhys. We are searching for anything whatever which may help. He has spoken to Joel, but it seems Joel feels Rhys was an unfortunate influence upon Arthur and Duke, and being the man he is, he cannot speak anything but the truth. I suppose I should admire him for that, and if it were of anyone else, I should be the first to applaud him." She bit her lip. "Which proves what a hypocrite I am, because I cannot. I wish desperately that he could bend a little, I suppose be less honorable. Isn't that a dreadful thing to say? I never thought I would hear myself say such a thing. You will be ashamed of me."

Wade put his arm around her.

"Never, my dear. It is only human to wish to protect those one loves, especially when there is no one else to do so. You are his mother. I should expect no less of you." He glanced at Rathbone, looking past Sylvestra. "How do you do, sir. I am Corriden Wade, physician to the family, and at present Rhys is in my care for his physical needs." He nodded towards Hester. "And Miss Latterly's care, of course. She has done excellently well for him."

Rathbone had risen when Sylvestra did; now he came forward and bowed in acknowledgment of Wade's introduction.

"How do you do, Dr. Wade. I am very pleased you have come. We shall need your medical assistance when the time comes. I believe you have known Rhys a long time?"

"Since he was a small child," Wade answered. He looked worried, as if he feared what Rathbone might ask him. "I wish, more intensely than you can know, that I could offer some testimony which would mitigate this appalling tragedy, but I have been unable to think of any." He still had his arm resting lightly on Sylvestra's. "What will be your defense, Sir Oliver?"

"I do not yet know sufficient to say," Rathbone replied smoothly. If he was as frightened as Hester felt, he hid it superbly. She thought he probably was. There was a stiffness to the way he stood, a hesitation in his voice which she had seen before, at the worst times in past cases, when it seemed there was no escape from disaster, no solution but tragedy and failure.

"What more is there to learn?" Wade asked. "Mrs. Duff has

told me what the police believe: that Rhys had been keeping company with women of the street, the lowest element in our society, spreaders of disease and depravity; that he had exercised a certain amount of violence in these relationships; and that Leighton had come to suspect as much. When he followed him and taxed him with his behavior, they fought. Rhys was injured, as you know, and Leighton, perhaps being an older man, taken by surprise, was killed. Is it any defense to suggest the fight was not intended to go so far and that death was accidental?" He looked doubtful even as he said it.

"If two men fight and one of them dies, unless it can be demonstrated that it was accidental," Rathbone replied, "it will be proved to be murder. For it to be manslaughter, we should have to show that Leighton Duff tripped over by mischance, or fell on some weapon he was carrying himself, or something of that nature. I am afraid that was very clearly not so. The injuries were all inflicted by fist or boot. Such things are not accidental."

Wade nodded. "That is what I had feared. Sir Oliver, do you think we might continue this discussion in private. It can only be most distressing for Mrs. Duff to listen to."

"No," Sylvestra said sharply. "I will not be excluded from . . . something which may affect my son's life! Anyway, if it is evidence, I shall hear it in court. I should prefer to hear it now and at least be prepared."

"But, Sylvestra, my dear——"

"I am not a child, Corriden, to be protected from the truth. This will happen, whatever I choose to ignore or pretend. Please give me the dignity of bearing it with some courage, not running away."

Wade hesitated, his face dark.

"Of course," Rathbone said with admiration. "Whatever the outcome, you will have peace of mind only if you know that you failed in nothing that could conceivably have been of help."

Sylvestra looked at him, a moment's gratitude in her eyes.

"So the charge will be murder, Sir Oliver?"

"Yes. I am afraid there is no possible defense of a charge of accident."

"And it is not imaginable that Leighton attacked Rhys or that Rhys in any way was defending himself," Wade continued gravely. "Leighton may have been appalled by Rhys's behavior, but the most he would have done would be raise his hand. He may have struck Rhys, but many a father chastises his son. It does not end in murder. I know of no son who would strike back."

"Then what defense can there be?" Sylvestra said desperately. For a moment her eyes flashed to Hester, then back to the men. "What else is left? Who else is there? Not Arthur or Duke, surely?"

"I am afraid not, my dear," Wade said, dropping his voice. "Had they been involved they would be injured also, very profoundly so. And you and I both know that they were not. Unless the police can find two or three ruffians in St. Giles, there was no one. And if they could have done that, they would not have come here to accuse Rhys." He took a deep breath. "I am truly grieved to say this, but I think the only defense that is believable is that the balance of Rhys's mind has been affected, and simply he is not sane. That, surely, will be the path you will follow, Sir Oliver? I know of excellent people who may be prevailed upon to examine Rhys and give their opinions—in court, of course."

"Insanity is not easy to prove," Rathbone answered. "Rhys appears very rational when one speaks to him. He is obviously a young man of intelligence and conscience."

"Good God, man!" Wade said with an explosion of emotion. "He beat his father to death, and very nearly at the cost of his own life. How can any sane person do that? They must have fought like animals. He must have been frenzied to . . . to do such a thing. I saw Leighton's body—" He stopped as abruptly as he had begun, his face white, eyes hollow. He took a deep, shuddering breath and let it out in a sigh. "I'm sorry, Sylvestra. I should never have said that. You did not need to know . . . to hear it like that. I'm so sorry! Leighton was my best friend . . . a man I admired enormously, with whom I shared experiences

I have with no one else. That it should end like this is . . . devastating."

"I know," she said quietly. "You have no need to apologize, Corriden. I understand your anger and your grief." She looked at Rathbone. "Sir Oliver, I think Dr. Wade could be right. I should be obliged if you would make every effort you can to find evidence, testimony, which will substantiate Rhys's imbalance of mind. Perhaps there were signs beforehand, but we did not understand them. Please call upon the best medical men. I am informed that I have funds to meet any such expenses. It . . ." She laughed jerkily, painfully. "It seems preposterous that I am using the money Leighton left for us to defend the son who killed him. If that is not insane, I wonder what is? And yet I have to. Please, Sir Oliver . . ."

"I will do all I can," Rathbone promised. "But I cannot go beyond what is provably true. Now, I am sure you wish to see your patient, Dr. Wade, and I would like to take my leave and consider my next step forward."

"Of course," Wade agreed quickly. He turned to Hester. "And you, Miss Latterly. You have been of extraordinary strength and courage in the whole affair. You have worked unceasingly for Rhys's welfare. No one could have done more—in fact, I doubt anyone else would have done as much. I will stay with Rhys tonight. Please allow yourself a little time to rest, and perhaps spend it doing something to enjoy yourself. Mrs. Duff and I can manage here, I promise you."

"Thank you," Hester accepted hesitantly. She felt a trifle uncertain about leaving Rhys. Sylvestra was obviously more comforted by Wade than anything Hester could do for her. And Hester would dearly like to go with Rathbone to persuade Monk to accept the case. She had every confidence in Rathbone's powers of argument, but still she wished to be there. There might be something, a thought, an emotional persuasion she could try. "Thank you very much. That is most thoughtful of you." She looked at Sylvestra, just to make sure she agreed.

"Please . . ." Sylvestra added.

There needed no more to be said. Hester bade them goodnight and turned to leave with Rathbone.

"What?" Monk said incredulously as he stood in the middle of his room facing Hester and Rathbone. It was very late, the fire was almost dead, and it was pouring rain outside. Rathbone and Hester's coats were both dripping onto the carpet even though they had come directly from Ebury Street in a hansom.

"Investigate the case to see if there is any evidence whatsoever to mitigate what Rhys Duff has done," Rathbone repeated.

"Why, for God's sake?" Monk demanded, looking at Rathbone and avoiding Hester's eyes. "Isn't it plain enough what happened?"

"No, it isn't," Rathbone said patiently. "I have undertaken to defend him, and I cannot begin to do that until I know every whit of truth that I can—"

"You can't anyway," Monk said. "It is as indefensible as a human act can be. The only possible thing you can say to procure anything except the rope for him is that he is insane. Which may be true."

"It is not true," Rathbone replied, keeping calm with some difficulty. Hester could see it in the muscles of his jaw and the way he stood. His voice was very soft. "In any legal sense, he is perfectly rational and not apparently suffering any delusions. If you refuse to take the case on the grounds that it horrifies and appalls you, then say so. I shall be obliged to accept that." He also did not look at Hester. There was anger in him, almost as if he would provoke the very answer he did not want.

Monk heard the sharpness. He swiveled to look at Hester.

"I suppose you put him up to this?"

"I asked him to defend Rhys," she replied.

Rathbone's acceptance, and Monk's refusal, hung in the air like a sword between them.

Hester thought of a dozen things to say. She wanted to excuse Rathbone. He had undertaken an impossible case because she had prevailed upon him. She had persuaded him to see Rhys, to feel some of her own pity and protectiveness for him. She felt guilty for it, and she admired him for not placing his own reputation, and the failure he faced, before it.

She wanted Monk to feel the same compassion and accept

the case, not for her but for Rhys. No . . . that was not wholly true. She wanted him to accept it for her also, as Rathbone had. And she would be ashamed of herself if he did.

And all that ought to matter was Rhys. It was his life.

"You were finding out about the rapes," she said to Monk. "Now you could find out about Rhys himself, and his father. Discover if Leighton Duff did know what Rhys was doing and followed him to try to stop him."

"That will hardly help your case," Monk pointed out bitterly. "Not that I can think of anything that will."

"Well, try!" Suddenly she was shouting at him, helplessness, anger and pain welling up inside her. "I don't believe Rhys is wicked or mad. There has to be something else . . . some pain, some . . . I don't know . . . just something. Look for it."

"You're beaten, Hester," Monk said, surprisingly gently. "Don't go on fighting anymore. It is not a kindness to anyone."

"No, I'm not . . ." She wanted to cry. She could feel tears prickling in her eyes and throat. It was ridiculous. "Just . . . try. There has to be something more we can do."

He looked at her steadily. He did not believe it, and she could see it in his face. He pushed his hands deeper into his pockets.

"All right, I'll try," he acceded with a little shake of his head. "But it won't help."

"Thank you," Rathbone said quickly. "It is better than doing nothing."

Monk let out his breath in a sigh. "Stop dripping on the floor and tell me what you know. . . ."

11

Monk was convinced that any attempt to find mitigating circumstances to explain Rhys Duff's behavior was doomed to failure. Rhys was a young man whose lack of self-control—first of his appetites, then of his temper—had led him from rape to the situation of murder which he now faced. Curiously, it was the beatings for which Monk could not forgive him. They, of all the crimes, seemed a gratuitous exercise of cruelty.

Nevertheless, he would try—for Hester's sake. He had said he would, perhaps in the emotion of the moment, and now he was bound.

Still, as he set out for St. Giles, it was more at the edge of his mind than at the center. He could not rid himself of the memory of the expression of contempt he had seen in the eyes of the people who had known him before—and liked Runcorn better, felt sorry for him in the exchange. Runcorn, as he was now, irritated Monk like a constant abrasion to the skin. He was pompous, small-minded, self-serving. But perhaps he had not always been like that. It was imaginable that whatever had happened between them had contributed to a warping of his original nature.

If anyone had offered this thought to Monk as an excuse for his own behavior, he would have rejected it as precisely that—an excuse. If he did not have the strength, the honesty or the courage to rise above it, then he should have. But he would soften the judgment towards others where he could not for himself.

He was in Oxford Street and going south. In a moment or two the hansom would stop and let him down. He would walk the rest of the way; he was not yet sure precisely to what goal. The traffic around him was dense, people shouting in all directions, the squeal of horses, rattle of harness and hiss of wheels in the rain.

He should turn his attention to Rhys Duff. What could he look for? What might a mitigating circumstance be? Accident was impossible. It had to have been a deliberate and sustained battle fought until both men were incapable even of moving. Provocation? That was conceivable for Leighton Duff, in the rage and horror of discovering what his son had done. It was not believable the other way around.

Unless there was something else, some other quarrel which happened to have reached a climax in Water Lane. Would that excuse anything? Were there any circumstances in which such violence ending in murder could be understood? He could imagine none. Leighton Duff had not died of a blow to the head which could have been one dreadful loss of control. He had been beaten to death, blow after blow after blow.

The hansom stopped and Monk alighted and paid the driver, then turned and walked in the rain towards the first alley opening. The smell of dirt was becoming familiar, the narrow grayness of the buildings, the sloping, leaning walls, the sense of imminent collapse as wood creaked, wind flapped in loose canvas or whistled thinly in broken glass.

The Holy Land had been like this twenty years before, only more dangerous. He turned his collar up, then pushed his hands deeper into his pockets. It was useless trying to avoid stepping in puddles; everywhere the gutters overflowed. The only answer was to keep old boots specifically for this purpose.

What had made Leighton Duff follow Rhys on that particular evening? Had he discerned something which, with a horrifying shock, made him realize what his son was doing? What could that be, and why had Evan not found it? Had Leighton Duff destroyed it, or taken it with him in order to confront Rhys? If so, then why had it not been found on his body?

Rhys had not left. Then had Arthur or Duke Kynaston taken it with them, and presumably destroyed it?

Or did it not exist, and Leighton Duff had known before, or at least suspected? What had decided him that night to follow Rhys?

Was it possible he had followed him before?

Monk crossed a narrow yard with a smithy in the building on the far side. He could feel the warmth from the furnace yards away, and smell the fire, the burning metal and the damp hide and flesh of horses.

A new idea occurred to him as he hurried past before the warmth could ensnare him. Might Leighton Duff also have used prostitutes, and that was how he had learned of Rhys's behavior? And to reason on the subject, how had he learned? Had Rhys returned injured and been obliged to explain to his father the blood on him, or scratches, or bruises? Surely not. He would have sufficient privacy for that not to be necessary— or for another simple explanation to be given. He could pass it off as a bout of boxing taken a little too far, a riding mishap, a scuffle in the street, a fall, a dozen things. Monk should check with Sylvestra Duff and see if any such thing had happened.

But what if Leighton had been there himself, perhaps with one particular prostitute? That could at one stroke explain his knowledge of both Rhys's presence in St. Giles and the series of rapes and beatings; and also perhaps explain something of Rhys's rage at being chastised by his father. The sheer hypocrisy of it, in his eyes, might infuriate him.

And on a darker note, if he knew of his father's association with such women, might it explain his own violence towards prostitutes, a sense of the violation of his family, especially his mother? That would be the beginning of some kind of mitigation . . . if it were true . . . and provable.

The answer was to see if anyone in St. Giles recognized Leighton Duff from any night except that of his death. Was he known in any of the brothels? It would be by sight. A man as sophisticated in the ways of the world was hardly likely to use his own name. While society knew perfectly well that a great many gentlemen took their pleasures in such places, it was still another matter to be caught at it. One's reputation would suffer, perhaps a great deal.

He stopped abruptly, almost tripping over the edge of the curb. He all but overbalanced, memory came to him so sharply. Of course, a man could be ruined, become the butt of social jokes, not so much from his carnal weakness as the absurdity of being caught in a ridiculous position. The man's dignity was shattered forever. His inferiors laughed, respect vanished. He could no longer exert authority.

Why had he thought of authority?

A man with a brazier of roasting chestnuts was staring at him curiously. A coster girl giggled and disappeared around the end of the alley into the thoroughfare, carrying a bag in front of her.

A magistrate. It had been a magistrate caught in a police raid in a brothel. He had been in bed with a fat, saucy girl of about fourteen. When the police had gone in, he had come running out of the room in his shirt tails, his hair flying, his spectacles left behind, and he had tripped and fallen downstairs, landing at the police officer's feet with his shirt over his head, very little left to the imagination. Monk had not been there. He had heard about it afterwards, and laughed till he was blind with tears and his ribs were aching.

Why did he remember that now? It was still funny, but there was a certain injustice to it, a pain.

Why? Why should Monk feel any guilt? The man was a hypocrite, sentencing women for a crime in which he himself was the abettor, for selling goods which he only too obviously bought.

And yet the sense of regret remained with Monk as he turned left and crossed the road again. He was unconsciously heading towards one of the bigger brothels he knew of. Was it to ask about Leighton Duff? Or was this where the old raid had happened? Why would the police raid a brothel in St. Giles— or the Holy Land? It was riddled with them, and no one cared. There must have been some other reason—theft, forgery, perhaps something more serious, kidnapping or even murder. That would justify storming into the place without warning.

He passed a man with a bundle of walking sticks, threading his way through the alleys to a main street where he would begin to sell them. A beggar moved into a doorway to shelter himself from the rain. For no particular reason Monk gave him a threepence.

It would be more intelligent to go to the police station and get a picture of Leighton Duff from Evan. Thousands of men matched his description. It would be an extremely tedious job to comb St. Giles for someone who had seen Leighton Duff and could recognize him, but he had nowhere else to start. And there was only a day or two before the trial began.

But while he was still in St. Giles he must see if he could trace his own history there with Runcorn. It was what he needed to know. Vida Hopgood was satisfied. He thought, with a smile, of her face when he had told her about Rhys Duff and his friends. It was less than perfect that Arthur and Duke Kynaston should escape, but it was not necessarily a permanent state of affairs. They would be unlikely to return to Seven Dials, and if they did, they would find a most unpleasant reception awaiting them. Perhaps Monk should go and warn them of that? It might save their lives, which did not concern him overmuch, but it would also free his own conscience from the stain of accessory to murder if they should be foolish enough to ignore him.

He reached the station and found Evan, now engaged in a new case.

"May I borrow your pictures of Rhys and Leighton Duff?" he asked when they were in Evan's tiny room.

Evan was surprised. "What for? Isn't Vida Hopgood satisfied?"

"Yes. This isn't for her." He would prefer not to have to tell Evan that he was trying to save Rhys Duff, that he was, in a sense, working against the case Evan had built with Monk's own help.

"Then who?" Evan watched him closely, his hazel eyes bright.

Evan would find out sooner or later that Rathbone had taken up the defense. Evan would testify at the trial; he would know then, if not before.

"Rathbone," Monk answered tersely. "He would like to know more about what happened before that night."

Evan stared at him. There was no anger in his face, no sense of betrayal. In fact, if anything he looked relieved.

"You mean Hester persuaded Rathbone to defend Rhys, and you are working to that end," Evan said with something that sounded like satisfaction.

Monk was stung that Evan imagined he was working for Hester, and in a hopeless cause like this one. Worse than that, it was true. He was tilting at windmills, like a complete fool. It was totally out of character, contrary to everything he knew of himself, and it was to try to ease the pain for Hester when she had to watch Rhys Duff convicted of a crime for which they would hang him, and this time she would be helpless to offer him even the remotest comfort. The knowledge of her pain then twisted inside Monk like a cramp. And for that alone he could hate Rhys Duff and his selfish, obsessive appetites, his cruelty, his stupidity and his mindless violence.

"I'm working for Rathbone," he snapped at Evan. "It is a total waste of time, but if I don't do it he'll find someone else, and waste poor Mrs. Duff's money, not to mention her grief. If ever a woman did not need a further burden to carry, it is she."

Evan did not argue. Monk would have preferred it if he had. It was an evasion, and Monk knew that Evan knew it. Instead he simply turned away to his desk drawer with a slight smile and a lift of his shoulders, and pulled out the two pictures. He gave them to Monk.

"I had better have them back when you are finished with them, in case they are required for evidence."

"Thank you," Monk said rather less courteously than Evan deserved. He folded them up carefully in a piece of paper and put them in his pocket. He bade Evan good-bye and went out of the police station quickly. He would prefer it if Runcorn did not know he had been there. The last thing he wanted was to run into him by chance . . . or mischance.

304

It would be a long and cold day, and evening was when he would have the best chance to find the people who would have been around at the time to see either Rhys or Leighton Duff, or, for that matter, either of the Kynastons. Feeling angry at the helplessness, his feet wet and almost numb with cold, he went back towards St. Giles, stopping at a public house for a hot meat pie, potatoes and onions, and a steamed pudding with a plain sauce.

He spent several hours in the area searching and questioning, walking slowly along the alleys and through the passages, up and down stairways, deeper into the older part, unchanged in generations. Water dripped off rotting eaves, the stones were slimy, wood creaked, doors hung crooked but fast closed. People moved ahead of him and behind like shadows. One moment it would be strange, frightening and bitterly infectious, the next he thought he recognized something. He would turn a corner and see exactly what he expected, a sky-line or a crooked wall exactly as he had known it would be, a door with huge iron studs whose pattern he could have traced with his eyes closed.

He learned nothing, except that he had been there before, and that he already knew. The police station he had worked from made that much obvious to anyone.

He began with the larger and more prosperous brothels. If Leighton Duff had used prostitutes in St. Giles, they were the most likely places to find them.

He worked until after midnight, asking, threatening, cajoling, coercing, and learning nothing whatever. If Leighton Duff had been to any of these places, either the madams did not remember him or they were lying to protect their reputation for discretion. Monk believed it was the former. Duff was dead, and they had little to fear from answering Monk. He had not lost so much of his old character that he could not wring information from people who made their living on the edge of crime. He knew the balance too well not to use it.

He was walking along a short alley up towards Regent Street when he saw a cabby standing on the pavement talking to a sandwich seller, shivering as the wind whipped around the corner and caught him in its icy blast.

Monk offered a penny and bought a huge sandwich. He bit into it with pleasure. Actually, it was very good, fresh bread with a sharp crust to it, and a thick slice of ham, liberally laced with a rhubarb chutney.

"Good," he said with his mouth full.

"Find yer rapists yet?" the cabby asked, raising his eyebrows. He had very sad, rather protuberant eyes of pale blue.

"Yes, thank you," Monk replied, smiling. "You been on this patch long?"

"Baht eight years. Why?"

"Just wondered." He turned to the sandwich seller. "And you?"

"Twenty-five," he answered. "More or less."

"Do you know me?"

The man blinked. " 'Course I knows yer. Wot kinda question is that?"

Monk steeled himself. "Do you remember a raid in a brothel, a long time ago, where a magistrate was caught? He fell downstairs and hurt himself quite badly." He had not finished before he saw from the man's face that he did. It creased with laughter and a rich chortle of pure joy escaped his lips.

"Yeah!" he said happily. "Yeah, 'course I 'members it. Rotten bastard, 'e were, ol' Gutteridge. Put Polly Thorp away for three years jus' 'cos some feller wot she were doin' a service fer said as she'd took 'is money—w'en 'is trousers was orff!" He laughed again, his cheeks puffing out and shining in the lamplight from across the street. "Got caught proper, 'e did . . . trousers down an' all. Leff the bench arter that. No more 'andin' down four years 'ere an' five years there, an' the boat all over the place. Yer could 'ear 'em laughin' all over the 'Oly Land, yer could. I heard Runcorn got the credit for that one, but I always wondered if that was really down ter you, Mr. Monk. There was a lot o' us as reckoned it were. Yer just wasn't there at the time, so ter speak."

"Did you?" Monk said slowly. "Well, it's a long time ago now." He wanted to change the subject. He was floundering.

306

He could not afford to show his vulnerability to these people. His skill depended on their fear and respect for him. He pulled the picture of Leighton Duff out of his pocket and showed it to the sandwich seller. "Have you ever seen this man?"

The sandwich seller tipped the picture over a little towards the light of the distant street lamp. He thought for a few moments.

"Yeah, 'e were the geezer wot were done in Water Lane. A rozzer showed me this afore. W'y d'yer wanna know fer?"

"Just wondering if he came here any time before that," Monk replied.

The cabby looked at it curiously.

" 'Ere, jus' a minute," he said, his voice quickening. "I seen 'im. Not the night 'e were done, I din't, but I see'd 'im afore that, 'bout a couple o' weeks, or mebbe less. It were the night afore Christmas Eve, I know that. I'd swear ter it."

Monk felt his body tighten and his heart beat a little faster. It was the scent of victory, familiar and sharp. "The night before Christmas Eve, and he was here, in St. Giles?"

"Yeah. Din't I jus' say so? 'E looked rough, real rough then, like 'e'd bin in a fight. Blood on 'is face, there were, an' on 'is sleeves."

Monk swallowed. "Look carefully. Are you sure?"

"Yeah, I'm sure. Ears, yer see?" He looked at Monk with a smile. "I likes ears. Ears is all different. 'Ave yer ever noticed that?"

"Yes. Yes, I have. And what was it about the man's ears that you remember so well?" As he said it he moved his hand over the picture to obscure the ears.

"Long," the cabby said without hesitation. "Long an' narrer, wi' 'eavy lobes ter 'em. Yer take yer finger orff an' look. I'm right."

Monk obeyed. The man was right.

"And he had blood on him? Did you see any injury?" He did not want to ask. He almost did not. It was too easily disproved. He could feel the new thread slipping out of his grasp again.

"No, on'y blood. Don't 'ave ter be 'is blood. Could 'a bin someone else's. Looked kind o' drunk, 'e did. Staggerin' abaht a bit, but 'appy enough, like 'e'd just won summink. So maybe the other geezer got orff a bit worse, eh?"

"Yes, maybe. Was he alone? Did you see anyone else?" Had Rhys been with him, close behind, or left wherever the fight had taken place? This evidence was almost too good to be true. Perhaps he would be able to take Hester something after all. Or rather take Rathbone something.

"Saw someone else," the cabby said thoughtfully. "But couldn't say 'oo. Jus' a shadow. Tall, like, an' thinnish, though it in't easy ter say, in a good coat. Covers a lot, a good coat does."

"Tall . . . and thin," Monk said slowly. "And his face? Was he dark or fair? Young or old?" Surely it must have been Rhys? "And was he injured too?"

"Don' rush me!" the cabby protested. "Can't answer more 'n one thing at a time."

"Did you see his face?" Monk said, controlling himself with difficulty.

"Sort o'—'alf."

"Dark or fair?"

"Dark. Very dark."

Monk swallowed. "And was he hurt, that you could see?"

"Yeah, come ter think on it, 'e 'ad blood on 'im too. Not so much, as I could see. But yeah, 'e were messed around. I reckon 'is coat were torn, an' looked sort o' wet. W'y, guv? Wot does it matter now? Yer've got 'im, in't yer?"

"Yes. It's just a matter of tidying it up, for evidence in court. You are positive about the date?"

"Yeah, I told yer."

"Thank you. You have been a great help. Now, will you please take me to Ebury Street. Have another sandwich." He gave the sandwich seller threepence and took two more. "And have one yourself," he added cheerfully to the seller. "They're very good." He gave one sandwich to the cabby, and set out at a stride to climb up into the hansom. His only regret was he had nothing for the horse.

At Ebury Street he alighted, paid the cabby and thanked him again, then went up the step and rang the bell. When it was answered by Wharmby, looking grim, he asked to see Mrs. Duff.

"I am sorry sir, but Mrs. Duff is not receiving," Wharmby said firmly.

"Please inform her that I am working for Sir Oliver Rathbone, and I have a question I must ask her regarding the case," Monk replied, equally unflinchingly. "It is important that I receive an answer before I can proceed. It is in Mr. Rhys Duff's interest."

"Yes sir, I will tell her." Wharmby hesitated. There was nothing more to say, and yet he did not move.

Monk waited. He wanted to prompt him, but he was afraid if he were too direct he could break the moment and lose it.

"Do you remember Christmas Eve, Wharmby?" he said quite casually.

"Yes sir." Wharmby seemed surprised.

"And the night before?"

Wharmby nodded. "Yes sir. How can I help you?"

"Who was here that night?"

"No one, sir. In the evening Mrs. Duff went with Mrs. Wade to a concert. Mr. Rhys went to the Kynastons' to dinner, and Mr. Duff went out on business."

"I see." The taste of victory was there again. "And how were they all when they returned home, or the next time you saw them?"

"How were they, sir? Quite normal, considering it was Christmas Eve."

"Was no one hurt in any way? Perhaps a slight traffic accident, or something of the sort?"

"I believe Mr. Duff had a scratch on his face. He said it had been a flying stone from a carriage going much too fast. Why, sir? Does this mean something? Can you . . . can you help Mr. Rhys, sir?" His face was crumpled with curiosity, his eyes frightened as if he dreaded the answer. He had been almost too afraid to ask.

Monk was taken aback. Such concern did not fit with the picture of Rhys Duff that Monk had formed. Was the man not more moved by the violent death of his master? Or was it now Sylvestra for whom he grieved, imagining her second loss, so much worse even than the first.

"I don't know," Monk said honestly. "I'm doing everything I can. It is possible this may . . . mitigate things . . . a little. Perhaps you do not need to disturb Mrs. Duff. If you say that Mr. Rhys said he was going to the Kynastons' that evening, I can ask them to substantiate that. Can you give me their address?"

"Certainly, sir. I shall write it down for you." And without waiting for agreement, he disappeared and came back a few moments later with a slip of paper, an address written out in copperplate on it.

Monk thanked him and left, seeking another cab.

At the Kynaston house he asked to speak to Mr. Kynaston.

He was received, reluctantly, in the library. There was no fire burning, but the ashes were still warm. Joel Kynaston came in and closed the door behind him, looking Monk up and down with distaste. He was a highly individual man with thick, very beautiful hair of an auburn color, a thin nose and an unusual mouth. He was of average height and slight build, and at the moment he was short of patience.

"What can I do for you, sir?" he said briskly. "My butler informed me you wish to make an enquiry about Rhys Duff, to do with the forthcoming trial. I find the whole matter most disturbing. Mr. Leighton Duff was a close personal friend, and his death is a great tragedy to my whole family. If I can assist the cause of justice, then it is my public duty to do so, and I do not shirk from it. But I must warn you, sir, I have no desire and no intention of involving myself in further hurt to the Duff family, nor will I injure or cause unhappiness to my own family in your interest. What is it you wish of me?"

"Did Mr. Rhys Duff visit your home on the evening of the day before Christmas Eve, Mr. Kynaston?"

"I have no idea. I was not at home myself. Why is it important? Leighton Duff was perfectly well and unharmed at that time. What affair is it of yours if Rhys was here?"

310

Monk could understand the man's desire to protect his sons, whom he might well fear had been involved deeply and tragically with the Duff family. He might feel he was to blame for not having been aware of their behavior, as apparently Leighton Duff had been. But for chance, had he been the one to know instead, he could have been beaten to death in Water Lane and Monk could have been asking these questions of Leighton Duff. It was not difficult to see Mr. Kynaston was tense, unhappy, and unwilling to have Monk, or anyone else, prying further into the wound. Perhaps he was owed some explanation.

"It seems to me possible that the night of Mr. Duff's death may not have been his first quarrel with his son over his conduct," Monk replied. "There is evidence to suggest they met and had some heated disagreement on the night before Christmas Eve. I would like to know if that is true."

"I cannot see why," Kynaston said with a frown. "It seems tragically apparent what happened. Leighton realized what Rhys was doing, that his behavior was unacceptable by any standards at all, let alone those of a gentleman. His temper and self-indulgence had gone beyond all control, his latest weaknesses had slipped into open vice. His father followed him and remonstrated with him, at which Rhys became vicious with rage and attacked him . . . with the consequences which we know only too well."

"Did Rhys always have a temper, Mr. Kynaston?"

"I am afraid so. When he was a boy it was held in check. He was never permitted to lose it while in my charge. What he was allowed at home, of course, I do not know. But his father was concerned about him. He confided that much to me. I do not wish to speak ill of the poor woman, who, God knows, has more grief than any person should be asked to bear, but Mrs. Duff has indulged the boy over the years. She hated to discipline him, and his character has suffered for it."

"I see. Is there someone I could ask if Rhys was here on that evening?"

"You might ask my wife, I suppose. She was at home, as, I believe, were my sons."

Monk was disconcerted, but not set out of countenance. It was just possible Rhys had gone alone on this occasion. Or more likely Kynaston was wrong about all of them.

"Thank you," Monk accepted, uncertain whether Mrs. Kynaston's word would satisfy him. As soon as Kynaston turned to the door, Monk made to follow him.

Kynaston stopped. "You are on my heels, Mr. Monk. I should prefer if you were to wait here, and I shall ask my wife and inform you of the answer."

"Possibly," Monk agreed. "Then I shall have to inform Sir Oliver that I was not permitted to speak to Mrs. Kynaston personally, and he may feel the necessity to call her to testify in court." He looked at Kynaston squarely and coldly. "However, if I speak to her myself, and to your sons, then that may prove sufficient."

Kynaston stiffened. "I do not appreciate being threatened, Mr. Monk."

"Few of us do," Monk said with a thin smile. "But most of us take heed."

Kynaston looked at him a moment longer, weighing Monk's nerve and his intent, then swung on his heel and led the way.

Monk was startled by Fidelis Kynaston. He had not had any particular expectations of Kynaston's wife, but this woman of extraordinary composure, with her asymmetrical face and her calm, very lovely voice, took him utterly by surprise. The inner repose of her fascinated him.

"This is Mr. Monk," Kynaston said tersely, without looking at him. "He requires to ask you a question about Rhys Duff. It is probably advisable that you answer him."

"How do you do, Mr. Monk," she said graciously. Unlike her husband, her face was filled with sadness rather than tension or anger. Perhaps she was completely unaware of her sons' part in the crime, or the pattern of behavior which had led up to it. Kynaston might have shielded her from it, in which case there was more in him to be admired than Monk had supposed. And yet Monk could tell, from looking at Fidelis's face, that there was knowledge of pain beneath her composure, and a kind of stillness in her eyes which springs from self-mastery in the experience of deep unhappiness. Was it conceivable that they both knew, and yet each shielded the other, and the whole tragedy was never shared?

"I am sorry to disturb your evening, Mrs. Kynaston," he said sincerely. "But I need to ask you to cast your mind back to the night before Christmas Eve. Can you tell me if you were at home, and if so, who was with you, and until what hour?"

"Certainly," she said with a shadow of puzzlement in her eyes. "I was at home, and my sons were here, and Rhys Duff, and Lady Sandon and her son, Mr. Rufus Sandon. We played cards and talked a great deal about all manner of things, Egyptian exploration in particular. Rufus Sandon was most enthusiastic about Monsieur Champollion and his discovery of the Rosetta stone, and its meaning. Rhys was fascinated. I think he would willingly have listened all night."

"What time did he leave, Mrs. Kynaston?"

"About two o'clock, I believe," she replied. "It was very late indeed. But the following day was Christmas Eve, and they intended to lie in, and be late the evening after as well. I remember them saying so. Marmaduke retired to bed earlier. He was less interested, but the rest of us remained long into the night. May I ask why you wish to know, Mr. Monk? Can it in some way help Rhys now?" There was no need to ask if that was something she wished; it was plain in her entire bearing.

"I don't know, ma'am," he answered frankly. "It is not what I had expected you to say. I admit, this throws me into some confusion. You have no doubt whatsoever about the date?"

"None at all. We were discussing the fact that it was Christmas Eve the following day," she affirmed.

"Thank you. I appreciate your courtesy."

"Then we will not detain you any further, Mr. Monk," Kynaston said abruptly just as Fidelis was about to speak again.

Monk bowed and took his leave, thoroughly puzzled. If Rhys had been at the Kynastons' until two in the morning, then it could not have been he with whom Leighton Duff had fought in St. Giles shortly after midnight. Monk did not doubt Fidelis, but it would be simple to check with Lady Sandon. He had not

313

asked for her address, but a woman of title would not be difficult to locate.

As soon as he reached his rooms he went to his desk and took out all his notes on the times, dates and places of the rapes he had investigated. They were in chronological order, and it took him only moments to ascertain that his memory was correct. There had been a particularly brutal rape and beating on the night before Christmas Eve, shortly before midnight, as near as the victim could tell, probably two men rather than three.

The conclusion was startling, and inescapable. Rhys could not have been guilty of this one. Leighton Duff had been there, and had been involved in a struggle of some sort. Marmaduke Kynaston could have been there. Arthur Kynaston, like Rhys, could not. Monk must be absolutely certain. There were more facts to check—with Lady Sandon, and with Sylvestra Duff, and for extra certainty, with the servants in the Duff house.

Had Leighton Duff followed and confronted Marmaduke Kynaston and his companion in rape, whoever that was . . . or was he himself the companion? And had Rhys, usually the third, on this occasion been more spellbound by something else, and remained in the Kynaston home listening to tales of Egypt and the Rosetta stone? Was it even possible that the three men who committed the rapes were not always the same ones?

He went to bed with his mind racing, and slept fitfully, haunted by dreams.

In the morning he arose, dressed, and after a hasty breakfast, went out barely feeling the cold. By two in the afternoon he had ascertained his facts. Rhys Duff had been at the Kynaston house until two in the morning and had returned straight to his own home, where he had remained until midday of Christmas Eve. He could not have been in St. Giles.

Leighton Duff had gone out at half past nine in the evening and had returned at an unknown hour. The footman had not waited up for him. Mr. Duff was always most considerate and never required the servants to remain out of their beds on his account.

It was confirmed that Duke Kynaston had retired before the end of the party, but whether he had then gone out or not, no one could say. While he was at the Kynaston house, Monk took the opportunity to deliver a warning. He had doubted whether to do so, or to leave justice to fortune. Now, as the picture grew even less certain in his mind, the doubt vanished. He asked to see both brothers and learned that Arthur was out, but Marmaduke could give him a few moments if he cared to go to the morning room.

Duke looked at him with a mixture of interest and scorn.

"A private agent of enquiry, eh?" he said with a lift of the eyebrow. "What a curious way to make one's living. Still, I suppose it is better than catching rats, or repossessing the furniture of debtors."

"There are times when it bears a closer resemblance to catching rats than one might wish," Monk answered with a corresponding sneer.

"I hear you were the one who caught up with Rhys Duff," Duke said quickly, cutting across him a little. "Do you think the court will find him guilty?"

"Is that why you consented to see me?" Monk asked with amusement. "Because you think I might know what the outcome will be?"

There was a faint flush on Duke's cheeks. "Do you?" he demanded.

Monk was surprised. Under the bravado, was it possible Duke actually felt some concern and some responsibility—or guilt?

"No, I don't," Monk said more gently. "I thought I knew the answer without doubt, but I have since discerned some information which makes me less sure."

"Why did you come here?" Duke frowned. "What do you want from us?"

"When you left the party on the night before Christmas Eve, where did you go?"

"To bed. Why? What does that matter?"

"You did not go to St. Giles with Leighton Duff?"

Duke's utter amazement was too profound to disbelieve.

315

"What?"

Monk repeated what he had said.

"With Leighton Duff? Have you lost your wits? I've been whoring in St. Giles, certainly—with Rhys, for that matter, and my brother Arthur. But Leighton Duff! That pompous, dry-as-dust old stick!" He started to laugh, and it was harsh, critical, but as far as Monk could tell, perfectly genuine.

"I take it you think it unlikely Mr. Duff would have gone to St. Giles in search of a prostitute?"

"About as likely as Her Majesty appearing on the stage of the music halls, I should think," Duke replied bitterly. "Whatever gave you that notion? You must be very out of touch with the case. You really have not the least idea, have you?"

Monk took the picture of Leighton Duff out of his pocket.

"Is that a good likeness of him?"

Duke considered it for a moment. "Yes, it is, actually. It is extremely good. He had just that rather patronizing air of self-righteousness."

"You did not like him," Monk observed.

"A crashing remark of the obvious." Duke raised his eyebrows. "Do you really make a living at this, Mr. Monk?"

"You would be surprised how people betray themselves when they imagine themselves safe, Mr. Kynaston," Monk said with a smile. "But thank you for your concern on my behalf. It is not necessary. What I came for was to warn you, and your brother, that the people of St. Giles, and of Seven Dials as well, are aware of who committed the recent rapes in their areas, and if either of you should return there, it is very probable you will meet with most unpleasant ends. You have been there. You know or can imagine how easily that could be accomplished and your bodies never found . . . at least not recognizable ones."

Duke stared at him with a mixture of shock and incomprehension, but there was marked fear in it as well.

"Why do you care if I get murdered in St. Giles?" he said truculently, then passed his tongue over dry lips.

"I don't," Monk replied with a smile, but even as he said it, it was not entirely true. He disliked Marmaduke Kynaston less

316

than when he had come in, for no reason that he would have been prepared to explain. "I don't want the people of St. Giles to be pursued by a murder enquiry."

Duke took a deep breath. "I should have known. Are you from St. Giles?"

Monk laughed outright. It was the first time he had felt like laughing for days.

"No. I come from Northumberland."

"I suppose I should thank you for the warning," Duke said casually, but his eyes still held the shock, and there was a reluctant sincerity in his voice.

Monk shrugged and smiled.

He left the house even further confused.

Time was desperately short.

He took Leighton Duff's picture to Seven Dials and showed it to cabbies; street peddlers; a running patterer; sellers of flowers, bootlaces, matches and glassware; and to a ratcatcher and several prostitutes. It was recognized by at least a dozen people, and some without any hesitation at all. Not one of them was prepared to identify Rhys.

By the second night Monk had only one more question in his mind. He returned to St. Giles to pursue the answer, and walked the alleys and courtyards, the dripping passages and up and down the rotting stairs, until dawn came gray and bleak at about seven o'clock and he was exhausted, and so cold his feet were numb and he could not control the shaking of his body. But he knew two things. Rhys Duff and his father had come to St. Giles on the night of the murder from different directions, and there was no proof they had met until the fatal encounter in Water Lane.

The other thing he learned by chance. He was talking to a woman who had been a prostitute in her youth, and had saved sufficient money to purchase a boardinghouse, but still knew a remarkable amount of gossip. He went to her partly to confirm certain dates and places, but mainly from his compulsion to probe the darkness in his own mind, the fear that gathered every time Runcorn's face came to his thoughts, which it did so

317

often in these dark, slippery paths. It was not Runcorn as he was now, graying at the temples, a little broader at the waist, but a younger, keener Runcorn, shoulders straight, eyes clearer and braver.

"Do you remember the raid in the brothel when the magistrate, Gutteridge, was caught with his trousers down?" He was not sure why he asked, or what he expected the answer to be, only that it lay at the back of his mind and would not leave.

She gurgled with delight. " 'Course I do. Why?"

"Runcorn led it?"

"You know that. Can't tell me you've forgot." She looked at him narrowly, her head tilted to one side.

"Did he set it up?" he asked.

"Wot's this, a game or summink? You set it up, an' Runcorn took it from yer. Yer let 'im, 'cos yer know'd poor ol' Gutt-'ridge was gonna be there. Runcorn walked right iner it, daft sod."

"Why? It was Gutteridge's own fault. Did he expect the police to hold off just because he was indulging himself?"

Her eyes widened. "Yeah. 'Course 'e did. Or at least warn 'im. Upset a lot o' people, that did . . . important people, like. None o' us, mind. Laughed till we creased ourselves, we did."

"What people?" Monk paused, knowing something eluded him, something that mattered.

" 'Ere, wot's this abaht?" she said with a frown. "It's all dead an' buried nah. 'Oo cares anymore? It don't 'ave nuffink ter do wi' them rapes 'ere."

"I know it doesn't. I just want to know. Tell me," he pressed.

"Well, there was a few gents wot felt theirselves a bit exposed, like, arter that." She laughed hugely at her own joke. "They'd always trusted you rozzers to keep yer distance from certain 'ouses o' pleasure." She wiped her eyes with the back of her hand. "Arter that they din't trust no one. Couldn't. It kind o' soured relations atween the rozzers and certain people o' influence. On'y time I ever thought as I could like Mr. Runcorn. Bleedin' pain, 'e is, most o' the time. Worse 'n you. Yer a mean bastard, but yer was straight, and yer weren't full o' cant. I never knowed yer ta preach one thing an' do another. Not like

318

'im." She looked at him more closely. "Wot is it, Monk? W'y d'yer give a toss abaht a twenty-year-old raid in a bawdy 'ouse?"

"I'm not sure," he said honestly.

"Arter yer, is 'e?" she asked with a note of something which could even have been sympathy. He was not sure whether it was for him or for Runcorn.

"After me?" he repeated. "Why?" It sounded foolish, but she knew something about it or she would not have leaped to such a conclusion. He had to know. He was too close now not to grasp it, whatever it was.

"Well, yer dropped 'im right in it, din' yer?" she said incredulously. "Yer knew all them folk was there, an' yer never tol' 'im. Let 'im charge in an' make a right fool of 'isself. Don't suppose nuffink was said, but they don' never fergive that kind o' thing. Lorst 'is promotion then, an' lorst 'is girl too, 'cos 'er father were one of 'em, weren't 'e?" She shrugged. "I'd watch me back, if I was you, even arter all this time. 'E don' fergive, yer know? Carries a grudge 'ard, does Runcorn."

Monk was barely listening. He could not remember doing it, even after her retelling of it. But he could remember the feeling of victory, the deep, hot satisfaction of knowing he had beaten Runcorn. Now it was only shame. It had been a shabby trick and too deep a revenge for anything Runcorn could have done to him. Not that he knew of anything.

He thanked her quietly and walked out, leaving her puzzled, muttering to herself about how times had changed.

Why? He walked with his head down into the rain, hands deep in his pockets, ignoring the gutters and his wet feet. It was fully light now. Why had he done such a thing? Had it been as deliberate and as calculatedly cruel as everyone else thought? If it had, then no wonder Runcorn still hated him. To lose the promotion was fair enough. That was the fortune of war. But to lose the woman he loved must have been a bitter blow, and one Monk would not now have dealt to any man.

The trial of Rhys Duff had already begun. The information he had was highly pertinent, even if it offered little real help. He should go and tell Rathbone. Hester would be hurt. How

Sylvestra Duff would take the news that her husband was also a rapist, he could not even imagine.

He crossed Regent Street, barely noticing he was out of St. Giles, and stopped to buy a hot cup of tea. Perhaps he should not tell Rathbone? It did not clear Rhys of the murder of his father, only of one rape, with which he was not charged anyway.

But it was part of the truth, and the truth mattered. They had too little of it to make sense as it was. Rathbone had paid him to learn all he could. He had promised Hester. He needed to cling to his sense of honor, the integrity, and the trust of the friends he had now. What he had been was acutely painful to contemplate. He had no memory of it, no understanding.

Did Rhys Duff understand himself?

That was irrelevant. Monk was a grown man, and whether he remembered it or not, he was responsible. He was certainly in possession of all his faculties and answerable at present. His only reason for not facing himself was fear of what he would find, and the gall to his pride of facing Runcorn and admitting his remorse.

Had he what it took—courage?

He had been cruel, arbitrary, too hasty to judge, but he had never been a liar, and he had never ever been a coward.

He finished the last of his tea, took a bun and paid for it, then, eating as he went, he started towards the police station.

He was obliged to wait until quarter past nine before Runcorn arrived. He looked warm and dry in his smart overcoat, his face pink and freshly barbered, his shoes shining.

He regarded Monk soberly, his gaze going from Monk's dripping hair and his exhausted face, hollow eyes, down his wet coat to his sodden and filthy boots. Runcorn's expression was smug, glowing with rich satisfaction.

"You look on hard times, Monk," he said cheerfully. "You want to come in and warm your feet? Perhaps you'd like a cup of tea?"

"I've had one, thank you," Monk said. Only a sharp reminder inside himself of his contempt for cowardice kept him there, and the thought of what Hester would think of him

320

if he were to fail the final confrontation now. "But I'll come in. I want to talk to you."

"I'm busy," Runcorn replied. "But I suppose I can spare you fifteen minutes. You look terrible!" He opened his office door and Monk followed him in. Someone had already lit the fire and the room was extremely pleasant. There was a faint smell of beeswax and lavender polish.

"Sit down," Runcorn offered. "But take your coat off first, or you'll mark my chair."

"I've spent the night in St. Giles," Monk said, still standing.

"You look like it," Runcorn retorted. He wrinkled his nose. "And, frankly, you smell like it too."

"I spoke to Bessie Mallard."

"Who is she? And why are you telling me?" Runcorn sat down and made himself comfortable.

"She used to be a whore. Now she has a small boarding-house. She told me about the night they raided the brothel in Cutters' Row and caught the magistrate, Gutteridge, and he fell downstairs—" He stopped. There was a tide of dull purple spreading up Runcorn's face. His hands on the smooth desktop were curling into fists.

Monk took a deep breath. There was no evading it.

"Why did I hate you enough to let you do that? I don't remember."

Runcorn stared at him, his eyes widening as he realized what Monk was saying.

"Why do you care?" His voice was high, sounded a little hurt. "You ruined me with Ellen. Wasn't that what you wanted?"

"I don't know. I've told you . . . I can't remember. But it was a vicious thing to do, and I want to know why I did it."

Runcorn blinked. He was thrown off balance. This was not the Monk he thought he knew.

Monk leaned forward over the desk, staring down at Runcorn. Behind the freshly shaved face, the mask of self-satisfaction, there was a man with a wound to his esteem which had never healed. Monk had done that . . . or at least part of it. He needed to know why.

321

"I'm sorry," he said aloud. "I wish I had not done it. But I need to know why I did. Once we worked together, trusted each other. We went to St. Giles side by side, never doubting the other. What changed? Was it you . . . or me?"

Runcorn sat silent for so long Monk thought he was not going to answer. Monk could hear the clatter of heavy feet outside, and rain dripping from the eaves onto the windowsill. Outside was the distant rumble of traffic in the street and a horse whinnying.

"It was both of us," Runcorn said at last. "It began over the coat, you could say."

"Coat! What coat?" Monk had no idea what he was talking about.

"I got a new coat with a velvet collar. You went and got one with fur, just that bit better than mine. We were going out to the same place to dine."

"How stupid," Monk said immediately.

"So I got back at you," Runcorn replied. "Something to do with a girl. I don't even know what now. It just went from one thing to another, until it got too big to go back on."

"That was all? Just childish jealousies?" Monk was horrified. "You lost the woman you loved—over a coat collar?"

The blood was dark in Runcorn's face. "It was more than that," he said defensively. "It was·. . ." He looked up at Monk again, his eyes hot and angry, more honest than Monk had ever seen them before. For the first time he knew, there was no veil between them. "It was a hundred things—you undermining my authority with the men, laughing at me behind my back, taking credit for my ideas, my arrests . . ."

Monk felt the void of ignorance swallowing him. He did not know whether that was the truth, or simply the way Runcorn excused himself. He hated it with the blind, choking panic of helplessness. He did not know! He was fighting without weapons. He might have been a man like that. He did not feel it was himself, but then how much had his accident changed him? Or was it simply that he had been forced to look at himself from the outside, as a stranger might have, and seeing himself, had changed?

"Did I?" he said slowly. "Why you? Why did I do that only to you? Why no one else? What did you do to me?"

Runcorn looked miserable, puzzled, struggling with his thoughts.

Monk waited. He must not prompt. A wrong word, even one, and the truth would slip away from him.

Runcorn lifted his eyes to meet Monk's, but he did not speak immediately.

"I suppose . . . I resented you," he said at last. "You always seemed to have the right word, to guess the right answers. You always had luck on your side, and you never gave anyone else any room. You didn't forgive mistakes."

That was the damning indictment. He did not forgive.

"I should have," he said gravely. "I was wrong in that. I am sorry about Ellen. I can't take it back now, but I am sorry."

Runcorn stared at him. "You are, aren't you," he said in amazement. He took a deep breath and let it out in a sigh. "You did well with the Duff case. Thank you." It was as close as he could come to an acceptance.

It was good enough. Monk nodded. He could not allow the lie to remain. It would break the fragile bridge he had just built at such a cost.

"I haven't finished with it yet. I'm not sure about the motive. The father was responsible for at least one of the rapes in St. Giles himself, and he was in Seven Dials regularly."

"What?" Runcorn could scarcely believe what he seemed to have heard. "That's impossible! It doesn't make any sense, Monk."

"I know. But it is true. I have a dozen witnesses. One who saw him smeared with blood the night before Christmas Eve, when there was a rape in St. Giles. And Mrs. Kynaston and Lady Sandon will swear Rhys Duff was with them at the time, miles away."

"We're not charging Rhys Duff with rape." Runcorn frowned, now thoroughly disturbed. He was a good enough policeman to see the implications.

Monk did not argue further. It was unnecessary.

"I'm obliged," Runcorn said, shaking his head.

Monk nodded, hesitated a moment, then excused himself and went out to go home and bathe and sleep. Then he must go and tell Rathbone.

12

THE TRIAL OF RHYS DUFF had commenced on the previous day. The court was filled and an hour before the trial began the ushers closed the doors. The preliminaries had already been conducted. The jury was chosen. The judge, a handsome man of military appearance and with the marks of pain in his face, called the court to order. He had come in with a pronounced limp and sat a trifle awkwardly in his high, carved chair in order to accommodate a stiff leg.

The prosecution was conducted by Ebenezer Goode, a man of curious and exuberant appearance, well known and respected by Rathbone. Goode was unhappy with proceeding against someone as obviously ill as Rhys Duff, but he abhorred not only the crime with which he was charged but the earlier ones which had provided the motive. He willingly made concession to Rhys's medical needs by allowing him to sit in the dock, high above the body of the court and railed off, in a padded chair to offer what comfort there was for his physical pain. He also had made no demur when Rathbone had asked that Rhys not be handcuffed at any time, so he might move if he wished, or was able to, and sit in whatever position gave him the least discomfort.

Corriden Wade was in court and could be called should he be needed, and so was Hester. They were both to be allowed immediate access to the prisoner if he showed any need for their attention or assistance.

Nevertheless, as the testimony began, Rhys was alone as he

faced a bitterly hostile crowd, his accusers and his judges. There was no one to speak for him except Rathbone, standing a solitary figure, black-gowned, white-wigged, a fragile barrier against a tide of hatred.

Goode called his witnesses one after the other: the women who had found the two bodies, Constable Shotts and John Evan. He took Evan carefully step by step through his investigation, not dwelling on the horror but permitting it to be passionately conveyed through Evan's white face and broken, husky voice.

He called Dr. Riley, who spoke quietly and in surprisingly simple language of Leighton Duff's terrible wounds and the death he must have suffered.

"And the accused?" Goode asked, standing in the middle of the floor like a great crow, his arms dangling in his gown. His aquiline face with its pale eyes reflected vividly the horror and the sense of tragedy he felt unmistakably deeply.

Hester had liked him ever since first meeting him in the Stonefield case. Staring around the courtroom, more to judge the emotion of the crowd than to note who was present, she was lent a moment's real happiness to see Enid Ravensbrook, her face smoothed of its earlier suffering, her eyes gentle and bright as she watched Goode, a smile on her lips. Hester looked more closely, and saw there was a gold wedding band on her hand, not the one she had worn earlier, but a new one. For an instant Hester forgot the present ache of fear and tragedy.

But it was brief. Reality returned with Riley's answer.

"He was also very severely injured," he said quietly.

There was barely a sound in the room. There were faint rustles, tiny movements, a sigh of breath. The jurors never took their eyes from the proceedings.

"A great deal of blood?" Goode pressed.

Riley hesitated.

No one moved.

"No . . ." he said at last. "When a person is kicked and punched there are terrible bruises, but the skin is not necessarily broken. There was some blood, especially where his ribs

326

were cracked. One had pierced the skin. And on his back. There the flesh had been ripped."

There was a gasp of indrawn breath in the room. Several of the jurors looked very white.

"But Sergeant Evan said that the accused's clothes were soaked in blood, Dr. Riley," Goode pointed out. "Where did that come from, if not from his injuries?"

"I assume from the dead man," Riley replied. "His wounds were more severe, and there were several places where the skin was broken. But I am surprised he bled so badly."

"And there were no wounds on the accused to account for such blood?" Riley pressed.

"No, there were not."

"Thank you, Dr. Riley."

Rathbone rose. It was a forlorn hope, but he had nothing else. He must try anything, no matter how remote. He had no idea what Monk would produce, and there were always the possibilities that involved Arthur and Duke Kynaston.

"Dr. Riley, have you any way of knowing whose blood it was on Rhys Duff's clothes?"

"No, sir," Riley answered without the least resentment. The smooth expression of his face suggested he had no conviction in the matter himself, only a sadness that the whole event should have happened at all.

"So it could belong to a third, or even a fourth, person, whom we have not yet mentioned?"

"It could . . . were there such a person."

The jury looked bemused.

The judge watched Rathbone anxiously, but he did not intervene.

"Thank you." Rathbone nodded. "That is all I have to ask you, sir."

Goode called Corriden Wade, who reluctantly, pale-faced, his voice barely audible, admitted that Rhys's injuries could not have produced the blood described on his clothes. Not once did he look up to the dock, where Rhys sat motionless, his face twisted in an unreadable expression, a mixture of helpless bitterness and blazing anger. Nor did Wade appear to look towards the gallery, where Sylvestra sat next to Eglantyne, both of them watching him intently. He kept his eyes undeviatingly on Goode, confirming that the events of the night of Rhys's father's death had rendered Rhys incapable of communication, either by speech or by writing. He was able only to nod or shake his head. Wade expressed the deepest concern for Rhys's well-being and would not commit himself to any certainty that he would recover.

Goode hesitated, as if to ask him further as to his knowledge of Rhys's personality, but after the vaguest of beginnings, he changed his mind. There was nothing for him to prove but the facts, and to explore the growth of motive only opened the way for Rathbone to suggest insanity. Goode thanked Wade and returned to his seat.

Rathbone took his place. He knew Wade was as sympathetic a witness as he would get, apart from Hester, whom he could find no excuse to call. And yet he had nothing to ask Wade which would not do more harm than good. He needed something from Monk as desperately as he ever had, and he did not even know what to hope for, let alone to seek or to suggest. He stood in the middle of the floor feeling alone and ridiculous. The jury was waiting for him to say something, to begin to fight back. He had done nothing so far except make a gesture about the blood, one which he knew no one believed.

Should he ask Wade about the deterioration of Rhys's character, and lay grounds for a plea of insanity . . . at least in mitigation? He thought that was what Sylvestra wanted. It was the only defense which was comprehensible for such an act.

But it was not a defense in law, not for Rhys. He might be evil, acting from a different set of moral beliefs from anyone else in this crowded room, but he was not insane in the sense that he did not understand either the law or the nature of his acts. There was nothing whatever to suggest he suffered delusions.

"Thank you, Dr. Wade," Rathbone said with confidence he was far from feeling. "I believe you have known Rhys most of his life, is that correct?"

"I have," Wade replied.

"And been his physician, when he required one?"

"Yes."

"Were you aware of there being a serious and violent disagreement with his father, and if so, over what subject?"

It was a question which Wade would find extremely difficult to answer in the affirmative. If he admitted it, it would seem incompetent that he had not done anything to forestall this tragedy. It would seem like wisdom after the event, and Sylvestra would see it as a betrayal, as indeed so might some of the jury.

"Dr. Wade?" Rathbone prompted.

Wade raised his head and stared at him resolutely.

"I was aware of a certain tension between them," he answered, his voice stronger, full of regret. "I thought it the normal resentment a son might have for the discipline a father naturally exerts." He bit his lip and drew in a deep breath. "I had no idea whatever it would end like this. I blame myself. I should have been more aware. I have had a great deal of experience with men of all ages, and under extreme pressure, during my service in the navy." A ghost of a smile touched his mouth and then vanished. "I suppose closer to home, in people for whom one has affection, one is loath to recognize such things."

It was a clever answer, honest and yet without committing himself. And it earned the jury's respect. Rathbone could see it in their faces. He would have been wiser not to have asked, but it was too late now.

"You did not foresee it?" he repeated.

"No," Wade said quietly, looking down. "I did not, God forgive me."

Rathbone hesitated on the brink of asking him if he thought Rhys insane, and decided against it. No answer, either way, could help enough to be worth the risk.

"Thank you, Dr. Wade. That is all."

Goode had already established the violence of the fight and the fact that Leighton Duff and Rhys had been involved, and there was no reason to suspect anyone else's being there. He called the Duff household servants, deeply against their will,

329

and obliged them to testify to the quarrel the evening of Leighton Duff's death and to the time both men had left the house. At least he spared Sylvestra the distress of testifying.

All the time Rhys sat propped up in the dock, his skin ashen pale, his eyes seeming enormous in his haggard face, a prison warder on either side of him, perhaps more to support than to restrain him. He did not look capable of offering any resistance, let alone an attempt to escape.

Rathbone forced himself to put the thought of his client out of his mind. He must use intelligence rather than emotion. Let anyone else feel all the compassion they could, his brain must be clear.

There seemed no way of casting the slightest doubt, reasonable or unreasonable, on Rhys's physical guilt, and he was struggling without a glimmer of hope to think of any mitigation.

Where was Monk?

He dared not look at Hester. He could imagine too clearly the panic she must be feeling.

Through the afternoon and the next day Goode brought on a troop of witnesses who placed Rhys in St. Giles over a period of months. Not one of them could be cast doubt upon. Rathbone had to stand by and watch. There was no argument to make.

The judge adjourned the court early. It seemed as if there was little left to do but sum up the case. Goode had proved every assertion he had made. There was no alternative to offer, except that Rhys had been whoring in St. Giles and his father had confronted him, they had quarreled and Rhys had killed him. Goode had avoided mentioning the rapes, but if Rathbone challenged him that the motive for murder was too slender to believe, then he would undoubtedly bring in the beaten women, still bearing their scars. He had said as much. It was only Rhys's desperate condition which stayed his hand. Fortune had already punished him appallingly, and the conviction for murder would be sufficient to have him hanged. There was no need for more.

Rathbone left the courtroom feeling he had been defeated without offering even the semblance of a fight. He had done nothing for Rhys. He had not begun to fulfill the trust Hester and Sylvestra had placed in him. He was ashamed, and yet he could think of nothing to say which would do Rhys the slightest service.

Certainly he could harass witnesses or object to Goode's questions, his tactics, his logic, or anything else; but it would serve no purpose except to give the effect of a defense. It would be a sham. He knew it; Hester would know it. Would it even be of comfort to Rhys? Or offer him false hope?

At least he should have the courage to go to Rhys now, and not escape, as he would so much rather.

When he reached Rhys, Hester was already there. She turned as she heard Rathbone's step, her eyes desperate, pleading for some hope, any hope at all.

They sat together in the gray cell below the Old Bailey. Rhys was in physical pain, muscles clenched, broken hands shaking. He looked hopeless. Hester sat next to him, her arm around his shoulders.

Rathbone was at his wits' end.

"Rhys," he said tensely, "you have got to tell us what happened. I want to defend you, but I have nothing with which to do it." His own muscles were knotted tight, his hands balled into fists of frustration. "I have no weapons. Did you kill him?"

Rhys shook his head, perhaps an inch in either direction, but the denial was clear.

"Someone else did?"

Again the tiny movement, but definitely a nod.

"Do you know who?"

A nod, a bitter smile, trembling-lipped.

"Has it anything to do with your mother?"

A very slight shrug of the shoulders, then a shake. No.

"An enemy of your father's?"

Rhys turned away, jerking his head, his hands starting to bang on his thighs, jolting the splints.

Hester grabbed his wrists. "Stop it!" she said loudly. "You must tell us, Rhys. Don't you understand? They will find you guilty if we cannot prove it was someone else, or at least that it could have been."

He nodded slowly but would not face her.

There was nothing left but the violence of the truth.

"They will hang you," Rathbone said deliberately.

Rhys's throat moved as if he would say something, then he swung away from them again, and refused to look at them anymore.

Hester stared at Rathbone, her eyes filled with tears.

He stood still for a minute, then another. There was nothing to say or do. He sighed, then left. As he was walking along the passage he passed Corriden Wade going in. At least Wade might be able to offer some physical relief, or even a draft of some sort strong enough to give a few hours' sleep.

Farther along he encountered Sylvestra, looking so distraught she seemed on the verge of collapse. At least she had Fidelis Kynaston with her.

Rathbone spent the evening alone in his rooms, unable to eat or even to sit at his fire. He paced the floor, his mind turning over one useless fact after another, when his butler came to announce that Monk was in the hall.

"Monk!" Rathbone grasped at the very name as if it had been a raft for a drowning man. "Monk! Bring him in . . . immediately!"

Monk looked tired and pale. His hair dripped and his face was shining wet.

"Well?" Rathbone demanded, finding himself gulping air, his hands stiff, a tingling in his arms. "What have you?"

"I don't know," Monk answered bleakly. "I have no idea whether it makes things better or even worse. Leighton Duff was one of the rapists in Seven Dials, and then later in St. Giles."

Rathbone was stunned. "What?" he said, his voice high with disbelief. It was preposterous, totally absurd. He must have misunderstood. "What did you say?"

"Leighton Duff was one of the rapists in both areas," Monk repeated. "I have several people who will identify him, in particular a cabby who saw him in St. Giles on the night before Christmas Eve with blood on his hands and face, just after one of the worst rapes. And Rhys was in Lowndes Square at a quiet evening with Mrs. Kynaston, Arthur Kynaston and Lady Sandon and her son."

Rathbone felt a sense of shock so great the room seemed to sway around him.

"You are sure?" he said, and the instant the words were off his tongue he knew how foolish they were. It was plain in Monk's face. Anyway, he would not have come with such news were he not certain beyond any doubt at all.

Monk did not bother to answer. He sat down uninvited, close to the fire. He was still shivering and he looked exhausted.

"I don't know what it means," he continued, staring past Rathbone at the empty chair opposite him, but mostly at something he could see within his own mind. "Perhaps Rhys was not involved in that rape, but he was in some or all of the others," he said. "Perhaps not. Certainly Leighton Duff did not follow his son in any sense of outrage or horror at what he had done, and then in righteous indignation confront him with it." He turned to Rathbone, who was still standing on the same spot. "I'm sorry. All it means is that we have misunderstood the motive. It doesn't prove anything else. I don't know what you want to make of it. How is the trial going?"

"Appallingly," Rathbone replied, at last moving to the other chair and sitting down stiffly. "I have nothing to fight with. I suppose this will at least provide ammunition with which to open up the whole issue as to what happened. It will raise doubts. It will certainly prolong the trial. . . ." He smiled bitterly. "It will shake Ebenezer Goode!" A well of horror opened up inside him. "It will shatter Mrs. Duff."

"Yes, I know that," Monk replied very quietly. "But it is the truth, and if you allow Rhys to be hanged for something of which he is not guilty, none of us can then undo that, or call him back from the gallows and the grave. There is a certain kind of freedom in the truth, whatever it is. At least your decisions are founded on reality. You can learn to live with them."

Rathbone looked at him closely. There was at once pain and the beginning of a kind of peace in Monk's face which he had not seen before. Monk's weariness held within it the possibility of rest.

"Yes," Rathbone agreed. "Thank you, Monk. You had better give me the names of these people, and all the details . . . and, of course, your account. You have done very well." Deliberately, he blocked from his mind the thought of having to tell Hester what he now knew. It was sufficient for the night that he should work out his strategy for Rhys.

Rathbone worked until six in the morning, and after two hours' sleep, a hot bath and breakfast, he faced the courtroom again. There was no air of expectation. There were even some empty seats in the spectators' gallery. The trial had degenerated from high drama into simple tragedy. It was not interesting anymore.

Rathbone had had messengers out all night. Monk was in court.

In the dock, Rhys looked white and ill. He was obviously in physical pain as well as mental turmoil, although there was now an air of despair about him which made Rathbone believe he no longer hoped for anything except an end to his ordeal.

Sylvestra sat like a woman in a nightmare, unable to move or speak. Beside her on one side was Fidelis Kynaston, on the other Eglantyne Wade. Rathbone was pleased she would not be alone, and yet possibly having to hear the things she was going to in the company of friends would be harder. One might wish to absorb such shock in the privacy of solitude, where one could weep unobserved.

Yet everyone would know. It was not as if she could cover it, as one can some family secrets. Perhaps better she heard it in court than whispered, distorted by telling and retelling. Either way, Rathbone had no choice in the matter. He had not told Sylvestra what he expected to uncover that day. She was not his client, Rhys was. Anyway, he had had no time, no opportunity to explain to her what it was he knew, and he could not foresee what his witnesses would testify; he simply had nothing to lose on Rhys's behalf.

"Sir Oliver?" the judge prompted.

"My lord," Rathbone acknowledged. "The defense calls Mrs. Vida Hopgood."

The judge looked surprised, but he made no remark. There was a slight stir of movement in the crowd.

Vida took the stand looking nervous, her chin high, her shoulders squared, her magnificent hair half hidden under her hat.

Rathbone began immediately. He was hideously unsure of her, but he had had no time to prepare. He was fighting for survival and there was nothing else.

"Mrs. Hopgood, what is your husband's occupation?"

" 'E 'as a fact'ry," she replied carefully. "Wot makes shirts an' the like."

"And he employs women to sew these shirts . . . and the like?" Rathbone asked.

In the gallery someone tittered. It was nervousness. They could not be any more highly strung than he was.

"Yeah," Vida agreed.

Ebenezer Goode rose to his feet.

"Yes, Mr. Goode," the judge said, forestalling Goode's objection. "Sir Oliver, has Mr. Hopgood's occupation got anything to do with Mr. Duff's guilt or innocence in this case?"

"Yes, my lord," Rathbone replied without hesitation. "The women he employs are profoundly pertinent to the issue. Indeed, they are the true victims in this tragedy."

There was a ripple of amazement around the room. Several of the jurors looked confused and annoyed.

In the dock, Rhys moved position and a spasm of pain twisted his face. The judge also seemed unhappy. "If you are going to demonstrate to the court that they were abused in some way, Sir Oliver, that will not help your client's cause. The fact that they can, or cannot, identify their assailants will distress them and give you nothing. In fact, it will only damage your client's sympathies still further. If it is your intention to plead insanity, then practical evidence is required, and of a very specific nature, as I am sure you know very well. You have pleaded 'not guilty.' Are you now wishing to change that plea?"

"No, my lord." Rathbone heard his words drop into a well of silence, and wondered if he had just made an appalling mistake. What was Rhys himself thinking of him? "No, my lord. I have no cause to believe that my client is not of sane mind."

"Then proceed with questioning Mrs. Hopgood," the judge directed. "But come to your point as rapidly as you are able. I shall not allow you to waste the court's time and patience with delaying tactics."

Rathbone knew how very close to the truth that charge was.

"Thank you, my lord," he said graciously, and turned back to Vida. "Mrs. Hopgood, have you suffered a shortage of workers lately?"

"Yeah. Lots o' sickness," she replied. She knew what he wished. She was an intelligent woman, and articulate in her own fashion. "Or more like injury. Took me a fair bit o' argy-bargy, but I got it aht of 'em wot 'ad 'appened." She looked questioningly at Rathbone, and then seeing his expression, continued with feeling. "They do a bit o' dolly mop stuff on the side . . . beggin' yer pardon, sir, I mean takes the odd gent 'ere an' there ter add a bit extra . . . w'en their children is 'ungry, or the like."

"We understand," Rathbone assured her, then explained for the jury. "You mean they practice a little amateur prostitution when times are particularly hard."

"In't that wot I said? Yeah. Can't blame 'em, poor cows. 'Oo's gonna watch their children starvin' and not do summink abaht it? In't 'uman." She drew breath. "Like I said, some of 'em was doin' a bit on the side, like. Well, first orff they got cheated outa pay. Got no pimps ter look arter 'em, yer see." Her handsome face darkened with anger. "Then it got worse. These geezers don't on'y cheat, they started roughin' 'em up, knockin' 'em around, like. First it were just a bit, then it got worse." Her expression twisted till the anger and pain in it were stark to see. "Some of 'em got beat pretty bad, bones broke,

336

teef an' noses broke—kicked, some of 'em were. Some of 'em was on'y bits o' children theirselves. So I got a bit o' money tergether an' 'ired meself someone ter find out 'oo wos doin' it." She stopped abruptly, staring at Rathbone. "D'yer want me ter say 'oo I got, an' wot 'e found?"

"No, thank you, Mrs. Hopgood," Rathbone replied. "You have laid an excellent foundation for us to discern from these poor women themselves what occurred. Just one more thing . . ."

"Yeah?"

"How many women do you know of who were beaten in this way?"

"In Seven Dials? Abaht twen'y-odd, as I knows of. They went on ter St. Giles—"

"Thank you, Mrs. Hopgood," Rathbone interrupted. "Please tell us only your own experience."

Goode rose again. "All we have heard so far is hearsay, my lord. Mrs. Hopgood has not been a victim herself, and she has not mentioned Mr. Rhys Duff. I have been extraordinarily patient, as was your lordship. All this is tragic, and abhorrent, but completely irrelevant."

"It is not irrelevant, my lord," Rathbone argued. "The prosecution's case is that Rhys Duff went to the area of St. Giles to use prostitutes there, and that his father followed him, chastised him for his behavior, and in the resulting quarrel, Rhys killed his father and was severely injured himself. Therefore what happened to these women is fundamental to the case."

"I have not claimed that these unfortunate women were raped, my lord," Goode contradicted. "But if they were, then that only adds to the brutality of the accused's conduct and the validity of the motive. No wonder his father charged him with grievous sin and would have chastened him severely, possibly even threatened to turn him over to the law."

Rathbone swung around to face Goode. "You have proved only that Rhys used a prostitute in the area of St. Giles. You have not proved violence of any sort against any women—in St. Giles or in Seven Dials."

"Gentlemen!" the judge said sharply. "Sir Oliver, if you are determined to prove this issue, then you had better be absolutely certain you are aiding your client's cause and not further condemning him, but if you are satisfied, then prove your point. Proceed with dispatch."

"Thank you, my lord." Rathbone dismissed Vida Hopgood, and one by one called half a dozen of the women of St. Giles whom Monk had found. He began with the earliest, and least severely injured. The court sat in uncomfortable near silence and listened to their pathetic tales of poverty, illness, desperation, journeys out onto the streets to pick up a few pence by selling their bodies, and the cheating, then the violence which had followed.

Rathbone loathed doing it. The women were gray-faced, almost inarticulate with fear and, in some cases, also shame. They despised themselves for what they did, but need drove them. They hated standing in this handsome courtroom facing exquisitely gowned and wigged lawyers, the judge in his scarlet robes, and having to tell of their need, their humiliation and their pain.

Rathbone glanced at the jurors' faces and read a sense of different emotions in them. He watched how much their imaginations conceived of the lives that were being described. How many of them, if any, had used such women themselves? What did they feel now? Shame, anger, pity or revulsion? More than half of them looked up to the dock at Rhys, whose face was twisted with emotion, but it was impossible to say what aroused his anger, or the revulsion which was so plain in his features.

Rathbone looked also at Sylvestra Duff and saw her lips puckered with horror as a world opened up in front of her beyond anything she had imagined, women whose lives were so utterly unlike her own they could have belonged to a different species. And yet they lived only a few miles away, in the same city. And her son had used them, could even, for all she knew, have begotten a child upon them.

Beside her, Fidelis Kynaston looked pale but less shocked. There was in her already a knowledge of pain, of the darker side of the world and those who lived in it. This was only a restatement of things she already knew.

On Sylvestra's other side, Eglantyne Wade was motionless as wave after wave of misery passed over her, things she had never imagined were rehearsed before her in sickening detail.

The following day the stories became more violent. The witnesses still carried the marks of beatings on their blackened and swollen faces, their broken teeth.

Ebenezer Goode hesitated before questioning each one. None of them had recognized their assailants. Every brutal act only added to his case. Why should he challenge any of it? To demonstrate that the women were prostitutes anyway was unnecessary. There was not a man or woman in the room who did not know it and feel their own emotions regarding their trade and its place in society, or in their own personal lives. It was a subject of emotion rather than reason anyway. Words were only a froth on the surface of the deep tide of feeling.

A particular wave of revulsion and anger swelled when the thirteen-year-old Lily Drover testified, still nursing her dislocated shoulder. Haltingly she told Rathbone how both she and her sister had been beaten and kicked. She repeated the grunted words of abuse she had heard, and how she had tried to crawl away and hide in the dark.

Fidelis Kynaston looked so ashen Rathbone thought she suffered more in hearing it than Sylvestra, beside her.

The judge leaned forward, his own face tight with distress.

"Have you not established all you need, Sir Oliver? Surely no more can be necessary. This is a horrifying matter of escalating violence and brutality. What more do you require to show us? Make your point!"

"I have one more victim of rape, my lord. This one was in St. Giles."

"Very well. I realize you need to establish that your assailants have moved into the relevant area. But make it brief."

"My lord." Rathbone called the woman who had been raped and beaten on the night before Christmas Eve. Her face was still discolored. She had difficulty speaking through her broken teeth. Slowly, her eyes closed as she refused to look at the people who were watching her as she told about her terror and pain and humiliation. She began to describe being accosted by three men, how one of them had taken hold of her, how all three had laughed, then one had thrown her to the ground.

In the dock, Rhys was gray-skinned, his eyes so hollow one could almost visualize the skull beneath the flesh. He leaned forward over the rail, his splinted hands stiff, shivering.

The woman described how she had been taunted by the men, called names. One of them had kicked her, told her she was filth, should be got rid of, the human race cleansed of her sort.

In the dock, Rhys started to bang his hands up and down on the railing. One of the warders made a move to stop him, but the muscles of Rhys's body were knotted so hard he did not succeed. Rhys's face was a mask of pain.

No one else moved.

The woman in the witness stand went on speaking, slowly, each word forced between her lips. She told how they had knocked her over till she was crouching on the cobbles.

"They were 'ard, an' wet," she said huskily. "Then one of 'em leaned on top o' me. 'E were 'eavy, and 'e smelled o' summink funny, sort o' sharp. One o' the others forced me knees up and tore me dress. Then I felt 'im come inter me. It was like I were tore inside. It 'urt summink terrible. I—"

She stopped, her eyes wide with horror as Rhys wrenched himself from the warders, his mouth gaping, his throat tortured with the sound it could not make, as if inside himself he screamed again and again.

A warder made a lunge after him and caught one arm. Rhys lashed at him, his face a paroxysm of terror and loathing. The other warder made a grab and missed. Rhys overbalanced, hysterical with fear, teetered for a moment on the high railing, then swiveled and fell over the edge.

A woman shrieked.

The jurors rose to their feet.

Sylvestra cried out his name and Fidelis clasped her arms around her friend.

Rhys landed with a sickening crash and lay still.

Hester was the first to move. She rose from her seat in the back of the gallery, on the edge of the row, where she could be reached were she needed, and ran forward, falling on her knees beside him.

Then suddenly there was commotion everywhere. People were crying out, jostling one another. Others had been hurt, two of them badly. Press reporters were scrambling to force their way out to pass on the news. Ushers were trying helplessly to restore some form of order. The judge was banging his gavel. Someone was shouting for a doctor for a woman whose leg had been broken by an overturned bench.

Rathbone swung around to make his way towards where Rhys was lying. Where was Corriden Wade? Had he been seized to tend to the woman? Rathbone did not even know if Rhys was still alive. Considering the height of his fall, he could easily be dead. It is not difficult to break a neck. The thought crossed his mind that perhaps it would be a merciful escape from a more prolonged and dreadful end.

Was it even suicide, in hearing the full horror of his crime told from the victim's view, her feelings of shame, humiliation, helplessness and pain? Was this the nearest Rhys could come to some kind of redemption?

Was this Rathbone's final failure, or perhaps the only thing he had truly done for him?

Except that Rhys had not raped the woman. He had been playing cards with Lady Sandon. It was Leighton Duff who had first raped and then beaten her. Leighton Duff . . . and who?

The uproar in the courtroom was overwhelming. People were shouting, trying to clear the way for a stretcher. Someone was screaming again and again, uselessly, hysterically. All around him people were pushing and shoving, trying to move one way or another.

Bent over Rhys's body, Hester, for one desperate moment, had the same thought that had passed through Rathbone's mind . . . was this Rhys's escape at last from the pain of body which afflicted him, and from the greater agony of mind which

341

haunted even his sleep? Was this the only peace he could find in a world which had become one long nightmare?

Then she touched him and knew he was still alive. She slid her hand under his head, feeling the thick hair. She felt the bone gently, exploring. There was no depression in the skull. She pulled her hand clear. There was no blood. His legs were twisted, but his spine was straight. As far as she could tell, he was concussed, but not fatally injured.

Where was Corriden Wade? She looked up, peering around, and saw no one she recognized, but there was a huddle of people where the bench was overturned and someone was lying on the floor. Even Rathbone was beyond the crowd jostling beside and in front of her.

Then she saw Monk and felt a surge of relief. He was elbowing his way forward, angry, white-faced. He was shouting at someone. A large man clenched his fist and seemed intent on making a fight of it. Someone else began pulling at him. Two more women were crying for no apparent reason.

Monk finally forced his way through and knelt beside her.

"Is he alive?" he asked.

"Yes. But we've got to get him out of here," she responded, hearing her voice sharp with fear.

He looked down at Rhys, who was still completely insensible. "Thank God he can't feel this," he said quietly. "I've sent the warder for one of those long benches. We could carry him on that."

"We've got to get him to a hospital," she said desperately. "He can't stay in the cell. I don't know how badly he's hurt."

Monk opened his mouth as if to reply, then changed his mind. One of the warders had come downstairs from the dock and was pushing people aside to reach Rhys.

"Poor devil," he said laconically. "Best for 'im if 'e'd killed 'isself, but if 'en in't, we'll best do for 'im what we can. 'Ere, miss, let me get 'im up onter the bench wot Tom's bringin'."

"We'll take him to the nearest hospital," she said, rising shakily and only just avoiding falling over her own skirts.

"Sorry, miss, but we gotta take 'im back to 'is cell. 'E's a prisoner . . ."

"He's hardly going to escape!" she said furiously, all her helplessness and pain welling up in useless anger for a moment. "He's totally insensible, you fool! Look at him!"

"Yes, miss," the warder said stolidly. "But the law is the law. We'll put 'im back in 'is cell, an' yer can stay wif 'im, if yer don' mind bein' locked in wif 'im? No doubt they'll send a doctor w'en they get one."

"Of course I'll stay with him!" she choked out. "And fetch Dr. Wade, immediately!"

"We'll try, miss. Is there anyfink as yer want for 'im? Water, like, or a little brandy? I'm sure as I could get a little brandy for yer."

She controlled herself with an effort. The man was doing his best. "Thank you. Yes, get me both water and brandy, please."

The other warder appeared along with two more men carrying a wooden bench. With surprising gentleness they picked Rhys up and laid him on the bench, then carried it out of the courtroom, pushing past onlookers and out through the doors and down the hallway toward the cells.

Hester followed, hardly aware of the people around her, of the curious stares and the mutters and calls. All she could think of was how badly Rhys was hurt and why he had fallen over. Had it been an accident as he tried to escape the warders and they attempted to restrain him, or had he intended to kill himself? Had he lost every last vestige of hope?

Or had he been lying all the time, and he had both killed his father and raped and beaten those women?

She refused to believe that . . . not unless and until she had to. As long as there was a flicker of any other possibility, she would cling to it. But what possibility? What other conceivable explanation was there? She raked her imagination and her memory.

Then one occurred to her, one so extreme and so horrible she stumbled as she followed the warders and all but fell. She was shaking. She felt cold and sick, and her mind raced for any way at all in which she could learn if it were true, and prove it. And she knew why Rhys could not speak, why even if he could . . . he would not.

She ran a step or two to catch up with them, and as soon as they were at the cells she swung around to face the warders.

"Thank you. Bring me the brandy and water, then leave us alone. I will do what I can for him." It was a race against time. Dr. Wade, or some other physician, would be bound to come soon. If she was right, it must not be Corriden Wade. But she must know. Anyone interrupting what she now meant to do would be horrified. She might even be prosecuted. Certainly she would jeopardize her career. If it was Corriden Wade, she might even lose her life.

The warder disappeared, leaving the door open, and his companion waited just outside. What could she begin doing to save time?

"Yer all right, miss?"

"Yes, of course I am, thank you. I am a nurse. I have treated many injured men before. I shall just examine him to see where he is most seriously hurt. It will help the doctor when he comes. Where is the brandy? And the water? A little will do, just hurry!" Her hands were shaking. Her mouth was dry. She could feel her heart lurching and knocking in her chest.

Rhys was still completely unconscious. Once he stirred there would be nothing she could do. She must not ask the warder to hurry again, or he would become suspicious.

She unfastened Rhys's collar and took off his tie. She undid the buttons of his shirt and eased it open. Very gently she began to examine the upper part of his body. There were no bandages. There was little one could do for bruising, except ointment, such as arnica. The worst of it was beginning to heal now. The broken ribs were knitted well, even though she knew they still caused him pain, especially if he coughed, sneezed or turned badly in the bed.

Where was the warder with the brandy and the water? It seemed like ages since he had gone.

Carefully she unfastened the waist of his trousers. This was where his worst injuries were, the ones which Dr. Wade had treated and not permitted her to see, for the sake of Rhys's modesty. She slipped the waist down a few inches and saw the blue and purple bruising, now fading. The abrasions were still marked where he had been kicked, but the edges were yellowish and far paler. She could feel no bandaging.

"Miss!"

She froze. "Yes?"

"Water, miss," the warder said quietly. "And a drop o' brandy. Is 'e 'urt bad?"

"I'm not sure yet. Thank you for these." She straightened up and took the dish of water from him, then the brandy. She set them on the small table. "Thank you very much. You can lock me in. I shall be perfectly all right. Come back and let me know when the doctor comes. Knock on the door, if you will. I shall get him ready."

"Yes, miss. Yer sure yer all right? Yer look terrible pale. Mebbe yer should take a sip o' that brandy yerself?"

She tried to smile, and felt the expression sickly on her face. "Maybe. Thank you."

"Right, miss. You knock if yer need ter come out."

"I will. Yes. Now I had better see what I can do for him. Thank you."

At last he went and she was left alone. She swung around to Rhys and started immediately. There was no time to be lost. They could return with a doctor any moment. There was no way on earth she could explain what she was doing, if she were mistaken. It would probably ruin her, even if she were right but could not prove it.

She pulled open his trousers and his underclothes, revealing his body as far as his thighs. There were no bandages at all, no plasters, no lint, no adhesives. There was only the most fearful bruising, as if he had been repeatedly kicked and punched. Sick in her stomach, she rolled him over to lie on his face and began the examination which would tell her what she needed to know, although the slow trickle of blood even now, and the purplish and torn flesh, was enough.

It took her only moments. Then, with shaking hands, fumbling, fingers stiff, she pulled the clothes back up and rolled him over, almost knocking him off the narrow bench. She tried

345

to fasten his trousers, but she had them crooked and they would not reach. She snatched his jacket and threw it over him just as his eyes fluttered open.

"Rhys!" She choked on the word, the anguish inside her spilling out, her throat aching, her hands trembling and clumsy.

He gasped, drawing in his breath. He was fighting her, trying to lash out, force her away.

"Rhys!" She clung onto his arms, above the splints, her fingers digging into his flesh. "Rhys, I know what happened to you! It's not your fault! You are not the only one! I've known soldiers it happened to, brave men, fighting men!"

He started to shake, trembling so violently she could not keep him still, even holding him in her arms. The fierceness of his anger shook her too. He sobbed, great racking, desperate cries, and she rocked back and forth, her arms around him, her hand stroking his head.

It was not until she had been doing so for several minutes, time she could not count, that she realized she could hear him. He was weeping with a voice. Something in his despair, in the fall, or in the knowledge that she knew, had returned his speech.

"Who was it?" she said urgently. "You must tell me." Although she was certain, with an aching coldness, that she knew. There was only one explanation as to why no one had known before, why Corriden Wade had not told anyone, not told her or Rathbone. It explained so much: Rhys's fear, his cruelty and rejection of his mother, his silence. She remembered with a sick pain the bell removed to the dresser, out of his reach.

"I'll protect you," she promised fiercely. "I'll see that the warders are with you all the time, or I will be, every moment, I swear. Now tell me."

Slowly, in agonized and broken words, in a whisper as if he could not bear to hear it himself, he told her of the night his father died.

The door burst open and Corriden Wade came in, bag in his hand, his face haggard, his eyes dark and furious. The two warders were just behind him, looming awkwardly.

"What are you doing, Miss Latterly?" Wade demanded, staring at Rhys's white, strained face and wild eyes. "Leave me to my patient, please. He is obviously deeply distressed." He turned to the warders. "I shall need clean water, several bowls of it, and bandages. Perhaps Miss Latterly can go and obtain those. She will be aware of my needs—"

"I think not," Hester said abruptly, moving to stand between Rhys and Wade. She looked at the warder. "Please will you fetch Sir Oliver Rathbone, immediately. Mr. Duff wants to make a statement. It is imperative you do this with all possible speed. I am sure you understand the urgency . . . and the importance."

"Mr. Duff cannot speak," Wade said with contempt. "This tragedy has obviously unnerved Miss Latterly, not surprisingly. Perhaps you had better take her out, see if you can—"

"Fetch Sir Oliver!" Hester repeated loudly, facing the warder. "Go!"

The man hesitated. The doctor's authority he understood. He would always obey a man before a woman, any woman.

"Fetch my lawyer," Rhys said hoarsely. "I want to make a statement before I die."

The blood drained from Wade's face.

The warder gasped. "Go get 'im, Joe," he said quickly. "I'll wait 'ere."

The other warder turned on his heel and obeyed.

Hester stood without moving.

"This is preposterous," Wade began, moving as if to push his way past, but the warder took him by the shoulder. Medicine was beyond him, but dying statements he understood.

"Let go of me!" Wade commanded furiously.

"I'm sorry, sir," the warder said stiffly. "But we'll wait for the lawyer afore we start any treatment on the prisoner. 'E's well enough for now. The nurse 'ere saw ter 'im. You jus' stand 'ere patient, like, an' as soon as the lawyer's done 'is bit, you can treat all yer need."

Wade opened his mouth as if to argue and saw the futility of it. He stood as if trapped, waiting for a moment to escape.

Rhys looked at Hester.

She smiled back at him, then turned and remained facing Wade and the warder. She felt sick with disillusion.

The minutes ticked by.

Rathbone came in, eyes wide, face flushed.

"I want . . ." Rhys began, then took a shuddering breath. "I want to tell you what happened. . . ."

Silently, Corriden Wade turned and left, although there was nowhere now for him to go.

Court resumed in the afternoon. Rhys was not present, having been taken back to the hospital and put in the care of Dr. Riley, but under a police guard. He was still accused of a fearful crime.

The gallery was surprisingly empty. There were spare seats in every row. People had assumed that Rhys's pitch over the railing had been an attempt at suicide, and therefore a tacit admission of guilt. There was no longer any real interest. It was all over but the verdict. The three women, Sylvestra Duff, Eglantyne Wade and Fidelis Kynaston, sat together, very clearly visible now. They did not look at each other, but there was a closeness in them, a silent companionship which was apparent to anyone who regarded them carefully.

The judge called the court to order and commanded Rathbone to proceed. The jurors looked grim but resigned, as if their duty had been taken from them and they were there only as a matter of form, but purposeless.

"Thank you, my lord," Rathbone acknowledged. "I call Mrs. Fidelis Kynaston."

There was a murmur of surprise as Fidelis, white-faced, walked across the floor and climbed the steps. She took the oath and looked at Rathbone with her head high, but her hands on the railing were clenched, as if she needed the railing's presence to support her.

"Mrs. Kynaston," he began gently, "did you have a party in your home on the night before Christmas Eve?"

She had known what he was going to say. Her voice was hoarse when she answered. "Yes."

"Who was present?"

"My two sons, Rhys Duff, Lady Sandon, Rufus Sandon and myself."

"At what time did Rhys Duff leave your house?"

"About two o'clock in the morning."

There was a sudden rustle of sound in the gallery. One of the jurors started forward.

"Are you certain as to the time, Mrs. Kynaston?" Rathbone pressed.

"I am positive," she replied, looking straight ahead at him as if he were an executioner. "If you were to ask Lady Sandon, or any of my household staff, they would tell you the same thing."

"So the group of men who raped the unfortunate woman in St. Giles at around midnight could not possibly have included Rhys Duff?"

"No . . ." She swallowed, her throat tight. "It could not."

"Thank you, Mrs. Kynaston, that is all I have to ask you."

Goode considered for a moment or two, then declined his opportunity.

Rathbone called the cabby, Joseph Roscoe.

Roscoe described the man he had seen leaving St. Giles, his hands and face smeared with blood. Rathbone produced a picture of Leighton Duff and showed it to him.

"Is this the man you saw?"

Roscoe did not hesitate. "Yes sir, that's 'im."

"My lord, this is a likeness of Leighton Duff, whom Mr. Roscoe has identified."

He got no further. The noise in the court was like the backwash of the sea. Sylvestra sat frozen, her face a mask of blank, unbelieving horror. Beside her, Eglantyne Wade supported her weight. Fidelis was rigid, still staring at the cabdriver.

The jurors stared from the witness to Rathbone, and back again.

The judge was grave and deeply disturbed. "Are you certain of your ground, Sir Oliver? Are you claiming that Leighton Duff, not Rhys Duff, was the rapist in all these fearful cases?"

"Yes, my lord," Rathbone said with conviction. "Leighton

349

Duff was one of three. Rhys Duff had nothing to do with them. He did indeed go to St. Giles, and there use the services of a prostitute. But he paid the price asked, and he exercised no violence whatever. It is a practice about which we may all have our moral judgments, but it is not a crime, and it is certainly not rape, nor is it murder."

"Then who murdered Leighton Duff, Sir Oliver? He did not commit suicide. It seems apparent he and Rhys fought, and Rhys survived while he did not."

"I shall explain, my lord, with your permission."

"You must do more than explain, Sir Oliver, you must prove it to this court and this jury beyond a reasonable doubt."

"That is what I intend, my lord. To that end I call Miss Hester Latterly to the stand."

There was a slight stir of interest. Heads craned as Hester walked across the floor and up the steps, faced Rathbone and took the oath.

"What is your occupation, Miss Latterly?" Rathbone began almost conversationally.

"I am a nurse."

"Do you presently have a patient?"

"Yes. I have been employed to nurse Rhys Duff since he returned from the hospital after the incident in Water Lane."

"Was there also a doctor in attendance?"

"Dr. Corriden Wade. He has been the family physician for many years, I understand."

The judge leaned forward. "Please restrict yourself to what you know, Miss Latterly."

"I'm sorry, my lord."

"Have you any experience in the army of men injured in the same manner and degree as Rhys Duff was, Miss Latterly?"

"Yes. I nursed many injured soldiers in Scutari."

There was a murmur of approval around the gallery. Two of the jurors nodded.

"Did you treat his injuries yourself, or merely nurse him, keep him clean, feed him, attend to his wants?" Rathbone must be careful how he phrased his questions. So far no one else seemed to have the slightest idea what he was seeking to prove. He must not lead her, neither must he leave any doubt in their minds, once he had shown them the truth.

Goode was listening intently.

"I treated those wounds above the waist," Hester replied. "They were bruises, very severe, and the broken bones in his hands, and two broken ribs. There was very little to be done for them. The injuries below the waist Dr. Wade told me he bandaged. This was for the sake of Mr. Duff's sensibilities."

"I see. So you never observed them yourself?"

"That is correct."

"But you accepted Dr. Wade's word for their nature and degree, and that they were healing as well as could be expected?"

"Yes."

The judge leaned forward again. "Sir Oliver, does the nature or site of Mr. Duff's wounds have any relevance to whether he was responsible for his father's death? I admit, I fail to see it."

"Yes, my lord, it does." Rathbone turned to Hester. "Miss Latterly, was Mr. Duff subject to any unusual degree of emotional turmoil during the time you cared for him?"

Goode rose to his feet. "My lord, Miss Latterly did not know Mr. Duff before the tragedy. She cannot know if his distress was usual or not."

The judge looked at Rathbone. "Sir Oliver? Mr. Goode's point is a fair one."

"My lord, I meant was he subject to emotions extraordinary in a man in his condition. Miss Latterly has nursed many men who were severely injured. I think she is in a better position than almost anyone else to know what to expect."

"I agree." The judge nodded. "You may answer, Miss Latterly."

"Yes, my lord. Rhys had the most appalling nightmares when he would try to cry out, beat his arms, even though his hands were broken and it must have caused him fearful pain, and he would try to scream. And yet when he was awake, he refused absolutely to respond to questions about the incident and became extremely distressed, to the point of violent reaction against people, especially his mother, when any pressure was placed upon him."

"And what did you conclude from that?" Rathbone asked.

"I did not conclude anything. I was puzzled. I . . . I feared perhaps he had indeed killed his father, and the memory of it was unbearable to him."

"Are you still of that opinion?"

"No . . ."

"Why not?"

She drew in a deep breath and let it out slowly.

In the courtroom no one moved. Goode was frowning, listening to her intently.

"Because after I saw him fall this morning," she replied, "I remembered for an instant something I had learned of in the army. It seemed too appalling to be true, but in his cell, where they carried him, I was alone with him for several minutes before the doctor came. I made a very brief examination of his injuries . . . below the waist." She stopped. Her face was filled with pain.

Rathbone wished he did not have to make her say this, but there was no possible alternative.

She saw it in his eyes and did not flinch.

"He had been raped," she said very quietly, but very clearly. "Rhys was the rapists' last victim."

There was a gasp, and then utter silence except for a moan from Sylvestra as such pain of mind tore through her as was beyond bearing.

"Rhys and his father quarreled because Rhys knew a little of what was happening. His father had criticized him for using prostitutes, and the hypocrisy of it infuriated him, but for his mother's sake he could not be open about it. He flung out of the house and went to St. Giles. By chance, so did his father."

She took a breath and her voice became huskier.

"The three of them set on him in Water Lane," she went on, and although it was hearsay, Goode did not interrupt her. His extraordinary face was creased with horror. "They knocked

352

him down and raped him," she continued, "as they had done the women—and perhaps other young men. We may never know. Then as he struggled and cried out, one of them stopped, realizing who he was. . . . It was Leighton Duff, who had just raped and beaten his own son." Her voice was hoarse. "He attempted to defend him from further beating, but his companions had gone too far to retreat. If they let him live, he would stand to accuse them. It was they who killed Leighton Duff—and who believed they had killed Rhys."

Eglantyne Wade sat helplessly. Fidelis held Sylvestra and rocked her back and forth, oblivious of the crowd whose pity welled around them.

"How can you possibly know this, Miss Latterly?" Rathbone asked.

"Because Rhys has regained his speech," she answered. "He told me."

"And did he know the names of his other assailants?"

"Yes . . . it was Joel Kynaston, his old headmaster, and Corriden Wade, his physician. That was a partial reason why he could not even attempt to tell anyone what had happened to him. The other part was his total shame and humiliation."

Eglantyne's head jerked up, her eyes wide, her skin ashen. She seemed to choke for breath. There was no outward change in Fidelis, as if in her heart she was not surprised.

"Thank you, Miss Latterly." Rathbone turned towards the judge, about to make a plea, and then stopped. The judge's face was engraved with horror and pity so deep the sight of it shocked.

Rathbone looked at the jurors and saw the same emotions mirrored in them, except for the four whose disbelief could not grasp such a thing. Rape happened to women, loose women who invited it. It did not happen to a man . . . any man! Men were inviolable . . . at least in the intimacy of their bodies. The horror and incomprehension left them stunned. They sat staring blindly, almost unaware of the room around them or of the strange, shifting silence in the gallery.

Rathbone looked at Sylvestra Duff. She was so white she

looked barely alive. Eglantyne Wade sat with her head bowed forward, her face covered by her hands. Only Fidelis Kynaston moved. She still held Sylvestra, moving very slightly back and forth. She seemed to be saying something to her, bending close to her. Her expression was tender, as if in this last agony she would bear some of it for her, share both their burdens.

"Have you anything further to add, Sir Oliver?" the judge said, breaking the silence.

"No, my lord," Rathbone answered. "If anyone has doubts, I will have further medical evidence obtained, but I would very much rather not subject Mr. Duff to any more pain or distress than he has already suffered. He has sworn a statement as to what happened in Water Lane the night of his father's death. No doubt there will be further trials at which he will be required to testify, which will be ordeal enough, should he recover sufficiently both his health and his balance of mind. In the meantime, I am willing to rest on Miss Latterly's word."

The judge turned to Ebenezer Goode.

Goode rose to his feet, his face grave. "I am familiar with Miss Latterly's nursing experience, my lord. If she will verify for the court upon what she bases her judgment, apart from Mr. Duff's word, I will abide by that."

The judge turned to Hester.

With a bare minimum of words, very quietly to a silent court, she described the bruising and the tearing she had seen, and likened it to other such injuries she had treated in the Crimea, and what the soldiers themselves had told her.

She was thanked and excused. She returned to the body of the court feeling too numb with pity to be more than dimly aware of the press of people near her. She did not even move immediately when she felt a man close to her and an arm around her.

"You did the right thing," Monk said gently, holding her with surprising strength, as if he would support her weight. "You could not change the truth by concealing it."

"Some truths are better not known," she whispered back.

"I don't think so, not truths like this. They are only better learned at certain times and in certain ways."

"What about Sylvestra? How will she bear it?"

"Little by little, a day at a time, and by knowing that whatever is built upon now will last, because it stands on reality, not on lies. You cannot make her brave; that is something no one can do for someone else." He stopped, still holding her close.

"But why?" she said almost to herself. "Why did they risk everything to do something so . . . pointless?" And even as she said it remarks of Wade's came back to her, with utterly different meaning now, remarks about nature refining the race by winnowing out the unfit, the morally inferior. And she remembered Sylvestra's stories of Leighton Duff's love of danger in his steeplechasing days, the excitement of risks, the elation of having taken a chance and beaten the odds. "What about Kynaston?" she whispered to Monk.

"Power," he replied. "The power to terrify and humiliate. Perhaps the righteous image he created for his pupils' parents was more than he could endure. We'll probably never know. Frankly, I don't care. I'm a damned sight more concerned for the families they leave to struggle on . . . for Sylvestra and Rhys."

"I think Fidelis Kynaston will help," she replied. "They will help each other. And perhaps Miss Wade too. They all have something appalling to face.

"Perhaps they will go to India?" she thought aloud. "All of them, when Rhys is better. They couldn't stay here."

"Maybe," he agreed. "Although it is amazing what you can face, if you have to." He would tell her about Runcorn some other time, later on, when they were alone and it was more appropriate.

"They'd like India," she insisted. "There is a great need for people out there who know something about nursing, especially women. I read it in Amalia's letters."

"Do they know anything about nursing?" he asked with a smile.

"They could learn."

He smiled more widely, but she did not see it.

The jury declined to retire. They returned a verdict of not guilty.

Hester slid her hand into Monk's and leaned even closer to him.

Don't miss the next William Monk novel:

A BREACH OF PROMISE

by ANNE PERRY

Barrister Sir Oliver Rathbone is representing brilliant young architect Killian Melville in a sensational breach of promise suit filed by his alleged fiancée's parents.

But Killian will not even explain to Rathbone his reasons for rejecting Zillah, and, utterly baffled, Rathbone enlists the help of William Monk and Hester Latterly. But even as they scout London for clues, their investigation suddenly and tragically ends...in murder.

Available this October in hardcover
from Fawcett Books.

The William Monk Novels by Anne Perry

THE FACE OF A STRANGER
The First William Monk Novel

His name, they tell him, is William Monk, and he is a London police detective—but the terrible accident he experienced has erased his memories of his past. Struggling to hide his amnesia as he returns to work to investigate the murder of a Crimean war hero, Monk begins to find the answers he seeks about himself.

A DANGEROUS MOURNING

Inspector William Monk is assigned the delicate task of looking into the fatal stabbing of the beautiful widowed daughter of a London aristocrat. Handicapped both by lingering traces of amnesia and by the craven ineptitude of his supervisor, Monk—with the intelligent help of nurse Hester Latterly—gropes warily through the silence and shadows that obscure the case....

DEFEND AND BETRAY

When an esteemed general suddenly dies—apparently due to a freak accident—at a London dinner party, his wife, Alexandra, readily confesses to killing him. Sensing that the truth is more complex than this, her attorney, Oliver Rathbone, hires former-policeman-turned-private-investigator William Monk to uncover what really happened.

A SUDDEN, FEARFUL DEATH

William Monk is engaged to investigate the strangulation of a talented Crimean War nurse, Prudence Barrymore. With the assistance of Hester Latterly, a nurse who knew Prudence on the battlefield, Monk assembles the portrait of a remarkable woman—and discerns the shadow of a tragic evil that darkens every level of society.

THE SINS OF THE WOLF

Nurse Hester Latterly's simple job of accompanying an elderly Scottish lady on a train trip to London takes a grave turn when the woman dies during the night. And when an autopsy reveals a lethal dose of medicine, Hester is charged with murder. Forced to stand trial in Edinburgh, she calls upon William Monk and Oliver Rathbone to prove her innocence.

CAIN HIS BROTHER

Angus Stonefield was a gentle, loving man—but now he has disappeared, and it seems likely that his brother Caleb, a creature long since abandoned to depravity, has murdered him. Hired to find the missing Angus, Monk scours the dank streets of London for clues to Angus's fate and his vicious brother's whereabouts.

WEIGHED IN THE BALANCE

Against his better judgment, Sir Oliver Rathbone agrees to defend Countess Zorah Rostova against a charge of slander. She insists, without a shred of evidence, that the prince of her small German principality was murdered by his wife. Though William Monk and Hester Latterly establish that the prince was indeed murdered, the likeliest suspect seems to be Countess Zorah herself....

The William Monk Novels
by Anne Perry

Published by Ivy Books.
Available at your local bookstore.